y. me

SILKEN SENSATION

While she was lost in thought, warm moist lips rolled over hers with such a light, arousing touch that Erica feared she would faint. She was dizzy with delight as Dante's sinewy arms slid about her waist, fitting his solid six-foot-two-inch frame to the slightness of hers. There was a subtle magic in his embrace, the likes of which she had never known. Tidal waves of pleasure rolled over her, leaving her relaxed and responsive in his arms.

She had been kissed before, but never like this! The taste of brandy was on his lips, and Erica drank her fill, amazed at her own abandon. She was consumed by odd sensations that trickled down through her to her toes. A sigh of pure pleasure tumbled from her lips as his wandering kisses traveled down her neck, blazing a path to passion that could be denied no longer. . . .

SATIN SURRENDER
CAROL FINCH

ZEBRA BOOKS
KENSINGTON PUBLISHING CORP.

ZEBRA BOOKS

are published by

Kensington Publishing Corp.
475 Park Avenue South
New York, NY 10016

First printing: August 1986

Printed in the United States of America

This book is dedicated to
David Laudick
Joe and Linda Strecker
Bill and Marilyn Walker
Mike and Cynthia Caldwell
Lloyd and Nancy Menz

May dear friends never be forgotten. The
warm memories are countless treasures.

. . . And to my husband, Ed.
You are always there to add creative imagination
when I bog down and to help with the plots of my books.
Your assistance is priceless!
Love you . . .

Part I

The efforts which we make to escape from our destiny only serve to lead us into it.

— *Emerson*

Chapter 1

Fat Tuesday, 1838
New Orleans

Indignant blue eyes clashed with determined gray ones as Erica Bennet drew herself up in front of her father and thrust out a proud chin. "I think it very unfair that you berate me just because I am a woman. I cannot help what I am and I do not appreciate being punished because of it."

Avery Bennet surveyed his twenty-one-year-old daughter with a mixture of amusement and chagrin. They had locked horns on this touchy subject so often in the past few months that their differences had almost become a daily ritual. Although Erica was the picture of feminine poise and breathtaking beauty, educated in the finest finishing schools in the East, she was a mite too big for her breeches. Indeed, Avery reflected that he would not have been the least bit surprised to see her wearing that garment since she had begun to consider herself a man's equal.

Somehow, in the past two years he had completely lost control of his daughter. He now found it a full-time chore to steer her in the direction he wanted her to go. But Erica, stubborn and headstrong as a mule, set her feet and refused to be prodded by anyone, even her father.

Propped against the wall, muffling a chuckle, stood Jamie Bennet, Erica's younger brother. He made it a point never to miss one of these family squabbles. His fiery sister was a constant source of amusement to Jamie, who delighted in watching her storm their father's defenses. Once she had broken down the barriers, Jamie had always been able, casually, to follow in her footsteps without doing battle. It was not that Jamie was a coward, only that he was clever enough to take advantage of any opportunity to avoid a clash with his battle-weary father, and he knew that Erica was rebellious enough for both of them.

Gathering his unraveled patience, Avery focused his narrowed gray eyes on his raven-haired daughter. "Your brother and I are very capable of managing the family business," Avery countered, in that patronizing tone that could make the hair bristle on the back of Erica's neck. "A woman's place is in the home, not on the rowdy docks of New Orleans, buying and selling crops and fussing over book work."

"My ability to manage business dealings is as good as Jamie's," Erica argued. Her snapping blue eyes swung to Jamie who seemed to be the only one enjoying the debate. "He is a year younger than I, and yet it is *he* who works beside you while I am left with the mundane responsibility of deciding what the cooks should prepare for dinner. You wasted your money sending me to those fancy schools if jotting down menus is all you expect of me." Erica sniffed disgustedly and then flounced across the room to glare at her reflection in the mirror. "I do not feel the least bit inferior to Jamie. It is humiliating to be stashed at home when I am quite capable of working. I have a need to be useful, just as Jamie does."

"She does have a point," Jamie interjected, only to be cut off by his father's derisive snort.

"You stay out of this," Avery ordered curtly. "If Erica declared that the sun had risen from the west, you would agree with her without even poking your head outside to check on that possibility."

When Erica cast her brother a discreet smile, he shrugged helplessly and then gestured for her to voice another protest in her own defense. And so she did. "Women have rights, just as men do. I see no reason why I should be denied mine."

Avery threw up his hands in exasperation. Their mansion would soon be swarming with guests who would join them in celebrating the Mardi Gras, and here he was in Erica's room, debating women's rights, an issue Avery was beginning to detest. "You have been reading too much propaganda," he grumbled, casting Erica a condescending frown. "One week you are raving over the abolition of slavery and the next week you are filling other females' heads with this nonsense, hoping they will revolt against their husbands and our way of life. Dammit, child, you have become a troublemaker."

Erica wheeled to face Avery, her delicate features alive with irritation. "Sarah Grimké's *Letters on the Equality of the Sexes and the Condition of Woman* are *not* propaganda," she declared heatedly. "Women were meant to be men's equals, to share their lives in more than servants' capacities. Since you and I constantly disagree on this matter, I think it might be wise if I moved to Natchez to stay with Aunt Lilian. I'm sure she would be more than happy to hire me in her dry-goods store, which, I might remind you, she has been successfully managing for over a decade."

His mouth narrowed into a hard line. "You are going nowhere, young lady. Besides, you have no funds; I have seen to it that you cannot touch your trust fund until the day you wed. When you consent to marry Sabin Keary, then you will receive your inheritance." His arm shot toward the door, and his voice became graveled with agitation. "Now you march yourself downstairs and prepare to meet our guests. And I do not want to see you waving your flag of women's independence in their faces when they come through the front door." Since Erica refused to budge, Avery clamped his hand around her arm, uprooting her from the spot on which she'd fixed herself and propelling her into the hall.

"It was an excellent speech." Jamie complimented his irate sister quietly as he fell into step beside her. "Next time, I suggest you put more emphasis on the fact that you have a better head for numbers than I. That should crumble his rebuttal. It is difficult for him to deny the truth."

Erica made a mental note to do just that. Although Erica did not wish her brother to fight her battles for her, she was not averse to employing his suggestions. Jamie was silently rooting for her, and she knew it. There was no reason for him to clash with Avery; she was the one who had to fight for her rights. Jamie had been granted his without debate.

"If I had not promised you to Sabin I would have suggested that you seek out some wealthy, but lazy, aristocrat who would not bat an eye at allowing his wife to wear the breeches or manage his business," Avery went on to say as he steered Erica toward the steps.

The caustic ring in his voice made Erica hiss like a disturbed cat that confronted a growling bulldog. "Perhaps I should do just that," she snapped back at her father. "A mealy-mouthed lush would be far better than matching me with that despicable viper you have selected. I would not wish that beast on my own worst enemy."

"Unfortunately, Sabin has decided that he wants you, and he means to have you," Avery replied, hustling Erica along beside him.

"He is an intolerable tyrant," Erica muttered, her expression making her look as if she had bitten into something sour and was unable to wash the bitter taste from her mouth. "I have twice refused his marriage proposal and I will continue to do so. I will not be ordered about by the likes of that disgusting man." She shivered uncontrollably at the thought of the homely aristocrat who was twenty-five years her senior. The mere thought of wedding Sabin Keary was enough to tie Erica's stomach in knots. She could not tolerate his touch, and she was repulsed when he came within ten feet of her. For the life of her she could not imagine why her father had consented to the ridiculous match. "You know as well as I do that Sabin and I would forever be at each other's throats."

Speak of the devil! Erica froze in her tracks when she glanced down to see Sabin draped over the banister at the foot of the stairs. He reminded her of a sun-dried prune. Even the welcoming smile that dangled on one side of his mouth could not overshadow his harsh, hollowed features. His thin tuft of sandy red hair framed his long face and sagging jowls. His close-set eyes—a physical characteristic that Erica had surmised denoted lack of intelligence until she'd met Sabin, who was as wily and conniving as a fox—were fixed on her. They were dark and beady, and staring into them for too long made Erica nauseous. His nose was long and thin, and Erica had considered planting her fist in it on several occasions when Sabin had attempted to stick his snout into her affairs. She could not think of one nice thing to say about Sabin Keary except that she might be able to tolerate him if he lived in another hemisphere.

Erica always found it necessary to guard her tongue when she was in Sabin's company. The man was plagued with a nasty temper. She had seen him flog his slaves for reasons that seemed ludicrous to her. She knew that Sabin dispensed painful punishment to anyone who dared to disobey him. Why Sabin wanted to marry her was beyond Erica. They had nothing in common, except the fact that they'd been born into the same species, and even then, Erica found herself wondering if Sabin had somehow been misplaced.

Resolutely, she pasted on the semblance of a smile. But she felt inclined to spin about and leap up the steps two at a time to avoid the malevolent plantation owner.

"My lovely Erica . . . You are breathtaking," Sabin drawled, his beady eyes slithering over the scooped neckline of her extravagant costume.

The gown had been authentically styled to depict the elegant dresses her great-grandmother had worn in the previous century. Suddenly Erica found herself wishing she had selected something that would have called less attention to her figure. Her father's costume ball would be intolerable if Sabin spent the evening drooling over her.

When Avery felt Erica tense, he leaned close to offer her a few words of advice. "Temper, my dear. The man is only paying you a compliment. If you were not so bewitching he would not take notice."

Jamie rolled his eyes when he overheard his father's words, but before he could call Avery's attention to the difference between an appreciative glance and an outright leer, he found himself whisked down the remainder of the steps and thrust at one of the available maids who had arrived during the debate in Erica's boudoir.

Damnation, Erica muttered under her breath when her father, who was dressed in pirate's garb, abandoned her to that slimy snake, Sabin Keary. How could he do this to her? Because she had provoked her father's temper, she reminded herself. Each time they broached the subject of Erica taking an active part in the family business, Avery refused to give her an opportunity to prove herself. He behaved as if being a woman was tantamount to contracting leprosy so she should be quarantined in her own home.

Erica was bored to death with sophisticated balls and fittings in dress shops. She wanted to do something purposeful in life before she lost her self-respect. There had to be more to living than making out menus and strutting through sprawling ballrooms. Erica hungered for a challenge, the excitement and thrill of galloping across the meadow on the back of a horse without her father's servants tattling on her. She wanted to select her own husband—a man whose touch would set fires alight inside her. She didn't want to be Sabin Keary's wife and she resented her father because he was shoving her into that disgusting man's lap!

"My dear Erica," Sabin cooed as he drew her down beside him and then wrapped a bony arm around her waist. "You know how anxious I am to make you my own. When will you relinquish your coy games and consent to become my wife?"

Never! Erica shouted to herself, wondering as she did so why she was too polite to state her response. She should blurt out her reply and put an end to this absurdity once and for all.

"This would be the perfect opportunity to announce our engagement," Sabin rasped as his hawkish gaze circled her, dwelling overly long on the creamy skin of her breasts, which rose and fell with each breath she took.

Before Erica realized what had happened, Sabin had pulled her around behind the stairs. Her alarmed gasp died beneath his bruising kiss, and a wave of nausea washed over her. The sticky sweet scent of his cologne and the pungent taste of liquor invaded her senses. It was obvious that Sabin had already begun celebrating the holiday, but Erica wanted no part of his brand of festivities. She would never become Sabin's feast. Never!

His hand swam across the bare flesh of her breasts, making her skin crawl with disgust. And then his mouth opened on hers. Sickered by his embrace, Erica twisted away from the repulsive kiss.

"Keep your hands off me!" she spat, attempting to rid herself of the disgusting taste of brandy. "I will not tolerate your manhandling."

"I will touch you whenever I please," Sabin assured her, pawing at her again.

Infuriated, Erica shoved him away with all the strength she could muster. When he resisted her efforts

16

to free herself, she kneed him in the groin. Yelping, Sabin doubled over, and before he could recover, Erica sprinted to the stairway. As she clutched the balustrade to dash up the steps, she heard Sabin growl viciously. Lifting her hampering skirts, she scaled the stairs, with the fuming Sabin Keary hot on her heels.

"Damn you, woman!" He declared malevolently. Shaking his fist at her departing back, he leaped after Erica.

"What is going on here?" Avery turned to stare up at the commotion on the stairs. The arriving guests were every bit as startled as he was.

Erica shrieked when Sabin grabbed the hem of her skirt and attempted to knock her off balance. Then she grasped the banister, pivoted on one foot, and ground her heel in his sunken chest, sending him clattering back down the steps. His dignity badly bruised, Sabin hoisted himself to his knees to find several amused faces gloating over the fact that he had been duped by a woman.

His self-control frayed and then snapped, and Erica could have sworn she saw smoke rolling from his ears as he stood erect and charged back up the steps like an enraged bull, muttering disrespectful curses as he did so. Erica desperately surveyed her surroundings, then flew toward her room to lock the door behind her. But that proved to be a wasted effort, for Sabin rammed his foot against the wood, splintering it and ripping the lock from the doorjamb. When he appeared inside her boudoir, he was like a madman, his dark eyes spewing fire, his mouth twisting murderously, and his sunken chest heaving as if he would breathe fire at any moment.

Feeling threatened, Erica frantically rummaged through her dresser drawer to retrieve the small handgun she kept for protection. Pointing it at Sabin's heart, she faced him.

"Don't come near me or I'll shoot," she assured him in a deadly tone. He looked as ominous and threatening as Satan himself, and Erica had taken as much as she could stand. If he dared to touch her she would blow him to smithereens.

"You haughty little bitch," Sabin spat furiously. "I should have bedded you long before now. Then you would not be so feisty. Soon I will become your master, and if you ever turn a gun on me again I'll thrash you for it."

"I would rather die than suffer your repulsive hands on me, you lecherous old man!" Erica hissed. She clasped the pistol more tightly in her hand when she heard her father's shocked gasp from the hallway.

"Erica, put that pistol down and apologize this instant!" Avery ordered once he had found his tongue.

"Sabin is the one who should apologize for taking outrageous privileges," she snapped defensively.

"From where I stand it seems the other way around," Avery contradicted. "You shoved him down the steps, insulted him, and now you are holding him at gunpoint. Put that thing down before someone gets hurt."

Erica was livid with rage. Her father had sided with that groping scoundrel. How could he?

"I demand a public apology!" Sabin declared as he took a bold step forward, his knobby fingers curled as if he meant to fasten them around Erica's neck.

"Stand your ground, Sabin," Avery advised, his gaze darting back and forth between his perturbed daughter and his wealthiest customer. "Erica is upset and she knows how to use that pistol. Don't provoke her."

18

"She wouldn't dare shoot me," Sabin scoffed, ignoring the warning as he stalked toward her, intent on punishing her for humiliating him in front of New Orleans' aristocracy.

"I'm warning you for the last time," Erica growled, her eyes narrowing to take careful aim.

The look in Sabin's eyes would have had a mountain lion cowering in his den, but Erica was as irate as he was. She had been backed into a corner and she refused to surrender. If Sabin won this round she would lose all future skirmishes; her stubborn pride would not allow that. Sabin Keary would never dominate her!

As Sabin stormed toward her, Erica took aim and fired at his leg. She cringed when he clutched his knee, howled like a wounded banshee, and then lunged at her again; but she threw the pistol at him, catching him on the side of the head. Then she shot past both startled men to flee down the hall, her mind racing frantically. God! What had she done? She had shot a man. No, not a man, she reminded herself as she wheeled around the corner into her father's bedroom and then stared at the balcony doors standing ajar to allow fresh air to drift into the room. Sabin was a beast who meant to harm her. She was justified in taking a shot at him. If she had not been so kindhearted, she would have aimed her pistol at his chest instead of his leg. If she had not fired he would have beaten her. She had seen Sabin abuse others who had crossed him, and she knew better than to expect him to be lenient with her. No, Sabin thirsts for my blood, she told herself. She had seen the murderous look in his eyes.

Harsh voices in the hall sent Erica scurrying onto the balcony to hide in the shadows.

"That little bitch will pay for this!" Sabin sneered

spitefully as he limped down the hall with Avery one step behind him.

"You swore to me that you would never lay a hand on Erica," Avery reminded him as he clutched at his chest to keep his heart from popping out after watching his daughter blow a hole in Sabin's leg. "You know Erica is feisty. You must have frightened her. If you will—"

"I want your promise of marriage, even if she does not consent," Sabin growled, ignoring Avery's remarks. "Furthermore, I want a public apology, or I'll take my business elsewhere and expose your carefully guarded secret. That woman needs to be taught proper manners, and I intend to instruct her since you have allowed her to run wild."

Avery's face blanched. "Now, calm down, Sabin. I'm sure we can come to a workable agreement. I'll—"

"Calm down?" Sabin hooted like a screech owl. "Your daughter knocks me down a flight of stairs in the presence of your most distinguished guests and then practically blows my leg to bits and you ask me to calm down?" His dark, vengeful gaze pried into every swaying shadow. "Where is that little termagant? We will settle this matter here and now."

"What the devil is going on up here?" Jamie demanded breathlessly.

He had heard the pistol discharge and had elbowed his way through the crowd to dash up the stairway. When Sabin swiveled around to face him, Jamie realized the man had been the recipient of the bullet. It did not take a genius to surmise who had been the donor. Erica, Jamie mused, silently applauding his sister's fortitude. Someone should have shot Sabin years ago, he thought, biting back a smile of wicked glee. The man was a scourge.

"That crazed sister of yours shot me," Sabin scowled furiously.

Jamie stared at Sabin's bloodstained trousers. "So it appears. What a pity," he remarked in a tone that implied otherwise.

Sabin was so indignant over Jamie's lack of concern and Erica's unmitigated gall that he smoldered with vindictiveness. "I swear I will have that girl's humble apology and her hand in marriage or I will see her hang from the tallest tree in New Orleans," he spewed out.

Erica flattened her back to the wall and attempted to swallow her heart, which had catapulted into her throat, cutting off her breath. She had overheard the conversation, and she had the sinking feeling her father would back down before Sabin as he always did. She envisioned herself swinging from a tree limb, suffering the same agonizing beating Sabin inflicted on his slaves. Then the impulse to flee overwhelmed her and Erica yielded to it.

When footsteps echoed through her father's bedroom, Erica tiptoed across the balcony and swung her leg over the edge to peer down at the ground. As she did so, her stomach fell the full fifteen feet to splatter on the rock wall that lined the garden. Erica was painfully reminded that she feared only one thing—height. Choking down her queasiness, she clutched the supporting beam and prayed she would not take the same spill she had as a young child when she'd walked along the balcony railing and failed to maintain her balance. The ground was swimming below her, pulling her to it like an invisible force that sought to pry her hands from the beam.

While Erica remained paralyzed, staring at the ground that, she remembered, could come at her with incredible speed, Avery, Sabin, and Jamie appeared on the balcony.

Even while danger stared her in the face, Erica was recalling the first fall that had jarred every bone in her body. It had been hours before she had regained consciousness. But the tormenting memory fled when Sabin stalked toward her, his mouth watering in anticipation of seizing her in a stranglehold. Gathering her courage, Erica squeezed her eyes shut and slid over the rail, shinnying down the supporting column until her feet touched solid ground.

"Come back here, you little twit!" Sabin bellowed, the anger in his voice as biting as a double-edged sword. "Don't think you can escape me. By God, I'll hunt you down and you'll wish you'd never crossed me!"

Erica darted across the lawn as if the devil himself were chasing her, afraid to look back, certain that demon, Sabin Keary, had left his human form and was winging his way toward her like a vampire bat that thirsted for her blood. When she heard her father call to his servants to pursue her, she quickened her pace, determined to lose herself in the throngs of onlookers who had lined the streets of New Orleans in anticipation of the celebration.

Finally pausing in her flight, Erica glanced about her, uncertain of her destination. Where could she go to escape Sabin? He would turn the city upside down to find her. There has to be some place where I can hide until this blows over, she told herself, only half-believing it. A fox like Sabin could sniff her out with that long nose of his. Lord, what was she going to do now? Unable to answer that question, Erica again headed away from her father's mansion, trying desperately to get a grip on herself and decide what to do. She had made a mess of the evening, but what else could she have done? She would not bow to Sabin Keary, not now, not ever!

As Sabin limped back down the hall to have his wound tended and to send servants after his runaway fiancée, Jamie stood on the balcony, watching his sister become one of the swaying shadows. "God's speed, *chère soeur*," he breathed softly.

A muddled frown plowed Jamie's brow. Why had Avery consented to this ridiculous marriage in the first place? Erica and Sabin were as different as dawn and midnight. It baffled Jamie that Avery would wish a ruthless old man like Sabin on his own daughter. Heaving a sigh, Jamie prayed that Erica's flight would be a successful one. She deserved better than Sabin Keary. If she could not find a way to intervene, Jamie fully intended to do so. The thought of Sabin as a brother-in-law was quite distasteful to him. Erica would wither and die if she were forced to become Sabin Keary's wife, and Jamie could not tolerate the thought of his vibrant sister being forced to submit to such a man.

Pushing away from the rail, Jamie wandered down the hall, praying that Erica would manage to escape. Even if he never saw her again, that would be better than seeing her tied to a man like Sabin, he reminded himself.

Chapter 2

New Orleans' boardwalks were bulging with celebrants as Erica pushed her way through the crowd, losing herself in the swarm of humanity. The city had come alive for the festivities in which costumed knights paraded down the streets like minions trailing behind a king. Two floats wobbled down the street just then, and Erica peered around the shoulders of the men who blocked her view. But she apprehensively shrank back when she spied two of her father's black servants threading their way along the avenue in search of her. Moving with the flow of the crowd, Erica kept a low profile, considering she was the only spectator garbed in a costume and mask. Although the guests in her father's home had intended to join the parade, Erica was not about to set foot in the street and risk being spotted by the servants.

Now, as the parade moved down the avenue, all the balconies were filled with people watching the celebration. The crowd roared its appreciation of the floats and the gay costumes. But within a few minutes the rowdy gathering was throwing flour at the marchers, and laughter rang through the street as the celebrating city began to look as if it had been hit by a blizzard.

Erica sputtered as flour sifted from the balconies, coating her raven hair with several layers of white. As she paused to brush off her gown she glanced sideways to find three surly roustabouts leering at her. Erica gulped hard. She had seen such men before, rowdy deckhands who carried cargo onto steamships from the docks, men who were notorious for drinking and carousing when they were off duty. Erica had also run into her share of predatory stares when she'd ventured to her father's office in the New Orleans Cotton Exchange, but she had always stashed a pistol in her purse and one or two servants had escorted her. Now she was unarmed and unprotected, and it was not difficult to tell what these scraggly rogues had on their minds. Their intentions were boldly stamped on their stubbled faces.

"Well, ain't we got a perty one here." Timothy Thorpe chuckled as his eyes raked Erica's seductive gown and he visualized what lay beneath it. "Why ain't you marchin' with the rest of them highfalutin' aristocrats?" His eyes danced with deviltry. "Was you lookin' for somethin' more entertainin' than a stroll down the avenue with Rex and his costumed knights?"

Erica shrank away when one of the men made a grab for her; then she rattled off several sentences in French, hoping her nemeses would think she had been unable to translate their suggestive remarks.

"Looks like we got us a real French countess." Ethan Morris snickered as his hand snaked out to snatch the rose that was stitched to the bodice of Erica's gown.

A shriek flew from her lips and Erica's temper exploded. She bared her claws and scratched his face as he grabbed for her. When Ethan howled and covered his cheek, Denby Eldwin lunged at her, but Erica reacted just as quickly. She planted her doubled fist in his toothy grin, and Denby staggered back, his eyes bulging from their sockets.

For the second time in less than an hour, Erica grabbed her skirt and ran for her life. With no regard for courtesy, she shoved bodies out of her way to escape the three men who stalked after her, calling her names that would have burned the ears off a priest.

After darting a backward glance at the roustabouts who were giving chase, Erica inhaled a breath and broke into a run. She had hoped the men would give up and turn their attention to the parade, but since her luck had been traveling on such a rocky course that evening, she was not surprised to see her would-be attackers weaving their way through the crowd to catch up with her.

Ducking down to hide in the throng, Erica shot into the first open door she encountered and then crouched behind a chair to glance about her. A muddled frown knitted her brow as she surveyed the plush red velvet chairs that lined the parlor. She peered up at the huge crystal chandelier suspended from the high ceiling. It was decorated with likenesses of nude women. She groaned in dismay. She had stumbled into an abandoned brothel. Suddenly a mischievous smile found the corners of her mouth. The men pursuing her would never expect her to seek refuge in a house of ill repute. She was safe at last. Carefully, she inched her way behind the sofa to keep a close watch on the open doorway; then she panicked when she saw the three men lingering just outside. While their backs were turned, she made a mad dash

26

for the stairs, ascended them in record time, and then collided with a man who was impatiently pacing in the shadowy hall.

"Pardonnez-moi, monsieur," Erica apologized breathlessly as she hiked up the front of her drooping bodice which had so recently almost been ripped off. She darted an apprehensive glance at the open door, noting that her burly pursuers had entered the parlor. "There are three men waiting for me down there and I . . ."

On lifting her eyes, Erica saw a wry smile part the stranger's lips, and her gaze locked with the most incredible pair of green eyes she had ever seen. As the scant light from the room below glistened in them, Erica forgot what she had intended to say.

Dante Fowler stared down at the bedraggled beauty who was caked with flour and whose ripped bodice was dangerously close to revealing what lay so temptingly beneath it.

"I can see why," he murmured.

He had become impatient after waiting a quarter of an hour for the proprietress to send one of her doxies to his room. Dante did not know that the women and their male customers had wandered outside to view the parade, and so he suddenly decided that this extraordinary bit of fluff was worth the wait. Indeed, this rosy-cheeked vision whose satin dress was embroidered with gold had transformed his impatience into lust. Her form-fitting gown complemented her creamy skin, and her blue eyes and raven hair, even when sifted with flour, were drawing him ever closer. Dante had drunk just enough at the casino to leave him thirsty to appease another need, so he doubted that his indulgence in liquor could be playing spiteful tricks on his vision. The masked woman was by far the most attractive minx he had laid eyes on in all his thirty-three years. Around her swanlike neck lay a diamond necklace that sparkled in the faint light. An expensive gift from one of her regular customers, Dante concluded as his eager gaze wandered at will, drinking in the tantalizing sight of her.

When he opened the door to the room in which he had been waiting and gestured for her to join him, Erica glanced toward the parlor. Upon seeing the roustabouts milling around the doorway, she slipped into the room. Her gaze took in the ruby-colored drapes, the plush chairs, and the ornately carved bed. So this is what the inside of a den of iniquity looks like, she thought. The room actually had a seductive appearance in the dim lantern light which cast hazy shadows on the gold-flecked walls.

Wheeling about to explain her dilemma, Erica found herself speechless when she looked into Dante's bronzed face. Strong lines creased his forehead, and dimples dived into his cheeks and deepened the cleft in his chin when he smiled at her beguilingly. Crisp, wavy hair framed his face and a fringe of thick, dark lashes surrounded the large green eyes that pierced her, the living fire in them staggering her. Erica felt that she would melt into her satin slippers when an appealing look settled onto his strong, commanding features. A strange magnetism radiated from him, drawing her to him.

When she caught herself staring, she glanced away, but her eyes drifted back to the handsome stranger who was fashionably dressed in tan trousers and a white shirt which contrasted with his copper skin. Erica had seen her share of attractive men, but this one surpassed them all. It shocked her to realize that she was fascinated by a total stranger, and when he reached out to her, she felt that she had been branded with a hot iron.

His lean fingers investigated the laced bodice of her gown and then trailed across the curve of her breast. Becoming aware of his intimate caress, she flinched and then retreated a step. His touch was much too exciting, and a little frightening. He stirred far more complex feelings than the revulsion she had experienced when Sabin and the rowdy roustabouts had pawed at her.

Dante's dark brow shot up when he noticed her reaction, and a gentle smile hovered on his sensuous lips as his wayward hand scaled the slope of her shoulder and curled around her neck to tilt her face to his.

"Has the boisterous crowd disturbed you, *chérie?*" he murmured in a rich, baritone voice that flooded over her, leaving her knees weak.

"*Oui,*" she almost whispered, trembling beneath his gentle touch.

Meanwhile, his probing emerald gaze held her hostage and Erica could do nothing but stare back at him, wondering what strange power he had. Never had she been so devastatingly affected by the mere sight of a man.

"I can see why those men who tarried by the door were not anxious to sit and wait for you." Dante traced the delicate curve of her cheek, marveling at the creamy softness of her skin. It was like satin beneath his fingertips. "But I would imagine you are worth any man's wait," he mused aloud. Then he reached up to draw the mask from her face.

Erica was too dazed to understand the insinuation. She had been screamed at, yanked about, and pawed for the better part of the evening. This stranger's reassuring smile and gentle touch had lured her into a false sense of security. She, who had always voiced her desire for independence, felt the unfamiliar need to be consoled after her harrowing experiences, to be held in this stranger's capable arms, to allow him to chase away her fears. He would never allow those burly roustabouts to lay a hand on her.

While she was lost in thought, warm, moist lips rolled over hers with such a light, arousing touch that Erica feared she would faint. She was dizzy with delight as his sinewy arms slid about her waist, fitting his solid six-foot-two-inch frame to the slightness of hers. There was a subtle magic in his embrace, which made waves of pleasure roll over her, leaving her relaxed and responsive in his arms.

She had been kissed before but never like this! The taste of brandy was on his lips as Erica drank her fill of them, amazed at her own abandon. When Sabin Keary had kissed her, she was repulsed, but with this handsome stranger, she was consumed by odd sensations that trickled through her, right to her toes. A sigh of pure pleasure tumbled from her lips as his wandering kisses tracked across the trim column of her neck and then meandered across the swells of her breasts.

Her eyes flew open, and her mind reeled as she tried to recall the words he had whispered before he'd kissed her senseless. Just what did he take her for, a whore? A wench who had come for no other purpose than to share his bed? Of course he did. What else could he think? She had blundered into a brothel and this skillful stranger was visiting this house of ill repute to . . . Erica swallowed hard and stared up at him, seeing him now in an altogether different light. Whoever he was, he had come to this whorehouse expecting to do more than aid a dam-

30

sel in distress. This man wasn't her white knight. He was thinking the same lusty thoughts as the rest of the male population! She decided she would be in a worse state than distress if she didn't set the matter straight before this situation got out of hand.

Sweet merciful heavens! This just wasn't her night. Fat Tuesday had become a disaster, and if she didn't put a stop to this amorous assault she stood to lose more than her dignity. She had been mauled. She had shot a man in her bedroom, had endured a near brush with rape; and now she was about to be seduced by a whoremonger who was probably no better that those heathens she had eluded. Just because this dashing stranger was elegantly dressed and was scented with cologne did not mean he was a gentleman. What kind of man could one expect to meet in a bawdy house? Erica asked herself, and she quickly answered. A good-for-nothing rakehell, a woman-izer who has one thing on his mind. What he wanted, he didn't mind paying for, but she was not about to become his concubine, not to escape her other molesters!

Erica pressed determined hands to the hard wall of his chest and pushed herself back as far as his encircling arms would allow. Dante frowned disappointedly at the interruption. He was thoroughly enjoying the taste of this young woman's skin and her titillating fragrance had begun to warp his senses.

"Sir, I fear you misunderstand. You see, I—"

Dante's gaze was focused on her heart-shaped lips. They hypnotized him and he could not resist dropping another kiss on her mouth. Drawn like a bee to nectar, he craved a sweetness more addictive than cherry wine. There were more pleasurable experiences than talking, and Dante longed to pursue them. It had been weeks since he had been with a woman, and the taste and feel of this dazzling beauty clouded his mind, allowing raw emotion to raise its head like a sleeping lion.

Erica strangled on her words and then came up for air, gasping and sputtering when Dante finally dragged his lips from hers. "What you think is going on here isn't," she blurted out. "*Détrompez-vous!* This is a mistake. I am not what you think. I was—"

"No, you are far more than I anticipated," Dante assured her, his voice heavy with disturbed desire.

Again his mouth slanted across hers, stripping her breath from her lungs. It was too late when Erica realized that his deft fingers had moved across the back of her gown to unfasten the stays. Her gold satin gown fluttered to the floor to lie around her ankles.

His dark green eyes swam over the shapely contours of her body, and fiery desire rose in Dante's loins. Whatever price she demanded he would pay. This enchanting minx is worth the cost, he thought as his heart pounded against his ribs, in rhythm with the drums that throbbed on the street below.

Erica trembled beneath his all-consuming gaze. His eyes were so intense that she could have sworn he reached out to caress her. She felt as if she were on fire! The sensation shocked her. Never had a man seen her in a state of undress, and never had she allowed a man to kiss her the way this stranger had. What was the matter with her? Why was she standing there watching him devour her with those entrancing green eyes when she should have punched him in the jaw for taking unfair advantage? *Get a grip on yourself*, Erica thought frantically. *Say something!*

When Dante scooped her up into his arms and moved

toward the bed, Erica finally came to her senses. Indignantly she wormed free of his arms, leaving Dante to stand empty-handed, his mouth gaping, as she leaped over the bed and retreated to the far corner of the room. Her hair now tumbled wildly from what had once been a neat bun on top of her head, and her kiss-swollen lips were jutting out in an exaggerated pout as she crossed her arms over her thin chemise to shield herself as best she could from those emerald eyes.

"Good God, woman!" Dante hooted. "I had envisioned a night of incomparable passion. Perhaps your other clients delight in playing cat-and-mouse games, but I have no time for them."

Erica blinked bewilderedly as Dante peeled off his shirt. The golden lantern light flooded over the broad expanse of his chest, displaying the crisp matting of hair that trailed down his belly and disappeared beneath the band of his breeches. His massive shoulders tapered to a muscular abdomen and narrow hips, and Erica could have pinched herself for allowing herself to wonder how he would look in the altogether. She didn't want to know! And yet . . . her gaze thoroughly assessed his powerful physique, finding not one flaw. He was all man, every gorgeous inch of him—a dashing rogue, the type her friends would have swooned over if they had been viewing him as she was.

However, Erica clamped her hands on the back of the chair behind which she stood, and she prayed that he would not strip naked before her eyes. She blushed seven shades of red when Dante reached down to unfasten his breeches; then she held up a shaky hand to halt him.

"Monsieur, qu'avez-vous? Please don't do that! I . . ." Erica's words died on her lips when the waistband of his

trousers drooped on his hips, revealing the fact that his body was not tanned all over.

A rakish grin twisted one corner of his mouth as he swaggered toward her, his eyes hungrily devouring her full breasts which rose and fell with each frantic breath she inhaled. "Would you prefer to do it, *chère amie?*" Dante raised a suggestive brow as his gaze wandered over her satiny skin. He ached to caress what lay so temptingly before him. "I don't mind as long as I am granted the same privilege of unwrapping such an enticing package."

There they were again, the charismatic smile that rattled her, and the seductive timbre of his voice that crumbled her composure. Erica struggled to gather her wits and locate her tongue.

"*Vous avez la berlue!* I am not a whore. Actually I am—"

Dante glanced sharply at her and frowned. How many times had he heard that line? "I think we've played enough games." Seeing her in this state of undress was hard on his patience and blood pressure. He did not need to be enticed into bed when passion was gnawing at him. If he did not appease his ravenous need, and quickly, he could not trust himself to be gentle with this chit. Due to his abstinence this lively beauty need not resort to playful antics. He was well warmed and ready to tumble into bed with her.

"This is no game I play. Listen to me, *s'il vous plaît,*" Erica pleaded, her pulse racing as she calculated the distance to her discarded gown and the number of steps required to reach the door. "I came to the brothel to *escape* being mauled."

Dante didn't believe her for a minute. No respectable young woman would be caught dead in a New Orleans

34

whorehouse. Prim and proper ladies shied away from sinful establishments, and they detested the fact that their men frequented them. No, this lively bit of fluff was toying with him to fully arouse his desire, but there was no need for that. Dante already ached to lose himself in her soft, feminine body which had had him smoldering since he'd captured her in his arms.

When Dante moved deliberately toward her, however, Erica darted into another corner. "I am *not* taunting you," she insisted, as she edged around the stuffed chair and then covered herself as best she could. All she succeeded in doing was pushing her bosom upward, so that the ripe pink buds were breathtakingly close to spilling from the dainty lace of her chemise. As the garment glided up over her hips, exposing the shapely curves beneath it, Dante nearly gasped. "I don't work here. I have never been in this room before in my life!"

Dante heard not a word; he was immersed in a fantasy that was slowly driving him mad. But his head jerked up and he came to his senses when Erica streaked toward the door, planning to scoop up her dress on the run. With the quickness of a jungle cat Dante sprang at her, intercepting her, but his toe caught on the bedpost when she writhed in his grasp.

A surprised yelp bubbled from her lips when she found herself tumbling into an upholstered chair with Dante atop her. The chair reared on its back legs and then crashed onto the floor. Erica was more jarred by Dante's half-nude body smashing into hers than from the jolt of their fall. As his hair-roughened chest rubbed against her breasts and his muscular thighs pressed between her legs, frantic sparks danced across her skin. She had never been this close to a man before and the experience was devastating. When she should have punched him in the jaw or scratched his face, Erica just lay there, gazing up at him, her jaw sagging. Why did he affect her so?

Dancing green eyes peered down into alarmed blue ones as he braced the top half of his body on his forearms, allowing the taut peaks of her breasts to brush his chest. The feel of her supple body beneath him sent a bolt of desire sizzling through him. Perhaps I have been too impatient with her, he mused. Pursuing this adorable nymph had become an interesting challenge, one he found himself thoroughly enjoying.

"Forgive my impatience, minx," Dante rasped as his raven head moved steadily toward hers. "Had I known the pleasure of pursuing you, I would not have questioned your tactics. You seem to be a very imaginative lover."

For the life of her Erica could not find her tongue. Her wide eyes were fixed on his darkly handsome face, on the charming smile that curved his sensuous lips; and her heart was hammering so furiously that she swore it would crack her ribs. Being this close to a man made strange sensations course through her veins. His virile body, intertwined with hers, had opened the Pandora's box of physical desire, something Erica had never before known. His lips descended on hers, and they explored her mouth with deepening intimacy as his fingers delved into her tousled hair to tilt her head into his devastating kiss. He was overpowering her with gentleness. Indeed, when the pressure of his lips lessened and they feathered over her, Erica could not draw away from him, and she had the odd sensation that all was lost. He was studying her with incredible hunger; yet he held her with such heart-stopping tenderness that every barrier of defense she had sought to construct had fallen. She was aware that she was losing control, but she could not stop herself.

Inquiring hands ventured across the uncharted territory of her skin, leaving her hot and cold and tremulous in their wake. His bold caresses drew her into a riptide of emotion that went against all she had ever been taught. Erica was unsure where these dangerous sensations would lead, and she was a little afraid to find out. But his skillful seduction continued to melt her resistance as he learned her body by touch, seeking and finding each sensitive point, leaving her breathlessly exploring the world of passion, one she'd never realized existed. Still the rugged, handsome stranger swarmed over her, like an invading army, using tactics so bewildering that Erica didn't realize she'd been captured in his spell until it was too late. He offered no terms other than complete surrender, a condition that Erica was hard pressed not to accept. Wonderment flooded over her as her body instinctively arched to meet his exploring hands, yet she chided herself for yielding. She was painfully aware that she should have been shoving him away and vaulting to her feet, but her body paid no heed to the command.

Dante's head was spinning like a runaway carousel, his male craving aroused as Erica's writhing body responded to his questing hands. Mother Nature has been more than generous with this gorgeous creature, he thought to himself as his wandering caresses scaled the peak of her breast and then fanned across her abdomen to explore the shapely contour of her hips. His mouth languidly possessed hers, taking her breath away and then giving it back the instant before they both drowned in a torrent of bubbling sensations.

Erica drew a shuddering breath and placed her arms

over his shoulders as he rolled to his feet and carried her to the bed. Her disbelieving eyes were glued to his, mesmerized by the fiery sparkle of desire in them. Erica knew that she had come too far to turn back. She could not now escape him. Indeed, she found herself wondering if she truly wanted to. Fighting him now would enrage him, and if she had to compromise her virtue, she preferred to do so with a man who displayed tenderness.

All thought fled as Dante, who had quickly shed his breeches, stretched out beside her. The feel of his virile body drew her like a magnet, and she responded with abandon to his provocative kisses and caresses. Suddenly swept into a blaze that burned brighter than a thousand suns, she was driven closer to the source of the fire whereas logic would have fled from it. His hands splayed across her abdomen, and his knee gently guided her legs apart. Then his probing fingers found her womanly softness, and Erica gasped as his intimate touch inflamed her with a craving she did not fully comprehend. When his lips left hers, Erica's lashes fluttered up to see him hovering above her, the muscles of his arms bulging as he determinedly held himself at bay. Then his hips slid between her thighs, his bold manliness pressing against her tender flesh. The pleasure she had experienced became a searing pain, but Erica's cry was smothered by Dante's guttural groan as he entered her. Erica's instinctive physical reaction unintentionally fed his growing hunger, and he began to move within her as his quivering lips came back to hers. When initial pain ebbed, Erica realized that her body was rhythmically responding to a passionate melody that played somewhere in the distance. He took her higher and higher, spiraling and then gliding like an eagle drifting in the wind, searching for rapture's pinnacle amidst the puffy clouds.

For what seemed an eternity their bodies moved together, satisfying a craving, waiting for that indescribable moment when pleasure peaked and then exploded to scatter in all directions like the pastel colors of a rainbow. Erica dug her nails into the muscles of his back as a soul-shattering sensation swept through her, and above her, Dante shuddered and clutched her so tightly that she could barely draw a breath.

When Erica had fluttered back to reality, she opened her eyes and saw the embers of desire glowing in his, amid them her reflection. Sweet mercy! What had she done? She had fallen into bed with a total stranger. She had responded with abandon. Overwhelmed by caresses that had her dancing like a puppet on a string, she had yielded to the lurid desires of the flesh. Had she lost what little sense she had left? How could she ever face her father, especially after she had humiliated him in front of his guests? He would know that she had become a tarnished woman. Everyone would know. They would see it when they looked at her. And how could she live with herself now? She had surrendered to this man who clung to her as if he would never let her go, but soon he would move away and would act as if nothing had happened between them. How could she endure that mortification? Erica was so ashamed that she prayed the earth would open and swallow her up. She was afraid to look in the mirror for fear of seeing a tainted woman. She was soiled. She'd been seduced in a bawdy house after she'd taken a shot at the hot-tempered Sabin Keary and she'd scratched the eyes of the ruffian who'd placed his filthy hands upon her. God help her!

Erica's mind raced frantically. If Sabin caught up with her, he would force Avery to sign a marriage contract, and when Sabin learned that Erica was no longer a virgin, he would be even more furious. She hated to think of encountering Sabin when he was so angered. Their earlier confrontation had been quite enough. She considered throwing herself into the river and praying that her body would be washed out to sea. Her life might as well be over. There was nothing but a trail of disaster behind her and impending catastrophe ahead.

"Mmmm . . . you are delicious," Dante murmured. His butterfly kisses skimmed her pulsating neck, evoking an instinctive response.

Erica choked back a humiliated sob as he rolled away, allowing her to snatch up her gown and chemise. But when he strolled over in front of her, wearing nothing but a roguish grin, Erica blushed deeply. Although she quickly glanced the other way, his muscular physique was branded on her mind. He could put a Greek god to shame, she mused as she fumbled with the stays on the back of her gown.

"Allow me," Dante whispered, as he pushed her hands away to take up the chore.

His moist lips hovered over the back of her neck, evoking responses that Erica tried desperately to ignore, but the dark stranger seemed to have some mystical power which made her body react to his caresses. Great balls of fire! Had she taken a headlong dive off the deep end? How could she be so affected by his touch when she had condemned him and herself in the previous moment? Had he stripped her of every ounce of pride? How she wished she could erase the past few hours. The heated argument with her father had resulted in a catastrophe. And where will it end? she asked herself miserably.

Erica flinched when she felt his hand dip into her bodice to stash the payment for her services. She immediately retrieved the bills and handed them back to him.

"I don't want your money," she insisted, her voice registering a trace of bitterness.

Dante slipped the payment back into her gown; then he flashed her a roguish grin. "Keep it, love. I'll be back, and I would be disappointed if you shunned me for not paying for services received the first time we chanced to meet."

Erica slipped from his arms and hurried toward the door, but she paused to glance back at him, careful not to allow her gaze to dip below his waist. "Your name . . . I do not even know your name," she choked out.

"Dante," he whispered. "And yours, sweet angel?"

Erica opened the door and slipped outside, trying to block out the memory of the intoxicating kisses and tantalizing caresses that had been her undoing, hoping to elude the masculine scent that still clung to her. "I doubt that it would make any difference to you, *monsieur*. For you, tonight is like any other night."

Her quiet words drifted back to him as she closed the door and vanished into the shadows.

"Ah, but it does matter," Dante mused aloud, lost to the captivating image of the young woman who had thrilled and pleased him with her silky embrace.

Heaving a sigh, he strolled back to the bed to fetch his clothes and then stopped short when he spied the stains on the sheets. Lord, she *was* innocent of men! Dante squeezed his eyes shut, then cursed himself for not listening to her pleas. The bewitching minx had not lied or taunted him after all. He had deflowered a virgin! Never

41

in his life had he bedded a woman who knew nothing of men. He berated himself for not having realized it, but he'd been so caught up in the moment that he'd been oblivious to all that had transpired about him.

Dante scrambled into his clothes and whipped open the door onto an empty corridor. He pricked his ears and then scanned his surroundings, but the young woman had disappeared into the darkness. An ironic smile curled his lips as he strode back into the room to fetch his waistcoat and hat. For years he had avoided virgins like the plague. Determined to remain free and unattached, he'd had no desire to be pursued by irate fathers who might demand that he wed their disgraced daughters. Then he had come to New Orleans to ease his frustrations in a brothel, and he had unknowingly taken a young woman's innocence. Inexperienced though she had been, Dante had unleashed her passions, and she had responded eagerly to his touch, pleasing him as no other woman had. And he had known many women. He did not boast about it, but he had no objection to sharing a bed with a woman who caught his eye.

Dante buttoned his waistcoat and strolled down the abandoned hall. Then, on an impulse, he went in search of the captivating woman who had swept into his life and then disappeared without giving her name. Dante wanted to see her again, to learn her identity, to apologize. . . . A faint smile touched his lips at that thought. No, he could not apologize for a night that had brought him indescribable pleasure. The memory of that dark-haired enchantress would linger in his mind for days to come. He could not say he was sorry for sharing a moment of passion with such an exquisite beauty. That would have been hypocritical.

As he ambled along the street, searching the faces of the crowd, the young woman preyed heavily on his mind. He could not stop thinking of her, remembering how they had tumbled onto the floor and then stretched out in bed, touching, sharing a rapturous moment. . . . Dante felt his loins stir at the memory, and he veered toward a pub to buy himself a stiff drink. He needed one. The vision that remained just beyond his grasp had already begun to haunt him.

Chapter 3

Determined to escape without encountering yet another disaster, Erica darted through the shadows, surreptitiously making her way through the streets to the wharf. Relief melted the tension on her face when she spied the *Natchez Belle*. The magnificent steamboat looked like a floating palace, the glow of its torches casting golden light onto the rippling water of the Mississippi River.

The pilot house, enclosed in glass, was at least fifty feet above the river. From it, the pilot could see in all directions while he navigated the narrow channels to the north. The hurricane deck, just below the pilot house, was lined with white lattice railings and housed the ship's officers. A wide curving stairway at the front of the boat connected that deck to the boiler deck where the passenger's cabins were situated. Along the railings which were painted white, passengers often strolled, enjoying the view of the mighty Mississippi.

Erica studied the bustling activity on the main deck

where the cargo was usually carried. Many a time she'd seen the steamboat piled so high with bales of cotton that the pilot house and the smokestacks were barely visible. But tonight, the *Natchez Belle* had room to take on deck passengers: immigrants journeying upriver to new homes and jobs, peddlers, and rafters who floated lumber from the pine forests of Wisconsin and Minnesota to New Orleans on their makeshift flatboats and then returned home by steamboat. A number of these rough, unruly boatmen were strolling along the main deck, drinking and singing boisterous songs that drowned out the immigrants' quiet hymn.

In past years Erica had witnessed such goings-on. When she'd traveled to her aunt's home in Natchez, she had often strolled the decks, familiarizing herself with the ship, learning the locations of its many rooms. But the excitement and anticipation she'd experienced then escaped her this night. So much had happened that she was drained of emotion. She had decided not to throw herself into the river. She had reminded herself that she was a survivor and she had always refused to surrender without putting up a fight.

She intended to outrun her tormenting memories and make a new life for herself. She would learn to mask her emotions so no one would ever know she had yielded to the weakness of the flesh. Everyone is allowed a few mistakes, she told herself. Unfortunately, she added, I made all of mine on the same night.

With her mouth set in a grim line, Erica pushed her way through the crowd to confront the clerk who was haggling over payment with a German immigrant. They were having considerable difficulty overcoming the language barrier and Erica was too impatient to await her turn. She had to leave New Orleans if she were to survive.

"Sir, I wish to book passage on the boiler deck," Erica blurted out, tugging on the clerk's sleeve and wedging her way past the immigrant in tattered homespun clothes.

"Sorry, miss. All the cabins are filled to capacity. Most of the sightseers who came for the Mardi Gras have booked round-trip passage."

Erica's spirits sank to the bottom of the muddy Mississippi River. "Well then, I would be willing to sleep on the deck," she assured him.

The clerk heaved a sigh as he stared at the bedraggled beauty. "I wish I could help you, miss, but these people have been camped out here for several days and some of them will have an even longer wait ahead of them. Another ship will be sailing upstream on Thursday. Perhaps you could—"

"Thursday!" Erica groaned. "That will be too late." As she glanced about her, she remembered her father's advice. If one wanted results, he'd said, one should go right to the top, not waste time bickering with employees on the lower rungs of the ladder. "I wish to speak with your captain." Erica lifted a determined chin and stared the clerk straight in the eye. "Perhaps he can make arrangements for my passage."

"The captain is ashore, miss," the clerk informed her. "I'm afraid you will have to wait for the next boat. This one is already overloaded with passengers. I am trying to explain to this poor man that we cannot wedge all of his family and his brother's family in such cramped quarters." He turned to the stubble-faced immigrant who had resorted to Erica's tactic of tugging on his sleeve.

46

Damnation! Was she not to be granted even a smidgeon of luck? Wait indeed! Erica flounced through the crowd at the dock, silently fuming. Her hair and face were caked with flour. She was ankle deep in mud. Her exquisite gown was grimy and soiled, and she was exhausted from living a nightmare. To make matters worse, she had been refused passage to Natchez.

She gritted her teeth and stomped her foot, then cursed when mud splattered up the front of her dress. In the next moment, she decided she was going to Natchez even if she had to swim there! With calculating blue eyes, she surveyed the massive floating palace. Then she grinned slyly. Turning her thought into action, she stripped down to her chemise and tossed her petticoats into the river. After she had twisted her gown into a silken rope, she tied it about her waist so it wouldn't hinder her, and she leaped into the Mississippi.

When she had silently sidestroked to the far side of the steamboat, away from the crowd of immigrants, Erica clutched the paddlewheel. Then she silently made her way up the spokes until she grasped the rail on the boiler deck. Without daring to look back down at the water, she scaled the supporting beam and hoisted herself onto the hurricane deck.

It wasn't difficult to find her way around the ship. Erica had been aboard quite a few steamboats, and they were all of similar design. She probably could have located the captain's cabin if she were blindfolded.

Smiling in satisfaction, she padded along barefoot, then halted in front of the texas, the captain's private cabin, which would be unoccupied until the following morning when the *Natchez Belle* sailed upriver. No room indeed! Erica snickered at her ingenuity, feeling quite

47

pleased with herself. Once the ship was launched, no captain worth his salt would toss her overboard. She would explain her situation, would appeal to the man's sense of decency, and she would pay her way with the money she had received from Dante . . .

When her contemplation led her back to the distractingly handsome rake who had taken her virginity, Erica winced uncomfortably. She had been unable to leave him without learning his name. She had feared that the memory of bedding a stranger would haunt her even more if she could not even attach a name to the man who had made love to her.

Muffled voices and the sounds of footsteps jerked Erica from her silent reverie, and she squatted down behind the row of chairs that lined the deck. She held her breath until two members of the crew ambled past her hiding place. Then, plastering herself against the wall, she inched her way back to the door of the texas. Still smiling at her cleverness, she folded her hand around the doorknob, anxious to hide in her sanctuary.

When the door wouldn't budge Erica cursed her rotten luck. The door was locked! Determined to gain entrance to the unoccupied cabin nonetheless, she pried open the window and then slipped inside. She breathed a weary sigh. Now she could be alone with her thoughts.

Suddenly Erica frowned. She wasn't at all certain she cared to rehash the disastrous events of the day, and she did not want to wallow in self-pity. She would slam the door on yesterday and devise a plan for the future. The past would die a peaceful death if she refused to indulge in painful memories. Tomorrow would be a brighter day. After all, how could it be any worse than this one had been?

A contented moan tumbled from her lips as she

stretched out on the bed, enjoying the spacious room and the security of knowing she could sleep without being pestered. But then, like specters of the night, the angry faces of her father and of Sabin Keary appeared before her, and she bolted up in bed, her body glistening with perspiration. After squirming beneath the sheet to find a more comfortable position, Erica saw Dante's handsome face swimming above her in the darkness. She could almost feel his gentle hands gliding across her flesh, could taste the drugging kisses that had melted her defenses. . . . *Stop it!* she chided herself when her memories evoked the same exciting sensations she had experienced in his arms. You mustn't dwell on the encounter, she told herself firmly. You have plans to make.

For the next few hours Erica worked out a scheme to resolve her dilemma, and finally, satisfied with her plan, she lay back on the pillow and drifted off to sleep. But her lectures had been in vain. Dante converged upon her once again. He was beside her, his lips playing lightly on hers. He was whispering, telling her she had pleased and delighted him. She was responding, returning his caresses, her hands ranging over his hard male body, as his had explored her quivering skin. . . .

A disgruntled frown distorted Dante's rugged features as he peered out over the street of New Orleans, listening to the chants of the rowdy men and women who continued to celebrate though it was long past the midnight hour.

"Where are you, dark nymph?" he whispered into the wind.

Dante had torn the city upside down and had come up

empty-handed. No one had seen his Cinderella in the golden gown and slippers. He raked his fingers through his hair, then braced his arms on the railing of the balcony outside his room at the inn. As his keen gaze swept the waves of humanity that rippled through the street below, he half expected to see the young woman floating up to him. But she didn't, not even when he silently called out to her.

"Perhaps you were right, *chérie*," he mused aloud. "What difference does it make now?" What could he say to the mysterious goddess, even if he found her? Dante had no answer. If it had been his intent to court the comely maid in the customary fashion, he doubted that she would have permitted it. After all, how would a man woo a woman he had taken to bed the first time he'd laid eyes on her? How could he hold himself at bay once he'd viewed the exquisite beauty that even five layers of clothing could not disguise? He envisioned her skin glowing like honey in the lantern light. That memory would never be erased from his mind.

Was she a wealthy aristocrat's daughter? A lost sheep who had been tossed about by an unruly crowd, separated from her friends by a cruel twist of fate?

Dante's shoulders lifted and then dropped in a gesture of futility. The brief, enchanting affair was over as quickly as it had begun; he should let her memory fade. Besides, he had sworn he would never become involved with women. They were trouble. They could destroy men with their conniving and scheming. Perhaps it was best that he never encountered the lass again. Their relationship had begun in reverse, and Dante was certain he would never be content to keep his distance from her, not when he'd known the passion that had come to life when he'd taken her in his arms.

"Dante? What the devil are you doing out there?" Corbin Fowler asked as he weaved his way toward the balcony.

"Searching for an angel," Dante murmured, his thoughts transporting him back to those mystical moments with his dark lady.

"In this surly crowd?" Corbin snorted and then sipped his drink. When his younger brother did not respond immediately, Corbin frowned. "Did you meet someone who caught your eye? I thought you had sworn off women."

"Women, yes." Dante chuckled. "Angels, no." He turned to survey his glassy-eyed brother who had spent the better part of the night winning and losing money at the casino.

"And what is this lovely goddess's name?" Corbin's speech was slurred and he braced himself against the doorjamb. "Perhaps I know her."

"I don't know her name," Dante admitted as he offered his brother a supporting arm and guided him back into the room.

"A nameless vision of beauty?" Corbin cackled, then flashed Dante a lopsided grin. "I think you have concocted this story to confuse my befuddled mind."

"That wouldn't be difficult," Dante muttered as he propelled him toward the bed.

Corbin overlooked the gibe and the leg of a chair. The latter tripped him up. With a squawk he clutched at the lapels of Dante's coat to regain his balance; then he grinned sheepishly at his clumsiness. "Put me to bed, little brother. I fear I have celebrated enough for one night. You can expound upon this strange story of

51

elusive angels when I am in full command of my senses."

"There is nothing more to tell," Dante assured his brother as he loosened Corbin's cravat and gently shoved him onto the bed.

Corbin collapsed as darkness swirled about him, numbing him to all except his need to sleep off his bout with brandy.

Dante chuckled at the sight of his disheveled brother sprawled on the bed. Corbin's arms and legs dangled in midair, and his cap was set at a rakish angle on his ruffled hair. "I'm glad Leona is not here to see you. She would swear you weren't the man she married."

"I'm not sure I am," Corbin groaned, his stomach churning like waves on a stormy sea.

With an exasperated sigh, Dante tugged off his own clothes and stretched out on the empty bed on the far side of the room. The evening had not gone according to plan. He had left Corbin in the casino, intending to seek out a wench to ease his needs, but he had found more than he'd anticipated. He was satisfied, yet restless. Why can't I put that raven-haired vixen out of my mind? he asked himself, as he clasped his hands behind his head and stared up into the darkness. But the dark beauty continued to plague him, and it was several hours before he slept, not long before sunlight announced the approach of another day.

"Good God!" Corbin moaned as he pried open one bloodshot eye to greet the morning. "Why didn't you close the drapes?"

Dante snickered at his brother's unkempt appearance and hoarse voice. Corbin sounded like a sick bullfrog.

"Time to rise," he announced cheerfully, drawing another agonized groan from Corbin who cringed as Dante's voice thumped against the inside of his sensitive head.

"There is no need to shout," he muttered as he carefully hoisted himself into an upright position. "Will you grant a dying man wish? I beg you for a hot cup of coffee."

"Perhaps you would prefer a jigger of brandy," Dante taunted unmercifully, uncorking the bottle to allow its aroma to permeate Corbin's warped senses. On a number of occasions Dante had been the recipient of Corbin's teasing so he delighted in turning the tables on his older brother.

Corbin wrinkled his nose distastefully and shoved the bottle away. "Quit heckling me. Just fetch the confounded coffee, will you? I have to be alive within the hour, and you are retarding my recovery."

Dante bowed mockingly, sashayed across the room, and slammed the door none too gently behind him. He tarried outside to listen to Corbin curse before he descended the stairs to retrieve the life-resuscitating liquid his brother had requested.

"I suppose I deserve this," Corbin grumbled when Dante announced his entrance by letting the door strike the wall.

"For all the times you tormented me when I was in a delicate condition," Dante chortled as he extended the coffee to Corbin.

Shaky hands folded around the steaming cup, and Corbin lifted heavy-lidded eyes to study his brother. Dante was only two years his junior, but his worldliness more than compensated for the slight difference in their ages. At times Dante acted older than he did. Once his younger brother had been light and carefree, but now his smiles did not come as often and he worked tirelessly, refusing to seek out the pleasures in life. Corbin had insisted that Dante accompany him to New Orleans to sow a few wild oats. It had been three years since Dante had indulged himself, three years since he'd sailed from one continent to another, selling goods to China, England, and the West Indies. In the interim he'd dropped anchor and had consented to try his hand at running a plantation, but his heart still belonged to the open seas.

The bitter circumstances that surrounded their father's death had made him hard and cynical. When Corbin had taken it upon himself to tell his brother that he must forget what could not be changed, Dante hadn't responded. Corbin felt that he needed some distracting diversion, something to lessen his resentment. Thus far, however, Corbin had failed to breathe new life into Dante.

Carefully, Corbin rose to his feet, testing his wobbly legs. He then tucked in the hem of his shirt. "I think I will survive now. When I first awoke I wasn't certain." A bemused frown knitted his dark brow when fragments of the conversation he'd had with Dante on the previous night drifted back to him. "What was it you were babbling about when I returned last night? Did you tell me you had been visited by an angel or did I dream that?"

Dante chuckled at his befuddled brother, then gestured toward the door. "You must have been dreaming. Shall we go? I believe you said there were several things you should accomplish this morning."

Following in his brother's wake, Corbin strode down the hall, reasonably certain Dante had mumbled something about angels. But as usual, Dante kept his thoughts to himself. It was easier to pry information out of a clam than to drag secrets from his tight-lipped brother.

"Did you seek out Avery Bennet?" Corbin asked, carefully calculating Dante's reaction, but he was met with a blank stare.

"I decided not to seek him out on this trip." The subject soured Dante's mood. "But one day I intend to confront him. Believe that. I want an explanation, even though you were content to let the matter drop."

"It would be best for all concerned if you would bury the past," Corbin advised, flinging his brother a meaningful glance.

"I will never be able to bury it until my questions have been answered," Dante snapped, his voice harsher than he'd intended. "I want to know the whole truth, not just Sabin's version."

Corbin did not reply, knowing he had brought up a touchy subject. He wished Dante would close the door on the past and bury the memories that disturbed him. Yet he knew Dante would never understand and forgive until he overcame his cynical attitude toward women. It is a difficult situation, Corbin thought as he walked along beside his brother. The past and present went hand in hand for Dante. One dilemma could resolve the other, but separately, each played against the other. Corbin frowned. Was he making any sense? Finally he shrugged away his wandering thoughts. His tender head was in no condition for deep thought, not until the fog of liquor evaporated.

Dante's keen gaze swept the main deck of the *Natchez*

Belle, and then he berated himself for expecting to find the young woman among the immigrants crowded amidst the cargo.

"Captain Fowler!" The mud clerk strode toward both men who turned in response to his summons. "It's a pity you both have the same names," he said with a broad grin.

Corbin was in no mood to tolerate idle prattle. "Perhaps when Dante weds he will take his wife's name and solve our problem," he declared sarcastically. "Now, to whom do you wish to speak? The presiding captain or the co-pilot of this journey?"

The mud clerk sobered when he realized Corbin was in too foul a mood to enjoy humor. But it is a bit confusing, he thought.

The *Natchez Belle* was owned by these two men who shared the captain's duties. Corbin was in command during the first leg of the journey, whereas Dante usually navigated upriver to St. Louis while Corbin remained with his wife and children. Although the working arrangement allowed both men to be ashore for longer periods of time, it was difficult to know which one to approach when both captains chanced to be sailing on the same voyage.

"I have already taken on wood, and the chief clerk has gathered the tickets." The mud clerk dropped the heavy pouch in Corbin's hand. "As you can see we have taken on a full load of cargo and passengers. The engineer has fired the boilers, and we will be prepared to sail as soon as you give the command."

As the mud clerk, who aptly earned his name by leaping ashore at each landing to take on wood and cargo, invariably wading in mud up to his knees, strode away,

Dante cast Corbin a reproachful frown. "Don't you think you were a bit harsh on the lad? Just because you have a hangover, you don't have to bite off his ears."

"Don't preach," Corbin scowled. "I'm having enough difficulty navigating without being lectured." He stepped onto the landing stage and then glanced back at Dante who was silently surveying the crowd that milled about the deck. "Don't expect to find an angel in that conglomeration of people."

"I wasn't looking for her," Dante lied.

Corbin broke into a smug grin. "So a woman did fascinate you in New Orleans."

Dante muttered something, and then he appraised his brother's shabby appearance. "I'll fetch your clean jacket from the texas," he offered. "I fear that climbing into such high altitudes might render you useless to the passengers and crew."

"I would appreciate that," Corbin replied as he rubbed his abdomen. "My stomach is still pitching and rolling." As Dante walked toward the stairs, Corbin called after him. "And tell the pilot to stand by. We should be ready to embark in a few minutes."

Part II

There is a certain relief in change, even though it be bad to worse; as I have found in traveling . . . it is often a comfort to shift one's position and be bruised in a new place.

—*Irving*

Chapter 4

When Erica heard the key rattling in the lock, she bounded to her feet, scooped up her dress, and darted across the texas to hide in the closet. Her heart was drumming so furiously that she swore the intruder could hear it pounding, but she held her breath as footsteps crossed the cabin. Although she had intended to confront the captain, she had overslept and she dreaded being caught in his cabin, especially when she was so unkempt. How could she sound convincing when she looked like a drowned rat? Perhaps she could milk the captain's sympathy, but she doubted that he would believe her to be a gently bred young woman who could afford to pay her fare. He would probably herd her off the boat, and she could not risk a confrontation with Sabin, not yet, not until she had followed through with the scheme she had devised.

A curious frown furrowed Dante's brow when he glanced over at the unmade bed. It was not like Corbin to leave his cabin without seeing to that particular chore. His brother was neat and orderly except when he'd been drinking, and even that was an infrequent occurrence. Shrugging, Dante strode toward the closet to fetch Corbin's jacket, but he jumped as if snakebit when he found himself staring into the same face that had tormented his dreams.

"Damn!" he declared, his eyes wide as saucers and his heart catapulting into his throat. "You took ten years off my life."

Erica stood frozen, staring at Dante in astonishment. "I'm . . . sorry."

Dante had wondered how he would react if he ever laid eyes on this stunning minx again, but the moment he saw her, he found himself wanting to begin right where he'd left off.

A gasp escaped Erica's lips as Dante impulsively stepped into the closet and then closed the door behind him. His arms encircled her, and she was flattened against the rock-hard wall of his chest as his mouth slanted across hers, sending her senses reeling before she had recovered from the shock of staring into the handsome face of the rogue she'd had no intention of seeing again.

Was he mad? A gentleman did not closet himself with a skimpily dressed woman and then kiss her until she swooned! The scoundrel had deflowered her, and here he was again, appearing out of nowhere, trying to take advantage of her. Erica was furious with him for cornering her, and she was annoyed with herself when her body began to respond to his caresses. She felt as if an entire butterfly collection were fluttering about in her stomach. Her palpitating heart was about to tear loose from its moorings, yet she could not even draw a breath for his mouth was devouring hers. His bold embrace had sent her into a mindless whirl, and she was unable to make any sense out of the sensations that burned through her when this stranger took her in his arms. She had spent half the night trying to forget him, and she told herself that she would have done so if he had not appeared to rekindle the fires he had set the previous night.

Erica half-collapsed when Dante suddenly stepped back. She braced her hands on the walls to keep her balance, but even that failed to steady her when Dante's wandering hand strayed beneath the bodice of her chemise to tease one pink peak.

"What do you think you're doing!" Erica shrieked. Finally taking command of her reeling senses, she slapped his hand away. Yet his touch had already branded her with fire.

"What do you think I'm doing, *chérie?*" Dante rasped, his desire for her so fierce that his lips impulsively moved toward hers.

He drew her supple body back to his, keenly aware of the feminine softness that melted against him. His hands wandered over her back and then her buttocks as he pressed her closer, but it wasn't enough. The memory of lying beside her, caressing her silky skin, drove reason from his mind. He had no interest in conversation for his lips were pursuing an activity far more stimulating than speaking. His body was hungry for hers, and he could think of nothing but losing himself to the subtle feminine fragrance that invaded his senses.

In the recesses of his mind he vaguely wondered what was the matter with him? He had never before thrown caution to the winds when dealing with a woman. But here he was, shut in a closet, kissing this enchanting nymph. He didn't even know her name, but that didn't matter. He was stirred by sweet memories that compelled him to cling to the only real pleasure he had found in years.

Erica had suffered so many catastrophes during the past twelve hours that she was becoming hysterical. Suddenly the incident struck her as amusing. The mere thought of how ridiculous they would look to anyone who might walk in on them made her giggle beneath Dante's kiss. Then laughter bubbled from her, and Dante raised his head, wondering why Erica was chuckling when he'd been involved in a very passionate embrace. Had he lost his touch? He had been intent on seduction, yet this minx was laughing at him!

Inhaling deeply, Erica tried to compose herself. And she did for a split-second. But when she saw Dante's muddled frown she again burst into laughter. Her mirth was contagious, and in a moment Dante was laughing with her.

"I swear one of us is crazy. Now all I have to do is determine which one," he chortled, as he reached back to open the door and shed some light on the subject.

That was a mistake, he soon realized. Erica's chemise hugged her shapely contours and exposed her creamy flesh, and seeing her so undermined his good intentions. He ached to touch her, to run his fingers through her raven curls, and to kiss her soft pink lips. Had he been so long without a woman before finding this adorable wench in the brothel that he had become a lusting beast? Couldn't he control himself for one minute? He didn't even know her name, for Christ's sake! She probably thought him to be as disgusting as the three men she had attempted to elude before she collided with Dante.

Erica deciphered the gleam in his eyes. She had seen desire flicker in those fathomless emerald pools once too often, and she had no intention spending the remainder of the morning cornered in the closet. She snatched up her dress as meager covering, then wedged past him, striving to reassemble her dignity, or what was left of it. "I think you have some explaining to do, sir."

"Me?" Dante stared incredulously at her, and then his eyes bulged from their sockets as she bent over to drag the sheet from the bed, displaying her shapely derrière before she draped herself in a makeshift toga. "I have every right to be here. But why were you sleeping in my bed and what are you doing aboard my ship?"

"Your bed?" Erica wheeled around, her jaw gaping. "*You* are the captain of the *Natchez Belle?*"

"Actually, I share the bed with my brother," Dante explained and then grinned when Erica cast him a suspicious glance. "I did not mean to imply that we sleep together. We both own the steamboat and divide the duties. Usually we are not aboard at the same time." Dante strolled toward her. "You still have not answered my questions. What were you doing in my closet and why are you aboard the *Natchez Belle?*"

"I am looking for my husband," Erica replied glibly.

"Your hus . . ." Dante strangled on the word. He had bedded another man's wife? A dubious frown plowed his bronzed features. She was lying to him. She was a virgin and no man in his right mind would allow this breathtaking creature to remain untouched, especially when he had legal rights to her. "I don't believe you. Last night after you left I found proof that I was the first, although circumstances led me to believe you were a . . ." His voice trailed off, refusing to blurt out the word. Nor was he about to apologize for making love to her. Dante did not regret it, not one tantalizing, arousing moment of it.

Erica blushed profusely and then presented her back to the handsome captain. Damn his soul for not begging forgiveness! The *least* he could have said was he was sorry for robbing her of her innocence. But no, the big oaf had probably carved another notch on his belt, grinning all the while.

"The fact of the matter is I am looking for my husband, but I have yet to meet him," she reluctantly explained.

Dante's frown carved deep lines in his forehead, his expression becoming harsh and cynical. "So you are a fortune hunter," he grunted disdainfully. He knew this lovely goddess was too good to be true. She wasn't an angel at all, but rather a conniving witch disguised behind a mask of distracting beauty. Had she somehow learned who he was and sneaked into his room to demand that he marry her after what had occurred the previous night? What was this vixen up to? "I didn't realize open season had been declared on the male population." He wrapped the words around his tongue and flung them at her with biting sarcasm.

Erica whirled around to confront the contemptuous sneer that slashed across his tanned face. "I have my *own* fortune awaiting me when I take a husband. The man for whom I search is only a means to an important end. I must be married to obtain my trust fund. If I had another choice, I assure you, I would not search out a man." Her eyes raked over him, and then she sniffed distastefully. "Thus far, I have found them all to be very annoying creatures."

Amusement splashed through his emerald eyes as he propped himself against the wall and crossed his arms over his chest, appraising the bedraggled beauty who still had the power to arouse him when she was at her worst. "I see," he said with thoughtful deliberation. "And what type of man do you seek, Miss . . ." He paused, hoping she would divulge her name.

"Erica," she begrudgingly supplied, not mentioning her last name. She dared not risk having this rogue learn her identity for he might cart her home to her father. "I am looking for a man who will be satisfied with a reasonable compensation for allowing me the temporary use of his name, one who will not make trouble for me when we go our separate ways. This marriage must last long enough to fulfill the requirements of my trust, but after the financial transaction is made I wish to be free to pursue my own life."

Dante's measuring gaze sketched Erica's determined features. She seems to have as little use for men as I have for women, he mused pensively. Had she suffered a bitter romance at a tender age, or had their tryst of the previous night left a damaging scar?

"Have you some aversion to a true marriage, Erica?" He tried out her name, allowing it to flow from his tongue like a slow, languid caress.

Erica peered at him out of the corner of her eye and then lifted a proud chin. "Men consider their wives to be servants of sorts. I do not intend to become a man's chattel, and I will not tolerate that attitude," she assured him flatly. "After last night, I lost what little respect I had for men, which was only enough to fill a thimble to begin with."

My, she was a skeptic, but it was not difficult to imagine why. Her beauty and her shapely figure would attract men's eyes and their hands. How well he knew. A contemplative frown crept onto Dante's face as he ambled toward Erica, making her retreat a cautious step. She was all too aware of what could happen when their bodies made physical contact, and he had already squeezed the stuffing out of her in the closet. It was apparent that she had no intention of allowing that to happen again, much to Dante's dismay.

"You must be a very independent young woman," he concluded. "Am I to assume that your future husband will not be allowed to consummate this marriage of convenience before you shuffle him out of your way?"

"Your assumption is correct." Erica's gaze was glued to the wall, but a slow blush worked its way up her neck. She was not accustomed to discussing lovemaking so casually.

"You found the experience distasteful then?" Dante questioned point-blank.

Erica jumped as if she had been stung when Dante's warm breath tickled her bare shoulder. The cad! If he were a gentleman he would not approach her so, especially not in the wake of such a probing question.

"That is not the point," she said evasively, then sidestepped before he could capture her in his arms. "I am in need of a husband and I must be quick about obtaining one. Surely there is one man on the *Natchez Belle* who would agree to allowing me use of his name and to collecting payment for it."

A wry smile trickled across Dante's sensuous lips. "I would like to offer my assistance," he volunteered, his voice bubbling with laughter. "I can think of nothing more entertaining than watching you rummage through the male passengers in search of your future husband."

Erica did not trust him or his motives. If he had any

sense of decency, he would have offered his own name after he had . . . She stopped herself before the mere word triggered the memories she'd buried in a dark corner of her mind. "I am offering no fee for a match-maker," she assured him flatly. "I will see to this grizzly business myself."

Dante took her hand, bowed before her, and then placed a light kiss on her wrist. "My dear Erica, I would not expect payment. It is only that I am piqued by your unconventional method of selecting and discarding a husband," he explained, his laughing green eyes silently mocking her. "I will be only too happy to introduce you around the steamboat."

"Dante, where the hell is my—" Corbin swallowed his breath when he barged through the door of his cabin to find his brother bowing before a wild-haired young woman who was wrapped in his sheet.

After spinning around to whip open the closet door, Dante tossed the jacket at Corbin. "Forgive the delay. I was unavoidably detained."

"I can see that." Corbin smirked and then opened his mouth to protest, but Dante propelled him toward the door and locked him out.

Dante pivoted to peer at Erica who had turned several shades of red. "Now where were we?" he murmured provocatively as his arms encircled her waist, drawing her back against his muscular body.

Erica unfastened his clenched hands and glared at the dashing rake who was attempting to seduce her and carry on a conversation at the same time. She knew she couldn't think when he touched her. His bold caresses were too potent.

"You were questioning me about my reasons for a

69

whirlwind wedding," she prompted. "You see, I am in a bit of a scrape. Without a husband I will be forced to wed a most irascible man who intends to punish me for an unfortunate accident."

One dark eyebrow quirked. "Oh? What kind of incident? It would help if you could be more specific." Her evasive explanation fed Dante's curiosity and he preferred some direct answers.

"I shot him," Erica blurted out and then tossed Dante a meaningful glance. "He sought to take privileges without my permission."

Dante laughed aloud. "And he still wants to wed you?"

"He is a strange man," she answered with a shrug.

"A glutton for punishment," Dante snickered, visualizing Erica with a pistol in her hand, taking pot shots at her overzealous beau. Oddly enough the picture fit this wild witch. "I suppose you also imply that I should have been next in line for a firing squad after what happened last night."

"The idea has a certain sadistic appeal," she assured him tartly. "Had I been armed last night . . ." She let her remark dangle in midair, allowing Dante to draw his own conclusions.

Dante didn't doubt that this feisty vixen would delight in blowing him to smithereens. Yet, she fascinated him. None of the women he had known possessed this maiden's fiery spirit.

"You cannot hold me personally responsible for what happened," he protested. "How was I to know—"

"You could have listened to my explanation," Erica snapped, bringing quick death to his self-righteous defense. "But no, what you had on your mind had nothing to do with assistance or consolation. You wanted a body, not the personality and troubles that went with it. I was being chased by three drunken roustabouts, and I traded one calamity for another!" She was almost shouting when she paused to draw an angry breath.

Dante's attention fell to her heaving breasts which rose and fell above the drooping sheet. Then he reluctantly raised his eyes to her belligerent face, intending to cross-examine her before she completely lost her temper with him.

"How did you secure passage on this steamboat? There were no vacant rooms on the ship." Dante felt fortunate that he had distracted her with this question for she had looked as if she were itching to find a weapon and turn it on him.

"I swam aboard from the blind side of the ship," she informed him, tilting her proud chin. "But I intend to pay my passage."

An ornery smile tugged at one corner of his mouth. "With *my* money, I assume."

Erica puffed up like a disturbed cobra that would have delighted in sinking its fangs into his flesh. "I damned well earned every penny of it! What I lost to you was more valuable than your entire fortune!"

"And if I had paid you what you were worth, my lovely nymph, you would have no need of your trust fund," he murmured, his green eyes glowing with the same fiery desire she had noticed in them earlier.

The unexpected compliment rattled her, and Erica blushed up to her perfectly arched eyebrows. After recovering her composure, she reached into the top of her chemise to retrieve the cash she had stashed there. "This should be sufficient funds for my passage to Natchez."

Dante accepted the money she thrust at him. "Have you enough to replace your wardrobe? Surely you do not expect to attract your future husband with yonder gown." His disapproving gaze landed on the soiled, wrinkled gown that was the worse for wear due to its dip in the muddy Mississippi.

His comment took the wind out of her sails. She had not thought past her frantic search for a husband.

"I would imagine that you would find it difficult to attract men if you intend to traipse about the steamboat in your stylish sheet," he taunted caustically. "But I doubt that my brother and the members of the crew could keep their minds on their work." His tanned finger investigated the edge of the sheet that concealed her breasts. "And this garb might shock some of our straight-laced passengers."

Erica chewed thoughtfully on her bottom lip. "I had not thought of that, but I dare not go ashore. Search parties are looking for me, and I cannot risk being found until I have taken a husband."

Dante fished into his vest pocket to retrieve his watch. "If you trust my judgment, I will see to the matter for you. We have only a few minutes before we sail, but I'm sure I can find something suitable."

Why was he being so helpful? There was nothing between them except a night of passion that really should never have occurred. As if he had translated the dubious frown that captured her features, Dante blessed her with a blinding smile.

"It is my way of compensating for last night, Erica. What I took from you cannot be replaced." His smile became a rakish grin that made her blush profusely. "Though I will not apologize for a most delightful encounter, I will be happy to be of assistance in your hour of need . . . which is rapidly ticking by," he added as he glanced back at his watch. "Do you wish my help or will you make do with this costume of muddy gold?"

Erica had no choice. Extracting more money, she placed it in his hand. "I will be grateful for whatever garments you select," she assured him and then allowed a wan smile to ripple across her lips. "Thank you, Dante."

"It is my pleasure, my dear." Dante circled around her, silently assessing her voluptuous figure from all angles. "I will do my best to ensure a good fit." With that he pivoted away and then called over his shoulder, "Stay put. We will decide where to house you when I return."

As the door closed behind him Erica collapsed on the bed and breathed a relieved sigh. At least she was safe from her father and Sabin Keary. The five-day journey to Natchez would entail an exhausting search for a man who would agree to her terms without hampering her future, but Erica convinced herself that in this instance the means would justify the end. She would never marry Sabin! She detested all he stood for, and he was too quick tempered to tolerate her beliefs and her independent nature. Sabin bought, sold, and beat his slaves; Erica could never live on a plantation where human chattels were kept by such a tyrant. Nor could she return to her father when he allowed Sabin to manipulate him. She and Avery had clashed at every turn since she'd returned from school in Philadelphia. When she had suggested shipping merchandise by the increasingly popular railroads that had begun to connect them with the East, Avery had refused, informing her that he had made arrangements to use Sabin's schooner and he would be very upset with the change. When she'd mentioned

73

women's sufferage, Avery had muttered about his foolish mistake in sending Erica to Philadelphia for her education. He swore that she would not have become so headstrong and willful if she had remained with her own kind.

Erica heaved a frustrated sigh. Perhaps her father was right. Once she had viewed her corner of the world from the outside, it seemed to have major flaws. The North had turned to dependence on factories while the South relied upon slave labor to produce their sugar, cotton, and tobacco. After Nat Turner's rebellion against slavery, Erica had begun to fear an upheaval in the Southern way of life. Debates on slavery in the legislature were becoming heated, but most plantation owners clung to their convictions and traditions. Erica had become involved in political groups that rebelled against the South's dependence on slavery, much to her father's chagrin. But cotton was selling at twelve cents a bale and slaves were bringing twelve hundred dollars per head. Southerners were not willing to believe that their way of life might be threatened. Indeed, Erica was considered a misfit because she refused to conform to the Southern ways. What a fine mess she had made of things. Now she was an outcast, a hunted woman—a tainted woman.

Still grappling with her disturbing thoughts, Erica absently smoothed the wrinkles from her satin gown. Perhaps she should return to the East after she had secured her inheritance. At least she would not be a constant embarrassment to her father. Avery had refused to allow her to work at the New Orleans Cotton Exchange, and he vehemently disapproved of her speaking out against slavery. Erica was certain that her father hoped marriage to Sabin would stifle her protests. What could she say when she was the wife of a plantation owner who kept his share of slaves? Well, she would not become a hypocrite. After all, look what she had sacrificed to avoid a public apology and marriage to that black-hearted scoundrel.

A secretive smile pursed her lips as Dante's vision hovered about her. At least Dante had been a gentle lover. His hands had worked magic on her skin and she had . . . *Stop that this instant!* Erica told herself. The past is past, and all men are beasts. She decided that she was merely dazzled by Dante's striking good looks and skillful caresses. In the future she would treat him as an acquaintance, Erica told herself firmly. But how could she do that when they had been as close as two people can be? She would just have to work that out. She could learn to adjust to that approach, and so could Dante once he realized that they had had their first and last passionate encounter.

Chapter 5

"Dante, what the sweet loving hell is going on?" Corbin demanded as he hastened his step to catch up with his brother. "What is that woman doing in the texas?"

"I'll explain later," Dante called back to him as he hopped onto the landing stage and strode toward shore. "Just leave her alone until I return."

"Where are you going? We are ready to sail!" Corbin groaned and grabbed his throbbing head, scolding himself for using such a loud voice which made him feel as if he were caught in the middle of the percussion section of a marching band.

"I'll be back as soon as I can. Don't sail without me," Dante ordered as he weaved his way through the crowd.

Corbin exhaled in exasperation. He would have given his right arm to know what Dante was about and why he was grinning like a weasel that had just feasted on a plump chicken. Dante's smile was as wide as the Mississippi, and Corbin was curious to know what had brought such pleasure to his brother's chiseled features. For the past few years Dante had behaved as if he had misplaced his one and only friend. Now he had found himself a lovely wench wrapped in a sheet, had stashed her in the texas for safekeeping, and was trotting down the street on some mysterious mission. Corbin was burning with curiosity. Dante had some explaining to do and it could not be done quickly enough. Corbin was in no mood for games. His head was splitting and his stomach was rolling. Lord, he felt terrible, and by traipsing off to New Orleans without explaining himself, Dante wasn't helping his foul disposition.

Erica gasped as Dante opened the boxes and spread the elegant gowns before her. "I cannot afford these! You spent far more than I gave you."

"If you intend to woo a husband in less than five days, you must be adorned in eye-catching gowns," Dante argued, grinning outrageously. "I did not mind adding the extra funds to pay for these items since I will be fully repaid by watching you land a husband who meets your unusual requirements."

Erica flung him an irritated glance, and her annoyance increased when she spied the lacy, provocative undergarments he had selected. He is obviously a connoisseur of women's apparel, she thought resentfully. Evidently, he has undressed enough females to know what lies beneath the velvet and taffeta. If he had overlooked a single item, Erica could not imagine what it was.

"You do not approve?" Dante raised an eyebrow as he strolled up behind Erica, who was rummaging through the boxes to find slippers, petticoats, and a new chemise.

"Do you also make a living by fitting women with proper clothing?" she questioned, her tone heavily laden

77

with sarcasm.

"No, but I am not ignorant of women," he rasped as his hands glided over her curvaceous hips.

"Obviously," Erica declared bitingly, although shock waves were running up and down her spine. She wheeled about, her frown warning him to keep his hands to himself or risk losing them. "Now please grant me privacy. I would like to dress." Her arm shot toward the door. "I will call you when I am decent."

Disappointment melted his roguish grin. "There is no reason to affect modesty. I have seen you in far less than a sheet," he reminded her as his intense gaze flooded over her figure, visualizing her as he had seen her the previous night.

His brash remark triggered her temper and before Erica realized what she had done, she had grasped the intricately carved wooden schooner that rested on the night stand, and had hurled it at Dante. The missile grazed his shoulder and then struck the floor, shattering into a thousand pieces. Erica gasped in dismay and Dante growled furiously.

"Damnation, woman, we really must do something about that nasty temper of yours. That statue *was* a prized possession, a replica of my own schooner. But it has weathered no storm worse than hurricane Erica," he muttered as he stalked toward her, causing her to retreat. "If you intend to snare a husband, even a temporary one, you had better learn to control yourself. I am not certain your cherished inheritance can pay for the damages if you throw another tantrum and demolish the *Natchez Belle!*"

Suddenly he turned and left the cabin. When he slammed the door, the echo bounded off the walls and

78

came at Erica from all directions. Chiding herself for allowing Dante to rile her, she knelt down to scoop up the broken pieces of the statue. It was just that Dante's constant teasing brought out the worst in her. They shared a secret that greatly disturbed her, and she simply could not contain herself when he made reference to the night she had allowed herself to be seduced by a strikingly handsome stranger. *And I did allow it,* Erica reminded herself miserably. But there had been something magic in his embrace and in the exciting way he'd kissed her. His touch could defy logic, and she was vulnerable to it. The emotions that churned within her when he was near frightened her. She had always prided herself on being strong and independent, but when Dante stared at her, that provocative smile hovering on his lips and that compelling fire in his eyes, he could melt her heart. She felt a strange need to lash out at him, to deny the sensations his skillful touch evoked. Perhaps she had worn her feelings on her sleeve; nonetheless, she decided that regular doses of Dante could prove fatal.

As a gesture of friendship she would try to replace his keepsake. One day she would find a substitute and send it to him, along with a note of apology. After making a mental note to do just that, Erica drew the elegant blue gown over her head and smoothed it into place, determined to make herself presentable. Five days was a short amount of time to attract and snare a husband. She must focus her full attention on that chore, distasteful as it was.

"Now, if it isn't too much trouble, would you mind telling me what the devil is going on around here!"

79

Corbin had been waiting on the hurricane deck to pounce on his brother and, although he had begun pleasantly enough, his voice had risen testily, warning Dante that his short-fused temper was about to explode.

Dante swallowed his irritation with the feisty vixen who prowled about the texas and turned to confront Corbin. "My angel turned out to be a temperamental witch." He scowled. "We have an extra passenger on the boat, and tempted as I am to toss that little termagant overboard to drown my troubles, I cannot."

"If this is your idea of an explanation, you have failed miserably," Corbin grumbled, his head throbbing in torturous rhythm as he spoke.

Heaving a perturbed sigh, Dante sought to get a grip on himself and to make a less jumbled explanation of the situation. But since Erica had swept into his life like a misdirected disaster, he'd been having difficulty making sense of it himself.

"The lady . . ." He paused to reconsider the word he had employed to describe that raven-haired armload of trouble, and he decided that whatever Erica was, she was definitely not a lady. "Erica is a stowaway, running from a man who intends to do her harm. I have given her permission to travel to Natchez with us so I had to go ashore to purchase suitable clothes since the misplaced mermaid was without them."

Corbin frowned thoughtfully as he recalled seeing Dante hop aboard with his arms full of packages. "But where do you plan to stash the woman?" he demanded. "You know the staterooms are filled to capacity, and we have no other woman traveling alone so there's no extra berth."

A wry smile pursed Dante's lips. "You could move in

80

with me and offer Erica your cabin," he suggested.

"You should have approached me on that subject when I was in a better frame of mind," Corbin grumbled. "I am in no mood to share cramped quarters with you. The next time you decide to play the good Samaritan, I hope you have the decency to consult me before I am inconvenienced."

"I knew you were too tender hearted to allow a gently bred young woman to camp out on deck," Dante mocked dryly.

"So naturally you volunteered my spacious room for your indecent princess." Corbin snorted. "When will I be allowed an introduction? I should at least like to meet the woman who will be enjoying the luxuries normally reserved for the captain who commands his ship." His eyes narrowed suspiciously on his grinning brother. "Or do you plan to keep her all to yourself for fear someone will snatch her away from you?"

Dante ignored the gibe. "I imagine you will see a great deal of Erica. She is husband hunting. Wherever a crowd of men gathers, no doubt she will be in the midst of them."

"Husband hunting?" Corbin crowed in disbelief.

"And it is my responsibility to point out every man who might suit her purpose before she makes her selection." Dante swaggered across the deck and leaned against the rail to inhale a breath of fresh air. "I must thank you for insisting that I accompany you, dear brother. This could prove to be the most entertaining voyage I have ever taken."

A skeptical frown plowed Corbin's aching brow as he appraised his brother's wily grin and radiant expression. There was something strange going on, and Corbin was itching to know what it was. But before he could interrogate Dante, his brother strutted away, leaving Corbin's throbbing head spinning with unanswered questions.

"Erica and I will join you shortly for lunch. I will make a formal introduction then." Dante paused to toss Corbin another mischievous grin. "On closer inspection you may find it necessary to remind yourself that you are a married man. This creature is nothing short of stunning when she is wearing something more complimentary than your bed sheet."

Corbin let his breath out in a rush and then spun about, aiming himself toward the pilot house. He had a ship to navigate, and although he would dearly love to know what Dante was planning, there were pressing matters to attend. The Mississippi was a treacherous waterway, and a man needed his wits about him if he were to steer through the sand bars and the remains of wrecks that blocked the channel. Corbin had a challenging river to read, and no time to attempt to untangle the workings of Dante's complicated mind.

When Dante rapped on the door of the texas, Erica admitted him, but her humble expression caught him off guard since he had expected to go another round with her.

"I am very sorry that I lost my temper with you, Dante," she murmured. "I promise to replace your model schooner and I am most grateful for your assistance." Her lashes fluttered down to shield her from the vivid green eyes that so easily entranced her.

Dante was spellbound. The blue gown he had selected for her accentuated every curve and swell she possessed, and she had pinned her dark hair atop her head in a sophisticated fashion that permitted soft ringlets to curl about her face.

"You look stunning." Dante's appreciative gaze took in the slope of her bare shoulder and then lingered on her creamy breasts. "Your search for a husband may not last a day." His eyes ascended to her flawless face, and he was enthralled by the gentle curve of the lips that had melted like summer rain beneath his own. He felt a hunger gnawing at him, one that was difficult to control when he stared too long and hard at this bewitching minx. No one deserved to be as breathtaking as Erica, he thought resentfully. Her beauty bordered on the sinfully seductive, and he decided that he could not condemn the roustabouts who had chased after her the previous night. Who could deny his desire when this goddess crossed his line of vision?

As his probing gaze returned to the scooped bodice to feast on the tempting display it revealed, Erica pivoted away, unnerved by his blatant appraisal. She had hoped to make friends with Dante, but he was peering at her with something akin to lust. He was a rogue in every sense of the word, and he had the uncanny knack of undressing a woman with those penetrating eyes that could melt her soul. He alone knows what lies beneath the silk and petticoats, Erica thought acrimoniously. She and Dante had no secrets from each other, not after the previous night. She knew the exact placement of the long scar that wrapped itself around his ribs, and the smaller one that arched over his left knee; and he knew . . . Erica choked on the thought. Dante knew things about her that she hadn't known about herself until he'd stirred them to life.

Shoving her meandering thoughts aside, she glanced back as Dante's emerald eyes made a slow sweep of her backside. "Your selection of gowns was a bit daring, don't you think?" she admonished, for lack of much else to say when his gaze scorched her as surely as a caress.

"Daring enough to match the woman who wears it," he countered, flashing her a sly smile.

Erica favored him with a dismayed frown. "I feel like a strumpet peddling my wares," she breathed. Then she hiked up the bodice of her gown, but the fabric refused to stretch. "I wish just once a man would show some interest in a woman's intelligence and inner charm rather than her physical attributes."

"The bitter truth is that we men are attracted to lovely women, not misfits garbed in feed sacks or sheets," he parried as he ambled toward her, giving Erica the hemmed-in feeling that plagued her each time he came within ten feet of her.

"A misfit, am I?" Erica braced her hands on her hips and thrust out a proud chin. "I am a product of catastrophe, searching for a husband I would prefer not to meet and for no other purpose than to elude a fiancé I could never tolerate." Her blue eyes flashed in annoyance. "I am only trying to survive by using ingenuity and resourcefulness, however bizarre and ribald that may seem to you," she added flippantly.

Dante curled his hand around her chin, bringing it down a notch. "I'm sure there is method in your madness, and it should prove to be as entertaining as the madness itself," he replied, his voice bubbling with laughter. "Shall we tour the *Natchez Belle* and scout out prospective bachelors?"

Hesitantly, Erica slid her hand around his proffered

arm. Then she heaved a dismal sigh. "Never in my worst nightmare did I dream I would set about seeking some reckless scoundrel to be my husband. Yet, here I am, searching for less than a gentleman, perhaps a rakehell who will give me his name without expecting a wedding night with all the usual trimmings," she muttered sourly.

"That might prove to be an exhausting search," Dante pointed out, muffling a chuckle. "What man in his right mind would not seek at least one night of pleasure in exchange for the temporary use of his good name?"

How aptly stated, Erica thought, disheartenedly. She could not risk wedding a man in his right mind. What she needed was a dense, slow-witted ogre. But that sort of man could also prove difficult to manipulate. If such a man were blessed with no more intelligence than God granted a mule it might be impossible to reason with him on any subject.

This isn't going to work, Erica mused pessimistically. It had all seemed so simple when she was lying abed, staring up into the darkness. But now the scheme seemed full of loopholes. She was taking a great risk. She must have been moonstruck to have concocted this scheme.

Disturbed by those thoughts, Erica leaned heavily on Dante's arm. It gave her a sense of security to know he would be there to protect her if she encountered a man who proved more than she could handle.

While they strolled along the boiler deck, admiring the view, Dante directed Erica's attention to an elegantly dressed man who, immersed in thought, was peering out over the river. "Hiram Johnson is an available bachelor," he informed her. "He is rather notorious at the gaming tables, but I'm sure he can be bought if the price is right."

Erica scrutinized the older man who did not seem too

unpleasant to the eye, at least from a distance, and Erica Johnson sounded respectable enough. She nodded agreeably when Dante arched a quizzical brow.

"Hiram . . . I would like you to meet Erica . . ." Dante frowned, realizing he still had not learned the lady's surname.

Hiram assessed the lovely lass with his card-sharp's eyes, not missing the smallest detail. "It is my pleasure to make your acquaintance, my dear," he murmured, favoring her with a smile. "Is this your first trip by steamboat?"

"No, I have traveled by steamer several times in the past," she informed him, her attention focusing on the thin beard that rimmed his jaw and the narrow mustache that emphasized the length of his nose. This man is capable of charming women, she thought skeptically. Blind ones.

"I wonder if you would be so good as to escort Erica around the ship while I see to a small matter for my brother," Dante requested. Then he choked back a chuckle when Erica silently pleaded with him not to abandon her to Hiram, who was grinning like a starved shark.

"I would be delighted to take Erica off your hands," Hiram purred, his gaze swimming over the enticing sea of bare flesh her plunging neckline revealed.

When Hiram placed his arm around her waist to guide her through the crowd, Erica flinched. His touch unnerved her whereas Dante's had warmed her inside and out. Driving out the thought of Dante, Erica concentrated on making conversation, and she blinded Hiram with smiles when he sought to amuse her with what he considered clever remarks. If this man thinks he has a sense of humor he is deluding himself, Erica mused as Hiram propelled her across the boiler deck.

After half an hour, Erica was craning her neck for a glimpse of Dante. Relief washed over her when she spotted him, but it was short-lived for the curvaceous blonde on his arm was leaning very close to whisper something in his ear. Stung by jealousy, Erica quickly chastised herself for behaving as if Dante meant something to her. Why should she care if he was cavorting with an attractive young woman? She merely wanted him to rescue her from the card sharp who was practicing his sleight of hand tricks on her instead of on a deck of cards.

When Dante finally glanced in her direction, she discreetly signaled for his assistance. But he merely waved to her and then ambled away, leaving Erica smoldering. After what seemed an eternity, Dante did stroll up beside her, and Erica suppressed the urge to strangle him. The cad! He had abandoned her to Hiram's amorous advances.

"I see how you 'attend to a small matter for your brother,'" she mimicked. Then she sniffed distastefully as Hiram bowed out and moved across the deck. "Your clinging vine very nearly strangled you."

Dante's mouth quirked into a smile. "Did you expect me to be rude and order the young lady to keep her hands to herself?"

"If you cannot even ward off a woman I would hate to think how ineffective you would be in the face of real adversity." Erica made it clear that she considered his excuse a lame one.

"Did it occur to you that I might have been enjoying the lady's display of affection?" he countered, as he grasped her hand and threaded his way through the crowd. "And thank you for your vote of confidence." His voice had a caustic ring to it. "Remind me not to ask you for a character reference, should I find myself in need of one."

Erica heaved a sigh. She was annoyed with herself for verbally attacking Dante. She had no right to criticize him or to meddle in his personal life. "I did not mean to sound so harsh. I was just anxious to be rid of Hiram. You are a very attractive man, and I should not be surprised to see a collection of women hovering about you."

Dante stopped short, causing Erica to ram into him. "Have my ears deceived me? Have you offered me a compliment?" he taunted, feigning surprise.

"Do not press your luck," she advised. "I may be forced to retract it."

He lifted one shoulder in a careless shrug. "Ah well, perhaps there are other females aboard the steamship who will not be so stingy with their compliments—or their affection." Dante steered her toward the saloon which ran the length of the boat. "I intend to introduce you to my brother, but I must warn you that he is happily married. You need not bat your eyes at him."

Erica would have been insulted by his gibe if she had been paying attention, but she was awestruck by the magnificent saloon. Rich draperies adorned the windows and large mirrors hung on the walls, making the dining area seem larger than its ten-foot width. Crystal lamps hung from the high ceiling, which was decorated with gold carvings, and plush velvet chairs and sofas lined the far end of the room. Dining tables with white tablecloths filled the area to which Dante guided her. The *Natchez Belle* was by far the most magnificent steamboat Erica had ever seen.

"I have never viewed a boat quite like this," she breathed as her stunned gaze took in the luxurious saloon.

Dante smiled at the expression on her face, but he swore nothing in the room compared to this bewitching beauty in the sapphire blue gown. The dress had not seemed so exquisite when he'd noticed it in the boutique, but with Erica in it, the gown was dazzling. Dante knew that he was not the only man who thought so for he was aware of the admiring eyes fixed on Erica.

After searching the crowd, Dante spotted Corbin at his usual table. He was staring at Erica, his jaw sagging slightly.

"Erica, I would like you to meet my brother, Corbin," Dante said.

Corbin was dumbstruck. At a distance the young woman had been attractive, even in her sheet, but at close range she was bewitching. He gathered his feet beneath him to rise and then wilted back into his chair for Dante had already seated Erica.

"Had I known I was to sacrifice my cabin to such a lovely lady, I would never have complained," Corbin confessed to Dante, but he could not seem to unfasten his gaze from Erica.

"You're drooling," Dante mocked dryly as he leaned close to his brother.

Corbin snapped his jaw shut and colored slightly. "I retract all the dubious thoughts I have been thinking about you since you explained Erica's dilemma," he assured his brother before his attention again turned to Erica. He marveled at the vivid blue of her eyes. They sparkled with such liveliness that he stared at them in amazement. She might well be the fire Dante needed lit beneath him, Corbin mused as he noticed his brother openly admiring Erica.

"Dante favors you in his good looks," Erica observed. "It is not difficult to tell you are brothers, though I would hate to be forced to decide which one of you is more attractive."

Corbin beamed delightedly. This lady was the best medicine anyone could prescribe for his hangover. Indeed, his disposition had sweetened considerably already. "If you continue to shower me with compliments I will not only give you my private cabin, but I might be willing to put you in command of the ship," he teased with a playful wink.

"I have to beg for her compliments, yet she offers them freely to my brother," Dante muttered sourly.

Although Corbin was too dazed to digest the remark, Erica got the gist of it. A sticky sweet smile glazed her lips, and she shrugged nonchalantly. "Some men earn my respect with their good manners, others have to labor for it," she insisted breezily.

"And I, of course, fall into the latter category," Dante snorted as he shook out his napkin.

Before Erica could comment, Corbin began to interrogate her about her past, and she found herself tactfully talking around the truth to avoid divulging any pertinent information. Dante was itching to know about her family and the man from whom she was running, but Erica was too clever. She gave nothing away. Chagrined, Dante decided he would need a crowbar to pry the truth from her lips.

Erica enjoyed the pleasant company and the succulent food. When a fricandeau and platters of potato croquettes and green vegetables were placed before her, she realized she was famished. She ate until she was certain the seams of her gown would split asunder, even indulging in the jelly tarts. Once Corbin and Dante had realized that Erica was not about to divulge any secrets about her past, they'd begun to taunt each other, and Erica was thoroughly enjoying their raillery.

After the meal, the tables were removed and small card tables were set up. Swarms of men, including Hiram Johnson, gathered to pass the afternoon playing cards. Erica was surprised when Dante insisted that she join in a game, but she was not about to refuse him. She much preferred the challenge of cards to gossiping with the women who had congregated at the far end of the saloon. After the first three hands, Erica had a sizable stack of winnings, and Dante was grumbling to himself. She had put the men to shame so he decided it best to evict her from the game before she earned a reputation as a card sharp.

"Why couldn't we finish playing?" Erica complained as she allowed Dante to propel her toward the door. "I was enjoying myself."

"Where did you learn to play like that?" Dante scowled. His male pride was bruised. "Women are not supposed to be handy with a deck of cards. I thought Hiram's eyes were going to pop out when he watched you shuffle the deck as if you had been born with one in your hands."

Erica smiled wickedly and then lifted one shoulder in an evasive shrug. "I have not spent my entire life in a vacuum," she assured him.

"Obviously not," Dante grunted. "Is there anything you cannot do?"

"Honestly?" Erica raised her delicate brow. She wondered if he was fishing for the truth or merely being sarcastic.

"Yes," he insisted as he paused to stare down at her.

"No." Erica flashed him a grin that melted his heart. "I have tried almost everything once, just for sport."

In that moment, Dante forgot his wounded pride and countered with a smile. "Somehow I knew you would say that." His lean finger traced the luscious curve of her lips. "And you never do anything halfway, do you, Erica whoever-you-are?"

His light, exploring touch warmed Erica's blood so that she backed away before he triggered emotions she was carefully holding in check.

"No," she assured him, struggling to keep her voice from quivering due to the aftereffects of his caress. "Living life to its fullest is much more appealing than merely existing."

Her comment confirmed Dante's belief that this lively firebrand was afraid of nothing and no one, and a new respect for her blossomed inside him. Erica was incorrigible. Not a man on God's green Earth could tame her feisty spirit. She was like a wild, free bird who refused to be held in captivity and who did not know the meaning of compromise or defeat. Erica was one of a kind, a misfit of sorts. Although she had the face of a seraph, she had the heart of a lion. Dante didn't doubt that Erica would overcome the difficulties created by the mysterious man who pursued her. She was calculating and clever, and if he wasn't careful—

"Is something amiss?" Wide blue eyes peered up at him, attempting to decode the expression on his craggy features.

Dante's face melted into a secretive smile. "No, my dear. It is just that my mind was wandering," he explained as he took her arm and guided her through the door.

"My goodness, has senility set in?" she asked with mock innocence.

"Are you implying that I am old?" Dante challenged, enjoying her playful banter. Erica had finally begun to relax in his presence, instead of watching him out of the corner of her eye as though he might spring on her if she dared to let her guard down. "At thirty-three I am still capable of running circles around you."

Erica could not argue with that, so she didn't. She well remembered the night she had made a mad dash toward the brothel door, only to be grasped in Dante's powerful arms. He was as quick and agile as a panther. Deciding it was time to change the subject, Erica glanced about her.

"Have you another available bachelor for me to meet? I am running on a tight schedule, you know."

Dante gritted his teeth and then scanned the passengers meandering about the deck, finally locating one who would test Erica's ability to fend for herself. Godfrey Finley had as many arms as an octopus, and Dante was curious to know whether Erica would chop off a few of them. His conscience would not allow him to sic Godfrey Finley on a lesser woman, but Erica was a different matter. He even anticipated watching the fireworks when Erica and Godfrey clashed.

"Right this way, my dear," Dante purred, grinning devilishly.

Godfrey Finley was so plain looking that Erica was

certain someone had randomly splattered bland features on his face after using the attractive ones for Corbin and Dante. She was not surprised that Godfrey was still a bachelor after forty years. Even if a woman married him she would easily overlook him since he blended in with the woodwork. The man turned out to be a walking encyclopedia of little-known facts, most of which Erica would have preferred not to hear, but when she learned that Godfrey had a penchant for gambling and that he had won and lost a fortune at the gaming table, she immediately scratched him off her list of possible husbands. No doubt, he would keep popping up to ask for money before she could have the marriage annulled. And gambling wasn't his worst fault, Erica soon learned, for her love-starved companion propelled her into a corner and began to squeeze her. Erica grabbed the nearest weapon—a broom—and clubbed Godfrey over the head until the clumsy galloot became addled. Noting his condition, she gave him one last smack across the cheek and then stomped away, feeling positively murderous. Men, she thought cynically. Not one of them possessed refined manners. She would never find a suitable husband, not in five days or five years!

As Erica stormed across the deck, Dante stepped from his hiding place, his wry grin stretching from ear to ear. He surveyed the bruised and battered Godrey Finley who would now think twice before he again laid a hand on hurricane Erica. Then, chuckling to himself, Dante swaggered away to seek out Erica's next victim. Never had he enjoyed watching a woman as much as he delighted in viewing this firebrand in action. Erica was an enigma—a mystifying beauty with a quick temper. Her tempestuousness amused him. Verbally fencing with her stimulated him. And touching her . . . Dante suppressed the arousing tingle that rippled down his spine. There would be time to dwell on those tantalizing sensations later, he reminded himself. Now, he would concentrate on Erica's antics, which were far more entertaining than a three-ring circus.

Chapter 6

An appreciative smile on her lips, Erica peered across the mighty Mississippi to see a flock of long-legged herons perched motionlessly on the shore, in the shade provided by trees draped with Spanish Moss. As the steamboat breezed by them, the slate purple birds released explosive squawks and leaped high in the air, flapping their wings to skim over the waves that rippled toward them when the steamboat interrupted the quiet of the riverbank.

Perhaps the herons were annoyed by the intrusion, but Erica found the river peaceful. She propped her arms on the rail and continued to peer at the wild creatures along the banks, noting that most of them slipped into the dense undergrowth at the river's edge when the steamboat passed. Life did not seem so tedious in these tranquil surroundings.

"How is your search coming along?"

Erica was startled by the low, seductive whisper so close to her ear. She turned to find herself pinned between Dante's muscular body and the rail, his arms braced on either side of her. She was suffocated by his nearness; the mere inches that separated them made her uncomfortable. The man did strange things to her equilibrium, not to mention the physical distress he caused.

"Fine. And yours?" she managed to reply without sounding too breathless.

One dark eyebrow rose acutely, then returned to its normal arch. "Mine?" His tone registered the faintest hint of amusement. "I am not wife hunting."

"I have seen you with a blonde, a brunette, and a red-head today," Erica said tartly, having regained her composure. She was determined not to let this rakehell disturb her. "I thought perhaps you planned to check out the entire list of female passengers."

A low rumble erupted from his chest as he bent his head to hers, his emerald eyes dancing with deviltry. "But I have not been as intimate with them as I have been with you," he assured her, his voice a wandering caress that demolished every barrier she had attempted to construct.

Beet red splashed across her cheeks. "Must you keep referring to that disastrous night?" she muttered acrimoniously.

"Disastrous, *chérie?*" Dante pounced on her choice of words; then he delighted in watching her squirm with embarrassment. "I found it to be a very pleasurable experience. For one so innocent of men, you proved to be an excitingly passionate woman."

Erica gasped. Then flesh cracked against flesh, and she was pleased to see her hand print brighten his left cheek. The cad! She was ashamed of the way she had responded to him, and it perturbed her to have the incident brought to her attention. Her satisfaction was short-lived, however, for Dante's lean fingers soon bit into her forearms.

"If we weren't in a crowd I would take you over my knee and paddle your lovely backside, witch," he growled, his teeth clenched. "You can deny your true nature if you wish, but you are a very passionate woman. I know. I learned that in a dimly lit room when—"

Erica could stand no more! She pushed away from him with such angry force that she had to clutch the rail to avoid toppling overboard. But the rail was low and she was off balance. Panic gripped her when she glanced over her shoulder and saw the water below. She thrashed her legs then, desperately trying to achieve a solid footing so she wouldn't flip over the rail and plunge into the river.

"Dante!" she screamed as her grip on the rail weakened. She was going to fall. God help her! Dante didn't intend to stop her! He just stood back, grinning.

Suddenly, with the agility of a panther, Dante scooped her up in his arms the split second before she arched backward toward the water. She clasped him about the neck, and she buried her head against his shoulder, trying to block out the haunting sensation of falling.

An amused smile pursed Dante's lips when Erica practically squeezed the stuffing out of him. "If you wanted me to take you in my arms, all you needed to do was ask," he teased, loving the feel of her supple body pressed so tightly to his.

Erica was too close to the rail to let go of Dante so she did not react to his taunt. When she did not retaliate in her usual, fiery manner, Dante frowned down upon the shapely bundle who clung to him like a choking vine.

"Don't tell me you are afraid," he said when he realized why Erica had not indignantly squirmed free. "I could have sworn you feared nothing or no one."

Erica held on to him for dear life because Dante had not stepped away from the rail and he could easily toss her overboard if he had a mind to do so. "I have a dreadful fear of falling," she confessed, twining her arms even more tightly around his neck. "I once fell from the balcony outside my second-story room. Although I tried to grasp a nearby tree, I scraped against every branch before I landed on the ground. I have never overcome the fear of falling that resulted from that experience."

"And do you also fear *falling* in love?" Dante inquired, his sensuous lips lingering only a few breathless inches from hers.

Erica pulled away from his shoulder and glanced at the murky river below her. "Do you intend to throw me overboard?" she demanded. "If not, I cannot endure the suspense. Please move away from the rail. You are making me nervous."

"What will you give me if I do?" he murmured, his tone implying that he preferred a physical display of gratification.

Damn him! Erica was humiliated because the crowd was smiling at them, yet Dante was forcing her to hug him when she would have preferred to slap him silly. "You might well receive a black eye if you don't," she snapped, so low that only her nemesis could hear.

That sounds more like the firebrand I've come to know, Dante decided. "Then at least answer my harmless question," he insisted, as his piercing eyes focused on her soft pink lips. "Do you also fear falling in love?" As he said this, he leaned over the rail, forcing Erica precariously close to disaster.

"Yes . . . no . . . I don't know. I never found myself teetering on that threshold." Erica gasped. "Dante, please put me down. You are scaring the wits out of me."

To Erica, it seemed forever before his arm slid out from under her knees and he set her on her wobbly legs. Dante surveyed her white face; then he aimed her toward the steps. "Come along. I think you should lie down a bit."

Erica found herself propelled through a crowd of curious onlookers, herded up the steps, and then forced to lie on the bed in which she had spent the previous night. Dante edged down beside her, reaching out to trail his index finger over her cheek.

"Since my brother has consented, the texas will be yours during this voyage. Feel free to make yourself at home." His index finger traced the hypnotic curve of her lips. "Rest now. I will return later to take you to supper, unless one of your beaux has invited you to dine with him."

"I declined the offers," Erica declared. Then she swallowed hard as his tanned finger continued to investigate the soft curve of her mouth. Why was he tormenting her like this? Didn't he know that his touch could make mincemeat of her emotions? Did he not realize that he had embroiled her in a mental and physical tug of war? She was trying to dislike his forthright manner, yet she was drawn to him like a moth to a flame.

"Hiram and Godfrey did not meet your expectations?" he murmured as his sensuous lips followed the path of his finger.

"Hiram was educated beyond his intelligence, and Godfrey could not keep his hands to himself," she said breathlessly, struggling to keep her mind on the conversation though her heart was pounding. It did not occur to her that she had beaten Godfrey senseless for attempting to take the privileges that Dante was enjoying at this very moment.

"I'm sorry to hear that," he rasped before his mouth fitted itself to hers, stealing her erratic breath and then giving it back at the very instant when Erica felt she must gasp for air like a drowning swimmer going down for the third time. "Perhaps we can find someone else to your liking, this evening."

"I . . ."

Erica was not able to reply, for Dante's lips rolled over hers, his questing tongue probing the softness of her mouth. His wandering hand glided over the slope of her shoulder to trace the lace bodice of her gown, then dipped lower to reclaim territory no other man had explored. Erica was on fire, and even the waters of the Mississippi could not dampen that blaze. His bold caresses unleashed forbidden memories, allowing them to run rampant. When his hand molded itself to the full swell of her breast, then slid along her ribs to wander over her abdomen before retracking the same arousing path, deep inside Erica a coil of longing unfurled and traveled through her entire body, completely baffling Erica. No man had affected her like this. Dante Fowler had that special touch, and although she berated herself for being so responsive to him, she could not seem to control the desire that bubbled through her. He could melt her defenses with kisses and caresses, could make her body strain for intimate contact with his. Again his searching hand mapped her curvaceous figure; then it ventured beneath her skirt to trail over her thigh. His kiss deepened, became more demanding, more passionate, while his bold fondling continued to weaken her crumbling defenses.

Her hand involuntarily slid inside his jacket, the palm pressing against his hard chest and then sliding over his ribs to his back, where muscles tensed and then relaxed beneath her timid touch. Dante drew her closer, molding her body to his while his wayward hand roamed over her hip. Her lashes fluttered up then, and she looked into his penetrating eyes, eyes that could see into her very soul, and when his full lips melted against hers, he breathed a fire into her. He was the master of seduction, swaying her with intimate caresses and intoxicating kisses, compelling her to want him, calling forth a need she had not been aware of until she'd collided with this stranger at the head of the stairs.

It was as if she were sinking into the mattress, floating on a sea that gently rocked her and yet aroused her. Her inhibitions had drifted out with the waves, and she was kissing him back. She was using his skillful techniques on him, just as he had employed them on her. The spark of passion leaped between them, blinding them to reason, feeding a growing hunger that could easily burn out of control.

Dante finally dragged his lips from hers. "Rest now, Erica," he said.

He was burning with desire, and the primal urge threatened to demolish what was left of his good sense, but he was determined not to make the same mistake he had made the first time they'd met. He intended to tempt and taunt her, to arouse her without completely seducing her. The next time he came to Erica there would be no lingering fear in her. She would desire him, just as hungrily as he craved her. Patience man, he told himself. This delicious minx is worth the wait.

Rest? Erica blinked in disbelief when Dante unfolded

102

himself from the edge of the bed and strode toward the door. How could she sleep after being assaulted by such fervent emotions? She had to get herself in hand. Dante was only toying with her, using her to quench his thirst for women. It was obvious that he was unaffected by a kiss that was heated enough to make the boilers of the steamboat explode. If he had been as aroused as she, he would not have been able to strut away from her. The man is carved from solid rock, she decided, willing her leaping heart to thud at a more reasonable pace.

Her skin still tingled from his familiar touch and her lips trembled with the aftereffects of his devouring kiss. But she chided herself. Dante means nothing to you, and you know nothing about him except what only a wife should know about her husband. Sweet merciful heavens! She didn't know whether Dante had been hatched from an egg or had come unassembled. She didn't know where his home was, whether he was married, single, or widowed. She didn't know where he stood on political issues. Determinedly, Erica closed her eyes and mind to those laughing green eyes that could look right through her. It would be wise to avoid Dante Fowler, she told herself. He would only complicate matters. She needed a husband, one she could discard without regret. Clinging to that thought, Erica tried to sleep, but Dante's handsome smile kept popping into her mind and she was not able to rout his disturbingly attractive image.

"Your choice of women is as impeccable as your taste for vintage wine," Corbin commented while he watched Erica and her latest escort leave the saloon for a stroll in

103

the moonlight.

"She isn't my woman," Dante declared, but his eyes strayed to Erica's departing back, lingering longer than necessary on the graceful sway of her hips.

Corbin surveyed his brother for a long, silent moment. "Then exactly what is your interest in Erica whoever-she-is?" he asked. "Since that lovely whirlwind breezed into the texas you have been grinning like a weasel. What game are you playing?"

"I am merely introducing her to men she might wish to wed and delighting in watching her charm them out of their boots," Dante replied with a casual shrug.

"Hiram, Godfrey, and Shelby Turpin are *her* kind of men?" Corbin snorted in disbelief. "You have introduced her to gamblers and vagabonds who don't have a responsible bone among them."

"That is exactly the type of man she seeks," Dante explained blandly. "Erica wants a man with dollar signs in his eyes, someone who is not opposed to compromising for the sake of a few gold coins."

"What?" Corbin croaked, his eyes popping. He was certain Dante was lying. "Why would a respectable young woman want to be seen gallivanting around the steamboat with those shady scoundrels? And who the hell is she anyway?"

Dante's shoulders lifted and then dropped as he threw down the remainder of his wine. "Your guess is as good as mine, big brother. Now, please excuse me. I doubt that Erica is in need of a chaperone, even if I have matched her against Shelby Turpin. But since wolves are known to rear their heads when the moon is full, it would be advisable for me to keep a watchful eye on the lady."

"You have purposely thrown her into the hands of a

wolf of the worst sort," Corbin accused. "That Shelby Turpin sprouts two extra pair of hands when he comes within ten feet of a woman. Godfrey was bad enough, but Shelby?" Corbin rolled his eyes, then glared at Dante. "Good God, man, you have invited trouble."

"I would guess that our hot-tempered lass will chop off a few hands if Shelby should paw at her," he chortled. "Would you care to join me? It will be interesting to see what happens when the wolf's fur starts flying."

Corbin gave his dark head a negative shake. He was silently questioning Dante's intelligence. Lord, his brother was behaving strangely. The sun must have fried his brain, he thought.

As Dante paced the deck he heard muffled voices coming from the shadows, and he hastened to the source of these sounds. Suddenly, he paused, then stepped back, watching in amusement as a deck chair sailed through the air to catch Shelby in the midsection. With a pained grunt, Shelby tumbled backward. Then he howled in surprise when his furious companion launched another chair at him with enough force to snap his head back. Shelby took shelter behind the upturned chairs, cowering like a frightened ostrich.

"If you lay another hand on me, you groping lout, I'll sever it at the elbow!" Erica spouted, her blue eyes blazing, her face livid with rage. "We have only met and you behave as if we have known each other forever. You disgust me, Shelby Turpin! It would delight me were I never to see you again. Do you hear me, you miserable apology for a man?"

Shelby got to his knees and then stood amidst the broken chairs that had served as Erica's weapons.

"I thought you wanted me to kiss you," he said hesitantly. "You—"

"You thought?" Erica railed indignantly "You must have the intelligence of a potted plant if you interpret a look of disinterest as a beckoning smile." Erica wagged a finger in his peaked face. Shelby backed down so quickly she might have been pointing a loaded pistol at his chest. "Don't you come near me again unless you can behave like a gentleman. I will not be mauled, not by you or any man!"

When Shelby had scampered away, Erica sought to rearrange the gown that the groping galloot had practically torn from her breasts. Shelby was even worse than Godfrey.

"Men, what a despicable lot," she muttered, her expression sour as a lemon.

"Am I included in your cynical opinion of males?" Dante inquired. He was so close that his warm breath caressed the back of her neck.

Erica's heart skipped several beats. "Will you stop sneaking up on me," she snapped; then she eyed him disgustedly. "You are an expert at appearing immediately *after* I have escaped a near brush with disaster."

Dante chortled. This little hellion had supplied him with more amusement than he'd had in years. If Corbin had witnessed Erica's confrontation with Shelby, he would not have condemned him for allowing this chit to put her overzealous beau in his place. Indeed, Corbin would have delighted in watching Erica settle the score with that ornery river hound, Shelby Turpin.

"If you had required my assistance I would have sprung to your side, but, as always, you had the situation well in hand," he insisted, flashing her a face-splitting grin. "It was Shelby who emerged the loser, not you, my dear." Dante smoothed a renegade strand of raven hair back in place before allowing his index finger to trickle down the column of her throat and to inspect the ripped lace around the bodice of her gown. "I must assume that Shelby also failed to pass the test. It's a pity. I only know of one or two other men who might suit your purpose."

Too late Erica realized that she had pummeled Shelby for touching her as Dante just had. When that lecher had reached for her, Erica had retaliated like a she-cat, yet when Dante caressed her she almost purred like a contented feline. Why, for heaven's sake? Dante was a rogue by all descriptions. He wanted what all the other men wanted. It was just that he used subtle, persuasive means to dissolve the barriers she had devised to hold men at bay. This green-eyed devil's approach always catches me off stride, she thought. He can kindle fires within me before I can react.

Erica backed away before she was drawn into a swirling emotional vortex she did not care to analyze for fear of what she might discover. She felt it best not to delve into her responses to Dante, and to keep him at a safe distance before she forgot her purpose, one that could determine her future.

"This scheme seemed so simple when I devised it," Erica confessed, obviously disheartened. "But I cannot seem to approach the subject of marriage. Those three men you singled out are very similar, and they all have a one-track mind. Not one has any use for conversation, and I refuse to lower myself to snare them." Her tone was as deflated as her spirits. "But I cannot return home without a husband. Even legally married I will risk Sabin's wrath . . ." Erica bit her lip, wishing she had not voiced those thoughts.

"Sabin?" Dante's rugged features turned to stone when Erica unwittingly spoke the name of the man who tormented her. He knew of only one man by that name. "Sabin Keary?"

No wonder Erica had such a cynical attitude toward men. Sabin was the epitome of ruthlessness. Dante was momentarily ashamed that the rogues he had aimed in Erica's direction were such reprehensible creatures.

Apprehension evident on her exquisite face, Erica frantically grasped Dante's hand and peered beseechingly at him. "Please don't betray me. I would do most anything to elude Sabin. What he intends for me would be far worse than death. If you have heard of him then you must know of his notorious reputation. Can you condemn me for making this desperate attempt to elude him?"

A tender smile rippled across Dante's lips as he smoothed the worried frown from her flawless features. "No, I cannot, Erica. I, too, have an ax to grind with the man." He paused momentarily, fighting to control his emotions. "Sabin Keary killed my father in a duel. One day Keary and I will cross paths. When we do I will see to it that he does penance for the misery he has caused you."

The color seeped from Erica's cheeks when she absorbed Dante's words. Sabin had killed Dante's father? Why? The thought stunned her. She knew Sabin was capable of great evil, but effecting another man's death? Was there nothing Sabin hadn't done, wouldn't do, to have what he wanted?

"Why did he duel with your father?" she asked softly.

When Dante's expression became as hard as granite, Erica knew she had hit upon a very sensitive nerve. But

108

because of her connection with Sabin she could not allow the matter to drop. She had to know what had happened. She couldn't understand why Dante's father had entered into a duel with a man who never fought fairly.

"The reason is of little importance now," Dante insisted, masking his frustration behind a carefully blank stare. "My father died defending a cause that was worth far less than the price he was forced to pay. But I have no doubt that Sabin Keary carefully plotted my father's murder."

Dante was still too raw inside to discuss the incident that had brought about his father's death. He had brooded over it for three years, but the pain he felt was just as fresh as if his father had died yesterday. Dante had refused to discuss the incident with anyone but Corbin, and even that was a struggle for him. Corbin had become complacent, but Dante had not. The thought of allowing Sabin Keary's crime to go unpunished made Dante's blood run cold.

"But how did Sabin—"

Dante grasped her arm and herded her across the deck, clipping off her question. "I think it's time we put you to bed for the night, *chérie*. You have had a busy day."

Erica could tell by the look on Dante's face that the subject was closed. Confound it, why was he being so secretive? After a moment's consideration, she reminded herself that she had no right to pry. Dante had not pressed her when she'd refused to offer her surname, and she had no right to poke her nose into his business.

When they reached the door of the texas, Dante unlocked it and then caught Erica around the waist before she could slip into the cabin. A prisoner in his arms, she was the recipient of a kiss that very nearly swept her legs out from under her. As his lips began an unhurried exploration of her mouth hers parted instinctively, as if eager for the pleasure to come. While her mind asked what the devil she was doing, her body arched toward Dante's virile frame. She was drawn to him because it was impossible for her not to be. His arms tightened, molding his frame to hers, and he kissed her so thoroughly that her world turned upside down.

Finally one of his hands slid up her spine to tilt her head back; then his moist lips fluttered over her cheek to nibble at the sensitive point beneath her ear. Erica's skin tingled and her knees became weak as his lips roamed over her shoulder. Just when she was certain that she was about to melt like butter left in the summer sun, Dante released her and she had to brace herself against the doorjamb to keep from collapsing at his feet.

"Good night, Erica. I hope tomorrow's search will be short and successful."

Erica blinked bewilderedly as he pivoted away and disappeared into the shadows. Her heart was slamming against her rib cage, but her body was suddenly cold after being so warm the moment before. Why does he affect me so? Erica asked herself, as she placed a quivering hand on the doorknob. And why am I allowing myself to depend on him?

Erica had never leaned on a man in her life, yet here she was, adrift on the Mississippi, comparing every other man to Dante Fowler—and finding that he surpassed them all. This is nonsense, Erica told herself as she stripped off her gown. She had to stand on her own two feet, to remind herself that Dante did not fit into her plan. Handsome rake that he was, he was not for her. It didn't matter that his kisses could send the stars spinning in the heavens or that his caresses inflamed her. He was a man and that entire lot was trouble.

An exasperated sigh escaped her lips as she plopped down on her bed. Her well-meaning lectures sounded convincing when she was alone, but they were as empty as the wind when she was caught in the seductive web of his embrace. *Forget him,* Erica told herself. Then she wondered how she could when they had been as close as two people could get. Perhaps she was just uncomfortable with a relationship that had started backward, she mused as she stretched out in bed. She was searching for something that wasn't there. Their first encounter meant nothing to Dante, not really, and she was making more of it than she should. But tomorrow would be another day. Surely the memory would fade. It just had to; that was all there was to it!

Dante leaned back against the outer wall of the texas and drew a deep, shuddering breath. Turning away from Erica was worse than tearing off an arm. He was determined not to let her forget how hot the fire between them could burn, but the flame of desire that sizzled through him was almost painful. It was a mark of heroism that he had mustered the will to walk away from her when his entire body blazed with unappeased passion.

Each night, before he left her alone, he wanted to give her food for thought. He intended to leave behind sweet, arousing memories that would inflame her dreams. Dante craved this feisty minx with eyes the color of the sky and hair the color of midnight, but he wanted her on his terms. He would not allow her to forget their passionate craving for each other.

Chapter 7

By late afternoon Erica was no closer to finding a prospective husband than she'd been when she'd dreamed up the idea. Dante had escorted her to breakfast, had introduced her to another river-boat habitué, and had abandoned her. It annoyed her that she spent the majority of her time craning her neck to see what had become of him, but in truth, the men she had met could not hold a candle to the raven-haired rogue who attracted female passengers to him like a pied piper.

While Erica was attempting to keep her male companions at an arm's length and to steer the conversation toward a hasty marriage, followed by an annulment, women hovered about Dante like bees in search of nectar. And to Erica's annoyance, he seemed to be thoroughly enjoying the attention he was getting, though she was bored stiff.

When Dante finally tore himself away from his harem and came to escort her to lunch, Erica was relieved to see him. Although she wanted nothing to do with Dante, her present situation forced her to look to him for assistance.

His knowledge of the available bachelors on the *Natchez Belle* threw them together, Erica reminded herself. If it had not been for that she would have had nothing to do with him.

Slumping back in her chair, she stared at the dashing captain who sat across from her. I am kidding myself, she thought. I can rattle off a thousand excuses, but I will still find Dante more attractive and more interesting than any man I have met.

A concerned frown furrowed Dante's brow when he glanced up and noticed that the lively sparkle in Erica's eyes had gone out. "Is something amiss?"

"Only everything," she muttered deflated.

Dante leaned across the table. Placing his finger beneath her chin, he lifted her head and smiled reassuringly. "You aren't thinking of abandoning your scheme, are you? Take heart, my dear. We shall find you a husband. There has to be one man on this boat who will please you. Perhaps you have been a mite too particular. You may be forced to compromise to gain results."

Erica eyed him skeptically. "If you are suggesting that I subject myself to another mauling I would never—"

"Not even a harmless kiss for the sake of your cause?" Dante lifted a mocking brow. "You still have a great deal to learn about the male species, Erica. We cannot be content with the small amount of affection you offer. Perhaps if you—"

"I will not!" Erica insisted tersely, quickly negating what she anticipated as being a distasteful suggestion. "What I have in mind is a business proposition, not a tumble in bed."

Dante rose from his chair and then walked around to assist Erica to her feet. "Did you learn nothing from your

113

experiences yesterday?" he queried. "Man cannot survive on bread alone, or even money. But one basic need lures him when all else fails."

"I have already stooped as low as I intend to," Erica assured him flatly. "I will not cater to the need to which you refer."

"Well then, have you considered throwing yourself overboard?" he teased as he led Erica through the crowded saloon and back to the deck.

"Have you forgotten I have a fear of heights?" she grumbled.

Dante chuckled as he flicked the end of her upturned nose. "Perhaps we can find another method. I do have a suggestion." He caught her to him, holding her hostage with his gaze. "You might also find it distasteful, but I could—"

"Dante?" A man's voice rippled through the air. "Am I to be the only man on board who is not introduced to this enchanting young lady?" Elliot Lassiter inquired as he strode up beside Dante.

Actually, Dante had been avoiding Elliot, and he wished his longtime friend would take a swim in the river instead of interrupting him at this moment.

"Of course not," Dante lied. "I had been waiting for the proper moment, but since you have spoiled it, may I present Erica." He darted her a warning glance before his gaze circled back to his blond friend. "This, my dear Erica, is Elliot Lassiter, one of Natchez's wealthiest bankers."

Reluctantly, Dante bowed out, but not without flashing Erica a beware-of-the-wolf-in-sheep's-clothing look.

As Dante disappeared into the saloon, Erica sized up an attractive man whose smile was almost as disarming as

Dante's. If Elliot was as hot-blooded as the rest of her suitors, she was in for an exhausting afternoon, she mused.

"I have been admiring you from afar since I saw you on Dante's arm yesterday morning." Lassiter's pale blue eyes strayed over his shoulder to ensure that Dante was out of earshot. "And I am bewildered that Dante did not put up a fight when I sought to share your attention."

Erica wasn't. She knew it amused Dante to watch her frantically search for a husband before the steamboat docked in Natchez. "Dante and I are only friends," she assured him, and then watched Lassiter beam delightedly.

"That is comforting to know. I should hate to compete with an old friend—and compete, I would have," Elliot insisted, favoring her with a blinding smile as he took her arm to stroll the deck. "Are you traveling to Natchez or St. Louis, Erica?"

"I am on my way to visit my aunt in Natchez," she informed him, surprised that his touch did not repulse her as the other men's had.

"Perfect . . ." Elliot mused aloud as Erica's feminine fragrance infiltrated his senses. Not only would he have the pleasure of Erica's company during the journey, but he could pursue this extraordinary beauty on land as well as sea.

Heaving a weary sigh, Erica removed her shoes and then collapsed onto the chair. A muddled frown knitted her brow as she remembered that Dante had silently cautioned her to beware of Elliot Lassiter. But Elliot had proven to be a perfect gentleman, and Erica had enjoyed conversing with him. He was intelligent, quick witted, and charming. Was Dante afraid she would use his friend in her scheme and then discard him, leaving Dante guilt-ridden since he knew her intentions?

That must be it, Erica decided as she tugged at the stays on the back of her gown. An alarmed gasp escaped her lips and she clutched at her drooping dress when Dante unlocked the door and ambled in as if he owned the cabin. Well, he does, Erica thought, but if he had any manners he wouldn't have intruded without announcing himself.

"You could have knocked," she snapped, coloring hotly as his hawkish gaze swooped over her scantily clad body. This man constantly had her blushing, and Erica resented his ability to rattle her.

"Knock on my own cabin door?" Dante smirked with magnificent arrogance. "I have a right to *everything* within the confines of this room, dear Erica."

And he set about proving that statement. Erica wasn't certain what evil spirit possessed him, but he smelled of whiskey and tobacco, aromas that soon clung to her when he marched over to grasp her in his arms. He planted a ravishing kiss on her lips and clutched her to him as if he meant to squeeze her in two.

Erica was too bewildered to protest, and before she thought to do so, her body, as if it had a will of its own, responded to the feel of his hard-muscled torso. She arched to fit herself to the only man who had managed to inflame her with desire. His embrace was hungry and impatient, like that of a starving man who is pouncing on a nourishing morsel. Erica had considered him a gentle lover after he'd taken her innocence, but she found him changed now.

His mouth possessed hers as his exploring hands intimately investigated her every curve and swell, as if what

116

had once been unclaimed territory was now his simply because he had been the first man to discover it. I am not his chattel, Erica thought indignantly. That he was treating her as such infuriated her. And she was even more annoyed to find herself responding breathlessly to the bold caresses that tracked an arousing path across her flesh. Somehow she had become addicted to his brand of passion. His kisses fed a desire that blossomed and grew deep inside her, compelling her to move closer when she should have soundly slapped his face as she'd done when other men had set their hands upon her.

Dante had been sitting and sulking in the saloon. Imagining Erica in Elliot's arms, he'd become more irritated by the minute that she had not attempted to use her charms on him, but had turned them on every other man aboard. Each drink he downed left him craving the subtle scent of her, longing to see the raven-haired enchantress who had not tried to attract him. He wanted her because . . . Dante cast out that thought before it boggled his foggy mind. Damn! Erica was his. He had known her as no man had, and he hungered to reclaim the moments that had bordered on fantasy the night he had chased her about the burgundy-colored room and then had made love to a bewitching goddess who had spirited herself off into the night. He wanted to erase Elliot's touch, his kiss; to make her forget that she had spent the whole damned day with a man who could offer her all she wanted and more. Damnation, why hadn't Elliot bypassed the Mardi Gras and stayed home where he belonged, counting his confounded money?

"Did Elliot's kisses set fire to your blood?" he rasped as he lightly bit at her lips. "Did you succumb to the same desire I discovered when I first took you in my arms?"

Erica responded without thinking. "I did not permit his embrace."

An unseen smile bordered Dante's lips as he nuzzled the trim column of her neck. "Why, Erica?" he asked, as his warm kisses traveled over her shoulder to sensitize the creamy flesh of her breasts.

His tongue flicked at a roseate bud, teasing it to tautness, before his lips tracked across her skin to give the same tantalizing attention to the other ripe peak. Meanwhile his free hand languidly glided over her abdomen to push the drooping gown away from her curvaceous body.

A tiny moan escaped her lips as his hand splayed over her hips and then ventured over her thigh. She was hot and cold and shaky, unable to catch her breath, unwilling to draw away from an embrace that was so ardent and demanding. As his knowing fingers found her womanly softness Erica clutched him closer, her slender arms sliding over the lapels of his jacket to curl around his neck and draw his mouth back to hers. His bold fondling continued as his lips opened on hers, bringing their passion to a fervent pitch. Emotions that simmered just beneath the surface erupted, and Erica knew that whatever he demanded of her she would freely offer. Dante could make his will her own, could evoke wild cravings for fulfillment.

As his mouth abandoned hers to track across her collarbone his hand cupped her breast, teasing the pink bud until she cried out with the want of him. He was setting her entire body ablaze from the inside out. His touch, like a compelling massage, left her dizzy and relaxed in his arms. Again his free hand trailed over her abdomen to invade the softness of her inner thighs, driving her mad with a need that threatened to become uncontrollable. He left her aching for more than he offered so Erica strained against him, hungry and impatient to appease her maddening need. He was so close and yet so far away.

As his thigh pressed between her legs his mouth descended on hers, stealing the last of her breath from her lungs. His probing tongue sought to mate with hers as his hands tracked across her back and then descended to her hips, clutching her closer to the hardness of his muscular body.

And then, as if he were satisfied that she had melted beneath the heat of desire, he slowly withdrew, leaving her to burn with frustrated passion. He had coaxed her to the brink of surrender, only to leave her teetering precariously on the edge.

"I will be by to escort you to breakfast in the morning;" Dante informed her as she stumbled back, trying to keep her balance.

Erica stared at him in disbelief. Then she drew her gaping gown over her breasts. The man was crazed! He had stormed into her room like an invading army, had kissed her senseless, and then had invited her to breakfast. She hated to think how he would approach her if it had been his intent to take her to his bed. He had no scruples. He was never going to let her forget what they had shared that fateful night when she had ducked into the brothel and wound up in his arms. Why was he torturing her like this? Wasn't she having enough difficulty without the emotional havoc he created?

She licked her kiss-swollen lips and assembled what was left of her dignity as she tilted her chin a notch higher. How could he stand there so calm and collected when his embrace had left her quivering with emotion?

Well, if he could act as if nothing had happened between them, so could she. He had probably had years of practice with women so he could turn his feelings off and on when the mood suited him, but she was determined to beat him at his own game. If he could behave as if they had just been discussing the weather, then she would not allow this skillful rogue to think he had gotten the best of her, even if she was trembling like a leaf in a storm. Dante Fowler was as solid as the Rock of Gibraltar, she decided as she peered up into his wry smile, wishing she could smear it all over his handsome face.

"Thank you kindly, Dante, but Elliot has invited me to breakfast," she stated coolly, although she was fighting like the devil to keep her voice from quaking. She wanted to sound aloof. If wishing could make it so, she would have appeared as indifferent as a stone post.

The news did nothing to resolve Dante's bout with jealousy, yet he managed the semblance of a smile when he noticed the smug expression on Erica's lovely face. He could cheerfully have choked her for spending so much time with Elliot Lassiter.

"Then I will take you to lunch," he insisted. "I have one or two men I would like you to meet."

"Elliot has also requested my company at midday." Erica tugged her lopsided gown back onto her shoulders. "But thank you for the offer."

"And the evening meal as well, I suppose." Dante's tone carried an undertaste of mockery. "It seems you are no longer in need of my services since you have latched on to a man with whom you have consented to spend the entire day."

When his hard green eyes slid from her face to tarry on the décolletage of her gown, Erica hiked up her dress and flashed him a glare. "Do not use that sarcastic tone with me," she chided him gruffly. "I am doing what I must to survive. I know you disapprove of my tactics. If that weren't so, you would have offered *your* name when I explained my dilemma. Or perhaps you already share your name with a woman and have been taking unfair advantage of me since the night . . ." Erica was just gathering steam, but her anger was transformed into embarrassment when her tongue outdistanced her brain.

A rakish smile turned up one corner of Dante's mouth as he watched a becoming blush stain her cheeks. "My dear Erica, no woman claims my name, and I did not offer to share it with you because the man you sought was an irresponsible rogue." Dante bowed before her, displaying gentlemanly manners and a disarming smile. "Naturally, I did not consider myself among that distasteful lot, and I hoped that you didn't."

"Perhaps I misjudged you," she muttered, flashing him a scornful glower. "But why I have not lighted upon some suitable means of reprisal for all the times you have taken outrageous privileges, I will never know." It was disgraceful to realize that time and again she had exhibited lack of will power where Dante was concerned. This green-eyed devil could barge into her room to seduce her, and she continued to allow it. Perhaps I am the one who is crazed, she thought disgustedly. If I had a smidgeon of fortitude, I would punch his seductive smile each time he came within ten feet of me.

"Perhaps for the same reason you did not allow Elliot to kiss you," he chortled as he swaggered toward her, captivated by the way the dim lantern light danced in her raven hair, which had come unwound and now cascaded provocatively over her breasts. "You didn't answer my question. Why didn't you allow Elliot to touch you?"

"Because I have barely known him a day," she replied. Then she darted away before Dante could capture her in his arms.

Dante felt as if someone had lit a torch under him when the gaping gown parted to reveal her bare back and the shapely curves of her hips. Her creamy skin seemed to beg for his touch. She was so damned tempting that he felt he must drive stakes through his boots to prevent himself from pouncing on her.

"If memory serves, you and I had only known each other a few minutes before we . . ."

Erica wheeled to face his taunting smile, itching to pound him flat, stuff him in an envelope, and have him shipped to China! Why did he have to refer to that catastrophic night? Wasn't it enough that she had yielded to the desires of the flesh? Must he continue to throw that in her face when she preferred to let the memory die?

"That was an entirely different matter," she snapped back at him. "I was distraught and I was not in full command of my senses. Too much had happened and I . . ."

With the quickness of a coiled snake, Dante sprang at her. He clamped his hands on her arms, forcing her to look him squarely in the eye. "Are you too naïve to realize that there was and still is a strange attraction between us, minx? Don't make excuses for your response to me. It was a special night, one I have no intention of forgetting." His voice was softer now; his smile suggested things Erica was desperately trying to ignore. "You can deny it if you wish, *chérie*. You can search every deck of the *Natchez Belle* to find a man who meets your qualifications for a loveless, temporary marriage, but what happened between us is an entirely different matter. If it weren't you would have permitted Elliot to kiss you. But you have held a true gentleman at bay."

"Only because you suggested that he was a wolf in sheep's clothing," she parried, knowing that she had again disguised the truth. "After I learned that Elliot is every bit the gentleman, I consented to spend the whole day with him."

Her comment did not sit well with Dante, and Erica was certain that he didn't want her tampering with his good friend. After all, the two men had known each other since childhood and had remained close for many years. That much Erica had discovered by subtly questioning Elliot.

"And therein lies the problem," Dante muttered as he released his grasp on Erica. "Elliot is too much the gentleman."

As he spun away and strode off, Erica stared after him, a muddled frown furrowing her brow. How could Elliot's good manners be a problem, she wondered; then she threw up her hands in a gesture of exasperation. Was it because Dante didn't want to see Elliot hurt? Why did he talk in riddles? She could no more read that man's complicated mind than she could fly to the moon. He was an expert at dodging probing questions. No wonder he was still free and unattached. A woman would be forced to clip the wings of a man like Dante to keep him from eluding her, and Erica had no time for such challenges. She was husband hunting—and time was ticking by. In a few days she would be setting foot in Natchez, and soon after Sabin and her father would appear on her Aunt Lilian's doorstep, demanding that Erica return home to face the consequences of her rash actions.

As she grappled with that distressing thought, Erica climbed into bed. A wry smile pursed her lips as Dante's image formed above her in the darkness. She wished that he had stayed to distract her. When she was with him she had a tendency to forget the world existed. He could ignite her anger and passion so easily that it frightened her. They had only known each other a few days, yet he had touched so many emotions that she might have known him forever.

If she had not been so determined to follow through with her scheme, she would have found herself in . . . Erica reacted sharply to the word that flashed through her mind. Good heavens! Was she falling in love with Dante? No, she was physically drawn to him. That was all. Love and passion did not necessarily walk hand in hand. If they did, Dante would have been in love with every woman he had seduced. And Erica hated to venture a guess as to how many women he had taken to bed. No doubt the number was staggering. Indeed, he was probably laughing at her inexperience, thinking her a child-woman who was ignorant of men until he had educated her on a subject she had cautiously avoided.

Erica slammed her fist into the pillow and heaved a frustrated sigh. Even if she were not seeking a loveless marriage to acquire her inheritance, she would be forced in that direction by her tryst with Dante—in a bawdy house of all places! Erica groaned miserably. What decent, respectable gentleman would be satisfied with another man's leavings? All men did what they pleased. They used some women—frequented brothels, kept mistresses—they demanded that the women they married were above reproach. I'm doomed, Erica thought, suddenly disheartened. A whirlwind courtship followed by a hasty wedding and an annulment was the only solution to all her problems. Dante had unknowingly set the course of her fate, and it would take a miracle to change it.

What have I done to deserve this? she asked herself. Oh, she had her bad points, plenty of them. She was short tempered, a bit outspoken, much too daring for her own good, and much too independent. She had arrived at the shocking realization that her passion for living was only exceeded by her passion for *passion*. But perhaps Elliot Lassiter would make her forget Dante's brand of it, she thought whimsically as her lashes fluttered against her cheeks and she breathed a weary sigh. Elliot was everything a woman could want, and perhaps he would be her salvation, *if* he could overlook the fact that she had been intimate with another man. Clinging to that encouraging thought, Erica drifted off to sleep. But visions of a raven-haired, green-eyed rogue flashed across her mind, and her body recalled the ways Dante had made her burn when he'd taken her in his arms and awakened her passion and desire. Then he was bending over her, kissing her, sending her skyrocketing to castles in the air. . . .

Part III

Calamity is man's true touchstone.
                    —Beaumont and Fletcher

Chapter 8

Elliot froze in his tracks when he stepped inside the texas and saw Erica. She was dressed in a mint green gown with bishop sleeves; sparkling diamonds adorning her swanlike neck, and soft, tempting flesh rising above her ruffled bodice. As his appreciative gaze swept over Erica's curvaceous figure, he decided that he would be the most envied man on the steamboat. For the last two days he had heard the passengers murmuring when he'd escorted Erica around the ship. Many pairs of eyes had followed her, but Dante Fowler's were the ones that baffled Elliot.

Each time he'd spoken of Erica to Dante, he'd been tactfully cut off and quickly steered to another topic of conversation. Yet Dante watched Erica like a hawk, even while she was on Elliot's arm. Since he refused to explain his relationship with Erica, Elliot was itching to know how and when they had met, but he knew it would take a crowbar to pry information out of his tight-lipped friend.

When Erica moved gracefully toward him, Elliot lost interest in his pensive musings and felt his knees go weak. This blue-eyed enchantress could reduce him to jelly with one of her beguiling smiles. He had never met a woman who had made such a strong impression on him, one whose stunning beauty and sharp wits left him hungering to spend every hour in her company.

"Words fail me," Elliot breathed as he took her hand to place a kiss to her wrist. "You look indescribably lovely this evening."

On purpose, Erica thought to herself. She had decided to approach Elliot on the subject of marriage, and she had primped all afternoon to ensure that she looked her best. She hated to deceive Elliot, but she felt forced to do it. The thought of Sabin Keary stalking her was a strong incentive to snare a husband. Although she had no desire to hurt Elliot, she was becoming desperate and time was short.

"Thank you, Elliot," she murmured appealingly.

As they entered the dining room, however, Erica found her gaze circling the crowd in search of the handsome face that continued to visit her dreams. Dante was surrounded by attractive women. When he was not, he was escorting a different young lady each time she caught sight of him. Their eyes met, and the heat of his gaze flooded over her, sending tingles down her spine. Then he flashed her one of his most disarming smiles as he raised his stemmed glass in a silent toast.

When Elliot had seated her, Erica glanced up to see Dante threading his way through the crowd toward them. Why does he have to select this particular moment to intrude? Erica thought resentfully. It wasn't that she didn't want to see him again, only that she intended to divulge her need for a husband over dinner and she wanted Elliot's complete attention. If only Dante could have waited until she had sealed her future before he—

"You look stunning, *chérie*," Dante declared as he lightly kissed her hand, the touch of his lips assuring her that he was still the only man who could set her heart to racing. "But then I knew you would be breathtaking in this gown when I saw it at the boutique." His words, only loud enough for Erica to hear, provoked a slight blush.

The old, familiar spark leaped between them, and it was all Erica could do to appear unaffected. Oh, why did Dante have to rattle her when she needed to be in full command of her senses? She thought he had finally bowed out to allow her to see to this distasteful business of snagging a husband. But no, he had only been biding his time, waiting until she had built up her hopes before he strutted over to deflate her. Dante intended to cause trouble. She just knew it! He had an ornery look about him, and she had seen it often enough to know that he was up to no good.

"May I join you?" Dante parked himself in the vacant chair without awaiting an answer.

No, you may not. Go away, Erica thought in silent response. Dante was doing this on purpose. He knew what she was about, and he planned to botch up her scheme.

"It seems you and Erica have hit it off quite well," Dante observed, taking in the lovestruck expression plastered on Elliot's face.

The warm glow in Elliot's eyes mirrored his emotions as he gazed at Erica. "I cannot name another two days when I have found myself in such delightful company," he murmured as he peered adoringly at Erica, who had

131

begun to squirm uncomfortably in her chair. She was certain that mocking smile on Dante's lips spelled trouble.

"That is because Erica is so bubbly and refreshing, like a bottle of champagne." Dante uncorked the bottle and poured them all a drink. "She fogs a man's mind, not to mention what she does to the rest of a man's anatomy," he chortled, flashing Elliot a wink. "There is no other as fair and lovely on the Mississippi as our Erica, and there is not a deceitful bone in her body," he added, making Erica choke on her guilt. Dante reached over to whack her between the shoulder blades. "It is a pleasure to meet a young woman who possesses captivating beauty, charming wit, and, above all, the honesty that makes a man realize she is not out to snare him for her own conniving purposes." Dante leaned back in his chair and raised his glass in a toast while Erica was still having difficulty dealing with her irritation. "Ah, yes, our Erica is truthful and unpretentious."

Erica felt the knife twist in her back, and she hungered to yank it out and turn it on Dante. Damn him. The one time in her life that she stooped to deceit, he had to singe her conscience, the rascal. The last thing she needed was to be overwhelmed by feelings of guilt when her life was at stake. So potent was her inner turmoil that Erica lost her appetite, which she realized when the perfectly baked fish was set beneath her nose.

"The meal is not to your liking?" Dante purred in mock innocence, knowing full well what had soured her stomach. "Would you prefer that I have our chef prepare something else for you, my dear?"

Erica could cheerfully have shaken him until his flashing white teeth rattled and fell to the floor, but holding her glass in a stranglehold, she managed to produce a civil smile. "That won't be necessary. The meal is satisfactory. It is only that I am so thrilled to be in the company of two such handsome gentlemen that I can give little thought to food." Taking fork in hand, she choked down her guilt along with a smidgeon of fish, just to spite Dante who was trying very hard to spoil more than her appetite.

"Flattery will get you everywhere," Elliot beamed as he reached across the table to clasp her hand. "Ask and whatever you wish will be yours."

Dante rolled his eyes in disgust. The lovesick expression on Elliot's face was making him nauseous. Obviously Elliot was reduced to mush the moment Erica batted her big blue eyes at him. She had Elliot wrapped so tightly about her finger that he would never come unwound. If Erica wanted the moon Elliot would have leaped from his chair, dived into the Mississippi, and paddled off to retrieve it for her. Erica has set her trap, and Elliot is about to fall face down in it, Dante thought sourly. Elliot might be a mathematical genius, but Erica had him miscalculating.

"It is easy to make such a generous offer to such a sincere, honorable young maid, is it not?" Dante interjected. "It is so refreshing to know a woman with Erica's integrity." His tanned finger raised her chin, forcing her to look him in the eye. "Could you detect one ounce of deceit in this angelic face, Elliot?"

Elliot sighed as he studied Erica's flawless complexion. Erica was everything he had ever wanted, and more. "Not an ounce," he breathed as he gave her hand a loving squeeze.

Dante had done it again. He had just lodged another knife between Erica's ribs and then, wearing that charm-

133

ing smile, he had given the blade a painful shove, slicing a nasty gash in her conscience. How can I approach Elliot with a marriage proposal that grants him nothing more than a pouch of coins in return for his name when Dante has described me as a saint? Confound it, why couldn't he leave me alone tonight?

Forcing a weak smile, Erica pushed away from the table. "If you gentlemen will excuse me, I would like to return to my cabin. I seem to have developed a headache." And indeed she had—a six-foot-two-inch headache with devilish green eyes and coal black hair.

"Brought on by your lack of nourishment," Dante diagnosed. "You really should eat something, love. You will feel better."

The only thing that would make her feel better would be a bite of Dante. The man was giving her fits!

"Let me accompany you," Elliot offered as he scrambled to his feet. "There is something I intended to discuss with you tonight and I fear it cannot wait."

Dante's face fell like a rockslide, and then his hard gaze drilled into Erica. But, before he could take her hostage with his probing eyes, she turned her back on him and curled her hand around Elliot's proffered arm. A quiet sigh of relief escaped her lips as they weaved their way through the crowd, leaving Dante and his taunts in the distance.

As they walked along the deck that was splattered with moonlight, Elliot placed his arm around her waist and spun her about to face him. "Erica, you must know by now that I have become very fond of you," he said, and when she opened her mouth to respond, he pressed his index finger to her lips to shush her. "I know we have just met, but I have searched the world for you. It does not take a man long to know what he wants and you are everything I have wanted in a woman. Dante is right about you." His heart in his eyes, he traced the delicate line of her jaw and then brushed the back of his hand over her creamy cheek. "You are warm and wholesome and spirited and I—"

"Kiss me, Elliot," Erica demanded as she lifted parted lips in invitation.

Elliot clutched her to him, his lips hovering over hers with such tenderness that Erica felt like crying. Although he was gentle, there was no fire in his kiss. It was not like Dante's. Her skin did not tingle, and her heart didn't race in anticipation.

"Again, Elliot," Erica whispered as she curled her arms around his neck, pressing closer to him, hoping the feel of his male body would rouse her. But his embrace evoked no wild sensations, nor did it leave her breathless.

Erica felt safe and comforted in his arms, as if she were leaning on a dear friend for consolation. Elliot was a nice man who deserved more than she could offer him. Even if she decided to make a true marriage with him, she could never be the wife Elliot anticipated, not when she would continue to compare him to Dante. She couldn't insult Elliot by offering him money for the temporary use of his name. She was desperate, but she couldn't take unfair advantage of him.

"Marry me," Elliot breathed raggedly. "Make me the happiest man on earth. Please say yes, Erica."

Instantly, she backed from his arms to bless him with a rueful smile. "There is so much you don't know about me, Elliot, things that would shock you."

"For instance?" he prodded as he traced the sensuous

curve of her lips. "I can think of nothing about you that could disappoint me."

"I have a terrible temper. I am staunchly independent and occasionally I have difficulty remembering that I am supposed to behave like a lady," she declared. "And you know nothing about my background. You don't even know my last name, for heaven's sake!"

"It doesn't matter," he insisted, his pale blue eyes glowing down on her. "I hope that very soon your last name will be the same as mine. Will it, Erica?"

"I . . . I . . . have to think," Erica stammered. Then she pivoted away before he could recapture her in his arms. "Good night, Elliot."

"But Erica . . ."

As Erica scurried along the boiler deck, toward the steps that led to the hurricane deck, she paused indecisively. If she returned to the texas, Elliot would appear there tomorrow to assault her with the same question. As much as she needed his assistance, she simply did not have the heart to hurt him. Perhaps it would be best for her to slip ashore and take a coach to Natchez. She had enough funds left to pay her fare, and the steamboat had stopped to take on wood for the boilers. In Natchez, she could find a place to hide, then wait until her father had given her up for lost.

Deciding that the latter plan would serve her best, Erica wheeled about and headed for the main deck, certain that avoiding Dante and Elliot would help uncomplicate her life. Halfway down the steps, she froze in her tracks, for at the bottom were the same three roustabouts she had encountered that fateful night in New Orleans. Of all the rotten luck! Erica thought sourly; then panic

136

gripped her when the three men smiled like starved sharks.

Dante sighed heavily before giving his enthusiastic companion an indulgent smile. Reade Asher had sailed the high seas as his first mate for several years before striking out on some wild-goose chase. Dante wondered why Reade hadn't signed on with some other sea captain, since he preferred sailing to being ashore. But Reade had interrogated Corbin when he'd come aboard; then he'd made a beeline for Dante, hounding him each time he found him without a lovely lady draped on his arm. As usual, Reade had bent Dante's ear, spinning yarns of his adventures, but Dante was in no mood for Reade's long-winded tales. Erica preyed heavily on his mind; he could think of nothing else.

"I have listened to your tales of buried treasure since we sailed the seven seas," he grumbled. "If a man believed your concoction of lies, he would spend his life searching for legendary fortunes that never truly existed."

"I tell you this ain't no figment of my imagination," Reade persisted as he poured himself another brandy and then leaned his forearms on the table to peer soberly at the doubtful captain. "I was shipwrecked off the coast of Yucatán two years past. Me and my friend, God rest his soul, lived with them Mayan Indians. They showed us their pyramid tombs and talked of the Sacrificial Well that is heapin' with precious gems. I saw it with my own eyes! They've bin makin' sacrifices there for hundreds of years, and the fortune that lays buried in the mud would

137

stagger the mind."

Dante's curiosity had once been piqued, but he had lost interest in chasing dreams after his superstitious crew had convinced him to seek out Lafitte's treasure on the way back from their one and only unproductive venture in India.

"I relish my hide," Dante smirked. "Indians are notorious for sacrificing humans as well as precious gems, and I should not like to be among those who plunge headlong into this heaping well of treasure."

"Them Mayans are a friendly sort," Reade argued. "They took me and my sick friend in like we was one of their own. You ain't riskin' your neck, but you could gain yoreself a fortune, the likes of which you've never seen."

After easing back in his chair, Dante gave his raven head a negative shake. "I am content where I am, Reade. Besides, I sold my schooner long ago. I have planted my feet on solid ground, and now if you will excuse me, I have pressing matters to attend."

"Ones as excitin' as sailin' the seas?" Reade leaned toward him, displaying a grin that revealed the lack of several teeth. "I know where yore heart is, Dante. You love the sea and you always will. This steamin' tub can't compare to unfurlin' sails and ridin' on the wind. You may pride yoreself in puttin' ashore to run a plantation and navigatin' the Mississippi when you git lonely for the sea, but I know you come to life when yore standin' at the helm, gazin' at the horizon, lookin' forward to the adventures awaitin' you." Reade arched a bushy brow, daring Dante to deny the truth. "And it won't be long before word leaks out about the treasure in Yucatán," he continued. Then he flashed Dante a sheepish glance. "You know how my tongue starts waggin' when I've had a bit too much to drink. Fortune hunters will be swarmin' the coast of Central America and the treasure will be gone. I'm offerin' you a chance of a lifetime."

"Perhaps I could . . ." Dante frowned when he noticed Elliot picking his way through the crowd, his blond features etched with concern.

"Have you seen Erica?" Elliot asked. "She hurried off before I could escort her to her door, and when I pursued her, she didn't answer the knock. I fear something is amiss."

Dante was on his feet in a split second, cursing himself for introducing her to reckless characters who would not hesitate to take what they wanted from Erica without an invitation. She had warded them off in the past, but if she were caught unaware one of them might . . . Dante growled disgustedly. He didn't want to think what might happen to that delicious minx. With Elliot and Reade following in his wake, Dante rushed from the saloon and leaped up the stairway to unlock Erica's door. He scowled when he found an empty room.

"Elliot, check the hurricane deck," he ordered as he aimed himself toward the stairway. "Reade, search the boiler deck."

"I don't know what I'm lookin' for," Reade crowed, staring at Dante as if he were addle-witted. The man had listened to him weave an enticing story of fortune and adventure, his face plastered with an expression of disinterest, and then suddenly he had come to attention like infantry at a bugle call, shouting orders that were impossible to follow.

"You are looking for a dark-haired woman in a mint green gown," Dante hurriedly explained. Then he gave Reade a shove, propelling him in the right direction.

"Is she perty?" Reade questioned, half-turning as he was herded along the deck.

"Sinfully so," Dante assured him before taking the steps two at a time to reach the main deck.

Shadows leaped at him as he wedged through the narrow corridors near the sweltering boilers. His keen eyes circled his surroundings, as he waited, listening, wondering what had become of that feisty bundle of trouble in the alluring green dress. Damn, he should have known better than to garb her in such form-fitting attire. Who could resist her? Dante jerked up his head when he heard a muffled shriek coming from the darkness, and then he dashed toward the sound, his heart hammering, his senses tuned to the imminent danger that lurked in the shadows.

As Erica squirmed away from the grimy hands that tugged roughly at the bodice of her gown, the satin gave way, exposing her thin chemise and what it barely concealed.

"Since our French countess run off before we could show her the true meanin' of Southern hospitality, I think we ought to make up for lost time, don't you, boys?" Timothy Thorpe snickered as his beady eyes devoured Erica, leaving her in no doubt of what she was about to encounter.

"Take yer place in line, Timmy," Denby Eldwin mumbled, his tongue thick with rum as he clamped a hand on Timothy's shoulder and uprooted him from the spot. "I've bin dreamin' about this wench since we first laid eyes on her and now my dream's comin' true."

As Denby muscled Ethan and Timothy out of his way

to stand directly in front of Erica, her eyes filled with fear. The drunken lout leered down at her, and at that moment she knew she would die trying to prevent any of them from touching her. The mere thought of their calloused hands mauling her made her skin crawl. When Denby pressed his bulky body against her, the smell of whiskey and tobacco was overwhelming, and she reacted instinctively, clawing at him like a wildcat in captivity.

"Ouch!" Denby growled, as he jumped back to avoid having his face cut to shreds. "You little bitch!" He backhanded Erica, snapping her head back and making her curls tumble about her shoulders in disarray. "You fight me and you'll surely wish you hadn't!"

Erica bit into the hand that fastened over her mouth, disregarding his vengeful warning, and Denby howled in pain. She very nearly took a bite out of the heel of his hand.

"I warned you!" Denby sneered as he raised his arm to strike Erica's already bruised cheek.

"If you can't handle a mere slip of a woman, let me have her first." Ethan snorted as he caught Denby's arm in midair and then shoved his companion out of the way. Placing his index finger beneath Erica's chin, he tilted her furious face to his and gave her a coaxing smile. "Maybe you prefer a man with a gentle touch, eh, lass? Ole Ethan won't give you cause to fight him."

"Go straight to hell!" Erica hissed through swollen lips. Then she screamed bloody murder when his head came toward hers.

Her voice echoed through the dingy cubicle and then died when the locked door groaned and gave way before the intruder who barreled in.

The shaft of light that followed Dante was like hell's

141

fire glowing behind the devil himself. His face twisted with rage, he leaped at the unfortunate man in his path. With one well-aimed blow he rendered Timothy senseless, making him wilt to the floor like a dainty flower too long in the hot summer sun.

"We was just out to have a little fun," Ethan insisted as he backed away from Erica, forcing a congenial smile that did not dampen the flames of Dante's temper.

"Get off my ship!" Dante snarled furiously, his arm shooting toward the door. "And take your filthy friends with you."

Denby started to protest as he hauled Timothy to his feet. "But we ain't bin paid for our—"

"You have been paid exactly what you're worth—nothing," Dante shot back, his deadly voice dripping with venom. "If you aren't off this boat by the time we finish taking on wood, a duty you three were responsible for, I'll have you tossed overboard to fight your way through the alligator-infested swamps."

When Denby took a bold step forward, as if he meant to challenge Dante's authority, he found a pistol aimed at his heaving chest.

"Give me one more reason to blow you to bits. . . ."

Denby wasn't the brightest individual in the room, but he had enough sense not to argue with Dante's weapon so he led the way as the three roustabouts exited.

When they were alone, Erica flew into Dante's arms, choking back the tears that threatened to roll down her cheeks. He enfolded her and nuzzled his chin against her head. "They won't bother you again," he declared soothingly as he smoothed the renegade strands of hair away from her face.

Erica shivered uncontrollably, then huddled deeper in

142

his protective embrace. "I have to get off this boat," she insisted, muffling her words in the lapel of his jacket. "I can't face Elliot again."

"He asked you to marry him," Dante guessed.

"And it's all your fault that I can't," Erica muttered as she wormed out of Dante's arms and then clutched at her ripped bodice.

"My fault?" Dante's tone was so disgustingly innocent that it turned Erica's stomach. "What did I do?"

"You know damned well what you did." Her flaming blue eyes incinerated his mock-innocent expression. "You hailed me as something akin to a saint, you ranted on about my unblemished honesty while Elliot was an attentive audience, and you made me feel as tall as a table leg." She heaved an annoyed sigh and then buzzed past Dante, madder than a hornet. "I thought you were my friend, but apparently I made a gross error. You take pleasure in making me miserable."

Dante grabbed her arm as she breezed by, spinning her about to face his somber expression. "What kind of friend would I have been if I had stood idly by while you ruined Elliot's life? You are as farsighted as a mole if you can't see that the man is head over heels in love with you."

"I know." Erica dropped her head, refusing to meet his stony gaze. "And I cannot bring myself to hurt him. That is why I must leave this ship and find other transportation to Natchez."

"Then you don't love him." Dante's voice was low and husky as he raised her chin so her eyes met his. "Why, Erica? He has all the charm and wealth a man could offer you. Are you afraid of falling in love?"

Speaking of blind fools, Erica thought sourly. If Dante

couldn't understand why she wouldn't accept Elliot as her husband, why she had held all the other men at bay while allowing him to take outrageous privileges, then *he* was as blind as a bat. It was all Dante's fault that she couldn't accept Elliot's proposal. It was his fault that Elliot's kisses did not fire her blood. When she compared other men to Dante they all ran a distant second to that green-eyed devil who could make mincemeat of her emotions.

"I . . ." Erica caught herself the moment before she made some preposterous confession that would have provoked Dante's laughter. The last thing he wanted to hear was that she had fallen in love with a rake who met all the necessary qualifications for a temporary husband, one who did not seem to believe in commitments; yet that man made her wish her scheme required a permanent alliance. The irony of that realization sent Erica's spirits plunging. If she dared to profess her love for Dante he would double over in laughter, and she would be tempted to double her fist and plant it on his handsome face. It would be too humiliating to be ridiculed for telling him the real reason she could not light on a man to suit her purpose.

"Yes?" Dante raised a dark brow, patiently waiting for her to finish her comment.

"I'm leaving." Erica moved silently toward the door. "As you said, I cannot afford to pay for the damages I might cause on your steamboat. I have already cracked the lattice railing, upturned the deck chairs, and tampered with your best friend's emotions. It will be best for me to disembark and take a coach to Natchez."

Dante blocked her path, refusing to allow her to escape him. "If you walk off this boat you will risk another confrontation with those ruthless roustabouts," he reminded her grimly. "Surely facing Elliot cannot be as dangerous as that."

"Perhaps not, but it could be just as painful," she muttered. She felt trapped. What had she done to make fate treat her so badly?

"You could always reconsider Shelby Turpin," he said, biting back a grin when Erica flashed him a glare sour enough to curdle milk. "Well, he could be bought for a reasonable price." Dante quickly defended his suggestion. "After all, you wanted a wandering vagabond who would temporarily share his name."

"At *my* expense," Erica grumbled acrimoniously. "I almost think I could tolerate a beating from Sabin as easily as I could endure being the wife of Shelby Turpin, if only for a day."

"Come along, love," he encouraged as he steered her into the corridor. "The world won't look so bleak after you have had a decent night's sleep. Perhaps we can think of some way to ease your troubles."

Erica did not share his optimism. From where she stood, tomorrow looked no brighter than that night. She had conceived of several plans, but, distasteful as it was, her scheme to take a husband and then promptly discard him was the only logical one. Now she must face her father and Sabin; she couldn't evade them when she had no spouse.

"Erica is not accepting visitors," Dante explained as he stepped out of the texas to meet Elliot's apprehensive gaze and Reade's curious one.

"What happened to her? Is she hurt?" Elliot fired the

145

questions at him.

"Some of our roustabouts attempted to attack her, but she only suffered a few bruises and scrapes. I ordered them off the boat." Dante urged Elliot toward the saloon, motioning for Reade to join them. "I'll buy you a drink, and Reade can finish filling my head with tales of buried treasure."

"They ain't tales," Reade snorted defensively. "If you wasn't so busy savin' damsels in distress, you'd realize that I was offerin' to take you on an adventure like you ain't enjoyed in years."

Dante silently disagreed. Watching Erica blunder in and out of disaster was adventure enough. Now he must give disappointing news to Elliot and to Reade without souring either of them. Perhaps he would think of a kind way to do that while they chatted over a bottle of wine, he reflected as he aimed himself toward the saloon. Yet how did one tell a man that the woman he loved didn't return his affection, and how did one tell a crusty old sailor like Reade that buried treasure was better left in the mud of Yucatán?

Chapter 9

A heavy-hearted sigh tumbled from Erica's lips. Pensively, she stared up at the ceiling, watching a sea-faring spider creep toward the fly trapped in its web. She sympathized with its prey. She, too, had been snagged in a tangled web when she'd attempted to tamper with her fate. All she had received for her attempt to avoid disaster was a ferocious headache, brought on by spending hours futilely trying to untangle her life. And that life wouldn't be worth a penny when Sabin Keary got his hands on her.

That morning, when Elliot had rapped on her door to invite her to breakfast, Erica had declined, explaining that she had been badly shaken after her near brush with calamity. She had relied on that same excuse when Elliot had returned at midday to take her to lunch. Presently, she was contemplating throwing herself off the hurricane deck to end her misery, but she felt that she would botch that up too.

Thinking of Elliot tied her in knots and thinking of Dante . . . Erica squelched the vision that appeared above her. Contemplating her feeling for Dante was mind boggling so she had firmly told herself to forget him. He had only one use for her, and she was too vulnerable to indulge in lust for she was falling in love with the dashing rogue.

An incessant knocking at the door yanked her from her troubled musings and Erica frowned. "Go away," she called out.

Dante ignored her order, unlocked the door, and strutted inside, causing Erica to gasp indignantly since she was wearing only the sheer negligee he had purchased for her.

"I wondered when you would model that seductive garment for me." Dante broke into a sly smile as Erica buried herself under the sheet, drawing it up to her neck to block the view Dante found so enchanting. "Get up, sleeping beauty. The showboat is docked in Williamsport and you are going to accompany me to tonight's performance."

"I prefer to remain in my cabin," Erica sulked, flashing him an annoyed glance. "And I wish you would stop bursting in on me without giving me the opportunity to make myself presentable."

When Dante marched over to yank on the bottom of the sheet, Erica found herself losing a tug of war.

"Get up and stop pouting," he barked sharply, dragging the sheet steadily toward him.

Erica clutched at her meager covering. "Leave me be!" she shouted. "Dante! Stop that."

Deviltry sparkled in his eyes as he tore away the sheet and scooped her from the bed to deposit her on her feet. "Are you going to dress for the occasion or do you wish to go as you are?"

Erica glared daggers at him, but he deflected them with

his blinding smile. "I swear you would make the perfect nagging wife," she muttered. "Do you stay up nights devising new ways to torment me or are these merely spontaneous forms of torture? Is there no one else aboard for you to harass?"

"This is for your own good," Dante declared as he marched over to the closet to retrieve the stunning pink gown he had selected at the boutique in New Orleans. "We haven't much time and I should hate the entertainment to start without us."

Erica's jaw sagged when Dante returned and began to unfasten her negligee. She slapped his hands away, but, as usual, he was persistent.

"I am quite capable of dressing myself," she snapped irritably.

Dante expelled a disappointed sigh and then turned his back. "Then be quick about it. I am not a patient man."

"I am not getting dressed until you're gone and it is safe," she informed him curtly.

A pair of laughing green eyes swept over her captivating figure; then he graced her with an ornery smile. "Are you insinuating that there is something dangerous about me, *chérie?*" he queried, convincing Erica that the seductive tone of his voice should be labeled a criminal offense.

"Everything about you is dangerous," she admonished, flashing him a condescending frown. "Now please step outside and grant me privacy."

Dante didn't budge from his spot. "If I leave you will crawl back into bed, and I will have to begin this procedure all over again. I will turn my back, but I am not leaving. A compromise is all I intend to offer. Take it or leave it." When Erica tilted a stubborn chin and glowered at him, Dante broke into a devilish smile. "In that case, you force me to become your dressing attendant."

Erica retreated as he moved toward her, and she braced her hand on his chest before he could make a grab for her. "Very well, I will dress, but you keep your eyes pinned to yonder wall," she ordered firmly.

"You are taking all the enjoyment out of this," Dante grumbled resentfully, yet he pivoted away, crossed his arms over his chest, and stared at the bare wall, wishing it were Erica's bareness he was observing.

Erica rolled her eyes in disbelief. Dante refused to allow her a smidgeon of modesty. He was doing his utmost to annoy her. Keeping a constant vigil on him, she wiggled into her gown, muttering several epithets as she did so. After smoothing the trim-fitting dress over her hips, Erica fumbled with the stays. Her fingers seemed useless thumbs when Dante was within ten feet of her.

"Aren't you dressed yet?" he queried impatiently.

"Almost . . . there," she informed him, breathing a relieved sigh when she finished working the final button and then fluffed the taffeta skirt over the full petticoats.

When Dante spun around to inspect her attire, his mouth opened. "Lord, woman, you will steal the show," he said thickly.

"In this old thing?" Erica flashed him a teasing smile and then sashayed across the room to retrieve her diamond necklace. "You are too quick with compliments, Dante," she chided. "A woman never knows when you speak the truth or what your motive might be for dishing out flattery. I, for one, am a mite suspicious."

150

"I think you know what I want from you." Dante's long, swift strides took him to her side before she could reach the door. "Do not play coy or pretend with me, *chérie*. We know each other far too well for that. I have learned things about you that you did not even know about yourself until . . ."

As his words hung heavily in the air, Erica felt suffocated in the close quarters. Then her heart catapulted into her throat as he braced his forearms on the door, pinning her against his solid male frame. His warm breath caressed her cheek, sending a chill through her.

"You know as well as I do that our relationship started backward, and I find it next to impossible to proceed in reverse," he rasped as his head moved deliberately toward hers, his fiery green eyes focusing on the sensuous curve of her lips.

"Then you are no gentleman if you cannot forget the past and—"

Dante was not courteous enough to allow her to finish. "I never claimed to be a gentleman," he reminded her as his full lips hovered over hers, leaving her feeling as though butterflies were flying madly about in her stomach.

"And I am not your harlot. I refuse to be a name on your extensive list of conquered women," she blurted out, dodging his intended kiss. When Dante found himself kissing midair, she said sharply. "I thought you were in a rush. Shall we go?"

Dante gritted his teeth, annoyed at being outfoxed by this raven-haired vixen. For one so young she had certainly learned to maneuver around overzealous men, yet he supposed he should be thankful that she had not resorted to clubbing him with any available weapon as she so often did when she refused a man's attention. Reluctantly, he broke into a smile when he noticed the lively sparkle in her sapphire eyes. Who could resist this adorable nymph?

"I did say that, didn't I?" he chuckled as he stepped back to open the door.

"You did," Erica assured him; then she looped her hand around his elbow, relieved that they would be out in public so she would not be forced to battle the engulfing emotions that overwhelmed her when she and Dante were alone.

The moment Erica stepped onto the showboat, she forgot Dante's attempt to overcome her resistance. The Chapmans, a theatrical troupe from England, entertained the audience with their rendition of Shakespeare's *The Taming of the Shrew*, which they implemented with song and dance. Their floating theater was equipped with a stage and adequate seating, and although Shakespeare might not have recognized his work, Erica thoroughly enjoyed the Chapmans' version of it.

For several hours, she was so immersed in the light-hearted show that she forgot her problems. Her drooping spirits lifted, and she found herself blossoming into the lively, carefree young woman she had been before disaster had closed in on her.

As he watched the torchlight play on Erica's exquisite features, Dante was bewildered by the transformation in her. Later, he grinned in spite of himself as she bounded along beside him, bubbling with pleasure, babbling about the characters in the play, and singing the catchy tunes she had heard on the showboat.

"It was a wonderful evening," Erica assured Dante as they ambled along the riverbank, veering away from the crowd of passengers who filed back to the *Natchez Belle*. When she dared to peer up at Dante, his emerald eyes caught hers and held them hostage. "I . . . thank you for inviting me." She stumbled over the words, and then turned away before she became lost in the depths of those enthralling green pools.

Before she could head back to the ship, however, Dante's lean fingers curled about her arm, drawing her back to him. "No good-night kiss, Erica?" he murmured huskily as his powerful body came in close contact with hers. "It seems a fair payment for the price of a showboat ticket."

"I think we should find some other method of repayment," she declared as she braced determined hands on the hard wall of his chest. "I have found in my dealings with you that kisses lead elsewhere. You do not seem to enjoy taking *no* for an answer."

"You know me well." Dante chuckled devilishly. "When it comes to touching you, I do not like to be denied."

Erica sniffed distastefully, calling upon her drooping resistance before it failed her completely. "When it comes to seducing *any* woman," she amended; then she glanced uneasily about her. "Surely one of your clinging vines is draped hereabouts, someone who might eagerly accommodate you."

His smile broadened as he hauled her back into his strong arms. "What makes you think I have a penchant for women, Erica? You certainly aren't a very trusting soul. You always see the worst in me when I only have your best interest at heart."

Erica didn't believe him for a minute. She was certain Dante would play every situation to his advantage, just as he was doing now. Their harmless stroll in the moonlight was getting out of hand!

"I met you in a brothel," she reminded him, as she strained against his chaining arms. "You have a different woman draped on your arm each time I chance to see you on the steamboat. Your habits are the same as those of the rakehells to whom you have introduced me. You have taken privileges with me when I have sought—"

Erica's complaints died beneath a kiss fiery enough to set the night ablaze, as Dante's arms drew her into a tight cocoon in which her trembling body was fitted to his virile form. Her heart hammered like an imprisoned creature pounding against a confining cell, and Erica was certain she would never be able to breathe normally again. His wayward hands mapped the curves of her figure, their possessive touch burning her like a branding iron. Erica fought the delicious sensations that blossomed deep inside her, but they quickly spread through her. Dante was a wizard. He could breathe passion into her yet no other man had.

"No, Dante . . ." Erica gasped when he finally granted her a small breath of air. She could feel herself losing control, but she was determined to overcome her weakness for this man who was only toying with her affection.

"You want me as much as I want you," he whispered, his voice heavy with disturbed desire. "I can feel your body responding to the heat of mine. Yield to me, Erica. I crave to recapture that night."

His mouth came down on hers with hungry impatience as his wandering hands found her breasts and then dipped beneath the bodice of satin and lace. Instantly his

154

lips abandoned hers to trace a searing path along her rapidly pulsating neck before trailing to her taut peaks to tease them with his tongue.

The world crumbled beneath Erica as his skillful caresses stripped her of what was left of her senses. As usual, reason failed her when she needed it most, and all of her well-meaning lectures deserted her as a tiny moan of pleasure escaped her lips. Dante's manly fragrance swirled about her while his hands and lips rediscovered the sensitive points of her body. She wanted to deny him, but that was impossible. His lovemaking was a forbidden fantasy that made life sweet—the rapturous memory of it gnawed at her, leaving her hungry to appease the need that only he stirred.

Emotions long held in check shook her as his bold caresses set off a chain reaction that seemed to have no beginning and no end. Drawn into the thick grass that lay beneath a ceiling of stars, Erica found herself clinging to the very man she had sworn to avoid. When he lifted his head and stared into her eyes, she was spellbound by the liquid fire that flowed down upon her, pouring over her with such warmth that she trembled.

"Tell me you want me," Dante demanded as his lips hovered over hers. "Not to solve your dilemma, but because you hunger to relive a dream, because you long to spend the night in my arms."

Dante's nimble fingers freed the stays of her gown; then he recklessly cast it aside to admire the exquisite body he had memorized by touch. The silver moonlight sprayed down upon her, enhancing her creamy flesh and making him burn with desire.

Erica had lost the battle of mind over body. Dante's persuasive caresses had taken her past the point of no return. Now, as his practiced hands glided over the slope of her breasts to weave intricate patterns on her abdomen before venturing to her thighs, her skin tingled, and when his eyes and hands retraced their arousing path, then descended, again and again, she lay soft and pliant in his arms. Suddenly, it didn't matter what her future held. She could not see past those fathomless green pools that compelled her to throw caution to the winds. She wanted him, despite her better judgment, despite the knowledge that she was only another notch on his bedpost. Yet she was painfully aware that he would have taken any attractive woman in his arms. Nonetheless, I will make him remember this moment, she promised herself as she raised parted lips to his. She intended to be more to him than a smile and a pleasant memory. She wanted to make warm sensations flood over him when he wasn't carefully guarding his thoughts, to haunt his nights long after they had gone their separate ways.

Is it so vain to want to mean something special to him? she asked herself as her hand slid inside his shirt to explore the muscled wall of his chest. Perhaps, but this was the man she loved, and it would break her heart if he did not harbor fond memories of her in the future.

Reaching back to pull the pins from her hair, Erica shook her head and sent raven tendrils cascading about her like a dark cape. Like a feline curling and stretching, she arched against Dante then, tunneling her fingers through his hair as she brought his lips to hers. She was determined to use the seductive techniques he had taught her, and a few she had originated, to arouse in him the same fevered desire that set her ablaze.

Dante groaned softly as her sensuous lips melted like rose petals beneath his. Her curvaceous body, now molded to the hardness of his, was enough to drive a man mad. The sight, taste, and feel of her filled him with a passionate craving.

"Lord, woman," he chirped as her hand brazenly dipped beneath the band of his breeches to follow the contour of his hip. "I swear you are a witch." The sudden transformation was baffling. First she had attempted to hold him at bay, yet now she was coaxing him to make love to her as he ached to do. "I don't know what to make of you."

"I thought perhaps you wanted to meet the seductress you anticipated when you made your way to the New Orleans' brothel," she taunted as her hands moved up his thundering chest to push the jacket from his shoulders. "Is this not the type of reception you expected?"

Dante sucked in his breath as butterfly kisses skipped across the dark furring of hair that trailed down his belly, then gentle hands traced his ribs before working the buttons of his trousers. This woman fought off over-zealous beaux with any weapon she could get her hands on? Erica was an enigma, a walking contradiction. She could infuriate him and then fuel his passion in the next instant. She touched all of his emotions, leaving him in chaotic turmoil. His attraction to this raven-haired enchantress was madness, pure and simple, he decided as his arms crushed her breasts to his chest. His senses were warped by the titillating fragrance that was so much a part of her. He was addicted to her intoxicating kisses, dizzy and light-headed from drinking his fill of them. Yet, he could not stop himself. He hungered to possess her fiery beauty.

Erica was feeling sinfully wicked now that Dante's black magic had dissolved her resistance. For the first time in her life she set out to lure a man, this man who was a challenge and her secret desire.

Dante found the tables turned on him as Erica squirmed away to crouch above him. He had intended to entice this headstrong temptress into his arms, but he found himself being seduced. Erica divested him of his clothes and then her hands explored every inch of his trembling flesh, her caresses making him feel that he was adrift on waves that were drawing him out to sea. He groaned in tormented delight as her fingertips played over his hair-roughened thighs, experiencing a weak, helpless feeling that he had never before known. He had allowed no other woman to love him in this way, only Erica, in the heat of passion. And what passion it was! Dante burned as her lips and hands skimmed over his body, provoking rhythmic responses and, like an accomplished pianist, playing on his emotions. He gasped for breath, and his heart stampeded in his chest. He wasn't certain whether he was living or dying when her hand folded around him, guiding him closer, offering that which he had discovered one night in New Orleans— indescribable pleasure.

"Do you want me, my handsome rogue?" Erica murmured as she nibbled at the corner of his mouth. "Do you long to spend an uninterrupted night in my arms?" She used his very words, assuring him that he had met his match.

"What price am I expected to pay for this sweet torture?" he growled, his voice ragged with fervent desire as her bare leg slid between his thighs, fitting them together like two pieces of a puzzle that made no sense at all until they were molded together, body and soul.

A devilish smile pursed her lips and her blue eyes

sparkled as she gazed down at him. "Only your heart," she insisted as her index finger investigated the chiseled lines of his face and then traced the sensuous curve of his mouth. "We witches have no use for gold trinkets. It is the very essence of your being that I seek. Only then will I be satisfied."

Dante swore he had unchained a tigress when he'd broken down the barriers she had constructed between them since they had met again on the steamboat. For beneath Erica's controlled exterior lay a seductress, the likes of which he had never known. If she had demanded the world, he would have thundered off to retrieve it and place it at her feet.

"Take what you want," he breathed as her supple body melted against his, appeasing the need that had consumed him. "But don't deny me the fulfillment of this dream."

Erica denied him nothing. Her lips opened on his, giving and sharing a breath that merged as their bodies moved in rhythm to a melody that played only for them. Emotions that had simmered in her for days boiled through her veins as he agilely pressed her to the grass. The muscles of his arms bulged as he held himself above her, then came to her, gently at first, then demandingly. Erica met his driving thrusts, reveling in the rapturous sensations that sent her skyrocketing toward the distant stars spinning in the black velvet sky. His hard body crushed into hers, striving for the intimacy of total possession, as if he were overwhelmed by the primitive need that drove him. Erica responded with fervor, arching against him, surrendering all, unashamed of her passionate response. Beyond the unending circle of his arms, nothing existed. She wanted only to satisfy a need

159

that defied reason.

Like a shooting star blazing through the sky, they gloried in pleasure until the fire of their passion consumed itself and they plummeted back to earth. But for those rapturous moments when time stood still, they were one, giving and sharing. The past could not compare with this, and Erica knew she would never be the same again. No other man could take Dante's place in her heart. What she felt for him was all-consuming. There was magic in his embrace, and although she could not admit it to him, she knew if she searched the world over, no man could stir her as Dante had.

Bracing his arms on either side of her so he could peer into her exquisite face, Dante kissed her one last time. He was drained. If they had not been lying on a sea of grass and if Corbin had not intended to depart, he would have been content to remain where he was that night. But he called upon the last of his energy to roll away from Erica so he might don his discarded clothes. Instantly, she tugged on his arm, drawing him back to her, an impish grin lighting her face.

"This night is far from over," she purred as she trailed a dainty finger along his cheek, surprising him and herself with her suggestive tone.

Dante chuckled as he caught her hand and brought it to his lips. "If we tarry much longer on the bank of the Mississippi, Corbin will sail away without us . . . or come searching for us. I should hate to place you in such an embarrassing situation, *chérie*." He reached back to grab her gown, then offered it to her.

Her lip jutted out in an exaggerated pout. Erica was not eager to return to the steamboat. Elliot was aboard, and she would have preferred never to face him again. "I have no aversion to walking to Natchez."

After Dante had shrugged on his clothes, he drew her to her feet and he fastened the stays on her gown. "But I doubt that we would make good time. You have an uncanny knack for making me forget my direction." His hand closed around hers as he led her back to the path. "Come along, minx, and don't tempt me further," he scolded playfully.

Erica allowed him to draw her along beside him, but she could not overcome her desire to finish what they had only begun. If this was to be her last night with Dante, she intended it to last until dawn. Why should she deny herself the pleasure she found in his arms when she might have to spend the rest of her life as Sabin Keary's wife? Why shouldn't she cling to this moment, salvaging a few memories that would have to last her a lifetime? I deserve some happiness, Erica told herself as they walked along the hurricane deck. She had never expected to find a man who could make her feel the way Dante did, but she had and she wouldn't allow foolish pride to deny her the pleasure she could never find with another man. Perhaps Dante didn't love her, but he was physically attracted to her. She wanted more from him, but she had learned that she couldn't have exactly what she wanted.

Clinging to that thought, Erica stepped into her cabin and fumbled to light the lantern. When she turned back to Dante, a beckoning smile hovered on her lips.

"Now, where were we?" she murmured as she slipped from her gown and held it on one curled finger before letting it carelessly fall to the floor.

Dante's eyes widened as they took in her shapely figure. Was she offering herself to him without a fight? After three days of battling her stubborn defenses had

161

she realized that there *was* a strong magnetism between them? Or did she have some other purpose? He would have pursued that cynical thought, but it evaporated when Erica, wearing nothing but a provocative smile, sauntered toward him to place her slender arms about his shoulders. Instantly, he was afire again. Even the Mississippi could not extinguish the flames that shot through him. If Erica intended to offer herself to him, he would not question his good fortune. She had made him forget that he had sworn off women, and he could barely remember his vow to avoid entangling bonds with the fair sex. He only knew that he could not get enough of this raven-haired minx with lively blue eyes and a disarming smile.

"I believe we were here . . ." he prompted, his hands gliding over her hips to bring her shapely body into firm, familiar contact with his.

Erica melted in his arms as his full lips slanted across hers, reminding her that their tryst in the grass had been only the beginning of a long splendorous night. Pride be damned! She wanted Dante in ways she had yet to experience. He made her feel like a whole woman, a woman with needs, a woman with a purpose. Her love for him had somehow changed her perspective, and as she surrendered to his greedy kiss, Erica realized that what she had once wanted in life could not hold a candle to her maddening need for this dashing rake with dancing emerald eyes. Perhaps Dante was wrong for her, but when she was in his arms, he felt right. Nothing else mattered, not her father, not Sabin, not even her guilt-ridden feelings about Elliot.

"Erica! I have to see you . . . now." Elliot's explosive voice resounded about them, and Dante scowled at his friend's poor sense of timing.

A wry smile played on Erica's lips. She tossed back her head, and her dark hair cascaded over Dante's arm as she peered at the door, which would remain closed and locked for one uninterrupted night.

"I fear that will have to wait until morning," she insisted, her voice husky with desire. When she glanced back at Dante she was held hostage by the unmistakable passion in his eyes. "I was just on my way to bed."

"But, Erica, I must see you." Elliot's exasperation was obvious.

She leaned over to snuff out the lantern and then focused on the shadowed face above her. "Good night, Elliot . . ."

Dante scooped her into his arms and carried her to the bed, his eyes sparkling with roguish anticipation. "Now, where did I say we were, before we were so rudely interrupted?"

"Here . . ." Erica whispered as she kissed the sensitive point beneath his ear. "And here . . ." Her moist lips skittered across his cheek to settle on his mouth, and Dante succumbed to her.

He responded as if under her command, drifting and swaying to music that played somewhere in the distance, as her caresses flowed over his thighs and then tracked across his hips before tracing the crisp matting of hair on his chest. His heart thundered so furiously that he was certain it would beat him to death before he satisfied his maddening craving for Erica. Finally, when he could stand no more of her enticing caresses, he clutched her to him, trembling with the want of her.

"Erica . . ." he whispered breathlessly. "I need you. . . ."

His quiet words stirred her, and when their eyes locked, she saw that his desire matched her own. As her thighs opened to him, he lowered himself to her.

Then the world exploded in a kaleidoscope of colors as they were consumed by passion. He was a living, breathing part of her—*her* possession. But it didn't matter, for they were one, scaling rapture's mountain, discovering new soul-shattering sensations at each lofty plateau. Time and space collided, blending in euphoric suspension, as they took wing and soared even higher than Dante believed possible. Mindlessly, he responded to the tempestuous emotions that churned within him, reacting to the primitive need Erica's provocative caresses had evoked. He couldn't think. He couldn't breathe. He could only feel the heat of passion flowing through him, as if it originated in an eternal spring deep inside him.

And then he clung to her, moaning in pleasure as the ultimate force of it surged through him, using up all of his strength. His body shuddered above hers in the aftermath of their devastating lovemaking. He had longed for this enchantress to fulfill his dream, and he had received far more than he had bargained for. She had granted him a glimpse of heaven, taking him on pinioned wings to a paradise beyond the horizon.

Erica pressed a lingering kiss to his shoulder then sighed contentedly. She had thought their night together had been splendorous, but that could not compare to the heart-stopping sensations that had just consumed her.

"Is there always such pleasure in love, Dante?" she asked innocently.

His mouth quirked into an amused smile as he stared down into her lovely face and watched the coals of her desire dwindle into a glow of contentment. "Only when

164

you are in *my* arms," he teased.

Usually, Erica was quick to rise to his taunts, but this had been a most unusual night. She had never set out to seduce a man before, yet she enjoyed knowing that she could stir the man who held the key to her heart.

An impish grin pursed her lips as she unashamedly met his laughing green eyes. "Although there was no repeat performance on the showboat, I would like to replay this last scene," she insisted, as her hands curled over his hips and then traced his spine. "Since you have informed me that I will never experience such pleasure elsewhere, I would be a fool to sleep when you are so close at hand."

"Now?" Dante croaked in disbelief. Lord, this minx never ceased to amaze him. "I have yet to catch my breath. At least give me a moment to muster my strength."

Erica laughed softly, taunting him and loving every minute of it. Dante had teased her since he'd found her hiding in his closet, and she now delighted in doing the same. "Or perhaps you are not man enough to rise to the occasion."

Dante could cheerfully have choked her for doubting his prowess. His manhood had never been questioned, but then he hadn't met a woman like Erica. She defied every rule that applied to other women.

"I should have left you to those roustabouts," he muttered spitefully.

Her arms slid over his shoulders, and her slim fingers delved through his dark hair. Then a low chuckle tumbled from her lips, tickling his senses as she moved seductively beneath him. "Do you suppose three men would satisfy me whereas one has not?" Her warm lips lightly crossed his cheek then glided down his neck, traced the hard contours of his ribs, and finally found the narrow lines of his hips. "You have brought into being a hunger that half a night cannot appease, and I will not sleep until I know beyond all doubt that your embrace is magic, as you have often insisted." Her lips played lightly on his until he groaned with intense pleasure. "Come, my handsome pirate, show me some proof that the treasures of your embrace exceed a woman's wildest imaginings. . . ."

Her light touch rekindled fires of desire that Dante would have sworn were no more than cinders, and he felt their flames leap through his veins as her soft mouth fitted itself to his, breathing into him renewed strength. With gentle fondling and arousing kisses, she fueled his fierce need, and again they glided, like an eagle, toward the far horizon, sharing unbounded ecstasy, living and dying in the same breathless instant. At last they tumbled back to reality, their passion spent, their needs appeased for a time.

Dante enfolded her in his arms and blessed her with a strangely tender kiss. "Has your appetite been satiated, witch?" he breathed wearily, praying that she would have the courtesy not to poke holes in his male pride since it had suffered several bruises.

"Mmmmm . . ." Erica sighed in satisfaction. "I think perhaps now I can sleep . . . for a while at least. . . ."

Dante chortled drowsily and then cuddled her closer, molding her shapely body to his. Erica's daring and passion had surprised and amazed him. A man would have to stay on his toes with this lively vixen, he mused as his thick lashes fluttered against his cheeks. Erica was feisty and headstrong, yet so very desirable. Indeed, she was in a class by herself, and she no longer needed an instructor if it was her intent to seduce a man. She had taught him a few things about lovemaking even though her innocent, impulsive ways sent his senses reeling. She was a curious combination of strength and sentimentality, a mixture that intrigued him. Yet, just when he thought he understood her, she did something totally unpredictable. *Like turning the tables on me and coaxing* me *into* her *bed,* he thought just before he drifted off to sleep. He'd realized that he could never outguess her quicksilver moods. Tomorrow her temper might be ablaze. But that night she'd been his, and they had shared loving hours that were beyond compare.

When Erica heard his slow methodic breathing, she reached up to trace the chiseled lines of his face, now softened by repose. Perhaps she would never have Dante's love, but she had enjoyed what pleasure he could offer before they went their separate ways. Perhaps it was her fate to nourish a one-sided attachment while threading her way through a maze of men who vied for her attention. That thought dampened Erica's spirits, and she hastily tossed it aside. She was in Dante's arms, and would lie beside him until the sun intruded on them. This night might be all she would ever have of a wild, free spirit like Dante Fowler.

Chapter 10

Corbin Fowler crossed the hurricane deck with hurried strides. When Dante had not returned to their stateroom the previous night, Corbin had no trouble guessing where he'd slept . . . if he had slept at all. A wry smile curled his lips as he strode up to the captain's cabin—the room *he* had occupied until that lively bundle of trouble had mysteriously appeared on the *Natchez Belle*. Erica was the cause of his brother's about-face. Dante was himself again, but his attention was focused on the bewitching, raven-haired minx who had all the males on the steamboat buzzing, not to mention the women, who were a mite jealous of Erica.

Pushing aside these thoughts, Corbin focused on the problem at hand. Heavy rains upriver had caused the Mississippi to swell, changing the channel and forcing the steamboat into treacherous waters. Now they were on a hazardous course. The pilot had just informed Corbin of the dangers ahead of them, so he had immediately come to fetch Dante. His brother's expertise would be helpful if they were to make it through the maze of sandbars and fallen trees that dotted the receding waters. These hazards could rip the hull of the steamboat; then it would be stranded for days on end.

"We've got trouble," Corbin abruptly announced as he pounded on the door of the texas, making Dante and Erica bolt straight up in bed.

Erica blinked, then colored profusely when she realized that Corbin had known that his brother was with her in the cabin. The memory of their lovemaking was eclipsed by the bright light that glared through the window, and Erica's embarrassment deepened when Dante grinned outrageously at her.

"What's wrong, *chérie?*" he asked, amused by the blush that stained her cheeks, knowing she was humiliated because Corbin was aware of what had gone on behind the closed door. The previous night, Erica had played the temptress as if she'd been born to the role, yet now she looked as if she wished the river would part and then swallow him up.

"You know very well what's the matter," Erica hissed as she covered herself with the sheet, blushing up to her hairline. "You're here, and your brother is no fool. He knows we weren't playing an all-night game of chess, or cards, or . . ." Erica swallowed her humiliation and then groaned miserably. "I will never be able to face him again."

With no concern for modesty, Dante bounded to his feet and crawled into his breeches while he stumbled toward the door. "Corbin is not one to spread gossip. Our secret is safe with him," he assured her.

If Erica had been carrying a loaded pistol she would have turned it on herself in the hope of ending her misery. She had shamelessly seduced Dante, like a common trollop addicted to passion, instead of pursuing some riverboat habitué who might further her cause. Now the steamboat would dock at Natchez and she would have no husband. And Corbin would think . . . Erica groaned as she yanked the sheet over her head, too ashamed to face anyone. She was such a slave to Dante's magnetism that she had overlooked her dilemma when time was so short. Had she lost what little sense she had left?

When Dante opened the door just wide enough to peer at his brother, Corbin wedged one foot inside. "We were swept out of the main channel during the night. We're heading straight for the sandbars. I want you in the pilot-house, posthaste."

"I'll be with you in a minute," Dante replied. Indicating that Corbin should remove his foot, he closed the door and began to don the rest of his clothing. Glancing up, he saw Erica, draped in a sheet, scurry across the room, and disappear into the closet. A muddled frown plowed his brow as the closet door slammed shut behind her. "What the sweet loving hell are you doing?"

"Dressing," she snapped from inside the narrow cubicle as she wormed into her gown. "I'm going with you. If I am to be drowned in the river I would like to watch the disaster occur."

Dante chortled as he shrugged on his coat. "I have no intention of allowing us to sink," he insisted.

"I suppose, in addition to your other unusual talents, you can work miracles." Erica's voice dripped with sarcasm. When she emerged from the closet, she presented her back to him, silently requesting his assistance in fastening the gown.

His lips trailed along her neck, sending a chill down her

170

spine. "Perhaps . . ."

Quickly Erica moved away from him. Stifling the sensations he'd aroused, she retrieved her slippers, determined to keep the previous night in proper perspective. She had risked a great deal to spend an uninterrupted night in his arms, but now they faced impending doom and she still had found no way to elude Sabin Keary.

"I certainly could use one if you have some to spare," she muttered as she headed toward the door.

"We'll see to that later." Dante grasped her arm and hurried her along the deck. "At the moment we must run the chute and work our way out of the crooked channel to regain the main stream. *Then* we will see what can be done about your unwanted fiancé."

Erica doubted that anything could be done about Sabin Keary, even though Dante was optimistic about finding a way for her to elude him; but keeping that depressing thought to herself, she focused her attention on the problem at hand. If it were true that the Lord worked in mysterious ways, maybe He would see fit to let her sink tō the bottom of the Mississippi so she would not have to face Sabin.

I won't be that lucky, she thought to herself. I'll probably be snared by a protruding tree limb and just dangle until Sabin happens along and fishes me out of the water. He will then take the lash to me for blowing a hole in his leg.

When they stepped into the glass pilothouse, Erica gasped as she peered down at the narrow channel. It seemed a treacherous labyrinth of sand and gnarled cypress trees. Feeling that the clogged river was waiting to entrap them, Erica was depressed by the very real possibility that they would never be able to weave their way through this network of hazards to safety. Her wild eyes flew to Dante, whose expression was grim. Then her gaze circled to Corbin. Both men were staring at the challenge before them.

Two leadsmen were perched on the bow, tossing coils of cord into the river to check its depth. Erica waited anxiously as the deckhands hauled in the weighted ropes and turned to peer up at the pilothouse.

"Mark twain!" one of the leadsmen called back to them.

"Damn," Dante muttered. Then he gave Erica a hasty glance when she tugged on his sleeve, her eyes full of questions. "The channel is only twelve feet deep and the *Natchez Belle* requires at least seven feet to clear the sand." His gaze swung to Corbin whose hands were clamped around the wheel. "We'd better alert the passengers. If we run aground, someone could be injured or thrown overboard."

Corbin nodded bleakly, and without taking his eyes off the hazardous channel, he ordered the pilot to tell the crew and passengers that they should brace themselves in case the *Natchez Belle* lodged on a sandbar or struck one of the dead trees that obstructed her path.

Dante leaned toward the brass speaking tube to order the engineer on the main deck to reduce speed; then he poked his head out of the pilothouse as the leadsmen dragged the ropes from the water.

"Half twain!"

Corbin and Dante stared solemnly at each other while Erica grasped the window ledge. "How deep is the channel now?" She wasn't sure she wanted to know, but the apprehensive question had left her lips before she could bite it back.

"Six or seven feet," Corbin told her grimly. "Hang on, Erica. If we snag in the trees or the sand, you could be thrown right through the glass."

That was not the kind of news she wanted to hear. She choked down the lump of fear that had lodged in her throat, and stared straight ahead. This simply was not her week. She had stumbled from one catastrophe to another, and now it looked as though she was facing a disaster. She braced herself for the worst. She doubted that anything good would happen. She was working up to seven days of bad luck, and on such a roll, the best one could hope for was to be knocked unconscious. She looked at the sandbars and jutting trees ahead of them. They were a preamble to oncoming disaster!

"Trouble starboard," Dante informed his brother. "Hard left!"

Corbin spun the wheel and then attempted to veer back into the winding chute, but the flooding rains had silted the main channel shut. It was as dangerous as the meandering path they were forced to follow.

"Crack steam!" Dante yelled down to the engineer.

Erica stared, wide-eyed, at the mound of sand that enveloped the bow of the steamboat. The paddlewheels thrashed and the huge boat shuddered as it plowed into the sand. Planks creaked and groaned, and Erica was flung forward. As her head slammed against the frame of the pilothouse, the shriek of the leadsman reached her ears. He had been thrown off the deck and was treading water until his crew mate could drag him aboard.

Dante slumped as he watched the black smoke churning from the stack, casting a cloud of impending doom over them. "Reduce steam," he called through the speaking tube. Then he sighed heavily as he peered over at his brother who was still gritting his teeth and straining against the wheel. "We can't break the sandbar. It's a quarter of a league long." His somber gaze landed on Erica who was carefully inspecting the bump on her forehead. "How are your nursing abilities?" he asked as he strode over to pry her away from the window and propel her through the door. "You'd better check on the rest of the passengers after you've seen to your own injury."

"I . . ." Erica blinked, hoping her head would clear.

"Check with the clerk. He should have some bandages for you, and for the other unfortunate passengers who weren't prepared for the sudden jolt," Dante muttered absently; then he returned to his brother's side. Together the men stared at the sand that had engulfed them.

After Erica staggered off, Corbin propped his forearms on the wheel and gave Dante a sidelong glance. "Do you prefer to work from the river or from the pilot-house?"

Dante's shoulders lifted, then dropped. "Since you are the captain of this voyage I suppose you should have the privilege of supervising this ordeal. Besides, I was the one who ousted the roustabouts, leaving us short-handed. I'll man the timbers."

A wry smile tugged at Corbin's lips. "You are quite right. You deserve to do the dirty work." He smirked. "After all, you spent the night with the lady Elliot has announced that *he* intends to marry. Never let it be said that my dear brother wouldn't do *anything* for his best friend."

Dante's carefully blank stare revealed none of his thoughts. "I don't think this is the time for a brotherly lecture. In case you have forgotten, we are stranded on a sandbar. Now, do you intend to order the crew to lower the yawl from the hurricane deck or must I work the poles without the aid of a rowboat?"

"I never would have expected you to compromise a young woman's virtue." Corbin snorted derisively, ignoring Dante's attempt to steer clear of the subject of Erica and of his tryst in the texas. "How well received do you suppose you will be in Elliot's home when he discovers that he was not the first one to know his wife? Damnation, Dante, you'll have to marry that minx just to save face, but you will still have to smooth Elliot's ruffled feathers. I always thought you had a sensible head on your shoulders, but I'm beginning to think you've been too long in the sun. The heat has fried your brain."

This was neither the time nor place to discuss Dante's intelligence, or lack of it, but Dante realized his brother was determined to pry. "What exists between Erica and me is very complicated," he said evasively.

"You can count upon the fact that I will anxiously await your *lengthy* explanation," Corbin taunted, flashing his brother a mocking grin as he sauntered out of the pilothouse to collect the timbers needed to drag the steamboat from the sand. "If by chance we find ourselves marooned, you can elaborate and I will be all ears. I must say, you have been acting odd since that lovely little mermaid swam aboard." Corbin gestured toward the main deck. "Roll up your sleeves, little brother. You have work to do."

Growling in response to Corbin's remarks, Dante stalked out the door and headed toward the staircase. At least the hull of the boat was not ripped. There would be a delay, but both he and Corbin had faced similar difficulties in the past. They knew what they were up against. He was not about to wait for another ship to come along and tow them off the sandbar. He did not want Sabin Keary to get to Erica before her future was decided. Keary had caused him much misery, and if he could complicate the man's life, so much the better.

A determined frown cut deep lines into Dante's bronzed face as he made his way to the main deck. He was not about to spend the entire day bogged down in the sand. He had plans to make, just as soon as he freed the steamboat from the sandbar; and time was of the essence. He had been procrastinating for four days, counting on untangling his involvement with Erica at the last minute. He hadn't figured on being marooned on the river. Confound it! He had no patience with these inconveniences when his mind was on other matters.

Erica made certain that none of the other passengers had suffered greatly from the grounding. She inspected several bruises, bumps, and scrapes; then she made a beeline for the boiler deck so she could watch Dante and the deckhands row out to drive the heavy timber crutches into the sand. Once the huge planks were standing upright on either side of the ship, thick ropes were strung through iron rings on the main deck, drawn through the pulleys atop the crutches, then tied back to the deck. Every available man grasped the ropes and waited for Dante's order to pull.

The *Natchez Belle* groaned as the deckhands strained to lift her hull from the sand.

"Crack steam!" Corbin bellowed as the bulky ship floundered and then inched forward, only to run aground once again.

The paddlewheels screamed and thrashed as the ship spun sideways, burying itself deeper in the sand. Again, Dante set the teetering timbers and gave the signal to pull while the engineer tossed more logs on the fire so the boilers were blazing. As the cumbersome steamship lurched forward and then slid sideways into the channel, Erica's wide eyes flew to the bare-chested captain who was attempting to steady the timbers on the starboard side of the boat. She had heard of crewmen being crushed beneath collapsing timbers and ropes. She squeezed her eyes shut, forcing those pictures from her mind, praying that Dante would not become a casualty in their escape from the sandbar. She wished they had remained marooned until the water rose to float the *Natchez Belle* to safety.

"Erica, I must talk to you," Elliot insisted as he grasped her arm and spun her around to face him. "I want your answer."

Erica glared disgustedly at him. They were in deep trouble, but Elliot did not have the sense to wait until the danger had passed before he popped the question. "Your best friend is treading in quicksand and you have the nerve to demand my answer?" She sniffed distastefully as she drew her arm from his grasp, and when she peered down, she saw a huge pole swaying wildly just above Dante's head. "Dante! Be careful!"

The skidding ship put excessive strain on the timbers and Erica watched in horror as a rope snapped. As the pulley over Dante's head tumbled free, he looked up, then dived into the river the moment before the entire contraption collapsed on him. Erica nearly fell as the steamboat, its smokestacks rolling, groaned and then

177

shot sideways.

Cheers resounded on all three decks of the *Natchez Belle* as she veered diagonally across the sandbar, scraping half-submerged trees and then gliding into the mainstream. But Erica was still holding her breath. She could not locate Dante amidst the fallen timbers and ropes. Panic gripped her as she flung herself away from Elliot and dashed toward the steps, leaping down them two at a time in her haste to reach the main deck. Her fearful gaze swept the murky water as Reade Asher rowed back toward the paddlewheeler—alone.

"Where is Dante?" Erica choked out as she met Reade's dazed eyes.

"He didn't come to the surface," he muttered sourly. "And I can't swim a lick. Tell Corbin to git down here."

Erica ignored the command, and displaying no concern for her own safety, she dived into the water, aiming herself toward the fallen timber and the curled ropes half-buried in the sand. Her heart thundered furiously as she groped for some object that resembled a man's body. When her hand finally made contact with flesh she tugged with all her strength and finally brought Dante's limp body to the surface.

As Reade approached, she fought to remain afloat and tried to tow Dante toward the rowboat. After Reade had managed to haul Dante into the skiff, he clamped a firm hand around Erica's waist and hoisted her up beside him. She gasped and choked as she attempted to catch her breath. Then a dismayed groan escaped her lips when she wiped the mud from her eyes and saw the deep gash that slashed the side of Dante's head. He was deathly pale and he looked as if he were . . . Erica banished the thought

178

and hastily turned Dante face down. As she tried to force the water from his lungs, she prayed that it was not too late to revive him.

While Reade rowed toward the *Natchez Belle*, she frantically continued her ministrations, finally breathing a sigh of relief when Dante coughed and sputtered. She whacked him between the shoulder blades until he expelled water and then drew a breath.

When they reached the bow, Corbin lifted his brother up, and Erica immediately turned to Reade, her eyes spitting hot blue flame. "What in heaven's name were you doing in a rowboat with Dante if you can't swim?" she snapped angrily. "For a man who claims to have sailed the seven seas you certainly take an unreasonable risk by not learning to keep yourself afloat." She looked him over disdainfully; then she wagged a slim finger in his shocked face. "What use were you to your former captain when he needed your assistance?" She didn't wait for him to respond. "I'll tell you exactly how much help you were—none. I don't know why Dante kept such an incompetent man beside him for so many years."

"Let me tell you somethin', woman," Reade shouted indignantly as he bolted to his feet, causing the rowboat to rock precariously. "I've . . ."

Erica flapped her arms to maintain her balance, but Reade's abrupt movements sent her sprawling in the sand and water. She screamed and then quickly took a shallow breath before she sank in the murk. Reade's hand clamped around her arm to fish her from the water, and he jerked her back into the boat, intending to finish what he'd started to say before this wildcat had lashed out at him with her razor-sharp tongue.

179

"I've dragged Dante from a few disasters in my time and he's done the same for me," he declared. "I don't need some wild witch comin' along to rake me over the coals. I was on my way for help when you dived in like a crazed fool."

"A crazed fool!" Erica railed. She was itching to scratch the arrogant smirk off Asher's stubbled face. "It seems to me that the pot is calling the kettle black. If there are lunatics running around loose, *you* are among them. By the time you rowed back for assistance and then returned, Dante would have been a dead man . . . if he isn't already."

Reade puffed up like an indignant cobra sparring with a mongoose. "Why, you feisty little—"

"Erica, fetch some bandages," Corbin demanded, quickly ending their shouting match. "I'm taking Dante to the texas. Bring them there." Placing a supportive arm around his groggy brother, he propelled him through the crowd.

Erica flashed Reade one last glower before she scurried toward the boiler deck to get antiseptic and bandages. When she burst through the door of the texas Corbin, Elliot, and Reade were carefully depositing Dante on the bed. She wormed her way through the three men hovering over him and began to apply salve to his head wound. But Dante sucked in his breath and then slapped her hand away.

"Damn, that hurts worse than the gash in my skull." He scowled irritably.

"That is exactly what you deserve for being so careless," Erica grumbled, her expression sour as a lemon. "I thought captains were supposed to issue orders, not carry

180

them out. And why didn't you take someone with you who could swim instead of enlisting the help of your first mate who is nothing but dead weight?"

"Now, wait just a minute, witch!" Reade shoved Elliot aside. He wanted to shake the stuffing out of this bedraggled termagant who'd had the unmitigated gall to ridicule him in public for the second time in a quarter of an hour. "I ain't gonna stand here and let you slander my reputation. I—"

"Your so-called reputation." Erica smirked as she carefully wiped the mud from Dante's wound.

The faintest hint of a smile hovered on Dante's ashen lips as he listened to Erica verbally lynch Reade while she leaned over him like a protective angel. Her gown clung to her curvaceous figure, and her dark hair was a mass of tangles from which water dripped onto his cheek. Noting that her blue eyes were flaming, Dante was not too dazed to realize that this little spitfire was having difficulty containing her volatile temper.

"Let me at her!" Reade growled, poising himself to pounce on Erica.

But Corbin stepped between them, forcing Erica back to Dante's side when she started to rise to meet Asher's challenge. He grinned when he saw the muddled frown on Dante's face. Obviously his brother did not understand why Erica and Reade were itching to get at each other's throats.

"Why are you so upset with him?" Dante asked as he propped himself up on one wobbly elbow. "Reade managed to free me from the ropes and haul me to safety."

"It was Erica who saved you," Corbin put in. "She

181

fished you out of the sand, not Reade."

Dante's face registered his surprise; then he grimaced as white-hot pain shot through his head, forcing him to wilt back onto the bed. "Erica?" he breathed raggedly.

She forgot her irritation with Reade when she saw the color drain from Dante's features. "You must rest now. I will see if there is a doctor aboard."

As she hurried from the room, leaving a trail of water, four pair of eyes followed her, but Erica was too concerned about Dante to notice the attention she was receiving.

"That is a most remarkable woman," Corbin mused aloud as his gaze wandered back to his brother. "It is not so difficult to understand why you didn't return last—"

"Don't you have pressing matters to attend?" Dante asked sharply before Corbin unwittingly informed Elliot that his would-be fiancée had entertained a man in her cabin. He didn't need Elliot breathing down his neck when he could barely hold his head up without seeing double.

"I consider you my first priority." Corbin replied, but he shot Elliot a discreet glance to assure himself that he hadn't made Dante's situation worse than it already was. "Besides, the pilot can man the wheel."

"He's the one who got us stuck in the first place," Dante grumbled; then he squirmed about, seeking a more comfortable position. "I think he has been leaning too heavily on the bottle this trip. Perhaps you should have a word with him while I rest."

When the three men had taken the cue to exit, Dante heaved a weary sigh and gave way to the darkness that encircled him. He was not aware that Erica returned with a doctor to examine his injury. Indeed, it was late afternoon before his head cleared and he could muster the energy to prop himself into a semiprone position without becoming light-headed. For over an hour Dante simply stared at the walls, grappling with the thoughts that had converged on him. Although his mind was a bit scrambled he knew he had to make some quick decisions. He must set his plan in motion before the *Natchez Belle* docked.

Chapter 11

"Dante wishes to speak with you," Reade announced abruptly, stirring Erica from her troubled musings.

"Is he feeling worse?" she asked, pushing away from the railing and frowning concernedly.

Reade's shoulders lifted noncommittally. "I don't know. I'm just deliverin' the message like he asked me to."

Erica bowed her head, then raised it to survey Reade's weather-beaten face. "I want to apologize for being so hateful to you earlier. I was upset and frightened so I lashed out at you. I'm sorry. I had no right to speak to you the way I did."

A lopsided smile twisted Reade's mouth as his astute gaze slid over the shapely lass in yellow satin. "I guess trouble brings out the worst in all of us. I felt useless, and I was just as scared as you was." He extended a callused hand and arched a hopeful brow. "Friends?"

Erica grasped his hand and graced him with a disarming smile. "Friends," she affirmed. "My explosive temper is one of my worst faults. It invariably gets me into trouble, and later, I find myself wishing I had not allowed my tongue to outdistance my brain. Dante told me you were an efficient first mate. I had no right to berate you."

"All is forgiven," Reade insisted as he offered his arm. "Come along, lass. The cap'n has been plagued by a foul temper since he split his head open. I don't want to keep him waitin'."

When they entered the texas, Erica frowned bemusedly at Dante's extravagant attire. He looked as if he were dressed for his funeral, yet he lay flat on his back, staring unblinkingly at the same spider Erica had noticed walking upside down in its web on the ceiling. Had the blow scrambled Dante's brain? What the devil did he think he was doing? The doctor had assured her that he would be as good as new in a few days, but he was behaving very strangely for a man who had received a clean bill of health.

After Reade had taken his leave, Erica just stood for a moment, uncertain of what to expect from the mending captain who had yet to acknowledge her presence or even move a muscle.

"Was there something you wanted to see me about?" she finally asked hesitantly.

"Come here, Erica," he requested, his voice gravelly because he'd swallowed so much of the Mississippi.

Mechanically, she moved toward him then sank down beside him when he patted the empty space on the bed.

"We will be docking in Natchez after midnight," he informed her as he reached up to run a lean finger over her soft pink lips.

Her lashes fluttered down, and she sighed disheartenedly. "So I have heard." Erica did not need to be reminded that she was about to reach her destination, but she was no closer to finding a suitable husband than she'd been on the day she'd left New Orleans.

"I have found a way to solve your problem," he announced, a wry smile lifting one corner of his mouth.

Erica patronized him by smiling in return. There was no solution to her problem, and she doubted that Dante was thinking clearly enough to realize that, not after being pounded with poles and pulleys.

"I am going to marry you," Dante said matter-of-factly.

"What?" Erica drew back; then she peered at Dante as if he were a dreadful monster that was about to gobble her up. Sweet merciful heavens! She couldn't marry Dante. She had fallen in love with him. Wedding him and then leaving him would be too painful. "I can't marry you!"

"Why not?" Dante snorted indignantly. "You have been husband hunting and now I'm offering my services. Isn't this what you want, a temporary name so you can acquire your inheritance?"

"Well, yes, but . . ." Erica toyed nervously with the folds of her gown.

"But you do not consider *me* the prize Elliot would have been if you hadn't been stung by your conscience," Dante declared, his eyes scornful and mocking. "Have you decided to keep Elliot instead of throwing him back after he has served your purpose?"

Idiotic fool! Elliot isn't half the man you are, Erica thought. But she was not about to confess that, not to the handsome rogue who had captured her heart but who probably couldn't care less that he had done so. She was certain that Dante would ridicule her if he knew her little scheme had backfired.

186

"Why would you want to marry me?" Erica demanded, purposely avoiding his question.

"Because I owe you my life," Dante replied blandly. "Since I value my soggy hide as much as you value your inheritance it seems fitting that I should help you acquire what you want most."

If only he had sense enough to realize I would sacrifice my fortune just to have him as my true husband, Erica thought despairingly. But she could not swallow her pride and tell him so, nor would she drag the man she loved into her conflict with Sabin Keary. Since Dante had a personal grudge against Sabin, marriage to him would only serve to aggravate the situation. Erica knew that Sabin was a malevolent man, and she felt that Dante was no match for him. No one was.

Then too, if she accepted his proposal, Dante would think she didn't care about him, that she was only using him. Their marriage would be headed for catastrophe. Because of her love for Dante she could not wed him. A bemused frown knitted Erica's brow. Was she making any sense? How could she explain her refusal to Dante without exposing her deep feeling for him? She couldn't. She realized that she must hedge.

"A simple thank you would suffice," she told him, raising a proud chin. "I ask no more than that."

"Good God, woman." Dante snorted in exasperation. "I am offering a practical answer to your dilemma and you decline. Do you see me as such an unworthy catch? Fowler is a respected name in Natchez, and I have no intention of tying you down. Why can't you accept?"

Because *not* being tied to you forever would not be enough, not now, not after I have fallen in love with you, Erica thought, but she said, "Don't you realize that you

187

would be inviting trouble if you were to wed me? Have you forgotten what kind of man Sabin Keary is? You already dislike him, and he would be infuriated when he learned of our marriage. That was why I wanted a drifter for a husband. Sabin would not have been able to locate him, but you . . ." Erica didn't want to think of what might happen if Dante rose to Keary's challenge. And she knew he would. He did not back away from trouble. "Sabin has a ferocious temper, and I will not pit you against him. What if he—"

"I welcome the opportunity to face my father's"— Dante gritted his teeth and bit back the word that dangled on the tip of his tongue and then replaced it with another—"assassin."

"I will not be the cause of such a confrontation," Erica insisted, bolting from the bed to pace the confines of the texas. "I will just have to devise another plan of action."

Dante grabbed her hand as she breezed by, spinning her around to face his sly grin. "There is no need for an alternate plan. You and I know each other well enough to become husband and wife," he murmured, his eyes taking on the alluring glow that always held Erica hostage. "You will be free to come and go as you please after you have decided your future, and I will see to your defense when Sabin comes calling."

How could she decline his persuasive offer when her heart was insisting she accept? Yet, the voice of reason told her to refuse. Dante was asking for trouble. Confound it, the risk involved was too great. If something happened to Dante, she could never forgive herself, for she knew Sabin would resort to fiendish tactics to dispose of Dante.

"Sit here beside me, Erica," he coaxed, his tone soft

188

and compelling. Hopelessly lost to his tender smile, she eased herself onto the bed. Dante curled his index finger beneath her chin, drawing her ever closer, but she flinched when a spark bridged the narrow gap between them, igniting emotions that she had carefully held in check. He drew her reluctant body closer. "Say yes, *chérie*. We can both be of service to each other." His full lips held hers captive, strangling her hesitancy, playing havoc with her logic. "And we can give each other pleasure for a time. . . . Have you forgotten what it is like between us?"

When his mouth took possession of hers, Erica felt herself melting. She had come dangerously close to losing him earlier in the day, and she had risked her own life to save him. How could she resist him now? She couldn't. She longed to spend every spare minute with him, for as long as she could.

"Very well, Dante, for a time . . ." she whispered, striving to keep her churning emotions from filtering into her voice.

His arms came around her then, but as he pulled her against his solid frame, Corbin barged into the room.

"From the look of things, I assume the lady said yes," Corbin observed as he sauntered toward the affectionate couple. He had already decided that this raven-haired enchantress was just what Dante needed. Perhaps now his brother could put the past in proper perspective. "I have been anticipating the day I could perform your wedding ceremony and also serve as best man." His amused gaze settled on Erica who now sat erect on the side of the bed. "He is all yours now, my dear. I've been heckled by this ornery rascal for most of my life, but it is your turn to keep him on a tight rein." His eyes flickered over Erica, then he nodded slightly. "And I do believe you might be the one woman who can hobble this brother of mine."

"Did you come to deliver a sermon or to perform a wedding ceremony?" Dante grunted sarcastically as he struggled to prop himself up in bed. However, the room careened sideways when he was not in a prone position.

"Both," Corbin assured him, ignoring the taunt. "My only regret is that you refused to wait until Leona could join us for this grand occasion. You know how your sister-in-law loves to cry at weddings."

"Can we get on with this?" Dante scowled irritably as he staggered to his feet.

"A mite anxious, are you, little brother?" Corbin's teasing was unmerciful. "You have avoided matrimony for so many years that I can't imagine what difference another minute or two will make."

Dante gnashed his teeth and gave his brother the evil eye. Corbin was sorely testing his patience. "I will die of old age before I am able to repeat the vows," he snapped grouchily. "Proceed, Corbin. We must wedge in the ceremony and a honeymoon before we dock in Natchez."

Corbin struggled to keep a straight face while he rattled off the customary ritual, but his amusement vanished when Erica supplied her full name and began to recite the vows.

"I, Erica Michelle Bennet, do solemnly swear to—"

"Bennet?" Corbin and Dante hooted simultaneously as they peered at Erica in astonishment.

"Not Avery Bennet's daughter," Dante groaned.

A frown knitted her brow. Why were they looking at her as if she had suddenly contracted leprosy? Dante was white as a sheet, and Corbin looked as if someone had knocked the wind out of him. "Do you know my father?" It was not difficult to see that they did, and obviously neither of them had much use for Avery.

"Yes," Dante muttered. Then he motioned for Corbin to by-pass the remainder of Erica's vows, saying, "Get on with it. Time is of the essence."

"Are you certain?" Corbin stared soberly at his scowling brother. "Perhaps you would like some time to reconsider after this new twist."

"No, dammit." Dante flung him a black look. "Spout off the rest of this ceremony and be quick about it. My patience is running short."

Reluctantly, Corbin continued, meanwhile eying Erica apprehensively and silently studying his brother's reaction to the upsetting news that he was marrying Avery Bennet's daughter.

"And now to kiss the bride," Corbin announced as he strode over to plant a kiss on Erica's cheek while she was still baffled by the morose expression on Dante's face.

"I am quite capable of seeing to that myself," Dante grumbled as he placed a hand on Corbin's chest to hold him at bay. "I don't mean to sound rude, but don't let the door slam when you exit." Corbin opened his mouth to fire a question, but Dante hastily continued, "Please ask Elliot to join me. We have an important matter to discuss."

Corbin's worried expression deepened. It was going to be difficult to break the disturbing news to Elliot. Dante had finally explained his involvement with Erica so Corbin knew of the entire episode. He did not relish Dante's ticklish situation, one that would undoubtedly become even more strained now that he knew who Erica really was. Dante had waded in up to his neck. He would inevitably clash with Sabin Keary, not to mention Avery Bennet; and this whirlwind marriage would certainly strain his friendship with Elliot. Corbin prayed that Dante knew what he was doing, but he wasn't at all sure Dante was in full command of his senses after the blow he'd received that morning.

"I will fetch Elliot for you . . . if you are certain you want to see him just now," Corbin looked directly at Dante.

"I prefer to get this over with," Dante said absently, as he massaged his aching temples.

When Corbin left the room, Dante eased back onto the chair and sighed heavily. Being on his feet had drained him, and he needed his strength to confront Elliot.

"I think it best for you to join Corbin in the pilot-house," Dante advised. "Elliot and I must talk privately."

"Would you prefer that I tell him I—"

"No," Dante declared adamantly. "I will handle this my own way."

"But it is my fault that Elliot—" Again Erica was cut off.

"Be on your way. I don't want you to risk an encounter with Elliot before I give him the news. It will only make matters worse, Erica. Elliot is a proud man, and I don't intend to humiliate him more than necessary."

Although Erica was itching to know how Dante had met her father and why he seemed distraught at the news that he had married a Bennet, she bit back her questions. As she silently headed toward the door, she decided to interrogate him when he was in a better mood . . . whenever that would be. Judging by the sour expression on his face, he might never be cheerful again. Well, it was her fault. She didn't have the foggiest notion of what her father had done to earn Dante's animosity.

Heaving a despairing sigh, Erica closed the door behind her. She wondered why people said that a woman's wedding day was the happiest time in her life. Erica felt positively miserable, and she wasn't exactly sure why.

When Elliot tapped on the door, Dante braced himself for the upcoming confrontation. He had spent the last few minutes formulating his thoughts so he might gently put the news to Elliot . . . if that was possible.

"Are you feeling better?" Elliot inquired as he ambled toward Dante, who was still propped up in the chair.

Dante had grappled with several approaches to the sensitive subject he must broach, but he'd finally decided to dispense with excuses and just tell Elliot what the situation was. He was a grown man, after all, and although wealth had spoiled him, he had endured a few disappointments.

"I am recuperating," Dante replied. Then he smiled bleakly. "I only hope that you will."

A befuddled frown distorted Elliot's features. "I am not the one who has suffered a catastrophe." Had the fall scrambled Dante's brain? What the devil was he babbling about?

"I'm afraid you have, my friend." Dante sighed and then gestured toward the unoccupied chair. "Perhaps you should sit down." When Elliot had complied with the suggestion, Dante cut right to the heart of the matter. "Elliot, I know this will come as a shock to you, but Erica and I were married a few minutes ago. I know you had—"

"Married?" Elliot yelped in disbelief, and the color

drained from his face as his expression became a mixture of hurt and resentment. "Damn you, Dante, how could you do it? You knew I had asked for her hand in marriage, and you were aware of how I felt about her."

"But it was *my* proposal she accepted," Dante calmly declared.

"Why? Because you were injured?" Elliot's spiteful glare riveted on his so-called friend. "You played on her sympathy, didn't you?" he accused. "You were interested in her all along, and you went behind my back to steal the woman I have waited so long to find. I never would have believed this of you, Dante."

"Now, Elliot, don't make this more difficult than it already is," Dante coaxed. "You claim that Erica is the woman you have always wanted, but you know nothing about her, not really."

"And I suppose you do?" Elliot snorted disgustedly. "I knew everything I wanted to know. Her past didn't concern me. It was her future that interested me."

"I know a great deal more about Erica than you do," Dante muttered as he squirmed uncomfortably in his seat. "I don't want her to come between us. Our friendship has stood the test of time, and of differences far worse than this." He looked Elliot squarely in the eye. "Believe me when I say it turned out best for all concerned."

Elliot laughed bitterly. *"Best* for you." His tone was riddled with scorn. "You are putting me in the position of coveting my best friend's wife. Or perhaps I should say my *former* friend," he added disdainfully. "I think you took advantage of Erica in a vulnerable moment. I know she approved of me, and given time, she would have accepted my proposal."

"One you would have deeply regretted making," Dante interjected. "Erica is not what she seems."

"Then why did you marry her? To save me from this supposed witch?" Elliot asked caustically. "Spare me your honorable motives, Dante. You wanted Erica and you didn't care who you hurt, not as long as you got her. All's fair in love and war. Isn't that how the adage goes?"

Dante was being made the culprit, and although he didn't consider himself a proper target for Elliot's acrimonious gibes, he endured them. "In time you will come to realize that I have done you a favor, not a disservice."

Elliot bolted to his feet, his pale blue eyes flaming. "I seriously doubt that you will ever hear me thank you for marrying the woman I love. And in the future I would appreciate it if you would keep your nose out of my affairs," he said brusquely. "Don't think that because you have married Erica behind my back I will gracefully bow out. She is fond of me, and when the novelty of this hasty marriage wears off, she will see her mistake, the same one your mother . . ." Elliot clamped his mouth shut. He was furious with Dante, but he had not intended to become vicious. He realized that his remark was tantamount to stabbing Dante in the back when he saw his injured friend flinch. "I'm sorry, Dante. I did not mean to dig up the past. For that—that alone—I apologize. But Erica is dear to me, and I have watched you toy with too many women to expect you to be faithful to one, even one as captivating and remarkable as she. In my eyes, she is still available, and I would not be ashamed to take her as my wife should you tire of her." His penetrating gaze drilled into Dante. "Know this, I will always be close should Erica need a strong shoulder to lean on, and one day she will realize that it was *my* proposal she should have accepted."

As the door slammed shut behind Elliot, Dante growled. He had expected Elliot to be upset, but not vindictive. Elliot had been a reasonable man until Erica had come into his life. Damn, he had disturbed an entire den of rattlesnakes by marrying Erica. Sabin would be furious, not that Dante cared what that bastard thought. Avery Bennet would probably suffer a heart seizure when he learned of his daughter's married name, and Elliot . . . Dante expelled a perturbed sigh. Elliot still wanted Erica, even though she was Dante's wife. What a tangled mess had evolved from one night of pleasure. Dante had been tormented by that night until Erica had reappeared. Then she had turned his life into chaos. He was a fool for becoming involved with her after learning of her connection with Sabin, and he was a lunatic for going ahead with the ceremony when he'd learned her name. Great balls of fire! What had he gotten himself into? Yes, he had planned to play the situation to his advantage, but if he didn't watch his step, he'd never have revenge on Sabin and Bennet. Elliot would not be satisfied until Erica drifted back into his arms. Confound it, all this turmoil for the sake of a raven-haired enchantress? Dante rolled his eyes in disbelief. He must have been out of his mind!

"Dante?" Erica poked her head into the texas to glance apprehensively at her newly acquired husband. "Corbin asked me to tell you that we would be docking in Natchez within the hour." She paused to draw a quick breath and then eased into the room. "Was Elliot upset?"

He released a derisive snort. "Upset? That is putting it mildly, *chérie*. Had the man been toting a pistol I do

196

believe he would have blown me to smithereens."

A wave of guilt washed over Erica, and she humbly hung her head to stare at the floor as if something there had suddenly caught her attention. "Perhaps, when we separate, Elliot will realize that I—"

"You are going nowhere." Dante's temper was getting the best of him. "Don't think I intend to let you waltz away immediately after we dock."

Erica shrank away as his booming voice ricocheted around her. "You need not shout," she snapped. "I may be a fool, but I am *not* deaf."

He lowered his voice, but it still carried a harsh ring. "I am not allowing you out of my sight until your father and Sabin come looking for you. I want to see the look on Sabin's face when he learns the identity of your husband. You will not deny me that privilege."

Erica did not appreciate being ordered about, nor did she like his tone. His despotic attitude riled her. "Do not think because I repeated the vows that I have sacrificed my independence. I will not honor and obey your every whim," she informed him tersely, tilting her chin defiantly. "If I wanted to be browbeaten, I would have consented to marry Sabin Keary."

"You would have been well rid of me if you had allowed me to drown. Just why did you save my life?" Dante asked point-blank.

The sudden change of focus took the wind out of Erica's sails. "Because I thought someone should," she parried. "But I am beginning to think that was another of my many mistakes."

Her remark set his teeth on edge, and he found his mood darkening further. "You are using me to serve your purpose, so I deserve the same consideration. You will remain on my plantation until the *honorable* Avery Bennet and his satanic sidekick come to fetch you home!" he ordered, striking the night stand with his fist much as a judge would pound his gavel when delivering a sentence. "And that is the beginning and end of this debate."

Erica bristled at his words, yet they also disturbed her. He seemed to have changed the moment they were wed. Was this the man she loved? Although Erica had intended to object to the living arrangements he'd described for the sake of her own sanity, she was sidetracked by Dante's sarcastic reference to her father. Her curiosity piqued, she broached the subject she had filed in the back of her mind during the wedding ceremony.

"I demand to know what you have against my father. Where did you meet him? I have never heard him mention your name."

"For good reason." Dante smirked. "I suggest you interrogate him about the matter when next you meet." He struggled to his feet and held his splitting head, hoping to find at least one position that didn't cause it to throb. "Lord, this has been one hell of a day."

Erica puffed up indignantly, certain that Dante was implying their marriage did not agree with him. "Believe me, it has not been one of my favorites either." She sniffed distastefully. "I should have thrown myself overboard the first day I set foot on this boat."

A mocking smile parted Dante's lips as he headed toward the door to seek a breath of air. "A pity you have a fear of falling."

When Dante had hobbled past her, Erica glared daggers at his back. My, but the man had become sour as a lemon. No doubt, he was having misgivings about their marriage. Indeed, she was now wondering why she had agreed to it. Dante had something up his sleeve, she could sense it. He had been subtly persuasive when he'd proposed, but now that she was his wife, he intended to use her. Erica had the uneasy feeling that she wasn't going to like the scheme he was devising. She should have known better than to marry Dante Fowler, but she had allowed her emotions to sway her. She would probably spend the better part of her life paying for that mistake. She berated herself as she flounced down onto the chair and glared at the walls. When Dante had swaggered into her life, blinding her with his charismatic smile, she had lost what little sense she possessed.

Part IV

We are never so easily deceived as when we imagine we are deceiving others.

—La Rochefoucauld

Chapter 12

As dawn broke, the sky threatened to spill rain, but Erica was determined to venture from the plantation while Dante was inspecting the cotton and rice fields. For two days they had practiced civilized warfare, avoiding each other as much as possible and engaging in strained conversation only when the situation demanded it. When Elliot had come to call, Erica had found herself turning to him for companionship. At least he had spoken to her without making snide remarks, Erica mused as she nudged her mount into a canter. Dante was a master at flinging barbs, then flashing her an intimidating smile that set her teeth on edge. Yet she still loved the green-eyed scoundrel, and because of her deep feeling for him she had chosen to make this journey alone.

Erica cast her pensive deliberations aside when she spotted her aunt's dry-goods store. Eagerly, she headed toward it. At least here she would find a friendly face.

"Erica? Is that you?" Lilian exclaimed when her niece appeared in the doorway. "My goodness you're lovelier than you were the last time I set eyes on you . . . if that's possible!"

Erica gave the plump woman a loving squeeze; then she appraised her aunt. She was certain her mother would have been as bubbly and attractive as her older sister if she'd survived the birth of her son.

"You are looking well, Aunt Lilian," Erica observed.

"And feeling fit as a fiddle," Lilian replied, as she ushered Erica toward the parlor situated directly behind her mercantile store. "Mind the shop for me, Madeline." Lilian glanced over her shoulder as she directed her request to the gray-haired woman who sat inconspicuously amid the feedsacks.

Once Lilian had fetched two cups of tea, she planted herself in the velvet rocker and peered curiously at Erica. "What brings you to Natchez? The last time I heard from your father, he said you would be marrying soon. I would not have expected you to visit me in the midst of your wedding arrangements."

I married sooner than Avery expected, Erica thought. When he learned of her scheme, he and Sabin would hit the ceiling. Erica was not looking forward to the inevitable confrontation. "I am already married," she announced, forcing a smile despite her drooping spirits.

"My goodness." Lilian chuckled. "I should be insulted that I was not invited to the wedding, but knowing your father, I suppose I shouldn't be surprised. He has had very little to do with me these past few years."

Erica had sensed an underlying tension between Lilian and Avery, something she had never been able to comprehend, but it was easy to see that Avery's manner changed when he and Lilian were in the same room. Erica thought a great deal of her aunt; she looked upon her as a mother for she had never really known her own. She admired

Lilian's strength and her zest for life, qualities Erica had possessed before she'd met Dante.

"Papa did not send out invitations. We had a falling out," Erica informed Lilian as she glanced over the rim of the teacup.

"He didn't approve of the match?" A bemused frown captured Lilian's graying brow. "But I thought—"

"Papa doesn't even know who I married . . . yet." When Lilian appeared totally confused, Erica hastened to explain. "I ran away from home, married a man on the steamboat, and I expect Papa to come looking for me any day. This will be the first place he'll check." Erica assumed that Avery had taken the steamship that departed two days after the *Natchez Belle*. If her calculations were correct, he would be arriving very soon. By leaving the plantation without Dante's permission, she hoped to avoid a clash between him and Avery and Sabin. She wanted to spare Dante. "I hope you don't mind if I use your home for a battleground."

"It wouldn't be the first time," Lilian said with a shrug. "But who is the man you've impulsively married?"

"Dante Fowler."

Lilian gasped, and her face turned dead white. "Oh my God, child. Your father will be beside himself when he learns about this and if he sees—"

"When he learns about what?" Avery Bennet's demanding voice exploded like a cannon. Indeed, Erica would have dived for cover if she'd thought doing so would spare her the wrath he would direct at her when he learned the news.

"Well, Avery, this is a wonderful surprise," Lilian remarked as her anxious eyes flew past him to the store

205

she'd asked Madeline to attend in her absence.

A shadow fell across Avery, and Erica darted a hasty glance at Sabin's hateful face. The room was charged with tension, and Erica was thankful that she had spared Dante this confrontation. Sabin was every bit as vicious as she'd anticipated and whatever Dante's differences with him were, it would be better to settle them at a later date. One skirmish at a time was sufficient when Sabin Keary was the foe.

"Lilian, leave us alone. I want to speak with my daughter." Avery gestured toward the door, but Lilian held her ground until Erica nodded slightly, assuring her that she was capable of handling the situation.

When Lilian had exited, Sabin nudged Avery, indicating that he should continue. "Sabin and I have come to a decision during our journey," he announced as he drew himself up before his defiant daughter. "After your shenanigans at the party, the only way for any of us to save face is to seek a hasty marriage and to inform our friends that the two of you had a lover's spat. Sabin has assured me that he will forgive and forget the incident if you consent to become his wife. I have his word that you will not be punished for your transgression against him."

Sabin's word was worthless as far as Erica was concerned, and she considered her father a fool if he believed the man. Erica eyed Sabin skeptically. Keary would lie without batting an eye if it served his purpose. Why couldn't Avery see that beneath his expensive garments lurked a snake?

"I wouldn't marry Sabin Keary if he were the last man on earth!" Erica informed them in no uncertain terms. "And I am ashamed to call you my father. Why do you allow this despicable scoundrel to pull the wool over your eyes? He damned well intends to extract revenge from me. I would bet a fortune on that."

"Guard your tongue," Sabin hissed as he limped past Avery, leaning heavily on a cane, the ivory handle of which was carved into the head of a serpent.

How fitting, Erica thought bitterly; then she ducked as Sabin shook the cane at her.

"You are referring to your future husband," he reminded her, a sardonic smile twisting his thin lips. "Once we wed, my first duty will be to teach you proper manners, something your schoolmasters in the East must have overlooked."

Erica glanced at her father for support, but none was forthcoming. He just stood there. Erica suddenly realized that her father had lost his backbone. Once he'd been a strong-willed man, but Sabin seemed to have some mysterious hold over him. If Sabin informed Avery that the sky was falling, her father would accept the statement as fact. God, what had happened to him? He wasn't the man she knew before she'd gone East to attend school.

"I cannot wed you," Erica informed him icily. "I am already married."

"What?" Sabin howled as thunder shook the walls of Lilian's modest home.

As the spindly-legged Sabin limped toward her, favoring the knee Erica had wounded, she bolted from her chair, frantically seeking a weapon to use in self-defense. "Stay away from me, you loathsome beast!"

His hands clamped around her wrist before she could scamper away. "Do not think you can outfox me, Erica. I have dealt with obstinacy before, successfully. You can be certain of that. This husband of yours will bow out when I have set the matter straight with him."

"Take your hands off my wife." Dante's voice rolled across the room, as ominous and threatening as the clap of thunder that followed it.

Erica had not expected Dante and she would have preferred that he was not caught in the cross fire, but relief settled over her as his powerful frame filled the entrance to the parlor.

Sabin wheeled around, but his sneer froze on his bony features. "You?" he screeched in disbelief.

A tight smile split Dante's lips as he strode across the room to stand beside his wife. "So you thought to deprive me of this pleasure," he muttered only loud enough for Erica to hear; then he focused his stony gaze on Sabin. "I have been itching for an excuse to confront you again, *Uncle.*" He expelled the title as if it left a bitter taste in his mouth. "If you ever lay a hand on Erica again, I'll call you out, just as my father did. But this time you will not be equipped with a hairpin trigger and a witness who doesn't have enough nerve to speak out against you."

"Uncle?" Erica would have collapsed if Dante had not slipped a supporting arm around her waist.

Dante was insulting Sabin, taunting him into a duel. So that was the real reason he had married her. *She* was the pawn in Dante's scheme to extract revenge.

Sabin was far too clever to snatch up the gauntlet, however. He would get what he wanted, but he would play by his own rules, not his nephew's. Dante had investigated his father's death more closely than Sabin had anticipated. He knew too much. Eventually Sabin would have to dispose of him.

"Who is this man?" Avery asked, his apprehension increasing. The subject of Fowler's death made Avery uneasy, and he found himself tugging on his cravat to

208

relieve the pressure on his throat.

Sabin bent his gaze on Avery, a sardonic smile curling his lips. "Forgive me, Avery. This is a man who, no doubt, has longed to make your acquaintance, and he has gone to great lengths to do so. May I present my nephew, Dante Fowler. You do remember the name, don't you?"

Avery's face paled. His suspicions were confirmed. He staggered back as if Sabin had knocked a prop out from under him. Erica was completely baffled by her father's reaction. She had never seen him so rattled. What the devil was going on? Everyone seemed to be sharing a sordid secret, but she couldn't fathom what it was.

Amusement glistened in Dante's eyes when he viewed Avery's reaction. It did his heart good to watch him squirm.

"I demand that you have this marriage dissolved at once," Sabin blurted out, his pointed glare transfixing on the wilting Avery, who seemed to be having difficulty with breathing.

Avery could not find his tongue. His darting eyes slid from his daughter's bewildered expression to Dante's devilish grin; then they swung to the stubborn set of Sabin's jaw. He opened his mouth, but he still couldn't speak. There was a great deal at stake here, more than any of them knew, and he had guarded his secret carefully to ensure that no one discovered the truth.

Sabin ground his cane into the floor, then gnashed his teeth. Avery seemed to have been struck deaf, dumb, and blind just when he could have been useful in manipulating Sabin's pesky nephew. "You think yourself very clever, don't you, Dante?" he asked, his dark eyes raking his adversary mockingly. "But I will destroy you just as surely as I did your worthless father. I always maintained that my sister deserved better than the likes of him."

"You think to play God?" Dante hissed through clenched teeth. "That is impossible since you are the very devil, Sabin. Because of you, my mother vanished. She was too ashamed and humiliated to face her family again. Is that how you *saved* her from my father? What has she now, a life of seclusion, estrangement from her sons and grandchildren?" His voice was intimidating, for he was well aware that his remarks would stoke the fires of Sabin's notorious temper. He was waving a red cape in the face of a charging bull.

Sabin went for his nephew's throat, but Erica kicked at his cane, ramming it into his injured leg.

Howling like a banshee, Sabin clutched at his knee; then he glowered at Erica. "I'll make you regret you crossed me, woman." His blazing eyes turned to Dante who was silently applauding Erica for hobbling his despicable uncle. "And I will ruin you, Dante," Sabin growled vindictively. "Avery and I will see to it that you never sell another bale of cotton in New Orleans. Neither of you can defeat me. Erica was promised to me, and I intend to have her."

Avery paled. "But I have a contract to fill," he said, desperation in his voice. "Jamie has made arrangements with the West Indies Company to supply a schooner of cotton for delivery in France. If I lose the cotton contract our business will be in jeopardy."

Erica noted that her father had displayed a meager amount of courage. He had not defied Sabin's threat to blockade Dante's cargo, but he hadn't supported it.

As Dante grinned slyly, Erica frowned. That expression spelled trouble. The cogs of his brain were turning, and she didn't like the way he was staring at her.

"I suggest a challenge," Dante remarked, looking at Sabin. Then he lifted a lock of Erica's raven hair from her shoulder, letting it drift through his fingertips. "The stakes will be high, of course. We will play for that which you cannot seem to resist. The first one of us to transport enough cotton to the docks of New Orleans will receive payment for the contract *and* will claim Erica."

"What!" Erica was stunned. Dante *was* using her to bait Sabin. That had been his intention since she had accidentally mentioned the man's name. Why that miserable vermin. He would not barter her as if she were his slave, not if she had any say in the matter. "How dare you!" She slapped his hand away, repulsed by his touch. "I will not be a party to this ridiculous race for a cotton contract. All I want is the trust fund that is due me. The two of you can tear each other to shreds for all I care!"

Sabin was doing some fast thinking during Erica's protest. In order to meet Dante's challenge he would need to buy up cotton from the plantation owners near Natchez, order his overseer to haul his own crop to the New Orleans' docks, and then ship the remainder of cotton down the Mississippi before Dante could accomplish the same feat. If he succeeded he would have Erica *and* he would have put Dante into a serious financial bind. Sabin had many connections in New Orleans; he could ensure that Dante didn't sell his cargo. Then his nephew would be left with nothing but staggering debt.

A wicked gleam flickered in Sabin's black eyes. Dante is as big a fool as his father was, he thought arrogantly. When Sabin won the race, Erica would loathe the sight of Dante. The thought delighted Sabin.

"I accept your challenge, Dante. Winner takes all and

the loser forfeits any claim to Erica," Sabin announced, grinning like a shark about to gobble up a feast.

Erica was itching to claw their eyes out. How could she have fancied herself in love with Dante? He was a scoundrel of the worst sort, one who would use any means to achieve the ends he desired. He had planned all this, had used her to lure Sabin into accepting this insane challenge. Something inside her withered and died, like a fragile spring blossom destroyed by a late frost. Dante had betrayed her!

"You can't do this to me!" she railed, turning snapping blue eyes on Dante who did not react to her harsh tone. "We made a bargain, and you did not uphold your end of it. You are no better than Sabin. Evil seems to run in your family."

Her insult bounced off him. "We signed no written agreement, madam," he reminded her flippantly. "I will not consent to an annulment, and Sabin will not force me to it until we learn the outcome of our challenge. If I win, Sabin will relinquish all rights to you and you may have your freedom if that is what you wish." His calculating gaze appraised his treacherous uncle before returning to Erica. "And you will receive your inheritance, although I'm certain Sabin is counting upon claiming it as your dowry if you wed him. Greed breeds greed, does it not, Uncle?" Dante glared at Sabin. "Yet, you could never be satisfied with wealth alone, though you have accumulated a sizable amount of it, one way or another. You are also in the business of controlling the souls of other men, manipulating them as you do Avery."

Now what is he implying? Erica wondered. What was Sabin holding over her father? Dante knew something she didn't, and she would pry the information out of him, even if she had to use a crowbar.

Dante could read the questions in her eyes, and he deliberately directed them toward Avery. "Why don't you tell Erica what you have been hiding these past few years. As inquisitive as she is, I'm sure her curiosity is overwhelming."

Avery refused to meet his daughter's eyes. "I cannot say," he muttered, so quietly that Erica had to strain to catch his words.

"Cannot or *will* not?" she asked. "Surely I have a right to know why you would sacrifice your own daughter."

"One day perhaps you could understand, but not now." Avery's gaze swung to the muscular, raven-haired man who towered over his daughter, and their eyes locked for a moment before he made his request. "I ask you to be silent, Dante. It is not your place to divulge this information to Erica."

"Isn't it?" Dante raised an eyebrow. "Why should I remain silent? Your honor is at stake, not mine."

Erica would have given anything to know what they were trying *not* to say!

"If you care for the woman you took as your wife, no matter your true purpose in doing so, you will consider my request, for *Erica's* sake," Avery countered, his expression grim.

Wrong, Erica thought bitterly. If Dante had considered her feelings, he would not have used her as bait in this preposterous race against time. If he cared, even a smidgeon, he would have been open and honest with her. She had learned a valuable lesson when Dante had encountered his uncle. Dante Fowler was no gentleman, not by any stretch of the imagination. He thirsted for revenge, and he would not rest until he had settled the score with Sabin. Dante had pretended to befriend her, but he had just bided his time until she had become desperate. He'd fully intended to incorporate her into his scheme. That was what he'd meant when he'd said they could each serve the other's purpose. But he had overlooked her needs in order to satisfy his own, and he did not plan to release her from the marriage until he had what he wanted—revenge.

"Come, Avery. I have business to attend. Very pleasant business." Sabin chuckled wickedly as he flashed Dante a parting glance. "Destroying Dante will be pleasurable indeed."

When the two men had departed, Dante placed his hand on Erica's back and propelled her forward, but she slapped his hand away.

"I am staying here with Aunt Lilian. You are the last person I want near me." She almost spat the words.

"You will remain at my plantation until we sail for New Orleans," Dante told her firmly.

"I want nothing to do with you. You and that loathsome uncle of yours were cut from the same scrap of wood!" Erica declared, her voice cracking with contempt.

"And let's not forget that you are your father's daughter. If you shared his shame, no doubt you would become as spineless as he has." Dante caught Erica's hand the split second before it collided with his cheek. "It is ill advised to fling insults if you are not prepared to receive them, madam."

"Perhaps if you informed me of my father's reasons for allowing Sabin to manipulate him, we would be equally equipped for battle," Erica taunted as she wormed her hand from his grasp. "Or are you afraid I might side with my father?"

The words were on the tip of his tongue, but Dante swallowed them. Why? He wasn't quite certain. After all, Avery deserved no consideration, not after what he had done to humiliate the Fowler family. But the moment Dante peered into Erica's wide blue eyes, he knew he must obey Avery's request. She had already lost a great deal of respect for her father, and Dante knew what it was like to harbor a shame. It had made him cynical. Erica has enough problems without facing that, Dante decided.

"Your father lives in fear that you might learn the truth about him. That is *his* punishment. I will not divulge the secret he has sold his soul to keep."

Erica wanted to shake the stuffing out of him for refusing to enlighten her. Whatever she had felt for Dante was dead. The cad had offered her as a trophy, and she detested him for it.

"And you, too, have sold your soul to Sabin," she flung at him. "If you think you have a chance against that conniving demon, you are a bigger fool than I had thought you."

Dante clutched her to him, his arms like bands of steel. "I fully admit to being a fool," he rasped, his voice heavy with frustration and desire, something he was unable to curb when he touched her. "But my madness does not come from dealings with my uncle. I have begun to understand the workings of his fiendish mind."

Erica was hard pressed to ignore the sensations his embrace evoked, and she was humiliated because she was responding to him when she wanted to hate him. Why did he affect her so? He cared nothing for her. "As well you should," she threw back at him. "Since both of you have as much appeal as a poisonous viper." She longed to hurt

215

him, to destroy his pride.

Lord, she is gorgeous when she's in a fit of temper, Dante mused. He chuckled at the combination of outrage and unwelcome desire in her eyes. "And you have the beauty to charm even the deadliest of snakes, *chérie*. Perhaps if you employ your powers, you can dissuade me from my so-called madness."

Erica poked him below the ribs, momentarily knocking the wind out of him. "Why waste my time when Sabin will find a way to crush you?"

"Would you care if he did?" Dante's tone was soft, but his emerald eyes probed hers, searching for her true feelings.

"I . . ." Erica bit her lip, determined not to let her heart rule her head. Dante felt nothing for her, and if she had any sense at all, she would have no concern for him. "Take me home. I have better things to do than argue with a lunatic, and I have no intention of being dubbed a bigger fool than I have already shown myself to be by marrying a man like you."

"Home?" Dante pounced on her choice of words, flashing her a mocking grin. "I wasn't aware that you were so fond of my plantation."

"A careless slip of the tongue," she said quickly. "Since you refuse to allow me to stay with my aunt, I have nowhere else to call home. But, in truth, I detest plantations and all they stand for. I do not believe in slavery, *black* or *white*."

Dante caught the underlying meaning in her remark, but he was not about to liberate her, even if she resorted to waving the flag of independence in his face. "I have no slaves, only servants who were freed when my father

216

died. They are paid an honest day's wage for an honest day's work."

Erica raised a perfectly arched eyebrow. At least Dante was not an advocate of slavery. Perhaps he had one noble bone in his body. "A man after my own heart? I shamefully confess I would never have thought it," she sniped, her tone warped with sarcasm.

"And if I *were* after your heart?" Dante questioned as he inched closer, his seductive smile making her want to weaken. "What would be my chances of taming it?"

Determined not to be seduced by his charismatic charm, Erica thrust out her chin. This time she would not be soft-soaped. They could not go back; Dante had spoiled every chance of that. She had seen him too clearly. He was a vindictive man who would resort to any means to avenge the taking of his father's life. Her affection for this darkly handsome rogue may have been her downfall, but it most certainly would not be the cause of her defeat. She would never stop fighting him. No matter how devastating his charm, she would deflect it.

"Your chances are slim and none," she assured him; then she ducked beneath his arm to leave him hugging air. "The same chances you have against your uncle."

The muscles in Dante's jaw twitched angrily as his hand snaked out to snag her before she could put a safe distance between them. "I think you would like to see him win this challenge."

Erica looked him right in the eye. "Nothing would please me more than to watch Sabin Keary meet with defeat for the first time in his miserable life. I detest the man."

"More than me?" The faintest hint of a smile flitted across his lips as he traced her creamy cheek with a

217

tanned finger. "Would you believe that I am sorry I had to use you to get back at my uncle?"

Erica's defenses weakened beneath his gentle touch, but she shored them up before they fell. "Not for a minute," she insisted. "I am not as gullible as I once was." She interjected a bitter laugh, then favored him with a look of disgust. "I believed you were sincere when you said you would help me solve my dilemma. I even came alone today, hoping to spare you the confrontation with Sabin. I intended to keep my husband's identity a secret. But it was your intent to throw me to the wolves, and that is exactly what you did, all in the name of your cause."

When Erica flounced away, Dante simply stared after her. What the hell could he say? She had managed to make him feel like a cad. Perhaps he should have told her the truth, but he hadn't. He had done what he felt he had to do, for *her* sake as well as his. But she couldn't see that. Now he would have to find a way to return to this hell cat's good graces. He needed Erica on his side, whatever the outcome of his clash with that devil. Why couldn't she understand his reasoning? Didn't she realize what she would gain if he won the challenge? Did he have to spell it out for her? No. There were more subtle ways to lure her back to his side, and he was not opposed to employing them.

With that arousing thought dancing through his head, Dante followed in Erica's wake, forcing a charming smile as he greeted Lilian Gordon, who seemed far more receptive than his own wife.

When Erica emerged from the parlor, she found Lilian

218

alone, her expression apprehensive. Madeline, the small, gray-haired woman who had attended the store, was gone, as were Sabin and Avery, much to Erica's relief. Although Lilian assaulted her with a barrage of questions, Erica supplied only sketchy details of her conflict with Sabin. She was in no mood to rehash the incident for Dante was prowling about the store and she was unable to inform her aunt that she had impulsively married a scoundrel. Not that Lilian would believe me, Erica thought sourly. Dante had been the perfect gentleman and the model husband in her aunt's presence. It annoyed Erica that Lilian seemed to hold Dante in high esteem, but she credited that to the fact that he was one of her regular customers.

After graciously requesting that Lilian visit Erica at his plantation and extending an invitation to the ball he planned for the following night to formally announce his marriage, he ushered Erica to the door. A dismayed frown knitted her brow when she stepped onto the boardwalk for the heavens had opened up. Driving rain pelted down, and streams of water meandered through the street. She would be forced to join Dante in the carriage instead of returning to his plantation in the same manner she had come, on the back of a horse, whose companionship she would have much preferred. She did not wish to be confined in close quarters with Dante.

A wry smile twisted one corner of Dante's mouth as he surveyed Erica's sour expression. "It could be worse, my dear," he mocked.

"I cannot imagine how," Erica muttered as she lifted her skirts in preparation for a dash to the brougham.

A startled yelp escaped her lips when Dante scooped her up in his arms. He carried her through the maze of mud puddles, then deposited her on the cushioned seat. After he had tied her horse behind the carriage, he gave instructions to the driver, who had brought along suitable garments to protect himself from inclement weather. When Dante jumped into the brougham, Erica would gladly have exchanged places with the groomsman.

After casting him a foul look, she scooted as far from him as the carriage seat would allow. She then crossed her arms beneath her breasts, and stared huffily at the opposite wall. Dante had managed to destroy her chance for happiness, and Erica's mood was as bleak as the gray sky which was still spilling torrents of rain.

Erica flinched when Dante slid over to her, pinning her between his masculine body and the wall. "I have no need of your attention," she told him coldly, her tone icy.

Apparently he was immune to frostbite, for her frigid remark produced no ill effects. "Then perhaps you would indulge me by conversing," he softly suggested.

Erica sniffed. "You have said and done quite enough for one day. We have nothing left to say to each other."

His thumb and forefinger cupped her stubborn chin, bringing it down a notch. "If talking doesn't please you, perhaps this will. . . ."

Before Erica could object, his full lips claimed hers in an amazingly tender kiss. She berated herself for finding enjoyment in the arms of the very man who was willing to sacrifice her to Sabin. But she knew that no matter what had transpired between them, he still had the power to move her, to turn her ire into desire. Her traitorous body warmed to the feel of Dante's hard flesh, but before her resistance crumbled, Erica turned away from his passionate kiss and clamped a tight rein on her runaway heart.

"Don't think you can kiss me into submission. I may be forced to endure this dangerous game you are playing with your uncle, but I refuse to . . ." Erica's words faded as his wayward hand crept beneath the hem of her dress to glide over the velvety flesh of her thigh.

"Do go on," Dante prompted, his voice husky with desire. "I know I deserve to be reprimanded for my unscrupulous tactics." His moist lips investigated the trim column of her neck, assuring him that his deliberate ministrations had quickened her pulse. "You were saying?"

His arm slid around her back and then curled over her shoulder, his index finger tracing the scooped neckline of her gown, then lingering on the exposed swells of her breasts before ascending to her right shoulder while his left hand continued to explore the shapely contours of her thighs.

Erica was determined not to give in to his assault. If she could chastise him while he attempted to seduce her, he would think she was no longer vulnerable to his touch. Then, perhaps, he would crawl back to his corner and leave her be.

"I refuse to pretend to be your dutiful wife." She realized as she spoke that her voice was failing her when she needed it most, but she struggled to maintain her composure while Dante tried to make mincemeat of her resistance. "There can be nothing between us now."

"Can't there be?" he whispered against her quivering skin, as his searing kisses spilled over the slope of her shoulder to glide along the fullness of her breast. His right hand tunneled beneath the bodice of her gown and chemise, pushing them away so his all-consuming gaze could devour her creamy skin and his lips would have free access to the taut, dusky peaks that seemed to beg his attention. "I believe the lady protests too much. The magic is still there, Erica. You know it as well as I do."

Erica caught her breath as his teasing tongue flicked each roseate bud while his right hand played across her hip, unfurling the longing that had knotted her stomach. Dante twisted sideways in the seat, lifting Erica onto his lap as his mouth slanted across hers. His lips opened, and his questing tongue probed the soft recesses of her mouth as his devouring kiss sought to claim her and to feed her burgeoning need. As rain pattered against the carriage with impatient, drumming fingers, Dante's heart pounded in rhythm, his male body aroused by the feel of Erica's flesh.

He possesses more than the normal number of hands, Erica thought as tantalizing caresses transformed her into a trembling mass of barely contained desire. When Dante's probing fingers sought her womanly softness, she burned with the need his skillful fondling intensified. Gently, his hand ascended to her abdomen, then made a titillating descent to guide her legs apart. Maddening sensations riveted through her as his fingertips tracked intimately over her inner thighs and then delved deeper, heightening the sweet torture of having him so close and yet so far away. A tiny moan escaped her lips as he retraced the same enticing path across her abdomen, again slipping down to her thighs, to leave her aching and throbbing in the wake of his familiar touch. While his flowing caresses continued to melt her, his lips feathered across her breasts, suckling at each ripe peak, feeding a fire that was already blazing.

Flames of passion raged through her surrendering

body as he laid her back on the seat and braced himself above her. Her senses were keenly attuned to the sight and feel of the lithe, muscular man who hovered just inches above her. Emerald green fire blazed down upon her as his eyes hungrily ran over her partially naked body, picturing her bare flesh, the memory of which no amount of time could erase.

A small gasp escaped him as he came to her, and she clung to him in wild abandon, eager to satisfy the craving he had aroused. Though she was a fool for loving him, she could not resist him. She could verbally deny her need for him, but heart and soul she longed to be his. As he moved within her, Erica surrendered to the rapturous sensations that flooded over her, pulling her beneath reality's surface, to the depths of passion. As his hard body blended into hers, she gloried in pleasures that blinded her to all else. They were one, tumbling in a dark abyss, aware of nothing but the taste and feel of each other, gliding and swirling until the moment of complete satisfaction converged on them, freeing emotions that flooded to the surface to flow like the channel of a mighty river cutting its course to the sea. Sweet release poured through their souls, triggering every muscle and nerve ending until, simultaneously, their bodies shuddered and they were drained of strength.

As Erica's thundering heart slowed its frantic pace, Dante bent his head to hers, his warm breath brushing her lips. As reality again descended on her, Erica felt humiliated. Was she a whore at heart? Sweet merciful heavens! How could she have allowed this to happen? They were in his carriage, lying half naked in each other's arms. They had interrupted a heated argument to surrender to passion. Had she not one ounce of will power? Apparently not.

Stung by the realization that she could not control her primal needs, not since she had had the misfortune to cross paths with Dante Fowler, Erica pushed him away and struggled to rearrange her gown.

An amused smile tugged at Dante's lips as he watched his flustered wife attempt to behave as if nothing had happened between them. "Never in my wildest dreams did I imagine a journey in the rain could be so pleasurable," he remarked, his voice still raspy from the after-effects of passion.

Erica resented his comment, and since she could not get her hands on a heavy object, she was forced to resort to the only weapon at her command—her tongue. "And never in my worst nightmare did I imagine that I would be *forced* to submit in a carriage, on a road, in the rain," she snapped as she tugged to bring the bodice of her dress in place.

"Forced?" One dark eyebrow shot up as Dante's eyes strayed to her creamy breasts. "I do not recall having to exert strength, my dear."

Erica wished she had made him do that. She was angry with herself for surrendering like a witless fool. Perhaps she was as spineless as her father. She had allowed Dante to manipulate her, just as Avery submitted to Sabin.

Erica was most thankful that the carriage jerked to a halt before she found it necessary to defend her behavior. She had disgraced herself, so she leaped from the carriage to escape Dante's taunting grin. How could she face him again when they both knew that she was a slave to his desires? She couldn't. Something must be done and quickly, Erica decided as she raced up the stairs two at a time. She wondered if she should have shot Dante. He deserved it after the way he had deceived her. But giving the matter second consideration, she felt it would be more satisfying to strangle him, prop him against the wall, and *then* shoot him.

In a burst of fury, she slammed her bedroom door and then locked it. Dante and Sabin were tossing her back and forth like a yo-yo. It infuriated her that she had no control over her destiny, and to add insult to injury, she was helplessly lost to Dante's magic touch. Yet he had stripped her of her pride; now she could barely tolerate her own reflection in the mirror. What she saw was a faceless image, the picture of a hypocrite who spouted words of denial just before yielding to the physical pleasure Dante offered.

Flouncing on her bed, Erica frustratedly punched her pillow, wishing she could take her irritation out on its true source—Dante. He was turning her inside out. If she didn't get a hold on herself she would become a mass of exposed emotion.

"Dinner is ready," Dante announced as he knocked.

Glaring at the closed door, Erica snapped, "I'm not hungry."

"Strange, I would have thought otherwise when we were enclosed in the carriage," he teased, his voice bubbling with laughter.

"Ohhhh . . ." she snatched up the flower vase and hurled it at the door, muttering several epithets as porcelain scattered in all directions. It infuriated her further to hear Dante snicker as his footsteps faded in the hall. Erica jabbed her pillow until a cloud of feathers rose above her and then carelessly drifted to the floor like the strewn pieces of a dream.

Chapter 13

Erica braced herself when Dante rapped on the door of her bedroom and strode inside. His green eyes slowly and deliberately swept over the gown he had purchased for her to wear to the ball he was holding in honor of their marriage. His bold assessment unnerved Erica, who felt he was looking right through the elegant burgundy gown that hugged her curvaceous figure.

Although she'd been spared his company for the entire day, during which he'd traveled from one plantation to another, buying up cotton from his neighbors, she would be forced to tolerate his presence throughout the evening. Erica knew it would be difficult to pretend to dislike him when the mere sight of him had her heart playing leap frog; he looked so dashing and handsome in his charcoal gray waistcoat and the white linen shirt that accented his bronzed features. And the light gray trousers that clung to his muscular thighs made her vividly aware of the powerful physique that lay beneath his expensive finery.

"You are a vision of loveliness," he complimented as

he approached. He slowly circled Erica, viewing her from all angles. Then he paused in front of her, bowed, and brought her dainty hand to his lips. "I will be the envy of Natchez when we waltz across the ballroom together."

"We will waltz *once* for appearance's sake," she stated firmly as she glided past him, presenting him with a cold shoulder as she aimed herself toward the door. She could not risk more than one dance in his arms, for the feel of his body pressed to hers could erode her defenses.

"But you will be on your best behavior tonight." His remark was not a question, but a demand.

When Dante closed the distance between them and slid his hand around her waist, Erica winced as though his touch branded her. She recovered in time to toss him a smile that sparkled with deviltry.

"I will make no promises that may have to be broken."

"Better a broken promise than a broken vase," Dante parried, flashing her a mocking grin.

Tilting her chin higher, Erica ignored his reference to her temper tantrum. The less said about that afternoon the better. Erica was still sensitive about it, and she would have preferred to delete it from her life. She had succumbed to passion and she was ashamed of herself for yielding to his persuasive touch, especially when she'd been furious with him.

When the newlyweds reached the foot of the stairs Erica pasted on a smile for the curious guests who were anxious to meet the young woman who had, supposedly, stolen Dante's heart. Erica laughed bitterly to herself. How could anyone have Dante's heart? It was made of solid rock. She would need a hammer and chisel to etch her way into his stone heart, or she would have to wait for the forces of erosion to wear it down. Erica knew she would not last long enough to see him crumble or feel any affection for her, but their guests were not aware of that. She was tempted to tell them how and why her marriage had taken place, but she held her tongue and responded politely when she was complimented on her ability to change the ways of a confirmed bachelor.

"Trouble in paradise?" Corbin questioned as he watched his sober-faced brother pour himself a second glass of brandy and swallow it in one gulp.

Dante flashed Corbin a disgruntled frown. "She has been perfectly charming to everyone except me. Each time I go near her, she bristles like a disturbed wildcat," he confessed with a sigh.

Corbin chuckled at Dante's woebegone expression. "What did you expect? I must admit it took me awhile to warm to the idea of challenging Sabin to a race." His smile evaporated as he met Dante's gaze. "You placed her in a ticklish situation, and you stand to lose everything you have worked so hard to achieve. Sabin is ruthless. He will stop at nothing to defeat you." Corbin placed a hand on Dante's shoulder. "I do not mind using the *Natchez Belle* as your transport, but I am concerned about your welfare."

"Don't preach," Dante grunted as he reached for the brandy decanter. "I am well aware of the risks involved, but they do not override the advantages I have to gain by winning this challenge."

Reade Asher, who had been eavesdropping on the conversation, strolled over to voice his opinion. "If you ask me, you'd be wiser to take my offer and sink yore money into a voyage to Central America. Yore uncle sounds like a devil, judgin' by what you've told me about him." His eyes gleamed as he shot Dante a smile. "I swear to you gettin' buried treasure is easier than haulin' cotton on that treacherous Mississippi. And if it's true that absence makes the heart grow fonder, maybe that little she-cat will be purrin' by the time you come back to her."

"Not interested," Dante said flatly. "I have made my decision, and I intend to see it through to the end."

"No matter how bitter it might be?" Corbin snorted. "You should never have dragged Erica into this. She could well become an innocent victim, and I, for one, do not relish the idea of feeding such a lovely lass to that snake."

"Et tu, Brute?" Dante scowled irritably. Must his own brother take Erica's side? Dante had followed both his heart and his head in this situation, and he had arrived at the only workable decision. Couldn't anyone else understand that? "Erica is the one ace I hold." His voice was rigid with anger. "She is the one temptation Sabin cannot seem to resist. If he could, he would have bowed out when he learned that we had wed. But he wants her. She is his weakness, and the one advantage I must play."

Corbin heaved a sigh, then sipped his drink. "Little brother, I wish you luck. You're going to need all you can get in your dealings with Sabin *and* Erica."

Dante chuckled acrimoniously. "To be sure, this marriage was not made in heaven, but it may have taken up residence in hell. Sabin is the least of my worries at the moment. I need Erica's cooperation, and she refuses to give it."

"There are ways to woo a woman," Corbin reminded Dante, his eyes twinkling merrily. "Haven't you heard of gentle persuasion?"

"That didn't work." Dante's expression was sour enough to curdle fresh milk. "That firebrand is so headstrong and stubborn that she will do something contrary, just to spite me. I swear she is the most willful woman I have ever met."

"You knew that before you proposed," Reade interjected as he seated himself on the sofa beside Dante. "I coulda told you what kind of trouble you would be facin' if you woulda informed me of yore plans. But no, you blundered ahead without waitin' for advice."

Neither Corbin's nor Reade's counsel raised Dante's spirits. He had rehashed the matter until his head throbbed, so he sat and sulked, mulling over his unpopular decision to wed. Dammit. He had very good reasons for making that raven-haired beauty his wife, but no one else seemed able to see them. Well, he didn't have to answer to anyone. Dante admitted to himself that he was stubborn. But he came by it naturally, and if he didn't stand up to Erica, she would walk all over him.

Erica took an instant liking to Leona Fowler. She was a vibrant woman who immediately put Erica at ease.

"I cannot tell you how delighted I am to have a sister," Leona informed her as she dragged Erica to a secluded corner. Her eyes, her most beautiful feature, rounded with enthusiasm as she surveyed the shapely brunette. "And I'm even more elated that Dante has finally taken a wife. I had almost given up on him. He is a strong, determined man, but once you earn his devotion you will have no complaints."

Erica had given up on that, but she did have several complaints. Still, she was hesitant to criticize Dante for

Leona seemed so fond of him. Does everyone see Dante as a prize? Erica wondered. If he is, why am I having such difficulty?

Leona's blue-green eyes raced up and down Erica's trim form; then she nodded affirmatively. "Yes, I do believe you are just what Dante needs. Corbin says you don't cater to him as other women have. I admire your independence." A thoughtful frown knitted her brow, and then she smiled slyly. "But I imagine Dante has difficulty accepting such behavior because he's so headstrong."

"It is a source of trouble," Erica confided. "We seem to desire different things from life, and we are pulling in opposite directions. Neither of us seems to be able to compromise."

"But you do love him, don't you?" Leona asked point-blank.

Erica stared at the far wall, a rueful smile pursing her lips. "Yes, but sometimes that isn't enough. We have serious problems facing us."

Leona frowned at a faraway look in Erica's eyes. "Don't give up on him so quickly," she advised. "Matrimony is a strain on all of us, even those who have been married as long as Corbin and I, but despite all our differences, I know I could never be happy with another man." She chortled softly as she patted Erica's arm. "It seems we cannot live with them and we cannot live without them. They say women are temperamental creatures. No doubt, that statement was made by a man at the very instant that his wife was thinking the same thing about men, and her husband in particular."

Leona had an uncanny knack of making Erica smile, even when she didn't feel like it. "Corbin is a fortunate man, and I intend to tell him so."

"I have tried," Leona said saucily. "But he and Dante are cut from the same mold. Neither will listen to logic."

Amen to that, Erica mused. Dante had closed his ears to her pleas to call off this ridiculous challenge that could put her in a worse situation than her present one.

"I was hoping you would bring along your children," Erica commented as they strolled back into the crowded hall. "I am anxious to meet my niece and nephew."

"Madeline is watching them for me." Leona smiled curiously. "Have you met her yet? She is truly a lovely lady, and I am most thankful that she occasionally consents to play nursemaid to our children."

"I have not been formally introduced, but I saw her in Aunt Lilian's mercantile store," Erica explained without giving the details as to why there'd been no time for cordial greetings.

"Well, perhaps one day . . ." Leona's voice trailed off as Elliot Lassiter strode to them, his eyes glued to Erica.

"Will you honor me with a dance?" he asked, his tone a soft caress.

Before Erica could accept or decline, Elliot grasped her hand to lead her toward the ballroom. Leona frowned pensively. It was apparent that Dante had competition, judging by the expression on Elliot's face. Grappling with that disturbing thought, she pivoted away to seek out her brother-in-law. She didn't want another man to spoil his whirlwind marriage while he and Erica were having difficulty adjusting to each other.

When Elliot drew Erica to him, she felt suffocated by his nearness. His arms held her tightly, forcing her to lean against him, and their bodies brushed intimately. Although she didn't want to seem rude, Erica braced her hand against his chest, pushing herself back a respectable distance.

Elliot frowned disappointedly. "You know this will never be enough," he murmured as he inhaled her sweet scent which clouded his brain. "Each time I look at you, I realize how much I have lost and how deeply I care for you, Erica."

"Don't, Elliot," Erica pleaded as she resisted the pull of his arms which sought to lessen the space between them. "What's done is done and nothing can change it. Don't make this more difficult than it already is."

Was she implying that she was having second thoughts about her hasty marriage? "You *can* change things," Elliot insisted as he leaned his chin against the top of her head, his senses warped by the tantalizing feel and scent of her. "You can admit your mistake. I harbor no resentment, and I will always be there for you. Just say the word—"

"Thank you for keeping my lovely bride company." Dante's tone belied his words as he tapped Elliot's shoulder, then wedged himself between the pair.

As Dante whisked Erica across the room, Elliot's face fell. It took all his self-control to remain civil to the man who had taken the woman he loved right from under his nose.

"Did Elliot proposition you? I wouldn't put it past him," Dante muttered, his tone bristling with resentment. Didn't he have enough trouble without Lassiter moving in on Erica the moment he turned his back?

Erica stiffened and missed a step, unintentionally waltzing on Dante's toe. But she didn't regret tromping on his foot. After all, he had stomped on her so often that he had squashed her flat!

"He did, and I must admit it sounded appealing," she sniped.

Dante forced the semblance of a smile. "Don't test my temper, Erica. I will not tolerate infidelity."

"That is comforting to know, dear husband," she purred. "It should be interesting to see which one of us seeks comfort elsewhere when it isn't forthcoming at home."

His fingers bit into her ribs. "I have no complaint regarding your bedside manner . . . except that you have been reluctant to display it."

"You haven't been home long enough to view it," she countered. But her intimidating tone did not produce the reaction she had anticipated.

One dark eyebrow tilted to a mocking angle. "Had I known *you* were so eager to have me there, I would have spent my time beside your bed," he cooed. Then he grinned outrageously.

Angry red stained her cheeks as his teasing smile radiated down upon her. She would be damned if she'd allow this rascal to think she yearned for him when he had treated her so abominably.

"Don't delude yourself, Dante," she snapped. "I prefer to sleep alone."

"I will be sure to alert Elliot to that fact. At least I can rest easier knowing you will not be slipping away in the cloak of darkness to rush into his waiting arms."

"I wouldn't be so sure of that if I were you," she cautioned, flashing him a goading smile. "You have given me just cause to leave you. Why should I remain loyal to a man with a heart of ice?"

Dante's powerful arms fastened about her, molding the hardness of his body to the softness of hers. His warm breath whispered across her cheek, leaving her chilled in the wake of his feathery kisses. "I think you know the answer to that. But if you have forgotten, I will be all too happy to refresh your memory."

His wayward hand glided over her hip, pressing her lower torso to his, letting her feel his bold manliness against her thigh. Then his penetrating eyes focused on her lips as if he were fascinated by them. As his mouth possessed hers, his exploring tongue traced the curve of her lips before seeking out their inner softness. He took her breath away, then offered it back to her in such an arousing way that Erica trembled.

She needed no prompting. Her body was already afire. Each time he set his skillful hands upon her a compelling melody played somewhere in the distance, and Erica had experienced it often enough to know that this music did not come from the orchestra playing for the ball. This song strummed in her soul, as if a harpist's agile fingers tripped lightly over strings to create a hypnotic tune. For a moment there were just the two of them, flowing with the music, clinging to each other, touching, sharing, enjoying. She felt as if she were suspended in time and space, rapt in a hazy dream of gentle pleasure. She couldn't have pulled away if her life depended on it.

Dante could be so tender and affectionate when it suited him. That was what had drawn her to this lion of a man, the enigmatic mixture of strength and gentleness. When he cradled her in his arms it was as if he were handling fragile crystal. His tenderness chipped away at her defenses far more than brute strength could, and Erica could not control her instinctive response.

Involuntarily, her arms slid over his shoulders as his kiss became one of languid exploration. His lips mapped the sensuous curve of her mouth and then his questing tongue mated with hers, subtly implying that he was willing to offer more if she were inclined to accept. Erica was absorbed in the musky fragrance that clung to him, aroused by the erotic sway of his body.

A round of applause rippled through their guests, abruptly bringing them back into reality. Erica blushed profusely when she noticed that the dance floor had been vacated and all eyes were upon them. Self-consciously, she glanced about her, noticing the smiling faces of Leona and Corbin, the sly wink of a petite blonde who was silently assuring her that she heartily approved of Erica's public display of affection.

"You have the exceptional ability to make me forget where I am and what I am supposed to be doing," Dante rasped as he brought her hand to his lips. "You go to my head, sweet nymph, not to mention the devastating effect you have on the rest of my body." The devilish sparkle in his green eyes caused another wave of embarrassment to flood over Erica.

She looked away before she was caught and trapped in those colorful emerald pools, but she jumped as if she had been snakebit when she saw the tall, reptilian figure that hovered in a dark corner of the ballroom. Dante followed her eyes, and he scowled when he spied the cause of her uneasiness. An uninvited guest had slithered into the festivities. Sabin Keary sported a haughty smile as he stood propped against his cane, garbed in black from head to toe.

Dante suddenly knew why Sabin was so obsessed with this blue-eyed enchantress, why Sabin had gone to so much trouble and expense to have her. Erica was a challenge. She was the one woman who had enough inner strength to refuse to bend to his will despite impossible odds. Sabin craved power; he collected people like trophies, conquering their souls. He surrounded himself with people who suited that need, and he craved a woman of unmatched beauty and spirit. But, to him, people were like pieces in a chess game. They must be strategically placed to serve and attend the king. Each move Sabin made was carefully calculated; Dante knew his uncle's tactics. Sabin had come to anger him. He wanted Dante to lose his temper, to make a mistake that might send Erica flying from her roost. Sabin was hovering about them like a vulture, but Dante was determined not to let his treacherous uncle get under his skin.

Displaying his own taunting smile, Dante curled his fingers beneath Erica's chin. "Look at me as if you are madly in love with me," he commanded, his hushed voice only loud enough for her ears to hear. "For Sabin's benefit . . ." he added, just before he placed a possessive kiss on her quivering lips.

Her self-imposed restraint faded as Erica met Dante's compelling gaze. For once she could look at him with love shining in her eyes and not be ridiculed for it. And she returned his kiss, letting her emotion flow forth unhindered. When they finally drew apart, the orchestra struck up a lively tune and the guests returned to the dance floor. Sabin scowled like a thwarted devil; then he disappeared in the crowd like Satan fading back into the fires of hell. But his appearance served as an unsettling reminder that he was there, watching and waiting to claim the woman he had set his sights on.

Erica felt a shudder ricochet through to her very soul. The look in Sabin's eyes had signified impending doom, but Dante's daring challenge had made his uncle all the more determined. Erica had the uneasy feeling that if Sabin ever got his hands on her, she would surely wish she were dead. Death would be a blessing compared to life with that vile beast. He would suck the spirit from her, leaving her no more than an empty shell.

She didn't realize how tightly she was clinging to Dante until he squeezed her hand, demanding her attention. His expression was somber, his eyes probing. "No matter how much you detest me, Erica, I will never use you the way Sabin would, nor will I ever let him near you. I have heard stories of how he treats women, and I will not allow you to be subjected to such degrading tactics."

When Dante wheeled and walked away, Erica half-collapsed in the middle of the dance floor. If Dante had intended to console her with that vow, he had failed miserably. Indeed, he had made her even more apprehensive. He knew of the unspeakable evils Sabin imposed on women, yet he had served her up as a trophy to the winner of the race to New Orleans. Sabin had years of experience in achieving what he wanted. He was a master of deceit, a calculating man who utilized unscrupulous tactics. How did Dante think he could compete with the likes of his uncle? Her own father was living proof that the strongest of men could be broken by Sabin's satanic force.

When Elliot strode up beside her to request another dance, Erica found herself clutching him closer than she should have since he wanted more than she could give. Although she would have preferred to be consoled by Dante, he had wandered away, leaving her to seek sympathy elsewhere. And Elliot voiced no complaint when Erica practically squeezed him in two. Indeed, it delighted him to find Erica so responsive. When he led her to the terrace for a moment of privacy, she did not object so Elliot perceived her recent behavior as an invitation. He had been sampling Dante's fine stock of liquor and had not witnessed the kisses that indicated the strong attraction between husband and wife.

Erica's startled gasp was suddenly muffled by a very passionate kiss, and she found herself held hostage in Elliot's arms, her body crushed to his.

"You know how I feel about you," he breathed raggedly when he finally came up for air. "Do you realize how much I envy Dante, knowing he possesses what I want most? The thought of you, sleeping in his arms, torments my dreams."

"Elliot, please don't . . ." Erica beseeched him. She was afraid to lean on Elliot, for he offered more than a strong shoulder to cry on. If she turned to him it would mean that she had turned *away* from Dante, had run away from love, not toward it. "I am a married woman and it would not be proper to—"

"Dante's tactics were far from proper when he stole you from me," he argued. "But he is man enough to give you up if *you* request it. Request it . . . I need you."

When Elliot had the decency to unhand her, she stared bewilderedly at him as he backed through the terrace doors. Did she dare look to him for assistance? He was a powerful and wealthy man. He could come to her aid, but would he read more into her plea than a need to escape the tangled web of her existence? She grappled with the memory of Elliot holding her in his arms, offering love and protection. Then the picture of Dante kissing her senseless in the crowded ballroom tormented her. And finally the dark, hollowed features of Sabin's face came before her. As troubled thoughts gnawed away

239

at her, she was struck by the overwhelming impulse to flee. She was standing in jeopardy, and she had to escape while she still had a chance. She had to depend on the only person she could trust with her life—herself. Giving in to that thought, Erica hiked up the front of her skirt, swung a shapely leg over the terrace railing, and prepared to dash off into the night, to seek sanctuary somewhere—perhaps in a secluded convent!

"Madam, your behavior is unbecoming for a lady."

The amused voice wafted toward her from the shadows, provoking a surprised yelp from Erica. Then she lost her grasp on the railing and fell into the shrubbery that lined the terrace. Chuckling at the sight of flying legs and swirling petticoats, Dante swaggered over to peer down at his wife, who was unceremoniously sprawled on the bush, a giant blossom amidst the greenery.

"Really, my dear Erica, it would be advisable to use a net if you intend to sharpen your acrobatic skills," he chided mockingly. "Our wedding party is not the time or place for such daring foolhardiness. After all, you do have a fear of heights."

His taunting voice stoked the fires of her temper but she was in no position to worry about her dignity. When Dante leaned over the railing to extend a helping hand, she clasped it and yanked with all the strength she could muster. A startled squawk broke from his lips as he toppled forward to land on top of his wife. He enjoyed the feel of her body pressed to his, but seducing her in the bushes seemed a bit unethical, even for him. Nonetheless, upon giving the matter a moment's consideration, Dante decided to seize opportunity when it presented itself.

His full lips found hers, and his heavy body pressed her deeper into the shrubs. Instantly, Erica yelped with pain. A protruding limb was puncturing her back. "Get off me, you lout!" she hissed, her pain and fury obvious when Dante raised his head.

"You pulled me in here with you," Dante reminded her before his laughing green eyes focused on her pouting lips in preparation for the same thorough attention he'd given them in the previous moment. "Were you perhaps feeling a mite guilty after the way you allowed Elliot to kiss you in the moonlight?" Dante was aching to erase the taste of his friend's embrace, to reclaim Erica as his own. He had needed an iron will to stand in the shadows, watching the two of them, but he had managed to wait until he had Erica alone. Now that he did, he intended to chase every vision of Elliot from her mind. "Don't toy with him, Erica. It will only cause trouble."

"Dammit, Dante, I didn't—"

"Well, well, did you two lovebirds fall from your nest?" Corbin queried as he and Leona leaned out to survey the situation.

Dante maneuvered himself around so he could free himself from the bush; then he scooped his flushed-faced bride into his arms. "It seems a man and his wife cannot enjoy a smidgeon of privacy, even when they resort to stealing kisses in the bushes. Give our excuses to the guests, will you, Corbin? Erica and I have this maddening craving to be alone . . . you understand."

"Perfectly," Corbin snickered as he watched Dante march off toward the back door. "But whom shall I call upon to bid good night to your guests while Leona and I slip away into the shadows?"

241

Dante did not bother to respond. He had his hands full. Erica was frantically squirming for release. She had been startled, humiliated, frightened, and embraced one too many times in the course of the evening."

"Put me down this instant!" she hissed, her blue eyes blazing like torches. "Haven't you caused me enough distress? I—" Erica shrieked and then groaned when Dante abruptly deposited her on the ground before she was prepared to balance her own weight. She tripped over the hem of her skirt, twisting her ankle. "Now see what you've done, you clumsy buffoon! You always make *me* appear awkward, but it is *you* who makes me trip over my feet, fall into shrubs, and stumble into furniture. I considered myself reasonably agile and graceful until I had the misfortune of colliding with you. I swear you bring out the worst in me and leave me wobbling about like a newborn foal!"

As Erica huffily limped toward the door, Dante followed in her wake, but at a safe distance. She had already burned holes in his shirt with her flaming glower, and he decided not to chance being clawed since she looked as if she would delight in extracting revenge from his hide.

"Shall I escort you to your room?" he queried, his voice laced with mockery. "Since you seem to have been struck awkward, I should hate to see you trip on the stairs and fall willy-nilly into a heap in front of the servants."

Erica wheeled around on her good foot and glared at him. "I do not want you anywhere near me. I wish you were in hell—or even farther away," she declared, her temper exploding like a keg of gunpowder. She was so furious she was actually seeing red—red shrubs, red grass, and a red husband whom she would have preferred

242

not to see at all.

"Strange, I thought that was where I was." Dante snorted derisively. He had already cast aside diplomacy since it had proven ineffective in dealing with this spitfire. Damnation, she is certainly in a snit this evening, he thought sourly. "Thus far, life with you has been nothing short of hellish!"

"My thought exactly." Erica flung the words at him.

"At least we seem to agree on one thing," Dante snorted gruffly as he brushed a leaf from the shoulder of his jacket. "All the two of us appear to have in common is a dislike for each other."

"I couldn't have put it better myself," Erica assured him, her air now stilted and polite. "If you will excuse me, I should like to retire for the night. With any luck at all, you will be gone before I wake. We get along much better when we never see each other."

"Madam, I will ensure that I depart before my regal queen rouses," Dante growled as he mockingly bowed before her. "Indeed, your highness, I would crawl through a lion-infested jungle to avoid the possibility of facing you on the morrow."

Erica drew herself up proudly at this insult, and she retaliated in the same goading tone. "And I would swim through shark-infested waters to avoid you," she shot back. "I anticipate your absence."

"You will have it!" Dante shouted at her departing back as she limped up the back stairs.

"Good!" Erica called over her shoulder; then she rubbed her throbbing temples as she continued on her way. She had contracted a six-foot-two-inch headache and she had the dreadful feeling that it would never go away. Damn the man!

When Erica disappeared into the darkness, Dante slammed the fist of his right hand into the palm of his left, grimacing at the pain he had inflicted on himself and muttering several epithets. Blast it, he had employed every device he knew to soften that firebrand, yet nothing had worked. She had her heart set on making him miserable. No doubt, she stayed up nights devising new ways to torture him. She detested the sight of him, and she was bound and determined to punish him for using her in his scheme to get back at Sabin. Should he march right up to her, confess the entire truth, exposing his feelings, and explain the real reason why he had done what he had done? Why should I? his male pride asked. Dante smirked arrogantly. He was the master of his soul and the captain of his conscience. He didn't have to answer to anyone, not Erica, not Corbin, not Reade. Besides, Erica didn't give a fig about his reason for planning this race with Sabin. She was too busy hating him to attempt to understand. There were times when a man had to stick with an unpopular decision despite how the rest of the world viewed his methods. In the meantime he would grit his teeth and complete his preparations, calculating every possibility without being distracted by his fiery wife. "And what a distraction she is," Dante grumbled as he aimed himself toward his room and the bottle of brandy on his night stand. That bottle had become the object of his attention these past few nights that Erica wanted nothing to do with him. At least it didn't fling insults at him the way she did. The witch! Refusing to share his bed was her brand of torture. Visions of her materialized before him each night, and he was very nearly forced to drive stakes through his feet to keep from storming into her room and making love to

244

her, not on the carriage seat or in the shrubbery, but in her very own bed! The memory of the night Erica had seduced him preyed on his mind. He could never forget the pleasure she had given him. She'd had him burning alive and he hungered to recapture that night. But that was not to be. Erica had given him a glimpse of what it could be like between them; then she had forced him to live with memories that could drive a man mad with want.

Dante heaved an exasperated sigh and plopped down on the bed. He wondered if he and Erica would ever set matters straight. He doubted it. There were so many barriers between them it would take an army to break them down.

Part V

Ah, now the plot thickens very much upon us.
—Villiers

Chapter 14

As she sat in her fragrant bath, Erica lifted a handful of fragile bubbles and blew them away, watching them scatter and burst like her dreams. Then she breathed a disheartened sigh. After the wedding party, she had seen very little of Dante, as he had promised. He had been racing around Natchez, buying up cotton to ship to New Orleans, along with his own crop. While he had been making the necessary arrangements with Corbin and the other plantation owners, Erica had been left to her own devices. Each morning she had gone riding, acquainting herself with the workings of Dante's plantation, searching her soul, and purposely avoiding Dante, although he had seen to it that she was chaperoned each time she set foot out of the mansion. One of his trusted servants always watched her every move, ready to provide protection should she need it.

Erica had found herself in solitary confinement. She had too much idle time on her hands and she hungered for something to do. She didn't know where she belonged or what would become of the rest of her life. Although she had been furious at Dante and had informed him that the less she saw of him the better, she was bored stiff. Even an argument with her manipulative husband would be better than what she was enduring—deafening silence!

Slumping back to rest her elbows on the edge of the tub, Erica peered thoughtfully at the far wall, immersed in thought. There had to be an answer to her dilemma. She must focus her full attention on the matter. After several minutes, an idea came to her, and she smiled for the first time in days. It was so simple that she had overlooked it, but there was a way to halt the challenge. All she had to do was . . .

An alarmed gasp burst from her lips when her eyes swept the room to find an uninvited guest had sneaked in and parked himself on a nearby chair while she was concentrating on a solution to her problem.

"What do you think you are doing in my boudoir?" Erica snapped as she plunged into the bubbles to hide her nakedness. "You have your own room, and I will thank you not to come barging into mine, especially when you are most unwelcome."

It was a moment before Dante's eyes returned to the surface of the water which deprived him of the view of Erica he'd enjoyed before she had realized she wasn't alone. Finally, he met her indignant expression.

"Let's not forget whose home this is and whose tub you are soaking in." He smirked. "This door will never serve as a barrier. As distasteful as you might find it, we are still man and wife." A wry smile twisted one corner of his mouth as he rose from his chair to swagger toward her, sending her even deeper into the water. "That is a fact I have neglected while I have seen to business and one *you* seem to have completely forgotten."

Erica certainly hadn't forgotten. Indeed, that was the cause of her misery. The memory of his caresses invaded her dreams. "Our marriage is a mockery and you know it," she hastily retorted, scalding blue flame shooting from her eyes. As Dante squatted down beside her she raked him with a contemptuous look, using her anger as a shield against the devastating effect of his presence. "Don't you have a mistress hereabouts who could pacify you? Surely you are not fool enough to think I take pleasure in your company after that fiasco at Aunt Lilian's and the one at the pretentious party you threw. If you do, you are incredibly arrogant."

"And you are incredibly lovely," Dante murmured as his index finger trailed over her bare shoulder to trace the submerged peak of her breast.

If he was insulted by her gibe, he didn't show it, much to Erica's chagrin. She was trying to pick a fight with him, but he refused to cooperate. Dante had lived with celibacy as long as he could. All of his late-night lectures on avoiding Erica were no match for the memories of their times together. His temperature rose ten degrees at the mere thought of holding her in his arms. He was prepared to eat crow if need be, but he wasn't going to spend another night alone when Erica was only a few doors down the hall. Every man has a breaking point, and Dante had discovered his. He was on the rack. While he attempted to preoccupy himself with the business at hand, he was being twisted and stretched by desires that granted him no peace. He could endure Erica's lightning tongue if he must, but he would woo her into his arms if it was the last thing he ever did!

His light teasing caress set her on fire, and even the

water she was soaking in couldn't cool the heat that sizzled through her veins. Why was she so vulnerable to this man's touch? How much torment was she expected to withstand? What he wanted from her had nothing to do with sharing his life, only his bed, and she would never be content to be his whore.

I still have my pride, Erica reminded herself as she fought the response of her flesh to his hands.

"Leave me be!" she hissed, clinging to her weakening resistance. "I want nothing more to do with you."

"Don't you?" His raspy voice tickled her senses.

As he leaned closer, the manly scent of him filled her nostrils and fogged her mind. His caresses became bolder as his lips brushed over her flushed cheeks. As they explored the silky flesh of her thighs, her breathing became ragged.

"I wish I could say the same, my lovely nymph, but I cannot," he whispered against her quaking skin. "We said hateful things to each other in anger, but I will never deny my desire for you. I want you as I always have. Shall I show you how much?"

"No!" Erica gasped as she vaulted from the tub, showering him with bubbles as she made a mad dash for the wardrobe closet and promptly shut herself in it.

"My, but you have a strange penchant for closets." Dante chuckled as he pried open the door Erica fought to keep closed. When he won the battle of the door, he propped his forearm against the wall and chortled again as Erica wiggled into his oversize jacket and then stomped huffily from the closet. "I envy my garment. It holds what I crave," he said softly as his all-encompassing gaze surveyed the long, shapely legs that protruded from the coat and then the enticing swells of her breasts that were

252

barely concealed.

Lord, she is gorgeous, he thought, no matter what she is or isn't wearing.

Erica gestured toward the door, but only one dainty finger managed to poke its way through the sleeve of the jacket. "I order you to leave, Dante. I am in no mood for your suggestive taunts."

He pushed himself away from the wall and headed toward the door, but Erica's relief was short-lived for he merely locked it and then strode back to her. As he did so, she retreated.

"Dante, I'm warning you. . . ." Erica's eyes darted around the room, searching for a means of escape. She had been in this situation before, at their first meeting, and she remembered the result of her run for freedom.

With catlike grace, Dante sprang at her, capturing her in his arms. The protest she intended to voice was muffled by his ravishing kiss, and his hands slid inside the jacket to make bold contact with her bare flesh. As their bodies melded, she knew that he was quite ready to seek his husbandly rights.

His questing tongue probed the recesses of her mouth, while one hand cupped her breast, caressing, massaging, evoking sensations that made Erica quiver. She was hot and cold and weak. She wanted to push him away but her need for him won out.

When his mouth abandoned hers to trickle over the slope of her shoulder and then hovered on the pink bud of her breast, Erica would have wilted had he not been holding her so tightly. Her trembling legs did not seem to have bones to support them. Then his muscled thigh pressed between them, stirring a longing so fierce and ardent that Erica shuddered in his arms.

For a wild, reckless moment, she resented the clothing that separated them. She was fully consumed by a maddening hunger to mold her bare flesh to his, to forget the barriers that stood between them, and to revel in the pleasure she found when she allowed love to rule her heart.

When his adventurous hand descended across her belly, Erica gasped for breath, like a drowning swimmer on her way down for the third and final time. His intimate caress retraced the sweet, tormenting path to a rose-tipped crest before following the curve of her waist. His fingertips fired her skin, leaving her with a burning need, and her body was his, responding, arching, craving fulfillment. As spasms of pleasure rippled through her, she heard herself utter his name and she tunneled her fingers through his raven hair to bring his lips into firm contact with hers.

"Erica, can't you see how much I need you?" he breathed raggedly, the emerald green fire in his eyes pouring over her. "You are an addiction. When I'm with you, I can think of nothing but having you, warm and willing, in my arms."

At that moment, Erica, too, could think of nothing but her need for him. He had banished her convictions and had fueled primal desires, which were surfacing like the molten lava of an erupting volcano. Only Dante could quench her burning need. Denying him would mean denying herself, and that she could not do, not when his skillful hands had captivated her. The wild, willful woman she had once been was no match for love. And she did love Dante.

When he led her to bed, she obediently followed, knowing she shouldn't, but unable to stop herself.

Shamelessly, she watched him disrobe, openly admiring his physique. He was like a bronzed god, strong and awesomely powerful, his body finely tuned, his face ruggedly handsome. There was nothing gentle about his appearance, she realized as his lithe movements brought him to her side to rekindle the fires that still smoldered within her. He might have been a fierce, fearless knight of old, steadfast in his cause, unyielding in his beliefs. But he could be so tender when he took her in his arms. His lips were full and inviting, so much so that Erica was lost to his exciting kiss, craving and savoring the blissful pleasures of love.

It didn't matter what tomorrow held. She needed him now, as a woman needs a man, giving and sharing the private moments that defy description. If I lived to be one hundred I will never understand why I surrender to this man and to no other, Erica thought. *Because of love,* she suddenly realized, the words coming from the depths of her soul. Love filled her being, and she was whole and alive when Dante took her in his arms to take her on the most intimate of journeys.

And suddenly she was there, just beyond the realm of reality, staring up into emerald eyes that burned with a living fire, watching his masculine body descend upon hers to make them one. Then he was a warm, demanding flame within her, feeding a fire that raged out of control. She could not feel the crushing strength of him, only the wild, delicious rapture that seared through the essence of her. His male body strained as he thrust deeply within her, his ardent movement sweeping her into the swirling passion that enveloped them. She arched against him, aching to be closer, anticipating that ultimate moment when the crescendo of tumultuous sensation exploded and left her soaring through time and space.

It came, that heart-stopping feeling, washing over her like a roaring river flooding its banks it raced through her until it touched every part of her and left her shuddering in response. But the sensations did not cease. Over and over again they drained her of strength and emotion until she lay quietly in his arms.

Dante groaned in sweet torment as his release came, devastating him. He gathered her close in the aftermath of love, amazed at the way she could make him forget the worries of the past few days. At the moment he didn't care if he viewed another sunrise. He had soared to heaven, and nothing could compare to the quintessential pleasure he had found there. Despite the upcoming race to New Orleans, he was content merely to hold Erica in his arms.

Dante's fingers delved into her sable mane, combing renegade tendrils from her face before he dropped a feathery kiss on her soft lips. Then the nights he had gone without sleep caught up with him, and he slipped into a dreamlike state, reliving a moment that might have been fantasy or reality. He could not tell.

Erica stared unblinkingly at the ceiling, remaining as stiff as a board until she heard Dante's methodic breathing. Then she inched away to don her clothes. Hardly daring to breathe for fear of waking the sleeping lion, Erica tiptoed to the door and then blended into one of the shadows that swayed in the hall.

When she had sneaked to the stables to fetch a horse and had swung up onto the gelding's bare back, she took a deep breath. While she lay in Dante's arms, she had decided what she must do. She would go to Elliot for assistance, explain the entire situation in detail, and hope

256

that he would grant her refuge until she planned her next move. Elliot had sworn that he loved her; she only hoped that he cared enough to comply with her request. If Sabin wanted her badly enough, she would lead him on a wild-goose chase, sidetracking him and preventing the resolution of the ridiculous challenge that could cost Dante all he owned.

Although she might have hated Dante for the way he had used her, she was not thinking of revenge, only of his safety. If she couldn't have him, she would at least ensure that Sabin would not destroy him. Keary was a bloodthirsty savage, and Erica cringed when she thought of Dante being defeated by his wicked uncle's treachery. Dante was a proud man, and she could not stand to see him subjected to such humiliation.

Erica nudged her legs against the dun gelding's ribs, and thundered toward Natchez as if the devil himself were hot on her heels. When she reached Elliot's mansion on the outskirts of town, she slid to the ground, marched up to the door, and rapped impatiently upon it. After a few minutes, a sleepy-eyed servant greeted her and then directed her to the parlor to await his master.

"Erica?" Elliot took in her windswept appearance; then he smiled in satisfaction. She had finally come to him. The agonizing days of waiting had come to an end. "Lord, I've missed you."

His heart was in his eyes, and Erica was having serious misgivings about seeking his assistance. Obviously, he had read more into her sudden appearance than it warranted. In three quick strides he was beside her. Scooping her into his arms, he swung her around until the room was spinning about her.

Erica was suddenly struck by a fearful thought. What

if Dante suspected foul play when he found her missing. What if he stormed to Sabin's hotel? Dante would never believe that Sabin didn't know what had become of Erica. Great balls of fire! Her disappearance could cause a clash rather than a distraction. Why hadn't she left Dante a note informing him that she was running away? If Dante suspected Sabin of kidnapping her, sparks would fly. She had botched up her escape! Confound it, could she do nothing right these days?

Stung by fear that her disappearance would provoke a heated confrontation, Erica wormed free of Elliot's grasp and then held his hands in hers before he could grab her again.

"I should not have come here, Elliot," she declared hurriedly. "I must go back. Forgive me for disturbing you."

"But . . . ." Elliot let his breath out in a rush as Erica swept out of the room. "You don't want to go back to him, do you?" He almost fired the question at her.

Erica paused before closing the door behind her. "I have no choice."

Before Elliot could protest her departure, Erica was gone, leaving him grumbling with frustration. Dante had taken advantage of Erica in a weak moment. Now, she had come to him, wanting him, but she could not forget that she already had a husband. Cursing a blue streak, Elliot stalked back up the stairs, determined to find a way to free Erica from his best friend. Best friend? Elliot snorted derisively. Dante no longer deserved his respect. He was holding Erica captive in a marriage that she didn't truly want. He must find a way to make Dante release her, and he would not sleep until he did.

* * *

As silvery moonbeams rained down upon the low-hanging branches, Erica tugged on the reins, bringing her winded steed to a halt. A glance to the west revealed the silvery ripples of the stream that meandered through a stand of trees, and she could not resist climbing down to wander along the bank. As she did so, she decided to indulge in a midnight swim. Perhaps it would settle her jittery nerves; then she could confront Dante with some degree of composure. After shedding her clothes, she slipped into the creek, sighing appreciatively.

This was just what she needed, the opportunity to be alone with her thoughts, without someone spying on her. She was free at last, free to work out another plan whereby she could leave Dante yet avoid a conflict with Sabin. The next time she rode away she would leave Dante a note; then she would borrow enough money from Lilian to take her far away from Natchez.

"I swear you are part fish." The low voice came from behind her.

Erica shrieked and then swung around in the water. The shadowy figure of a man lurked beside her discarded clothes on the bank.

"I told you never to venture off alone. What the hell are you doing out here?" Dante's sharp voice sliced through her like a sword.

He had awakened to find that Erica had abandoned him, and after turning the house upside down, he'd galloped toward town, certain that she had wandered off and been snatched up by Sabin, if she hadn't run into some other varmint that prowled at night. When he had spied the riderless horse, his heart had seemed to stop beating, and he'd had visions of Erica meeting with disaster. But here she was splashing in the stream, humming a tune, as if she didn't have a care in the world. She looked so damned tempting and desirable that Dante was about to tear off his clothes and wade in after her.

But he clamped a firm rein on his lusty thoughts, reminding himself that she had disobeyed his orders and that she would have to be punished for doing so. He could not allow her to gallivant about the plantation and risk abduction. After all, he did have her best interest at heart, and there were times when a man was forced to exert his power over a woman, even one as staunchly independent as Erica.

"I forbade you to leave the house unescorted," he said gruffly. Then he wagged a lean finger at her. "Because of this, I will be forced to assign you a bodyguard who never allows you out of his sight."

Erica's spirits were soaring after her wild ride and the satisfying swim. She didn't care if Dante stood there, ranting and raving, for the rest of the night. She merely laughed at the stern frown stamped on his craggy features. "You presume too much, lord and master," she purred, her tone so sticky sweet that Dante feared he would develop a stomachache just listening to it. "You will never make me your submissive slave so don't waste your time trying. I will not be shackled by overprotective bodyguards. If I crave a midnight swim I will take one, whenever it suits me."

Moonlight glistened in her eyes, making Dante acutely aware that it would take more than threats to break this vixen's undaunted spirit. The defiant tilt to her chin and the challenging smile on her lips alerted him to the fact that she was not about to back down. A sly grin lifted the corners of his mouth as he swaggered to the water's edge.

"But at what risk, madam?" he asked, his hungry gaze following Erica as she cut through the water like a graceful swan.

"At any risk," she insisted, chortling recklessly. "I crave my freedom and I intend to have it."

"So that is the way of things, is it?" Dante's grin grew broader, revealing pearly white teeth.

"Yes, that is the way of it," Erica assured him, unaware that she had been baited. "I will not be dictated to." But her haughtiness evaporated when her gaze slid back to Dante. "Don't you dare!" she shrieked.

Dante's shirt landed on top of her wrinkled gown, then his boots and breeches. "I dare to do just as I please, as you do, *chérie*," Dante informed her, his eyes dancing with deviltry. He moved deliberately toward her, like a stalking predator, wearing nothing but his predatory leer.

Gasping, Erica stared helplessly at his magnificent body. His muscles rippled, and the sinewed columns of his legs flexed and relaxed as he walked into the water. The awesome sight of him paralyzed her, leaving her to sketch his granite shoulders and tapered hips with adoring eyes. *Don't let him near you*, her pride screamed, and gathering her waterlogged composure, Erica willed her sluggish body to retreat before she was forced into unconditional surrender.

Erica's backstroke failed her, and she was not about to turn away from Dante, not when he had that ornery gleam in his eyes. She had seen it aboard the *Natchez Belle* each time he'd introduced her to . . . Erica missed a stroke as awareness hit her like a dash of cold water. The lout! He had introduced her to such deplorable scoundrels that she would be forced to look elsewhere for a husband. What a deceitful, underhanded, manipulative rogue! And she had played right into his hands. She had fought off all their amorous assaults until, nearly ex-

261

hausted, she had fled back to Dante, only to succumb to *his* seductive pursuit. She had sought comfort and protection, leaning on him as she had no other man, and he had taken full advantage of the situation while pretending to befriend her. But all the while he had been plotting and scheming, snaring her in one trap after another, yet she, like a witless wonder, had fallen in love with him, had even stooped to seducing him in the hope that he would learn to love her in return. Good God, how could she have been so dense? It had taken a midnight swim to make her alert. And alert she now was, although somewhere between New Orleans and Natchez she had contracted a fatal illness—stupidity!

When Dante swam toward her, his arms outstretched, Erica jabbed him in the belly with her knee and then shoved his head into the water before he could take a quick breath. So furious was she that she entertained the thought of pounding him flat and then letting him float down the creek with the rest of the driftwood.

"I should drown you like the miserable rat you are!" she growled as she leaped on top of him, wrapping her legs around his back and ramming his bobbing head back into the water.

His flailing arms brought him back to the surface, but with Erica sitting on him and clubbing him, he was destined to settle to the bottom of the creek. Still Erica refused him air, waiting until the last possible moment before she spared him. When he suddenly became a lifeless heap sinking deeper into the stream, fear shot through her, as it had when Dante had been knocked unconscious on the sandbar by the falling timbers. My God, what had she done? She hadn't meant to kill him, only to pound some sense into his wooden head.

"Dante?" Erica's heart hammered against her ribs as she reached down to grab his hair and yank him back to the surface. "I didn't mean to—"

Her shrill cry of surprise woke the birds in the over-hanging trees, and they took wing as Dante miraculously came to life, trapping her in his arms. He dragged her down with him before she could catch a breath, and his hard body molded itself to hers as his lips claimed her mouth.

When Dante brought them back to the surface, Erica gasped, then declared irately, "You let me think I had drowned you. I thought you were dead."

"I was, but I recovered when blessed with a mermaid's kiss," he teased as his arms encircled her breasts. "Your shenanigans only served to remind me that there is a need as fierce and compelling as the instinct to survive."

Erica pushed back as far as his arms would allow, all too aware of the need to which he referred. "And you have the lust of a beast twice your size," she shot back at him.

"But you mermaids are blessed with magical powers," Dante parried, flashing her a grin of roguish anticipation. "You can transform this lusty dragon into a charming prince with a kiss."

"In your case, I think I shall conjure up a potion and turn you into a toad," she taunted, but she was unable to bite back the smile that curled her lips. Dante's light-hearted mood was contagious, and her anger was no match for his charismatic grin.

"Have a care for my plight, frightful nymph," he murmured as his moist lips sought out the sensitive point beneath her ear. "Can't you see that you hold my mortal soul in thrall?"

Erica's body was already betraying her, responding to Dante's wandering hands, which were parting her legs with gentle insistence. His caresses stoked the fires of desire, chasing the last protest from her lips, and Erica realized that there was no fight left in her. She was at home in his arms; she truly had no desire to be elsewhere. Everyone has at least one weakness, she rationalized. Dante is mine, and I may as well accept that since I can not seem to overcome it.

"Kiss me," he demanded, his voice heavy with desire. "Is that asking so much?"

It was asking a great deal, for Erica knew full well where that kiss could lead. But kiss him she did, with all the pent-up emotion that surged through her soul, offering to return the pleasure he had often bestowed upon her. As her arms slid over his shoulders, the taut peaks of her breasts bored into his heaving chest, driving him mad with want. His body shuddered as she moved closer, forging their flesh into one living, breathing essence; and they were drifted together, sharing passion's embrace.

"Love me, Erica. . . ." His plea was no more than a breathless whisper.

Warm, moist lips opened on hers, and he inflamed her with his darting tongue, bringing sweet desire to the surface. A coil of longing curled within her, making her entire body alert to the tantalizing sight and feel of him. Then his kiss blocked out the rest of the world, and sheltered them in love's cocoon.

Desire fogged his thoughts, and Dante could not appease the tormenting fire that burned in him. Though he was standing neck-deep in water, his temperature soared and nothing could extinguish the flames that devoured him but the spark that had set them. He drank the sweet nectar of her kiss. It satisfied a gnawing hunger, but created an even greater one. Her adventurous hands played over his hips, guiding him ever closer, shamelessly offering that which he craved. Her touch was embroidered with intimacy as she caressed every powerful inch of him, her gentle caresses limning hair-roughened planes and contours of his body, and evoking wild, titillating sensations.

Erica felt as if she were standing apart, watching herself seduce the very man she should have avoided. But she loved the feel of his masculine frame, and she reveled in the power of her touch. If only she could make Dante love her as totally and completely as she loved him . . . if only she could become the most important thing in his life . . .

Dante could not endure another moment of her seductive stroking. His need for her, now fierce and instinctive, demanded satisfaction. His hands curled around her trim waist, bringing her to him and then gently guiding her away. Again he drew her to him, seeking her ultimate depths, flowing in rhythm with the enchanting melody that played in his blood.

Erica was bombarded by fervent sensations as he thrust deeply within her, fulfilling passion's cravings. Suddenly she was spiraling toward the distant sparkling diamonds in the black velvet sky, reveling in the wild, reckless pleasures that consumed her. Words that had remained imprisoned in her heart tumbled forth as he drove into her, and a tiny moan escaped her before his greedy mouth seized hers. His arms crushed her to him; then they were floating, bobbing, on a rolling river that had no beginning and no end.

Tears of sheer delight scalded her eyes, and she clung

to him for what seemed an eternity before they toppled over a waterfall of stars and plunged back into reality. For a breathless moment she waited for her heart to slow its frantic beat; then she released him, only to see him smiling curiously at her.

"Did you mean what you said?" Dante asked softly.

A puzzled frown etched her brow. What had she said?

A low rumble erupted from his massive chest as he peered into her face. "You said you loved me," he prompted.

Erica turned a deep shade of red. Had she? Lord, have mercy! Erica frantically paddled toward shore, afraid to face the humiliation that would result from her careless admission. To allow Dante to have that knowledge was tantamount to handing her enemy a weapon to use on her.

"We had better be on our way. Our horses have probably wandered off by now," Erica insisted quickly changing the subject.

"Answer me," Dante demanded as he followed in her wake. "Will you deny it?"

Erica hurried ashore and wiggled into her gown. Then, bracing herself she spun to face him, only to find herself gawking at his virile physique. Willfully, she raised her eyes to meet his probing stare. "Have you never whispered words of love in the heat of passion?"

"Not even once," Dante declared, eradicating her attempt at defense.

"Then you are a better man than I am," Erica grumbled, wishing she hadn't put the question to him in the first place. She was still on the spot. She had no answer, except the truth, and she was not about to arm him with that!

266

"If you were a man, we wouldn't be standing here discussing the matter." A faint smile appeared on his lips as he cupped his hand beneath her chin, forcing her to look him straight in the eye. "Have you overcome your fear and fallen in love with me?" he asked point-blank.

Erica slapped his hand away and tilted her chin a notch higher. "You have taught me the meaning of passion *and* betrayal, but you have given me no reason to love you," she said harshly. "I was a fool once, Dante. I finally realized that I played into your hands. You introduced me to men I couldn't possibly tolerate, not even for the span of a week; then you *graciously* offered to marry me. But there was nothing honorable about your request. You only wanted to use me to achieve your ends. You are not deserving of my love. Do not expect more than I can give, and in return I will never expect more than I have gotten from you."

Dante's face fell, then his expression became ice-cold. "One day I will hear those words again, and you will gladly confess them," he declared.

Erica gasped at his arrogance. Did he see her as another challenge? Only that? She wanted Dante as a true husband, one who wanted her and her alone. Perhaps she was vain, but she would be damned if she became just another trinket on his chain of broken hearts. She wanted his love, and she would never settle for less, even if she had to leave the only man who had burrowed his way into her heart.

Dante ground his teeth as Erica flounced toward her mount. How could such a sweet encounter turn sour so quickly? Would he ever grow accustomed to this termagant's quicksilver moods? Dante doubted it. Erica could make him soar to dizzying heights of ecstasy; then she

267

could send him plummeting to the depths of frustration. Dante never knew in which direction he was headed until the moment was upon him.

For years he had lived with the misconception that he could predict a woman's moods, take what he wanted, and then waltz away when he had tired of her. But that was not so with Erica. She affected him deeply. Lord, he hated to count the ways! He couldn't keep his distance. He was like a moth winging toward perpetual flame, one that never died but burned brighter with each passing day. Grumbling to himself, Dante stalked over, put on his trousers, snatched up his clothes, and then swung himself onto his steed. He urged his mount into a gallop, intending to pursue the perplexing minx who thundered ahead of him.

When he reached the plantation he went straight to her bedroom to give her strict instructions never to set out alone again, but she had barricaded the door and she refused to answer his knock.

Dante stormed back to his own room, where he paced the floor, as he had each night since he'd brought Erica to his home. What did he have to do to wedge his way into that woman's wild heart? He had offered her protection and refuge. He had bought her the most exquisite gowns to be had in Natchez, and he had made passionate love to her. But that wasn't enough. That will never be enough, he thought dismally. He might as well hitch himself to a passing cloud, for that was what she was. Erica was as shifting as the wind, raging at one moment and gentle the next. She was constantly changing, forever moving, eluding him, tormenting him. Dammit, she should be grateful that he had kept her from Sabin, at least his uncle hadn't gotten his hands on her. But did she show any gratitude? Dante snorted disgustedly. Hell no, she only flung insults in his direction and then berated him for his tactics.

What is the use? he asked himself as he sank back onto the bed and stared into the darkness. It would take a lifetime to lure that minx, and even then Dante wondered if he would come up empty-handed for all of his trouble. The woman was damned near impossible!

Chapter 15

When the servant rapped on her door to inform her that she had a guest, Erica bounded down the steps, expecting to see her aunt. She came to a screeching halt when she saw Elliot Lassiter propped against the balustrade, peering up at her and displaying his most charming smile.

"Good morning." He greeted her in a cheerful tone. "I have come to take you on an outing. What would you like to do today?"

Erica smiled weakly. "I doubt that Dante would approve."

Elliot's shoulders lifted in an unconcerned shrug. "Your servant tells me that you are only allowed out of the house in the presence of a chaperone." Elliot bowed in the chivalrous manner of the knights of old. "I am at your service, my lady. Name your destination and I will see that you safely reach it."

Why not? Erica asked herself. She would like to visit her aunt. Surely Dante wouldn't complain about such a harmless excursion. Besides, he returned home so seldom that she doubted he would miss her.

"Thank you, Elliot. I accept," she said, blessing him with a smile that nearly melted him.

As they rode toward Natchez in Elliot's carriage, Erica inhaled a breath of fresh air and then relaxed. Elliot was gentleman enough not to mention her appearance in his home, and for that she was thankful. He was charming and attentive, giving her no reason to complain about his behavior. After he escorted her to her aunt's store and informed her that he would return within an hour to take her to lunch, Elliot took his leave and Erica glanced up to find Lilian staring at her.

"I thought Dante ordered you to remain at his plantation until the danger with Sabin had passed."

"I have a very capable chaperone," Erica assured her, letting her eyes stray to the plump, gray-haired old woman who sat in her usual position in the corner.

"Forgive my manners," Lilian chuckled as she followed Erica's gaze. She took her arm and led her toward Madeline. "Erica, this is Madeline Perkins, a dear friend of mine. And this is my niece, Erica. She has recently wed Dante Fowler."

From behind thick spectacles, Madeline gave Erica the once-over. "Dante's wife?" she murmured thoughtfully. "I doubted that the lad would ever wed. He is such a cynical sort."

Erica was startled by the woman's frankness, but she merely smiled. After all, what could she say to that? Madeline had Dante pegged as a skeptic, and he was skeptical about love.

"Erica, why don't you show Madeline to the parlor. The two of you can become better acquainted. I am expecting a customer momentarily, but I'll join you when I've finished my business transaction."

Erica spent the next quarter of an hour answering prying questions. The older woman was skilled in extracting information without seeming offensive. Indeed, her interest in Erica's past was very sincere. Nonetheless, Erica was relieved when her aunt joined them and brought a halt to Madeline's third degree.

"How are the two of you getting along?" Lilian inquired as she sank down in her chair and peered at Madeline.

"Your lovely niece seems to have led a very fascinating life. She was educated at the finest schools, brought up in a proper home," she remarked as she studied Erica from over the rim of her teacup.

"Erica has had her share of excitement," Lilian concurred, casting Madeline a sly smile. "But I would imagine that only began since she wed our notorious Mr. Fowler."

"A feisty one, he is." Madeline chortled. "I've watched him grow from a skinny-legged stripling into a strong, handsome man."

"Do you know him well?" Erica asked, for the lack of anything else to say.

Madeline shrugged nonchalantly, then drew her drooping shawl back on her shoulders. "I have only observed him from a distance. I lived near the Fowler plantation many years ago, and Dante and Corbin were a constant source of amusement. They were a lively pair."

Without seeming rude, Erica tactfully steered the conversation back to Lilian. She was hoping that her aunt had information about her father and Sabin, but Lilian had seen very little of her brother-in-law since the first day he had arrived in Natchez.

When Elliot returned, Madeline frowned disapprovingly. "I thought it was Dante you had wed."

The barb made Erica blush as she rose from her chair and started toward the parlor door. It was obvious that Madeline did not approve of her gallivanting about town on another man's arm. Erica wondered if the old woman was a gossip since she seemed to have little else to amuse her.

"Elliot is my husband's closest friend," Erica felt obliged to say. "Dante is very busy and I—"

"And I suppose you did not hesitate to inform your new husband that you had another male escort." Madeline focused intently on Erica, making her squirm uncomfortably. "He is very sensitive about that sort of thing. I would not think it wise to tempt history to repeat itself, my dear."

Erica eyed the old woman who was peering up at her. Why wouldn't someone tell her what had happened to Dante's family? People were always dropping hints but no one would expound on them.

"Madeline is quite right," Lilian put in. "It is not proper to be seen in the company of another man. Rumors can start trouble and after what happened to Dante's family . . ."

"What did happen to Dante's family?" Erica asked. "Everyone refers to an incident, but I have been left completely left in the dark."

"Dante has not told you the whole of it?" Madeline queried.

"No, he hasn't and no one else will provide information. I do not appreciate being treated like a child, as if the news were too harsh for my delicate ears. I assure you that is not at all the case."

A mysterious smile played on Madeline's lips as she bent her gaze on Lilian. "Your niece shows a great deal of spunk for one so young, and I tend to agree with her. She has a right to know."

"In time perhaps," Lilian amended. "But the question is from *which* source?"

Madeline chuckled. "Perhaps it would be easier coming from a stranger."

"Well, I wish someone would tell me and quickly," Erica blurted out. "I have lost my patience. Surely one of you can tell me . . ." Her words faded as she realized Elliot had tired of waiting in the store and had wandered back to the open door.

He tipped his hat to the two older women. "Are you ready, Erica?"

She would have preferred to park herself in the chair and hear about the incident that had soured Dante on women, but she bided her time, hoping that one day she would find Madeline alone and would pry the truth from her. One way or another Erica intended to uncover Dante's mysterious secret.

It was almost a relief when Elliot deposited her at the Fowler plantation, for Erica's mind had strayed to the conversation at her aunt's home so many times during the course of the afternoon that she had not fully enjoyed the outing. But her relief was speedily transformed into apprehension when she opened the front door to find Dante glaring at her and her escort, who was sporting a smug grin.

The muscles of Dante's jaw were tense, and his eyes were cold green chips. Indeed, the expression on his face startled Erica. She had seen him angry, but never like this! She swore the rage blazing through Dante would reduce him to a pile of cinders if he did not get a grip on himself. Perhaps Madeline was right, she thought nervously. Perhaps the skeletons in Dante's closet had pounced on him. Erica knew it wasn't jealousy that had him fuming. More likely, it was past torment mingled with pride. After all, he had no deep feeling for her.

"Where have you been?" Dante's voice was ominous and threatening, like thunder.

"I thought Erica was in need of an airing," Elliot answered, and he slid a protective arm about her when Dante scowled at the caustic reply. "You have kept her closeted since she arrived in Natchez so I thought I would show her the sights."

"I have my reasons for keeping her at the plantation," Dante replied coldly.

"Flimsy ones, no doubt," Elliot retorted.

By exerting his iron will, Dante corraled his stampeding temper and then ambled toward them. The smile pasted on his lips did not reach his eyes, and Erica knew that beneath his controlled exterior was a man who wanted to shake the stuffing out of her.

"If it appears that I have neglected my wife, that is because I have pressing business matters to attend," Dante explained with chilling tolerance. "But I assure you, Erica is constantly in my thoughts."

Erica would have protested that bald-faced lie if she had been allowed the opportunity, but she wasn't.

"You can count upon me to attend her when your priorities take precedence." A devilish smile flickered across Elliot's lips as he lifted Erica's hand to place a light kiss to her wrist. "I don't mind entertaining her, day or *night.* As a matter of fact, there is something intriguing about finding such a lovely vision on my doorstep, shrouded in darkness. . . ."

Erica froze, and the color seeped from her cheeks. Elliot was deliberately trying to cause trouble by implying that she had come to his home for some other reason than her true purpose. Damnation, didn't she have enough trouble without being tossed from the frying pan into the fire? Elliot was a rascal, and she'd thought him a perfect gentleman for not bringing the matter up. But he had waited until he had Dante as an attentive audience.

Dante's condemning gaze riveted over her as he conjured up a picture of Erica swimming in the stream. So that is the real reason she went out alone, he thought furiously. He was certain that she had flown to Elliot's arms and then had stopped at the stream to cleanse her sinful soul. When she had murmured words of love, Elliot's face hovered above her, not his! Dante felt an unfamiliar knot coil in his belly. It ate away at him, bit by excruciating bit. Had Erica decided that she'd made a mistake when she accepted his proposal? Hadn't she implied that on several occasions? Well, she was *his* wife whether she wanted to be or not. Damn her for traipsing off behind his back! Dante was itching to beat Elliot to a pulp for blurting out the disgusting truth.

The thought of Erica in his arms made Dante's blood boil. Was that why she was smiling and humming a merry tune? That night, had it been the first time she had sneaked away to meet Elliot or had there been other nights on which she had come and gone without being caught? God, his tormenting thoughts were turning him inside out!

Erica would have sworn she could have sliced the

dense silence with a knife. Dante was looking at her as if she were some wretched creature that had just slithered out from under a rock. It broke her heart to know that he didn't trust her.

"Thank you for escorting me home, Elliot," Erica said, her voice unintentionally sliding from low to high pitch.

"It was my pleasure." Elliot's face radiated mischievousness. Now Dante knew the tormenting sensations he had suffered when he'd learned of his marriage. "I shall anticipate seeing you again. . . ."

When the door closed behind Elliot, Erica dashed for the stairs, hoping to put a safe distance between herself and Dante before he exploded. But a lean hand clamped around her arm, dragging her up the steps at such a quick pace that she stumbled twice and would have fallen if Dante hadn't hoisted her up and herded her along ahead of him.

Dante slammed the bedroom door shut with his boot heel. Then he focused his glowering eyes on Erica.

"Is this how you seek to repay me for the injustices you *think* I have committed against you?"

His voice had such a deadly ring that it would have made a mountain lion cower in its den, but Erica refused to back away. She was not about to be condemned for wrongdoing when she was innocent.

"Yes, I went to Elliot, hoping my disappearance would delay this preposterous challenge. But when I stopped to reconsider my action I feared it might have the opposite effect, that it might cause another clash with Sabin." Erica plowed on before Dante could disclaim her explanation. "I left Elliot after a few minutes, and I intended to come directly to the plantation"—a sheepish smile lifted one corner of her mouth—"until I was tempted to indulge in a midnight swim. I simply could not resist."

Indecision etched Dante's brow. He wasn't certain he should believe her. It all sounded too innocent, and he was still mad as hell. "If there is nothing going on between you and Elliot, why did you accept his invitation today?" he demanded in a gruff tone.

"Because I have had little else to do except twiddle my thumbs. The confinement was playing havoc with my sanity," she informed him tartly. "Elliot offered me a breath of freedom. How could I resist the opportunity to visit my aunt, to dine in one of Natchez's exclusive restaurants, and to view the sights when I have been bored to tears?"

Dante grunted derisively. This minx was accustomed to doing what she damned well pleased, come hell or high water. She continued to pursue her whims, and she didn't give a fig what anyone else thought.

"Do you know what your trouble is, madam?" Dante shook a tanned finger in her defiant face as if he were scolding a naughty child.

Erica crossed her arms beneath her breasts and flung him a withering glance. Surely he wasn't about to lecture her on her faults. Her father had already listed her shortcomings and she could rattle them off without being prompted. "Pray, tell me, what is it? I am dying to know," she said coolly. How could he possibly narrow her faults down to one? She knew she had at least a dozen.

"You are used to having your own way and you intend to have it, no matter what the cost," Dante snapped.

His condescending tone got the best of her. "And you aren't?" Erica laughed humorlessly. "You are as spoiled as three-day-old fish, yet you have the nerve to tell me *I* must have my own way? Well, let me tell you something, Dante Fowler. Nothing has gone as I would have chosen since the day I laid eyes on you." Erica jabbed her index finger in his chest. "You have taken advantage of me from the beginning, and you, of all people, have no right to criticize my behavior. I cannot sit and stare at these walls day after day. If Elliot Lassiter comes to call, I will accept an invitation for any outing he suggests. Anything short of an afternoon tryst," she amended. "I am a married woman, and, happy or not, *I will not be intimate with other men!*" She was almost shouting in his handsome face.

A relieved smile hovered on his lips as he folded his hands around hers and watched the fire blaze in her indignant blue eyes. It was comforting to know that no matter what their differences were, she had not been unfaithful to him.

"Nor will I with other women," he assured her, his voice softer now, his gaze warm. "And I apologize for my inconsideration. It is just that I have a great deal on my mind and time is running short. I came home early today to invite you on a picnic. Will you come?"

His gentle touch and persuasive smile immediately melted her ire, and she would have followed him through the fires of hell if he had requested it. He was looking at her as if he cared, and that small ray of hope spurred her agreeable response.

"And a ride perhaps?" she queried, her eyes dancing with excitement.

Erica yearned to race against the wind. Her midnight ride had given her a taste of the freedom she had once known, and she craved to recapture it, if only temporarily.

His grin stretched from ear to ear. "Can you be ready

in half an hour?"

"Less than that," she assured him, her smile bubbling with happiness, something she had been deprived of lately. "If you will unlace me . . ."

A playful growl tumbled from his lips as his hands slid over her waist to work the stays on the back of her gown. "Perhaps an indoor picnic is in order."

Erica was in an odd mood. She had remained straight-laced with Elliot, but she suffered a flare-up of mischief when Dante was underfoot. Her eyebrows arched provocatively. "Just what did you have in mind?" she purred.

"I think you know what thought is buzzing through my mind," he murmured as his hands slid beneath the gaping gown to swim over a sea of bare flesh.

Darting away, Erica flashed him a saucy smile. "Why, picnics of course."

The pale blue gown cascaded over her hips to fall in a pool of silk around her ankles, and she stood before him in her short chemise, letting his all-consuming gaze wander over her at will. She was in a seductive mood. If she could not have Dante's love, then she would settle for that which he could offer, knowing that their time together would not last forever. Why shouldn't I enjoy the pleasure he can give? she asked herself. Her pride had stood in the way once too often, and this time she intended to be impulsive with Dante. Pride and vanity be damned.

Dante's eyes widened as they devoured her curvaceous body. Was Erica silently suggesting that she would not be opposed to spending the afternoon in his arms after he had attempted to fight his way through her defenses for two weeks? It was too good to be true, but Dante was not about to question such a stroke of luck. Yet, this could be another of her ploys, he reminded himself.

The heat of desire pulsed through him as Erica walked across her room and then bent over to retrieve her clothes. The short undergarment slid up higher as she did so, exposing the shapely curve of her hips and Dante swallowed hard. It was all he could do to stand his ground when he longed to touch what his eyes boldly caressed.

"Aren't you going to change?" Erica smiled when she noted the starved expression on his rugged features.

"Ah . . . yes . . . of course," Dante stammered as he backed toward the door, craning his neck for one last look at her enticing figure. "I'll join you downstairs."

Erica had done some serious thinking since the night she had thundered off to Elliot's mansion. She had then asked herself what she wanted most in life and had answered Dante. He had taught her the meaning of love and passion, and she longed to have him return her affection. She had finally decided to fight for him. Dante was battling time to defeat Sabin. No longer would she be a thorn in his side. She would offer her assistance. Surely two heads were better than one, especially when opposing Sabin Keary. Now, determined to assault Dante's senses, Erica dressed fittingly. If he didn't sit up and take notice, then she would know at last that she was wasting her time and energy. Today will be the test, she told herself as she carefully smoothed her garments into place. It would be a new beginning for them, or it would assure her that Dante had no real interest in her except for amusing himself until he had gotten what he wanted from Sabin—revenge for his father's death.

With that thought milling through her head, Erica checked her appearance in the mirror and then bounded down the steps. Dante gripped the balustrade when he saw her, for before him stood the essence of beauty. Erica's hair cascaded over her shoulders to curl temptingly over her breasts. A rose tinge heightened her cheeks, and her blue eyes glistened with the lively sparkle he adored. Beneath her gossamer, peasant-style blouse was nothing but bare flesh, and when she swayed provocatively as she came toward him, he could see that she wore no petticoats.

Dante was baffled by the abrupt change in Erica. She seemed reckless and carefree, not calculating as she had been on the steamboat when she had desperately sought a husband. But then why should her fickle moods surprise him? he asked himself. There were many facets to this complex young beauty. Indeed, it would take a lifetime to discover all there was to know about Erica.

While he was busy ogling her, Erica was thoughtfully surveying him. His white linen shirt, partially unbuttoned, revealed a touch of the dark furring of hair on his chest, and it accented his dark features. Black breeches clung to his hard thighs like well-fitting gloves, and black boots hugged his calves. Erica was overwhelmed by his lithe, powerful physique, his broad shoulders and narrow hips. An aura radiated from him, and it so intrigued her that she could not look away. She was suddenly lost to the giddy sensations that overwhelmed her. Dante made her feel wild and free and reckless. It is a strange feeling—exhilarating, Erica mused as she swept past him and headed for the stables. She wanted to leap onto her horse and chase the wind, shouting her love, holding nothing back.

And she did, but she galloped off ahead of Dante so the words she spoke were carried off in the breeze. Aware that they did not reach his ears, Erica found herself wondering why Dante should be the last person to know she loved him. That seemed odd. As she leaned against the dun gelding's neck, urging him to his swiftest pace, she reminded herself that her relationship with Dante had begun in reverse. Perhaps one day she could speak of her love and he would be prepared to accept it . . . if Sabin didn't spoil any chance of those things happening. Erica gritted her teeth and drove that depressing thought to the far corner of her mind. Today was too beautiful to be ruined by thoughts of Sabin.

Dante's breath caught as the sunlight struck Erica's sheer blouse, exposing her full, tempting breasts. Her raven hair was a waterfall of shiny tresses, and Dante longed to run his fingers through those lustrous strands. She had drawn the back hem of her shirt between her legs, tucking it into the front waistband so she could straddle the saddle, and her shapely legs were curled about the gelding's ribs. Dante was completely mesmerized by the stunning witch who urged her steed to leap the creek and then circle back toward him. Passionate desire now ruled him.

When Erica trotted back to him, he scooped her from the saddle and settled her in front of him, where she curled up like a contented kitten. As her silken hands wandered inside his shirt and settled against his ribs, his heart beat furiously. A beckoning smile hovered on her lips, an invitation Dante could not resist. His mouth clung to hers as she pressed closer, the taut peaks of her breasts gliding wantonly across his chest.

But the moment before he gave way to the impulse to make wild sweet love to her right on the back of his chestnut stallion, Erica slid from his arms and playfully bounded away, leaving him to follow her like a starved kitten on the trail of fresh milk, his emerald eyes fixed on the lively nymph who frolicked in the meadow. Suddenly all thought left Dante. He was in a dreamlike trance, his need for Erica so strong that it drove him to distraction. As she spun about, her skirt swirling, their gazes locked across the distance that separated them. Then the sparkle in her sapphire blue eyes turned to the glow of desire, assuring him that their thoughts had converged.

Brazenly, Erica loosened the ties at the front of her blouse, letting it reveal the swells of her breasts. She tossed her hair away from her face and then graced Dante with a smile that penetrated his heart.

A craving for her raged through him as Erica sauntered closer, and when her hands caressed his chest, Dante gasped. This spell-casting witch raised his temperature, so much so that Dante wondered whether Erica was a hazard to his health. Lord, he was so steamed up that his eyes had fogged over. Her wayward hand mapped the hardened contours of his belly and then dipped beneath the band of his breeches, causing him to respond with a quick intake of breath.

"It isn't Elliot who stirs my blood," Erica informed him as her bold caresses tracked across his hair-roughened flesh to bring his passion to a fervent pitch.

"No?" Dante sounded like a water-logged bullfrog who had swallowed his pond, lily pad and all.

"No," she murmured huskily as one delicate finger scaled his shoulder to trail over the chiseled lines of his face and then sketch the sensuous curve of his lips. "It is you, Dante. I will no longer deny that I find pleasure in your arms." She rose on tiptoe to spread butterfly kisses over the column of his neck, then let her lips melt like wine against his. "Make love to me as you have with no other woman."

Erica's assault on Dante's senses was so thorough that he was consumed by the heated sensations. As the scent of lavender engulfed him, he emitted a guttural groan and roughly clutched her closer, but it was not enough to hold this bewitching vixen. He hungered to shed the garments that separated them, to feel her satiny flesh forged to his.

"Must I voice my need for you?" His voice was a hoarse whisper. "You already know what you do to me, don't you?" He lifted her from the ground, his right hand slipping behind her neck as he focused on her inviting mouth. Then his lips took hers, and shock waves of pleasure rippled through her.

"Yes, but I need to hear the words," she whispered against his cheek. "I want more than a brief passionate affair. I want you to need me, to want me. . . ."

The expression in her eyes magnetized him. She had burrowed so deeply into his heart that plucking out the memory of this afternoon would be tantamount to pulling splinters from his soul, then leaving it to bleed. If he lost her to Sabin, he would be only half a man.

"Erica, I . . ."

Dante jerked back when he caught a movement in the brush.

"Good afternoon, Cap'n." Reade Asher urged his mount forward. Despite the cheroot in his mouth, he chuckled at Dante's glare, certain that he had interrupted a tryst in the meadow.

Erica hurriedly tied her gaping blouse as Dante's arms dropped to his sides, his hands clenched in annoyance.

"What do you want?" Dante grunted.

Without awaiting an invitation, Reade stepped from

the stirrup. "I met yore uncle last night," he commented as he strolled toward Dante. "He sent me with a message for you."

Like shattering crystal, the mention of Sabin broke the spell of the afternoon. Dante scowled irritably. "What does he want now?"

"He said to tell you he's contracted his shipload of cotton and is settin' sail tomorrow. He told me to tell you he would be waitin' on the docks when the *Natchez Belle* arrived in New Orleans."

The news soured Dante's mood. Although he had made arrangements to sail at dawn, he still had several wagon loads of his own crop to transport to Natchez. Dallying with Erica had cost him precious time, and he would be hard pressed to ensure that Sabin did not sail before he did.

"Keep an eye on Erica for me," he ordered as he snatched up the chestnut stallion's reins and leaped onto the steed.

Erica's spirits fell. She had hoped for some commitment from Dante, for some indication that the fragile bond between them had been strengthened by their secluded afternoon together. But it was obvious that revenge against Sabin Keary was foremost in his mind.

She sighed dejectedly. She should be able to recognize a lost cause when she was staring at its departing back. And Dante was a lost cause. She had lost her fighting spirit, something she had long prided herself on. What more could she do? If Dante felt something for her he would drop this challenge and find some other way to deal with Sabin. Instead, he had left her in his haste to load his cargo. Erica was playing second fiddle to a confounded steamboat laden with cotton! Hell and damnation. She would never be more than Dante's paramour, an occasional distraction. How many times did she have to be slapped in the face before she learned her lesson? Well, this is the last straw, Erica muttered under her breath as she glared at the rider who thundered out of sight. She decided to let Dante gallop out of her life forever, not to try to lure him back.

"Would you care to ride?" Reade inquired, jolting Erica from her troubled contemplations.

"I would prefer to be alone just now," she replied as she turned away, fighting tears.

Reade scanned the area and then shrugged. "If that's what you wish, lass, but I wouldn't stray too far. You never know who's wanderin' about."

Too lost in thought to catch his mumbled warning, Erica swung into the saddle and cantered away. This is my own fault, she told herself. If I hadn't lost my temper at the Mardi Gras I'd be in New Orleans fighting to be treated as a human being instead of a woman.

Certainly she would never have ended up in the arms of the one man who could make her realize that her life was incomplete. She had been satisfied until she'd stumbled onto Dante Fowler, that dashing devil with laughing green eyes and a smile that could melt a woman's heart. How ironic it was to be in love with a rakehell who was more interested in cotton than in her. She had wanted to become involved in his life, to share his innermost thoughts, but he wanted a mistress who would share his bed and then shuffle out from underfoot when his desires were appeased. Erica was willing to compromise, but not to be broken for the sake of love. Yet Dante wouldn't even bend. Her love had not mellowed him.

Erica heaved an exasperated sigh. When had she become so wishy-washy, swaying back and forth between a desire to earn Dante's love and a determined drive to put him out of her mind? Lately, she had done nothing but contradict herself at every other breath. One moment she was prepared to fight for him, and the next she was ready to throw up her hands and call it quits. Since she'd discovered that she'd fallen in love with Dante Fowler, she reminded herself. Love had infected her heart, distorting her thoughts and making her chase impossible dreams.

Enough of this! Erica chided herself. This is an open-and-shut case of one-sided love. I must forget him if I want to salvage my sanity.

Erica jumped when Sabin's wicked chuckle sliced through her silent musings. Then fear constricted her throat as she spied him and the three roustabouts Dante had ordered from the *Natchez Belle* converging on her. Timothy grabbed her before she could gallop away.

"You knew I would come for you, didn't you, my dear?" Keary asked. Then he declared, "This is only the first surprise I have in store for my arrogant nephew."

"Do you intend to turn your surly henchmen on him as well?" Erica hissed venomously as Denby tied her hands and feet, and then tossed her over the back of Timothy's horse like a feed sack.

"I have hired someone to deal with Dante," Sabin assured her, seemingly unaffected by her biting tone. "Having you disappear will serve as a distressing reminder that he is no match for me, and very soon Dante will be repaid for trying to stand in the way of what I want."

Erica desperately wished that she was safely tucked

behind the walls of Dante's mansion. She knew the abuse Sabin and his ruffians would inflict on her, but she would have given anything to know what Sabin had in store for Dante. She struggled to free herself from the ropes, but to no avail. Bound and gagged, Erica had to listen to Sabin's tormenting laughter as he weaved his way back to Natchez with her in tow.

Chapter 16

Dante's furious glare nailed Reade to the wall. "Dammit, man, I thought I could depend on you!" he bellowed, his voice bounding off the walls and coming at Reade from all directions. "Maybe you have changed in these past years." His flaming green eyes riveted on Reade in scornful mockery. "I am beginning to think I don't know you at all. Are you friend or foe, Asher?"

"How the hell was I s'pposed to know Sabin Keary wanted yer wife?" Reade yelled when Dante grasped the neck of his shirt, depriving him of oxygen.

"Suppose you tell me," Dante gritted out, his lips curling in a hateful sneer. "It seems odd that you would come around with a message from my uncle just before she was kidnapped. I know your lust for coins, Asher. How much did he pay you to leave Erica unattended?"

"Now wait a damned minute." Reade pried Dante's hand from his shirt and readjusted his clothing. "You got no right to accuse me of workin' for Sabin. I only just met him in the tavern."

Dante didn't know where to turn or what to think. He

and Reade had been close, but that had been some years ago, before Reade had drifted from ocean to shore and had begun to work at whatever would pay for his room and board. Dante had offered him a job on the plantation, but Reade was too restless to stay put for any length of time. Had he sold out an old friend for a pouch of coins?

Growling, Dante unwadded the note he had clenched in his fist, and he reread the message from Sabin.

No need to fret, nephew. Your lady is in very capable hands. My new wife and I will be waiting in New Orleans to greet you when you arrive.

Dante cursed the taunting image that rose above him, mocking him, jeering him. "If he abuses her, I'll kill him with my bare hands," he declared vindictively. Then he stalked into the hall, Reade scampering after him.

"What are you gonna do?" Reade asked.

"I'm going to round up the crew and sail for New Orleans," Dante muttered disgustedly. "I should have known that message you delivered was another trick."

When Dante reached the docks a roar of pure rage burst from his lips as he glared murderously at the silhouette of the steamship that had just left the dock for New Orleans. He stormed across the wharf in search of his crew, who had been lured from the ship by an offer of free drinks, while Sabin braced himself against the railing of *The Lucky Lady*, gloating over his cleverness. Erica was stashed in a stateroom with guards posted at her door, his ship was loaded with enough cotton to fill Avery's contract, and Dante was scurrying about Natchez in search of a crew that would be so drunk they would be little use to him.

Sabin pricked up his ears when Erica's indignant screams penetrated the silence; then he stalked toward her room, growling at her outburst. "Don't force me to abuse you here and now," he snapped as he reached down to replace the gag she had managed to loosen.

"I demand to see my father!" Erica spat out furiously. "You have no right to keep me here."

"Ah, but I do," Sabin countered as he smiled intimidatingly. "In one week your marriage will be annulled, and you will become *my* wife." As he traced a gnarled finger over her flushed cheek, Erica shrank away from his repulsive touch. "You shun me now, but before long I will teach you the manners that are becoming to a plantation owner's wife."

"I will never marry you." Erica's voice quivered with fury, and she itched to scratch out Sabin's beady eyes. "Your touch sickens me; I will never tolerate it."

A wicked smile curled Keary's lips as he rose to his full height. "You *will* endure my caresses, nonetheless. And don't think you can cry to Avery. He has troubles of his own."

"What is it you hold over my father?" Erica demanded to know.

Sabin ambled toward the door, then paused to lean on his cane. "That is between Avery and me, my dear. If he wanted you to know, he would have told you. That he has not is to my advantage." His hawkish eyes roamed over the sagging blouse that exposed the creamy swells of her breasts. "Avery will not stand in my way. Your beauty has bewitched me, but we will have to do something about your fiery nature. I intend to tame you. On that you can depend."

How she despised this corrupt brute! He was willing to

go to any lengths to have what he wanted. Damn him! One day he would receive a just reward for all the misery he had caused. Somehow, some way, Sabin would pay for manipulating people and sucking the spirit out of them like a starved leech draining blood from its prey. If ever a more hideous excuse for a man stalked the earth, Erica could not imagine who that might be. Sabin was rotten, selfish, and ruthless. He derived demented pleasure from devising unsavory schemes and watching them unfold, from entangling his victims in a web of treachery and deceit.

While Sabin paced the boiler deck, grinning smugly, Erica silently smoldered. Now, more than ever, she was aware of what had driven Dante to accept this risky challenge. It was hatred. Never in her life had she loathed another person, but she loathed Sabin Keary. No one is lower than he, she thought bitterly, and if anything happens to Dante, I will avenge him.

A tear formed in the corner of her eye and trickled down her stained cheek. What a selfish little fool she had been. She should never have criticized Dante for seeking his revenge on Sabin. She should have worked tirelessly beside him, helping him with his plan, overseeing the transfer of cargo to his ship, encouraging him instead of distracting him with her tantrums. Now it was too late. Dante could not possibly win this race, not when Sabin had several hours' head start. Her only hope was that *The Lucky Lady* would spring a leak. She didn't really care about the danger to herself, just as long as Dante was safe. Her gaze lifted, then she prayed for a stroke of fortune, wondering meanwhile if she had the right to ask for divine assistance after the mess she had made of things; her plea was met with silence. Maybe I don't deserve an answer, she thought despairingly. Perhaps Dante is thankful that I am off his hands so he can dedicate himself to his purpose.

Erica slumped back in her chair and squirmed into a more comfortable position beneath the restraining ropes. She would be forced to survive on sweet memories of Dante's intoxicating kisses and tantalizing caresses. They were all she had, all she would ever have, if Sabin got his way. But he would never break her spirit the way he had broken her father's, she vowed determinedly. Sabin could beat her within an inch of her life, yet she would go on loving Dante. No one could change that, not even the devil himself.

Dante raked his fingers through his hair and then let his arm drop to his side as he peered into the distance, hoping to catch sight of *The Lucky Lady* cutting through the water in the channel ahead of him. After three days of navigating a river choked with brush and bayous that could entrap a careless captain, Dante had almost given up hope of sighting Sabin's vessel. He had towed wood flats behind the steamboat to save time, veering to shore only when the woodpile became dangerously low; and he'd ordered the engineer to maintain the swiftest speed possible without risking an explosion.

"Yer mighty quiet tonight, Cap'n," Reade remarked as he ambled up beside Dante, whose eyes were glued to the channel ahead of him.

"I have a lot on my mind," Dante mumbled, gripping the wheel to steer through swampy waters from which tree limbs rose like ghostly hands eager to snare him.

"Yer lady, I'd guess," Reade mused aloud. Then he

cocked a wondering brow as he studied Dante's weary features. "I know you claimed you married that vixen to get back at yer uncle, but I got a feelin' there's more to it than that. I never saw you so distracted by a woman before."

Reade propped an elbow on the window sill and then tapped the ashes from his cigar onto the deck, provoking a furious growl from Dante.

"Dammit, what are you trying to do, send this ship up in smoke? I have enough trouble without fighting a fire on this tub."

Reade mashed his foot into the glowing ashes before returning to the subject he had broached before being scolded for his carelessness. "You feel somethin' for that feisty beauty, don't you, Cap'n?"

Dante was in no mood to be interrogated. He just wanted to wring Sabin's neck. He was stewing over the possibility of losing the race, and he was tormented by the thought of Sabin taking Erica to his bed. But he assured himself that the latter case would be a battle. Erica would claw Sabin to shreds if the opportunity presented itself. She detested the man, much as Dante did. But what would Sabin do to Erica if she injured him again? Dante hated to think of that.

"Have you nothing better to do with your time than harass me with prying questions?"

"You didn't take no passengers on this trip and I hate to drink alone." Reade snorted. He was undaunted by Dante's attempt to shush him. "Is this challenge due to that saucy wife of yores?"

Dante let his breath out in a rush. "Blast it, Reade. Talk of something else," he barked sharply. "Any subject would be better than this one."

"A sore spot, is it?" Reade taunted unmercifully. Then he sadly shook his head. "I never thought I would see the day you fell head over heels for a woman. Can't get her out of yore blood, can you, Cap'n? Did you ever stop to think what you would do if you lost this race?"

Dante's hands clenched around the wheel until his knuckles turned white. The thought of defeat tied his stomach in knots. "I do not intend to lose."

Reade was silent, his thoughtful gaze drifting to Dante as he relit his cigar and then followed the captain's anxious stare to the glistening waters of the Mississippi.

As the low-hanging branches parted to reveal the channel ahead of them, the lights of *The Lucky Lady* skipped across the darkness like a beacon in the night. Relief washed over Dante's face and his fierce grip on the wheel eased. After calling down to the engineer to maintain their speed, he stepped away to allow the pilot to take the wheel.

"I could use a drink," Dante breathed.

Reade smiled, revealing his lack of teeth. "Did I tell you about the time I signed on with that drunken Captain Sagefield to sail to China? Lord, I never thought to see land again. The man had charted his course over a bottle of rum." He grunted acrimoniously as he strode along beside his silent companion. "I swear that experience was enough to make a salty sailor seasick. We was becalmed in the tropics and me and the crew . . ."

Dante wasn't listening. His thoughts were centered on a pair of sea blue eyes that could sizzle with anger or glow with passion. Erica . . . Just thinking of her did strange things to him. He had been yearning for her since that afternoon when she'd asked him to make love to her as he had to no other. He could not forget the look in her eyes.

296

It had boggled his mind, yet he had been unable to decode the message in those fathomless blue pools. Then he'd been lured away, only to have Erica kidnapped from him and to go through three days of hell while he wondered what Sabin was planning and whether he had dared to force himself on Erica.

That is all part of Sabin's careful scheme, Dante reminded himself. He knew his uncle intended to anger and frustrate him, but Dante was determined not to let his thinking become clouded. In order to outguess Sabin, to consider every possibility, Dante needed his wits about him. The following morning he must pass *The Lucky Lady* and lead the way into the entangled channel north of New Orleans.

The self-satisfied smile faded from Sabin's thin lips as he strolled from his stateroom to see the *Natchez Belle* paddling toward him, its smokestacks rolling, its hull low in the water due to its cargo. Damn, how had Dante managed to catch up with them? Sabin had given the captain strict orders to keep rolling fires in the boilers.

"I see your meticulous plotting could not keep Dante at a safe distance," Erica mocked as she was ushered outside for a breath of fresh air.

Denby had made the mistake of removing her gag, and Sabin sorely wished he hadn't. He was in no mood for Erica's goading. In fact he regretted allowing the wench out of her confining cubicle, but Avery, having found a smidgeon of misplaced courage, had demanded that his daughter be granted a stroll on deck.

"I am disappointed that you doubt my capabilities, my dear," Sabin said smoothly after he had gained control of his quick temper. "Your lover has a surprise in store for him, or have you forgotten that I alerted you to that fact the day I stole you from his plantation? One can always find a traitor to sabotage a man's ship if he is willing to pay a price. And I was."

The devilish grin that split Sabin's wrinkled face made Erica's blood run cold, and giving no thought to her own safety, she stormed across the deck, catching Denby off guard. Sabin squawked as Erica charged at him, knocking the wind out of him. Although her hands were still tied behind her back, Erica's blow was painful. His temper fired, Sabin backhanded her when she kneed him in the belly the second time.

"You foolish bitch!" he screeched furiously.

"Don't you lay a hand on her again," Avery growled as he stepped between them. "You may have cowed me, but Erica will not suffer abuse. You swore to me that you would never beat her, and I will hold you to it or the wedding is off, no matter what the cost!"

Sabin laughed. "I will ruin you and you know it. You should know better than to cross me."

"Your word, Sabin," Avery demanded, his eyes clashing with Keary's dark, vindictive orbs.

"My word," Sabin begrudgingly agreed. He would have to humor Avery until the marriage vows were sealed, he reminded himself.

"Oh, my God!" Erica choked out as her wild eyes flew to the *Natchez Belle*.

Although the steamship had edged up beside them, flames were leaping from the main deck. Within a split second the fire had shot across the cotton bales towering above the hurricane deck, and quicker than a heartbeat, the entire cargo was a mass of glowing orange flame. The heat radiating from the blaze was so intense that Erica knew the boilers would catch fire at any moment and the steamboat would explode. Over the alarmed screams of the crew of the *Natchez Belle*, Erica heard Sabin's arrogant chuckle. The sound abraded her nerves and left her trembling with pure rage.

"You see, my dear, I had considered the fact that my skillful nephew might catch up to us. But even *he* cannot fight the dangers of this mighty river." Sabin beamed delightedly. "One never knows when a careless fire will crop up aboard ship, destroying the cargo and sending its crew overboard to avoid being charred beyond recognition." His glistening black eyes drifted to the floating inferno, and he thoughtfully stroked his pointed chin. "I wonder if our noble captain will go down with his ship. It would indeed save him a great deal of humiliation."

Erica couldn't believe what she was seeing and hearing! Sabin had set the *Natchez Belle* afire. The dastardly bastard!

When Keary expelled another round of goading laughter, Erica could stand no more of it. He might kill her for attacking him again, but she didn't care. She thirsted for his blood.

Sabin squealed like a stuck pig when Erica kicked him in the groin and then shoved him face down on the deck while he was doubled over. Deprived of the use of her hands, she pelleted him with her feet, kicking and jabbing at him until Denby pulled her away and, roughly grabbing her hair, shuffled her back to her cabin.

En route, Erica screamed curses at the man who refused his competition a sporting chance. What would Dante do, even if he managed to escape the flaming ship? He had lost his entire crop and his steamship. He had staked everything he owned on this race in order to buy up all the cotton in the area before Sabin did. Now what could he do? Erica burst into tears at the dreadful thought. Even if Dante did come out alive he wouldn't be grateful, not when he'd lost everything but the shirt on his back. This vicious trick might destroy his strong will. Where would he turn for help? Had he been killed? Erica cursed Sabin with every sobbing breath she took. How she hated the man! He was a vicious madman who delighted in crushing his enemies, even in watching them burn to death.

Choking fumes hovered about the decks of the *Natchez Belle* like clouds of doom as Dante gave the order to abandon ship. He and his crew had tried to douse the flames, but they hadn't a chance. The fire had consumed the cotton bales that were stacked on the steamboat, and now Dante feared that the boilers would become so overheated they would explode. He did salvage the yawl, but several crewmen had already dived overboard without waiting for it to be lowered onto the river.

As Dante stepped into the yawl and took up the oars, a mixture of rage and despair possessed him. His eyes were fixed on the flaming riverboat which carried a cargo and investment that could never be replaced. He had lost everything except the plantation, and even that would be difficult to maintain without payment for the cotton crop. He would have to repay Corbin for his half-interest in the *Natchez Belle,* but now that he and Elliot were at odds, he couldn't expect a loan, not without using Erica for collateral. He knew Elliot would demand her in return for a loan that Dante would spend years struggling to repay.

Then came the inevitable. The explosion sent waves rushing toward the yawl, and Dante instinctively ducked as the two smokestacks flew high into the air, then toppled end over end before crashing into the river. Another deafening roar resounded about them as the bow of the ship shattered into a thousand flaming pieces, scattering burning debris on the water. It sizzled and spewed as the riverboat sank, taking Dante's dreams to the depths with it. With pained eyes Dante watched the massive boat disappear as hissing steam sprayed above the blaze, watching until there was nothing left but a soul-shattering silence.

His agonized gaze drifted to Reade Asher who grimly rowed toward shore. "How do I explain this to Corbin? I don't even know what caused the fire," he mused aloud, his eyes circling back to the sinking ship.

"What are we gonna do now?" Reade's solemn voice penetrated Dante's troubled contemplations.

Dante stared at *The Lucky Lady* as she glided through the water on her way to New Orleans. "I don't know," he replied. He was too dazed to think.

Reade strained his ears to catch the words Dante muttered as he stepped ashore and pulled the yawl into the sand. Dante's eyes were still glued to the smoking embers of a dream, one that had collided with reality. Sabin had defeated him. That thought hummed in his head. He was stunned and disoriented. He had never considered defeat, but now . . . Sabin had left him no weapon with which to fight. Dante must forfeit any right to Erica, and before he could pick his way to New Orleans, Sabin would see to it that the marriage was annulled. Sabin . . . The thought of his treacherous

301

uncle set his teeth on edge. Dante would have bet his singed right arm that Sabin had had a hand in the mysterious fire that had caused the loss of his cargo and ship. Sabin was unscrupulous. He would stop at nothing to win. But how could he ensure? . . .

Dante's accusing gaze settled on his quiet companion as he recalled the previous night when Reade had carelessly allowed his cigar ashes to flutter to the deck of the pilothouse. It disturbed him that Reade had also been the one to deliver the message from Sabin and that he had been in charge of Erica when she'd disappeared. Sabin might have enlisted the aid of Reade Asher to sabotage the ship. Did Reade have a price? Had hard times corrupted his values?

"How much did my uncle pay you?" Dante's voice sliced through the silence like a razor-sharp dagger.

Reade's head jerked up and his jaw sagged. "Are you accusin' me of settin' that fire? We've been friends a long time, Dante."

"Acquaintances," Dante corrected, his eyes like cold chips of stone as he glared at Reade.

"But I've saved yore life." Reade was indignant. "Why would I sabotage yore ship?"

"Suppose you tell me the answer to that," Dante demanded harshly.

The implication hung heavily in the muggy air as both men glared contemptuously at each other.

"Oftentimes the greed for money brings out the worst in a man," Dante remarked. "It's like tossing raw meat to a pack of wolves. That always brings them to each other's throats. Maybe you were so eager to waltz off on another treasure hunt that you took the money Sabin tossed at you."

"And maybe you got exactly what you deserved." Reade snorted derisively. "Time changes men, and you ain't the man I thought I knew."

"Why? Because I don't happen to believe in *blind* loyalty?" Dante shot back at him. "I smell a rat and he fits your description."

"Of all the . . ." Reade howled. "Now I suppose yore gonna accuse me of cuttin' the rope when you was stuck in the sandbar so the timber would fall on you!"

"Strange that you should mention it." Dante's stormy green eyes narrowed on Reade's weather-beaten face.

"I thought yore uncle was part devil," Reade growled. "But I swear yore as sour as he is."

"So you *do* know him better than you would have me believe."

"Don't start shovin' words in my mouth, Fowler. I only said you inherited a few of his traits."

"No more than you have picked up these past years," Dante fumed.

"If I was you, I'd be figurin' out a way to get back at yore uncle instead of pointin' accusin' fingers at yore friends. You need money, Fowler. Now just how the hell are you gonna get it?" Reade grunted.

Dante grumbled under his breath as his eyes swept across the river to see *The Lucky Lady* disappear around the bend. Reade was right. He was facing a mountain of trouble, and it didn't matter whose side Reade was on at the moment. Dante wasn't sure he could trust his first mate, but he had little choice. Reade was all he had. The crew had scattered into the forest to pick their way back to civilization so he and Reade were left. Dante could accept defeat and crawl back to Natchez, or he could roll to his feet and come out fighting. Since he wasn't one to give up, Dante had some fast thinking to do.

"I'll find a way by the time I reach New Orleans," he muttered as he wheeled and stalked away, pushing through the dense underbrush that lined the river. "Sabin Keary hasn't seen the last of me. Two can play that bastard's game."

A secretive smile pursed Reade's lips as he fell into step behind Dante, but he said not a word as they weaved through the maze of thickets that lined the Mississippi.

Part VI

Evil often triumphs, but never conquers.

— *Roux*

Chapter 17

As he ogled his prize, Sabin smiled like a barracuda. His beady eyes took in Erica's exquisite features and her curvaceous figure, missing not the slightest detail. Although she had been belligerent since the day she'd seen the *Natchez Belle* go up in smoke, she had signed the annulment papers, dissolving her marriage to Dante Fowler. Sabin now had the world in the palm of his hand. His cargo was safely loaded on his schooner, and Jamie Bennet was prepared to set sail the following morning.

Very soon, Erica would become his wife. How he ached to get his hands on that feisty wildcat. She had become an obsession, and he vowed to drive every memory of his nephew from her mind. There are ways, he reminded himself as he displayed a satanic smile. He certainly had no qualms about employing them. Time and relentless persistence could conquer even the most rebellious heart, and once Erica realized he would never relinquish his claim on her, she'd bend to his will. After spending endless days in dark seclusion, she'd be begging for his company.

He had chosen Erica for her dazzling beauty and wealth, and Avery had played into his hands. Although Erica had been reluctant, she would soon become Sabin's wife; then the New Orleans Cotton Exchange would be under his control. He would force Avery to do business only with those who met with his approval. Those unwilling to reciprocate the favors Sabin extended to them would no longer find a market for their crops.

For too many years Keary had been snubbed by the aristocracy, but now they would bow to him or go hungry. He itched to see the look on his associates' faces when they learned that he was the reigning monarch of New Orleans.

While Sabin was indulging himself in delusions of grandeur, Erica was glaring holes in him. She had beseeched her father to take a stand against this despot, but Avery had backed down when Sabin had issued another of his venomous threats. Avery had then refused to explain his involvement with Sabin. Instead, he'd muttered something about the problem becoming even more complicated after she had met and married Dante Fowler. Erica breathed a heavy-hearted sigh. She had heard nothing from Dante, and it had been a week since his steamship had gone up in flames. Was he dead or alive? Erica didn't know, but she was sustained only by the hope that he had managed to escape the destruction of the *Natchez Belle*.

"In only a few more hours we will be man and wife," Sabin cooed as he strutted over and ran a bony finger across her cheek.

Erica flinched at his touch. "And you will regret marrying me," she spat at him, her tone dripping hatred. "I will see to that."

Sabin's smile became a contemptuous snarl. "Mind your tongue, Erica. Once we are wed I will not be so lenient with you."

"You think you've won, don't you?" Erica drew herself up in front of him, her blue eyes snapping. "The battle has only begun. I intend to take up where Dante left off."

"You can never win against me," Sabin growled as he grasped her arm and propelled her toward the stairs. "You will be staying the night to ensure that you don't attempt escape. And tomorrow. . . ." He let his words hang in the air to emphasize his intentions. "No lock will bar the entrance of your room, my dear Erica. We will be sharing far more than conversation."

Erica hungered for something to hurl at him, but there was nothing within reach.

"Don't be so sure of yourself," she warned, her voice quivering with disdain. "I will fight you with my dying breath." With those words, she stormed up the remainder of the steps and slammed the door.

She paced the floor, her mind racing. There *had* to be some way to escape. The window to her room had been barred from the outside, and Sabin held the key to the door she had slammed shut so forcefully that the entire mansion had rattled. Silently she padded across the room and eased open the door, hoping Sabin had remained downstairs so she might have an opportunity to sneak away before he locked her in for the night. But the scoundrel was clinging to the shadows in the hall.

"The guard will be here shortly," he purred sarcastically. "Until then, I will personally ensure that you do not leave me. I know what a nasty habit you have of fleeing in the middle of the—"

Erica slammed the door in his wretched face, wishing it had flattened his wrinkled features. God, how she detested that man! How Avery tolerated him was beyond her. No matter what dark secret Sabin held over him, it could not be as sinful as becoming Keary's puppet.

Nervous energy kept her pacing back and forth across the room long after she heard Sabin's key rattle in the lock, but finally she gave up hope of fleeing that night. Surely she would find a solution the following morning, she told herself confidently. Sabin couldn't keep her locked up until the moment before their wedding. Somehow she would elude him, just as she had before.

With that determined thought in mind, Erica climbed into bed and willed her eyes to close, but they kept popping open when she heard faint sounds in the darkness. If Sabin tried to sneak in and force himself on her, she would claw him to bloody shreds! But after an hour of tense waiting, all was silent, and she sank into dream-filled sleep.

She was in Dante's protective embrace, enjoying the pleasures that swept over her as she soared on rapture's wings to freedom. Warm, full lips feathered across hers, compelling them to respond to a kiss that stirred hidden desires. Gentle hands massaged away the tension that had claimed her, and Erica drifted on waves of tantalizing sensation. As her body instinctively strained toward the bold caresses that glided over her bare flesh, a tiny moan tumbled from her lips.

Dante's name escaped her as lips traced the delicate line of her jaw. Erica was experiencing the same enchanting dream that she had each night. Her emotions lurked just beneath the surface, waiting to rise and spill forth, like a river overflowing its banks, as soon as she closed her eyes.

She was deliriously content and yet . . . her eyes fluttered open, and she winced, suddenly aware that she couldn't be dreaming. The sensations were too real. The silhouette that hovered above her startled her, but her alarmed gasp was smothered by another kiss, one fiery enough to burn Sabin's mansion to the ground.

A soft chuckle bubbled from Dante's chest as he raised his head to peer into Erica's wide blue eyes. "Did you call to me in your dreams? Was it my name you murmured, or are my ears playing tricks on me?"

"How did you—"

Dante clamped a hand over her mouth before she awakened the guard who dozed outside her door.

"The question is not how, but why," he whispered back to her. "And the answer . . ." His face inched steadily closer as he drew his hand away from her mouth. "For this . . ."

The masculine hardness of his body molded itself to the feminine softness of hers, his lips telling her what he need not say. He had come to fulfill the dream that had haunted both of them during the days they had been apart.

Erica welcomed him with open arms, reveling in the feel of his virile body. Theirs was a wild coming together. Breathless impatience seized them, and they could not seem to get close enough to the tormenting flames that seared them. As Dante braced himself above her, fighting to keep from being too quickly consumed by his passion, Erica lifted her eyes to his. The scant moonlight framed his darkly handsome features and in his face she saw a hunger that mirrored her own needs.

"Dante . . ." Again his name formed on her lips, and

this time it brought him to her, satisfying the maddening craving that their bold caresses had stirred.

The muscles of his arms bulged as he settled between her thighs, raw instinct driving him to her yet tenderness holding him back. The way she gazed up at him bewitched him, called upon his gentler nature which he rarely displayed. But Erica moved him as no other woman did. He had never been able to receive her passion without giving something of himself. She was a rare, beautiful treasure, one to be adored and cherished. Lost to the warmth of that thought, his fingers delved into her silky hair while he drank the intoxicating sweetness of her mouth. With heart-stopping tenderness he kissed her for what seemed forever, languidly tasting her, drowning in the flood of pleasure he felt at forging his body to hers. The message he conveyed became living fire within Erica, its flames blossoming as he caressed her, and time stood still as they moved together, giving and taking, sharing the splendorous moment.

Erica had no time to analyze the reason for his strange tenderness. Her growing hunger for him scattered thought. And ever so slowly the rhythm of his lovemaking brought her from the dark abyss of rapture to the soaring clouds of ecstasy. She clung fiercely to Dante as he plunged deeply within her, striving for unattainable depths of intimacy.

And then they came, the wild, breathless moments when instinct and emotion converged. Her senses were alive with the manly scent and feel of him, her body arched to meet his, and his thrusts drove her to the quintessence of pleasure. Still the sensations continued to build, each more intense than the one before, blossoming into unique lovemaking.

Then the world split asunder, bringing sweet, satisfied release and showering Erica with contentment. Time and space ceased to exist, and they were one, suspended in the quiet universe that only lovers share.

Dante drew a ragged breath and waited several moments before he could muster the will or energy to move. Finally, he eased away and nestled against Erica's exquisite body, knowing danger hovered outside the door, but unable to bring himself to flee. If Sabin barged in on them, Dante knew he would, at least, die a contented man. Sabin would be enraged if he knew that his nephew had made love to the woman he coveted—in his own home, on the eve of his wedding. The irony of that situation brought a sly smile to Dante's lips as he bent to press one last kiss to Erica's soft mouth.

"Fetch your clothes, *chérie*. We have a long night ahead of us," he rasped as he groped for his discarded garments.

Erica did not ask about their destination. To be anywhere other than Sabin's mansion would be a blessing. Silently, she moved across the room to randomly select the gowns for her journey; then she followed Dante to the window he had pried open to gain entry.

Like a cat prowling on a ledge, Dante knelt on the window sill and then stretched out to grasp the tree limb that was just beyond his grasp. When he had scrambled into the overhanging branch, he motioned for Erica to toss him her pouch and then reach for the limb.

Her face paled as she leaned over the window sill and looked down at the ground. She swallowed hard and then raised her gaze to Dante, perched in the tree. "I can't make it," she said shakily, her heart fluttering against her ribs.

Dante sank back on his haunches and heaved an exasperated sigh. "It is time you overcame your fear of heights," he muttered. "There is no other way to escape."

Erica was well aware of that, but the knowledge didn't help her overcome her anxiety. Gritting her teeth, she slowly extended one hand, then retracted it and desperately grasped the frame of the window, certain that at any moment she would teeter off balance and plunge to her death.

"Hurry up," Dante whispered impatiently. He glanced around him, wondering if their delay would bring Sabin and his guards out of the woodwork.

"I wish you had to wrestle with these fears," Erica choked out. "Then you would know how I feel."

"Believe me, I *do* know." Dante sniffed. "I suffer from the unnerving fear of capture. And I assure you, my fear is far worse than a dread of sharing a lofty nest with sparrows or of peering down at the ground below. Now move!"

Erica tried to obey, but she was frozen to the spot. She reminded herself that she had shinnied down the supporting beam of her father's home to escape Sabin. Surely she could reach out to grasp that tree limb. With that encouraging thought planted in her mind, she pried one hand loose and reached toward Dante, but the overwhelming feeling that she was about to fall paralyzed her, and she plastered herself back against the side of the house.

Growling, Dante sought a better position in the tree and extended his hand. "Damnation, woman, you have braved far worse than this. Give me your hand."

She would have been more than happy to do just that,

314

but there was no way to offer him her hand without forcing the rest of her body to go along with it. And her fear simply wouldn't permit that.

Dante finally lost his patience. Before Erica could protest, he grasped the limb above him and swung out to hook his free arm around Erica's waist, forcing her to hang on to him or plummet to the ground below. Muffling her gasp against his shoulder, Erica clung to him like a choking vine as they sailed through the air. When Dante found solid footing, Erica let out a shuddering breath upon realizing she was still alive.

"Put your foot here." Dante indicated the branch beneath. He waited a moment for Erica to come to her senses and proceed down the tree, but she didn't move. She clung to him, afraid to let go. Dante rolled his eyes heavenward, as if summoning patience. "Erica, listen to me. Keep your eyes focused above you and feel your way down to the limb. I'll be right behind you."

Erica drew in a breath and gradually eased her grip on Dante's neck. Mustering her determination, she lifted her gaze to the window through which she had escaped; then she cautiously stretched out her leg to locate the branch Dante had indicated. Once they had weaved their way through a maze of limbs to reach the fork of the tree, Dante hopped to the ground and lifted outstretched arms, coaxing Erica to come to him.

Carefully, she squatted down, shut her eyes, and took the plunge. Relief washed over her when she found herself in the tight circle of Dante's arms. But as he set her on her feet, she clutched at him, unable to steady her wobbly legs.

Before she could get her bearings or stop her heart from thundering, Dante grasped her hand and aimed her toward the mounts tethered a good distance away from the mansion.

Only then did Erica break her silence. "Where are we going?"

"On a long trip, somewhere far away from Sabin," he answered evasively. "I need you with me, Erica. Without your help, we will be stranded in New Orleans."

When Dante scooped her up and set her atop the steed, Erica frowned suspiciously. Her help? Now what was he planning? Was she about to become bait for another scheme? The last one had proved disastrous. Damnation, why couldn't he have said he needed her and have left it at that? But no, he'd implied that she was merely a tool. Well, she wanted no part of whatever hare-brained scheme he had in mind. She wouldn't continue to follow this vagabond from one corner of the earth to another.

"I am not going with you," she informed him.

Dante stared incredulously at her. "You prefer to stay with my uncle?"

"Of course not." What an idiotic question, she thought sourly. "But I do not intend to strike off with you either. You have caused me enough trouble. Now that Sabin has had the marriage annulled, I can collect my trust fund and go my own way."

Dante swung onto his mount and then grasped the reins of Erica's steed, forcing her to follow behind him. "A ship awaits us, one I cannot board without your assistance and you *will* give it," he gritted out. "There is more than one way to skin a snake, and I haven't finished with Sabin yet. You are going to help me defeat him at his own game, once and for all."

"Dammit, haven't you learned your lesson!" Erica exclaimed. "Sabin calculates your moves. Don't you know he sabotaged your ship? You are lucky to have survived the explosion."

"I am aware of that." Dante's emerald eyes darkened at the reminder. "But I intend to give Sabin a taste of his own medicine. Nothing could make me happier than outfoxing a fox."

Erica flung Dante a withering glance. The man was a glutton for punishment. Either that or he was so incredibly stubborn he didn't know when he was whipped. Erica could not share his confidence, especially since he had no basis on which to conclude that Sabin Keary could be beaten. And yet . . . The semblance of a smile caught one corner of her mouth. How could she help but admire his determination. A lesser man would give up, but not Dante. He acknowledged no man as master. That was what had drawn her to him, even on that first night, the aura about him—the compelling quality that burned in his eyes, the window to his soul. He was noble and proud. He radiated strength and self-reliance. He was a champion—her champion. Dante rose to meet every challenge. While her father buckled beneath Sabin's iron will, Dante defied him, using his wits, daring to clash as often as necessary to defeat his wicked uncle.

If only Dante could see me as something more than a device, she mused whimsically. But this time I will fight beside him, she vowed. If he needs me it is better to be with him than not to have him at all. Erica slumped back in the saddle as Dante led her toward the docks, aware that again she was saying one thing and doing another. First she'd informed Dante that she wanted to go her own way, but the moment he'd protested and dragged her along with him, she had reversed her decision. God, she must be stark raving mad! She had fallen hopelessly in love with a man who only used her to suit his purposes. She had become indecisive and—

Her contemplation was interrupted when Dante leaped to the ground and then hauled her from the saddle, holding her to him longer than necessary.

A beguiling smile drifted across his sensuous lips as his touch became a wayward caress. "I missed you, nymph," he murmured before his mouth slanted across hers.

Stripping her of what remained of her self-control, Erica dissolved into a pool of desire as the feel of Dante's body stirred her compelling passion.

Suddenly, he released her, grabbed her hand, and, drawing her along, strode swiftly off. Dazed, Erica trailed after him, frowning bemusedly when Reade Asher emerged from the shadows with a menagerie of supplies and odd-looking equipment draped around him.

"Dante, what are you planning?" Erica demanded.

"I'll explain later," he assured her, turning his attention to Reade. "Where is the rope?"

Reade fished into a sack to retrieve the rope and then handed it to Dante, who grabbed Erica. When he bound her hands and feet, her jaw dropped. She was so dumbfounded that she couldn't speak. Dante was behaving like a maniac. Was this the man she thought she loved? Why had he snatched her from Sabin to hold her hostage?

"Release me this instant!" she snapped when she finally located her tongue.

In response to her harsh command Dante chuckled devilishly. When she attempted to scream, he stuffed a gag in her mouth, hoisted her in his arms, and strode toward the gangplank of the schooner. Her struggles were futile.

"Patience, *chérie*. You will be free soon enough," he

assured her as he tossed her to Reade and then leaped onto the ship to reclaim the squirming bundle that would have pounded him flat had her arms been free.

Jamie Bennet jumped as if he'd been stung when the door of the captain's cabin crashed against the wall. He twisted around in his chair to see his sister in a stranger's arms and a crusty-looking sailor poised beside them. Two pistols were aimed at his chest and one was pointed at a startled Captain Marshall who was choking on his brandy.

"Erica?" Jamie squeaked, his eyes bulging as he surveyed his uninvited guests and his fuming sister. "Are you all right?"

"She will be if you and the good captain do exactly as I command," Dante assured them in a deadly tone. "Otherwise, your lovely sister will become the sharks' next meal."

His remark made Erica retract everything nice she had ever said about him. The beast! She had expected to be used as bait for another of his crazed schemes, but for sharks?

"What is it you want from me?" Jamie cautiously rose from his chair and darted a sidelong glance at Captain Marshall, warning him not to provoke the darkly clad man who held his sister hostage.

"The use of your ship," Dante informed him. "You and the captain will go ashore with a message for Sabin Keary."

The color seeped from Jamie's young features. "And what about my sister?"

"She will remain my hostage until we return to port."

"You can't . . ."

When Jamie took a step forward, Dante cocked his pistol and grinned satanically, silently declaring that he was in a position to do whatever he damned well pleased. "Ah, but I can, you see," he assured Jamie, his tone dangerously calm and confident. He gestured toward the door; then he roughly set Erica on her feet, forcing her to prop herself against him to maintain her balance. "If you hope to see your sister again, you and the captain will walk down the gangplank and deliver my message."

Jamie's worried gaze focused on Erica's flushed face before drifting to Dante's bearded features. The man looked like a pirate who had just blown in from the high seas. His green eyes danced devilishly, his smile was dangerously challenging.

"Make your decision, Bennet," Dante ordered brusquely. "Does she live or die?"

Jamie felt he had no choice but to comply. His shoulders slumped as he nodded slightly. "I will take your message to Sabin." His pale blue eyes anchored on Dante. "But if any harm comes to Erica, there is no place where you can hide from me. I will hunt you down like the ruthless devil you are."

Dante silently admired Jamie's strength, something he and his sister possessed in abundance but their father sorely lacked. "We are wasting precious time, Bennet." Dante gestured toward the door and then tossed the note at Jamie's feet. "Be gone. I am not a patient man."

After flashing Dante a contemptuous glare, Jamie snatched up the note and stalked out of the cabin. When the two men had moved across the deck, Dante tossed Erica on the cot and then followed them, watching them march down the gangway and hop onto the dock. Dante and Reade promptly drew in the gangplank, then chuckled as Erica's brother glared furiously at them.

Jamie growled under his breath. He was feeling utterly helpless. He was not looking forward to a confrontation with Sabin or his father, nor did he approve of Erica being dragged off by a pirate.

Captain Marshall heaved a frustrated sigh. "I've had ships blown out from under me and one very nearly capsized in a storm, but I've never had one stolen right out from under my nose."

"The man has incredible nerve." Jamie scowled. "When Sabin learns that someone has stolen his would-be wife and his schooner, he will be in a rage."

Jamie wheeled around to storm across the abandoned wharf, clenching the message in his fist. While he worried about Erica's welfare, he wondered how he was going to explain the incident to Sabin. Damn, it wasn't going to be easy. The man was notorious for his fiery temper.

Although Jamie had no aversion to seeing Erica elude Sabin once again, he was apprehensive about her sailing off with a bearded pirate who had threatened to feed her to the sharks. Jamie had spent the better part of the evening trying to devise a way to prevent the upcoming wedding of his sister and Sabin. When he had approached his father about the matter, however, he'd been told to mind his own business. Avery had appeared content to let the marriage take place, but Jamie wasn't. He had even considered hiring roustabouts to aid him in storming Sabin's mansion and freeing Erica. A muddled frown suddenly creased his brow as he wondered how the pirate had managed to abduct his sister when Sabin had posted guards at her door. Well, however he had managed the feat, Erica was his hostage, and Jamie could be of no help to his sister.

Heaving an exasperated sigh, Jamie aimed himself toward Sabin's dwelling, thankful Erica had escaped her unwanted fiancé but concerned about her immediate future, and dreading his own encounter with that dragon, Sabin Keary.

Chapter 18

"What!" Sabin roared like an angry lion and then bolted to his feet. His dark eyes smoldered as he pinned Jamie and the captain to the wall with his fierce glare. "You mean to tell me that someone waltzed aboard *my* ship, caught you unaware, and sailed away with *my* cargo?"

"We had little choice, he—"

Jamie's attempt to explain was cut off by Sabin's derisive snort.

"Only a pair of fools would allow such a preposterous thing to happen."

Jamie gritted his teeth, bracing himself for another barrage of insults as Sabin stalked up in front of him. "He left you a message."

Sabin snatched the note from his hands, unfolded it, and glared furiously at the parchment.

Uncle,

Since you destroyed my steamship, I have decided to confiscate your schooner and its cargo.

It seems only fair, does it not? In compensation for my losses of time and money, I have taken your fiancée with me. My condolences, dear uncle. You can imagine how grieved I am that your wedding day will not be at all what you anticipated.

Dante

"Dante?" Sabin's breath came out in a shocked gasp. "But this is impossible! Erica is locked in her room upstairs."

"Not unless she has devised a way to be in two places at once," Jamie declared caustically. "I just saw her, bound and gagged, on your schooner."

Sabin wheeled around and charged toward the steps, taking them two at a time in his haste to reach Erica's door. Another furious growl burst from his lips when he lit the lantern and found an empty bed. How had Dante taken her from the house? It seemed that his nephew was more resourceful than Sabin had thought. But Dante would not make him the laughingstock of New Orleans. He would concoct some story about Erica being taken ill, say she had been sent away until she recovered. How else could he explain her disappearance? Dante would pay dearly for this, Sabin vowed as he crushed the note and then proceeded to rip it to shreds.

Erica was smoldering as she waited for Dante to return to the captain's cabin and untie her. The nerve of the man! How dare he tie her up and then abandon her, issue threats to her own brother, and set sail in the middle of the night without informing her of their destination!

While Erica was berating his behavior, Dante returned to the cabin, so absorbed in thought that he forgot about her until she pounded her feet against the wall to gain his attention.

Dante wheeled around to find Erica glaring furiously at him. His amused gaze focused on her heaving breasts, and his preoccupation evaporated. She was magnificent when she was angry, her flawless features alive with indignation, her blue eyes snapping, her dark hair glowing in the dim lantern light. He swaggered toward her, then knelt to untie her feet, leaving the gag until last for he knew he would be bombarded with a tidal wave of insults.

The moment her hands were free, Erica yanked the gag from her mouth, and words erupted from her lips. "Why did you scare my brother like that? And what are you planning? Where the devil are we going?"

His shoulders lifted in a shrug as he smoothed the agitated frown from her face. "Which question shall I answer first?"

"I demand to know what idiotic scheme you have embroiled me in this time? Dammit, Dante—"

Reade's intrusion quickly silenced her rapid-fire questions. "I informed the crew that they was under new leadership and that Erica was replacin' her brother on this voyage. They got no complaints so long as they get paid." He wandered over to pour himself a drink of brandy and then planted himself in the chair, even though he knew he was interrupting. "Tom Hyatt and Owen Grant are among the crew. They put in a few good words for you, and the rest of the men didn't bother to question why they'll be sailin' under a new captain."

Dante acknowledged the comments with a slight nod of

325

his head, but his eyes were still fixed on Erica, watching the enthralling way the golden light of the lantern was absorbed by the waterfall of dark hair that spilled over her shoulders. As her full lips parted and her long lashes swept up to meet his gaze, he was mesmerized. During the nights he had spent without her, she had preyed heavily on his mind, and Dante had come to the painful conclusion that one week away from this seductive minx was seven days of pure hell. Unable to get her out of his system, he had hungered for her. She was his addiction, a craving that granted him no peace. The sweet, feminine scent of her had become a part of him, and the memory of her touch sent his senses reeling.

"Would you leave us alone, Reade? Erica and I have several pressing matters to discuss."

A sly smile hovered on Reade's lips as he watched Dante ogle Erica. If they did get around to a verbal discussion, Reade would be surprised. What Dante had on his mind wasn't conversation.

"Whatever you say. Yer the cap'n." He snickered as he grabbed the bottle of brandy and swaggered toward the door. "I won't be disturbin' you the rest of the night."

As soon as the door eased closed behind him, Erica glared at Dante. "I demand some answers. I am not a witless twit to be used and manipulated when it suits you. Now what the hell is going on?"

One dark eyebrow arched as he surveyed her indignant features. "My dear Erica, I have always given you credit for being an intelligent young woman, but I must admit I am shocked by your language," he taunted. "You have been cursing quite a bit since you nested in Sabin's tree."

Erica vaulted to her feet to prowl about the cabin like a nervous, caged cat. "Then you will be further shocked to learn that I often sneaked to the docks as a child and that my vocabulary brims with the salty language of sailors and roustabouts. If you do not explain what is going on you may hear the full extent of my repertoire." Erica's voice rose until she was almost screaming.

Dante chuckled at her explosive temper. She certainly had the body and face of an angel, but when the devil had dished out fiery temperaments, this little wildcat had gotten a second helping. It was little wonder her father had not had control of her. It would take a strong-willed and determined man to keep this spitfire towing the line. They would often clash, but it would be a challenge to match wits with a woman like Erica. Perhaps that is one of the reasons why I'm so attracted to this raven-haired hellcat, Dante mused as his eyes mapped the enticing curves and swells of her shapely figure. Not only is she a distracting beauty, but she is clever, knowledgeable, and delightfully entertaining. Lord, he even enjoyed arguing with her. He had never been able to say that about any other woman. Most of them resorted to whining and bursting into tears to sway him, but never once had Erica succumbed to tears, even when she had every reason to cry. She stood firm in battle, and she could verbally lynch him when she felt she had just cause. And Dante could tell by her rigid stance and that fiery look in her eyes that she was itching to fling a round of barbs at him. Although he would have preferred to by-pass a trenchant argument and appease his ravenous desire for her, he could tell that he was about to be served a good piece of her mind. Not that he could blame her for being annoyed. She had been left in the dark about so many things these past few weeks. Perhaps it was time she learned the whole truth. After all, she couldn't race back to New Orleans to confront Sabin or her father when she was adrift in the Gulf of Mexico.

"I think perhaps a drink is in order," he announced as he strode over to fetch two glasses.

As he rummaged through the cabinet to find Captain Marshall's stock of liquor, Erica rolled her eyes toward the ceiling, summoning what was left of her dwindling patience. She didn't want a drink. She wanted answers! Her temper snapped, and she was seized by the uncontrollable urge to throw something. Clutching a nearby chair, she hurled it at Dante.

He yelped as the unwieldy missile jabbed him in the back and then crashed to the floor, causing him to spill wine down the front of his breeches. "Confound it, woman, do not demolish our cabin," he growled. "Sit down at the table and join me in a drink. It might douse your flaming temper."

"You are the cause of my sour disposition," Erica flared. "I don't want wine. I want an explanation. You have toyed with me long enough, and I will have no more of it!"

Relying upon his most disarming smile, Dante pulled out the chair beside him and motioned for Erica to avail herself of it. "I think it would be easier to digest what I have to say if you chase it with wine," he advised.

Erica threw him a skeptical glance and then marched to her chair. After taking a sip of wine she started to fire a question at him, but the bite of the wine had her choking. Chuckling at the stunned expression on her flushed face, Dante reached around to whack her between the shoulder blades.

"I doubt that the good captain allowed the wine to age a week, but after a few more sips you will not notice the difference." He snickered and then eased back to let the wine trickle down his throat.

Erica gasped for breath as she stared incredulously at Dante who seemed to be suffering no ill effects after swallowing the liquor. "How can you do that without choking? It is like swallowing fire."

His shoulders lifted and then dropped as he took up the bottle to refill both glasses. "I have acquired a lead-lined stomach," he replied, raising her glass to her lips. "Drink up. The second sip will not be as distasteful as the first."

Erica complied, and was surprised to find that he was correct. Her tongue and throat had been numbed by the first fiery gulp.

The amusement in Dante's eyes mellowed as he peered into her bewitching face. "What I have to tell you is the truth, Erica. You may not like what you hear, but you demand some answers and tonight you will have them. Your father will condemn me for divulging his secret, but you are not a child and I prefer that you know the truth. I will not keep it from you."

Erica braced herself for the worst, although she could not fathom what had reduced her father to a spineless excuse for a man. When Dante filled her glass to the brim, she took another sip and found the taste of the wine even more tolerable.

"Three years ago, my mother was invited to stay at her brother's plantation. My father detested Sabin and ordered my mother not to associate with her brother, but she traveled to New Orleans despite his objections, since she didn't have the heart to disown the man who was responsible for raising her. She claimed there was some good in Sabin, and she was determined to make amends for the years he and my father had been at odds. My

329

parents had a bitter argument, after which Maggie, my mother, journeyed to Sabin's plantation, where she remained for almost two months. She tried to persuade him to forget his grudge against my father."

Dante sighed as he glanced back through the window of time, wondering what had become of his mother after the incident. "Sabin is my mother's older brother. He idolized Maggie and openly claimed that Dominique, my father, was not good enough for her. Sabin tried in every way to split them apart, but my mother had taken the wedding vows and had devoted her life to my father." Dante smiled ruefully as he watched Erica down another drink and then peer at him with wide eyes. "I cannot say that they shared a great love, but they were content with each other," he murmured. "While my mother was at the plantation, Sabin saw to it that she kept company with a prominent gentleman from New Orleans. He threw that man and my mother together as often as possible, hoping that his matchmaking would sever my mother's allegiance to my father." Dante's pained gaze dropped to study the contents of his glass. "Sabin's scheme proved effective. My mother was drawn to the man Sabin had imported to keep her company. But Sabin was not content to leave it at that. He sent word to my father that . . ." His voice cracked, and it took a moment for him to get a grip on himself. "Sabin informed my father that his wife was having an affair with another man, one who was far more suitable for her. When Dominique arrived to deny the slanderous remarks and to retrieve his wife, Sabin goaded him into a duel."

Erica steadily sipped her wine, experiencing the dreadful feeling that the explanation would get worse before it came to an end.

"My father was furious. Sabin had counted on that," Dante muttered bitterly. "When Sabin arranged the duel, he called upon my mother's companion to serve as the witness. The man was trapped for Sabin swore he would reveal all the sordid details of the affair if he dared to speak out." The muscles of Dante's jaw twitched as he clasped his hand around his glass, took a sip, and then continued. "I have no proof that Sabin relied upon a hairpin trigger or that he furnished my father with a pistol that misfired, but I know Sabin well enough to realize that he never accepts a challenge unless he has an ace up his sleeve."

The color trickled from Erica's cheeks as she watched Dante fight to control his resentment. "And the other man? He was a witness to what you deem a murder?"

Dante nodded grimly. "Both he and my mother were there. Mother was destroyed by the incident. She left that day, never to show her face again. But her lover went about his business, shamefaced, living in fear that Sabin would expose the truth to his family, that others would lose respect for him if the incident were revealed, and that he would forfeit all he had worked to acquire if he didn't allow Sabin to manipulate him." He eased back in his chair to stare at the far wall. "I think Sabin must have intended to match Mother and her lover, but she fled. Sabin's conniving only hurt my mother. He tampered with her life, just as he has interfered with everyone else's."

Erica's shoulders slumped as she peered at Dante, then downed another gulp of liquor. "Do you suppose she actually fell in love with this man? Could you forgive her if she had?" she asked, her words somewhat slurred.

A rueful smile softened Dante's lips as he noted the

mellow expression on Erica's face. "When my father died, I blamed her for allowing this to happen. I loved and admired my father, but I knew their marriage began as a contractual agreement to satisfy both families. My mother was a young bride who was given little choice in the matter. She did not attempt to escape as you did, nor did she take a hand in her destiny." Dante braced his forearms on the edge of the table, and he peered solemnly into Erica's glassy gaze. "My bitterness has faded. I no longer condemn her for what happened, especially when I have seen firsthand how treacherous Sabin truly is. But because of the incident I was leery of women. I was determined not to devote myself to one unless I was certain that she would be faithful to me. I had to know that I was loved as deeply as I loved before I would ask a woman to remain at my side for a lifetime."

It was not difficult for Erica to understand why Dante was so cynical about love. He had cared deeply for his father and mother, and because of the incident he'd described he was cautious in his relationships with women, avoiding entangling bonds. Yet, Erica sensed there was more to be said, something Dante had tactfully avoided blurting out. She was too astute, even when she'd had a bit too much wine, to miss the underlying message.

"And do you despise my father because of his involvement?" she queried softly.

Dante's sooty lashes fluttered up, his expression somber. "I cannot respect him for allowing Sabin to hold this incident over him, for not speaking out against a cruel injustice. My family was torn apart yet Avery kept his silence, catering to Sabin for fear of losing his wealth when he has already sacrificed his pride. If a man forsakes his self-esteem he can be no more than half a man."

While Dante was condemning Avery's actions, or lack of them, Erica was asking herself *why* Avery had cowered away from the truth. Had he done it only to save his children from shame and disillusionment? His declining courage had caused Erica a good deal of heartache and inconvenience, but she didn't think her father was so vain and selfish that he'd willingly sacrifice his own daughter's soul to keep the truth buried.

"And what of you, Erica?" Dante asked. "You know your father has gone to great lengths not to allow this story to leak out. It is obvious that he would not tell you of his love affair. Can you forgive him for serving you up as the devil's bride?"

Erica chewed thoughtfully on her bottom lip, but she could not quite sort out her emotions. The wine had mellowed her, and she wasn't certain what she really thought.

"I believe your mother and my father are to be pitied," she murmured, her voice showing the effects of her drinking. "Yet I cannot condone what they did. Too many innocent people have been hurt, and Sabin has been allowed to manipulate too many lives. Because of their weakness for each other you mistrust love and I have been hastily wed, kidnapped, and my marriage annulled." Erica gestured at the cabin. "Now I am drifting on a ship that has no destination, closeted with a man who is my father's lover's son, embroiled in some secretive scheme . . ." Erica breathed out an exasperated sigh and then attempted to refocus on Dante's face, but it was becoming cloudier, as were her thoughts. "A month ago I thought I was in full command of my life but now I am a pawn. I want control of my future," she declared, "but am I allowed that privilege? No."

Dante reached across the table to take her small hand in his. He was strangely touched by the vulnerability he saw in her eyes. Erica seldom let her guard down. She was a willful woman who strongly objected to being manipulated, yet he had subjected her to that humiliation time and time again. Suddenly, Dante felt as tall as his glass of wine. Perhaps she was right. He was no better than Sabin.

"Would it help if I say I'm sorry for causing you so much distress?" he rasped as his touch became a lingering caress.

Erica pulled her hand away and then took a large swallow of wine. As her face puckered into an exaggerated pout, Dante coughed to disguise his amusement.

"No, it wouldn't," she insisted sluggishly. "You have been an inconsiderate scoundrel and you damned well know it." She hiccuped and then plowed on since the words seemed inclined to tumble off her loose tongue. "You pawned me off on all the vagrants on the steamship and then you wed me, letting me think you were doing me a favor when you were only plotting to get back at Sabin."

Although Dante was partly guilty as charged, he was determined to voice a few words in his defense. "But when I proposed you agreed," he countered. "And I would have allowed you to go your own way if Sabin had not sabotaged my steamboat and caused me to lose my cargo."

Erica took another swallow of wine and then pointed an accusing finger toward Dante's face. She was having trouble seeing it clearly. She had never partaken of so much heady brew before because it was impossible to keep a clear head when one was up to one's eyelids in wine.

"Admit it. You intended to use me for bait," she said accusingly, attempting to skew her face into a condemning frown.

Dante choked back a laugh when Erica weaved in her chair, her hair toppling over one shoulder and her frown drooping to the left side of her face as if it might slide off at any moment. "Would you prefer to postpone this argument until morning? I think you may have had too much wine."

"That's your fault too." Erica sniffed and then lifted the glass to her lips. "I didn't want it in the first place."

The little minx is intoxicated, Dante decided as he watched Erica's sylphlike movements become clumsy and disoriented.

"You are absolutely right. I have been a beast where you are concerned," he confessed, his eyes glistening with amusement.

Erica nodded affirmatively, but the gesture caused her chin to slip from her hand and she teetered precariously on the edge of her seat. A surprised yelp burst from her as she found the floor coming toward her with incredible speed. Then she was hoisted to her feet and steadied in Dante's arms. Had she been in full command of her senses, she would have been blushing profusely, but she wasn't and she didn't.

"We had better put you to bed." Dante chuckled as his deft fingers loosened the stays of her gown.

The feel of his hands on her bare flesh was arousing, and Erica snuggled against him, placing her head on his chest.

"But you still have not told me where we are going and

335

why." She sighed and her eyelids drooped, but she struggled to remain alert.

"We are sailing to the West Indies to deliver the cotton and then we will set out for Central America."

"That's nice," Erica murmured as she wrapped her arms about his shaking shoulders. She did not fully grasp the import of his words.

Dante shook his head in amusement. He knew Erica would not have been using him for her pillow if she had not drunk so much wine. But he had wanted the liquor to reduce the sting of learning of her father's involvement and of their destination. His plan had worked . . . all too well. Now he had an intoxicated beauty on his hands, and if he took advantage of her in this condition, Erica would be furious with him. They had been in the middle of an argument before he had coaxed her into drinking some wine, but now she was soft and pliant in his arms. He found his head moving deliberately toward hers, his lips tenderly molding themselves to the sensuous curve of her mouth. As her defenseless body melted against him, Dante groaned at the sweet, torturous strain of having her so close and yet so very far away.

Erica tilted her head back when his lips drew away from hers, and a raven cascade of curls tumbled over his arm. "I have always been intrigued by those green eyes and that enchanting smile that touches your every feature," she rasped indistinctly. "You are very handsome, Dante." A lopsided smile twisted one corner of her mouth as she lifted heavily lidded eyes to his. "And I wasn't sorry I married you, not really." The wine had become a truth serum, and her tongue was outdistancing her brain. Erica could not hold back the words that were effortlessly pouring forth. "Although you are a libertine who probably has a long list of conquered hearts to your credit, you are the only man I have ever allowed to touch me."

Dante could not suppress the grin that curved his lips. Erica was like a rag doll in his arms, and she was expressing thoughts she had never dared to voice. Although he should have stopped her from rambling, his curiosity was piqued. He had always wondered what went on in that complicated mind of hers, and this was the perfect opportunity to find out.

"I admire your discretion, *chérie*," he chortled softly.

"I wasn't quite certain why I granted you privileges in the beginning," she mused aloud, her relaxed features attempting to form a thoughtful frown. "But now I know the reason I was drawn to you. It was this magnificent body of yours." She giggled impishly.

"I'm happy you approve of it," Dante growled seductively.

"Mmmmm . . . very much so," she purred as her dainty finger traced the fullness of his lips and then trailed over his cheekbones, his features softening beneath her touch. "And when your ship was set afire, my heart went out to you. I wanted to strangle Sabin and would have if . . ." Erica hiccuped and then smiled sheepishly. "S'cuse me. But Sabin's ruffians pulled me off of him. He'd hired Ethan and Denby to do his dirty work." Droopy eyes peered up at him, so silly and yet so serious that Dante had to struggle to keep from laughing at her. "Do you know I actually considered disposing of that devil myself?"

"No . . ." Dante feigned surprise.

Erica's positive nod was greatly exaggerated. "I did. But the brutish knave wouldn't let me near a weapon. He kept me stashed in a stateroom."

"I do appreciate the fact that you were prepared to come to my defense," Dante remarked in an amused tone as he aimed Erica toward the cot. "You are a very courageous woman."

"But you could never love someone like me," Erica declared forlornly. "I suppose I am much too independent and outspoken—even a bit rebellious at times. Oops." Erica tripped over the hem of her drooping gown as she navigated across the spinning room. "And I even enjoy an argument occasionally."

"I never would have guessed," Dante said caustically as he steered Erica ever closer to the cot.

She nodded guiltily as Dante drew off her garments; then she posed another question. "Do you find me attractive, Dante?"

He was so mesmerized by her exquisite body that it took him a moment to reply. "Very much so," he breathed raggedly.

"I thought as much." Erica sank onto the cot, stretching leisurely, oblivious to the fact that she was stark naked. "But then you would find any female attractive," she declared.

"My dear Erica, you wound me to the quick. I have always considered myself a selective man." Dante snorted indignantly, but his irritation quickly mellowed as his hungry gaze traveled over her silky flesh. "But you, *chérie*, are a rare gem." He knelt beside her, his hand following the gentle curve of her hip. "And I swear you have bewitched me. . . ."

Erica's defenses had been eroded long ago, and she immediately responded to his tantalizing caresses. They were so gentle, so deliberate, that she felt she was floating on a puffy cloud. A sigh of pleasure escaped her as her heavy eyelids drifted shut.

Dante's mouth was exploring her bare flesh, tracking a warm path over the slope of her shoulder to reclaim her lips. His eyes flew open when Erica did not respond, then he cursed under his breath. The enchanting nymph had fallen asleep in his arms. She found him attractive? Dante snorted derisively. More likely she was comfortable with him, so much so that she fell asleep when he had something far more arousing on his mind.

A frustrated groan rattled in his chest as he grabbed a quilt and covered his sleeping beauty. He had been dreaming of this night since he'd planned to kidnap her from Sabin's mansion—Erica warm and willing in his arms, enjoying and returning his caresses, taking him to ecstasy. And what had he received for all his meticulous plotting? Dante snorted disgustedly. Now he couldn't pry Erica awake with a crowbar.

He stalked over to the table, intending to drown his annoyance in drink, but it didn't help. He had visions of making wild sweet love to Erica, yet now he would have to settle for merely sleeping beside her. What I need is a cold bath, he thought sourly. Determined to ease his unappeased need, Dante marched outside to fetch some water. For an hour he soaked in it, sulking, until he had shriveled up like a prune. Finally, certain that he had gained control of his passion, he returned to the cabin to take his place beside Erica, who had not moved since Dante had tucked her into bed.

So this is to be my torment, he grumbled to himself as he sought to find a comfortable position. Having and yet having not was far worse than being stretched on the rack. *His* pain came from within. It was a maddening need that could never be drowned, no matter how cold the bath or how long it lasted.

Chapter 19

Erica acknowledged the dawn with a doleful groan. No matter how she held her head, an agonizing throbbing kept painful rhythm with her pulse. Her stomach lurched and rolled when she tried to move, and every muscle complained as she attempted to push herself into an upright position. Her bloodshot eyes circled the empty cabin and then came to rest on the drained wine bottle. Erica moaned again. The mere thought of liquor nauseated her.

As the door burst open and sunlight fell across the room, Erica fumbled to cover herself, but not before Dante grinned appreciatively at what had been exposed.

"Good morning. I have brought your breakfast."

His cheerful voice did nothing to raise her sagging spirits. She felt ghastly.

"I don't have the stomach for food," she squeaked, turning green around the gills.

Dante noisily set down the tray. As it clanked, Erica cringed.

"A bit under the weather, are we?" he teased.

Erica was in no mood for his taunts, and she flung him a disgruntled glare. "Go away and let me die in peace," she muttered, easing herself back onto the bed and dragging a pillow over her head. When Dante sank down on the mattress, Erica squirmed away, refusing to be pestered. "Just go away . . . please."

"No, now sit up here," Dante commanded. "The best cure for a hangover is food. Try this." He tugged at the pillow, pulling it away from her peaked face; then he waved a sea biscuit under her nose. "We will have you back on your feet in no time at all," he declared.

Erica doubted it, but she propped herself up on an elbow to munch on his remedy since he obviously had no intention of leaving her to her misery.

A muddled frown furrowed her brow as she tried to recall their conversation of the previous night. "Did you say we were on our way to the West Indies or did I dream that?" she questioned hoarsely.

Dante nodded affirmatively and then offered her a sip of tea. "I did. That is our destination."

"But how will that rid us of Sabin? You will be considered a pirate, and you will never be able to dock in New Orleans without fearing that Sabin will have you arrested."

A devilish smile skipped across his lips. "I intend to spring a surprise on my uncle. Even the wiliest fox can sometimes be snared in his own trap."

"That is wise advice." Erica stared pointedly at him. "You would do well to remember that."

"Truth will win out," Dante insisted confidently.

Erica silently nibbled on her meal. Then she tested her sea legs, finding them a bit wobbly after her bout with wine. If she survived the day, it would surprise her. She felt positively miserable.

"I found these for you." Dante fished some garments from a bag and then held them up for her inspection.

After surveying the garb, Erica managed an appreciative smile. "Thank you. I have nothing but silk and velvet gowns, which would be impractical for stepping over ropes and around kegs and barrels," she murmured, careful to keep her voice soft for fear of causing her throbbing head further distress.

"I doubt that the crew will complain about any garment you choose. The sight of a lovely woman, no matter what she is wearing, will draw their attention." Dante chuckled.

But when Erica had slipped into the breeches and shirt, he instantly regretted his choice of apparel. The thin shirt revealed the taut peaks of her breasts, and the tight trousers hugged her shapely hips. The crew would find it impossible to concentrate on their chores with Erica roaming the deck. He would have his hands full, keeping the men at arm's length. There simply aren't enough cold baths to go around, he thought dismally. Swallowing his apprehension, however, Dante stood aside to allow Erica to precede him through the door and up the steps to the quarter-deck. He grumbled under his breath when all work on the schooner came to a halt.

Reade Asher chortled at the challenging glare on Dante's face, but the entire crew, blinded by Erica's appearance, did not notice their scowling captain standing in her shapely shadow.

Although Reade had tried to dissuade Dante from bringing Erica along with him on this voyage, Dante had refused to listen, especially when he'd learned that Sabin was planning a hasty wedding. But Erica is goin' to cause trouble, Reade mused as he watched the men gape at her curvaceous figure, which filled out men's clothing with distracting effectiveness. Nothing could camouflage Erica's beauty because every garment she wore complimented it, from a provocative gown to a feed sack.

Erica breathed deeply and then gazed about her. Finding herself the focal point of attention, she felt a bit like a lamb amidst a pack of wolves. Usually, she would have been infuriated by such suggestive glances, but now she was inclined to use them to her advantage.

As she sashayed across the deck to join Reade at the helm, she heard Dante growling behind her.

"What are you staring at? Have you never seen a woman before? Get back to work," he barked sharply. Then he stalked up behind Erica. "What the sweet loving hell are you doing? Inviting molestation?"

Undaunted by his scolding, Erica was pleased by his possessive attitude. Perhaps he is a wee bit jealous, she thought. If other men find me attractive, he might become more interested. A quiet smile lifted her lips as she faced into the wind, marveling at the exhilarating feeling that washed over her. Not so long ago she had considered herself an island, an entity, someone who could survive alone and be content to do so. But Dante had changed all that. She found herself leaning on him, looking to him for consolation, and for passion the likes she'd never realized existed. She felt whole and alive when he was beside her. Yes, she had complained about being whisked off to the schooner, but she would be miserable without Dante. At least he'd cared enough to snatch her away from Sabin's clutches. And caring might lead to love, she thought hopefully. She would make him learn to love her, to depend on her as she depended on

343

him. She would become the smile that lingered on his lips when no one was around. She would be a warm, tender sensation that flowed through him, a memory that would never fade. Dante is worth fighting for, Erica told herself. She could no longer imagine life without him.

Slowly, she turned to face him, a mischievous grin settling on her delicate features. "I have no fear of your crew," she informed him. "You need not be so harsh with them."

Dante snorted derisively. "Couldn't you read their lurid thoughts on their faces? If you don't watch your step you'll be stewing in your own juice, witch," he warned, giving her a disgruntled glance. "You can't *strut* across the deck without expecting trouble."

Her shoulders rose in a careless shrug. "I can defend myself when there is a need, but"—her blue eyes danced with deviltry—"there may be some among the crew whom I would like to help me while away the hours aboard ship." Erica smoothed Dante's tousled hair away from his forehead. "Perhaps a woman should not condemn a man's promiscuousness, but should try some experimentation of her own. After all, how can she make comparisons without it?"

The muscles of Dante's jaw went rigid as he glared at the saucy chit facing him. "I will not have you gallivanting about this ship with my crew," he snapped gruffly.

His firm command slid off her like water from a duck's back. "If a man can frequent brothels and keep mistresses, I see no reason a woman cannot observe the same standards. I think it's time I investigated that possibility, for experience' sake, of course," she added breezily. "Since I am no longer a married woman I have the right to pick and choose as I please." Let him chew on that possibility and see how he likes it, she thought.

It was immediately obvious that Dante didn't like it. "Erica, I'm warning you. . . ."

She took in his rigid stance, silently admiring his powerful physique, intrigued by the way his beard and shaggy hair changed his appearance. He reminded her of a swashbuckling pirate, a bit rough around the edges, but very attractive in a rugged sort of way. Although she was drawn to him, she had no intention of letting him know that he aroused her.

"I never did back down from dares," she assured him as she sauntered away, bringing a halt to the workings on the ship as surely as a bolt of lightning striking the mast.

Dante scowled as his eyes followed the seductive sway of her hips. What the devil had come over the woman? The previous night she had admitted she found him desirable, yet at first light she set her sights on the entire crew! Well, if she thought for one minute that he'd allow another man to touch what belonged to him, she was sorely mistaken. The ornery witch!

Reade snickered as he stood aside, watching Dante's mood turn as black as pitch. "I told you not to cart that little hellion on this schooner. She's too much of a woman, even for you, Cap'n."

"I would appreciate it if you would keep your thoughts to yourself." Dante grunted disgustedly as he wedged himself between the helmsman and the wheel.

A taunting grin surfaced on Reade's weather-beaten features. "It might be wise to remember that a man in passion steers a mad ship, Cap'n."

Dante's angry glare nailed him to the mast. "Don't you have something better to do than spout your opinions?"

"Nope." Reade swaggered toward the steps. "Not

unless yore ex-wife would like to experiment with a man with a lot of miles on him." His eyes twinkled, curdling Dante's already sour mood. "Maybe I'll suggest the idea to her. It might be to her likin'. After all, the two of us should get to know each other, don't you think?"

"If you dare touch her you will answer to me," Dante hissed, his green eyes flaming.

"Yore oversteppin' yore bounds, Cap'n." Reade chuckled as he watched Dante silently smolder. "The choice belongs to the lady."

Dante growled under his breath. Damn the woman! Just when he thought he had her purring like a contented kitten, he awoke to find her prowling about his ship, seeking new conquests. Didn't he have enough on his mind without wondering who she was luring into the shadow of the companionway?

His knuckles turned white as he grasped the wheel in a stranglehold, wishing he could clamp his hands around Erica's lovely neck and shake some sense into her. Confound it! She was worth her weight in trouble!

For an agonizing week Dante watched Erica charm the entire crew out of their boots. Their faces lit up each time she strolled over to chat with them, inquiring about their duties, requesting instruction so she could learn about the chores on a schooner, joining in their card games to pass idle time. The men followed after her like obedient pups, toting buckets of water for her baths, serving her breakfast in bed, treating her like a queen. Dante was so frustrated he feared he would explode. He felt that if Erica planned a mutiny he would be tossed overboard when she snapped her fingers.

He had planned a romantic candlelight dinner the previous night, intending to lure her back into his bed after Reade had graciously consented to forfeit his cabin to her and bunk with the crew. But while Dante sat watching the candles melt, Reade had come to inform him that Erica had been detained by one of the crew members and that she would be unable to join him.

From that time Dante had begun to lean heavily on the brandy, locking himself in his cabin to converse with the walls when he was not on duty. Like a nightly ritual, Erica's vision came to haunt his dreams. He was a man on the rack, stretched to the limits of his patience, taunted by a pair of sparkling blue eyes and a compelling smile. He had taken so many cold baths that he felt like a pickle soaked in brine. But nothing helped ease his frustration. His craving for Erica had begun to affect his sanity, and he swore if he spent another night without her he would lose his already deteriorating mind.

Dante stalked the confines of the captain's cabin like a restless jungle cat. Although he had vowed he would not chase after Erica the way the rest of the crew had, he found his footsteps taking him through the corridor to Erica's cabin. A dim light filtered through the curtain at the window and Dante gritted his teeth, visualizing Erica with another man. Agitated, Dante charged through the door without knocking, and his glazed gaze circled the room to find Erica curled up with a book, her head propped on her hand, her ebony hair flowing about her like a lustrous black cape. She was clothed in one of Dante's shirts, which barely concealed the enticing curve of her hips.

A welcoming smile captured her lips, and the hypnotic curve of her mouth lured him closer. "Good evening,

347

Captain," she murmured as she drew her legs from beneath her and swung them over the edge of the cot.

Dante drank in the sight of satiny skin which glowed like honey in the lantern light. Then his ravenous gaze tracked upward to settle on her gaping shirt. As he watched the creamy swells of her breasts rise and fall with each breath she took, shock waves of desire shot through his body, sensitizing every nerve and muscle. Lord, he ached to touch what his eyes hungrily devoured. He was a man who had been too long on a desert, and Erica was a mirage that compelled him onward. He could not have turned and walked away if his life depended on it.

Erica rose and gracefully approached him, raking her nails over the beard that covered his tense jaw. She could feel the tautness in his powerful body, and she smiled secretly. He was very nearly at the end of his rope. He would not have come if he didn't need her the way she needed him.

And she did need him. A week of longing had built that need into one of incredible proportions. She had flirted with the crew and had allowed Dante to believe that he couldn't just snap his fingers to find her groveling at his feet. She longed for him to see her as an equal, a woman whom he could depend upon for more than appeasement of his desires. She could only hope that the days they'd spent apart had been as difficult for him as they had been for her. Would he ever realize that she wanted to be his friend and companion as well as his lover? Was she expecting too much from a man so leery of love?

Erica smiled up into his flaming green eyes and then took his hand. "I was about to bathe. Perhaps you would be gracious enough to test the water temperature for me."

Dante's body caught fire as he watched her sylphlike movements. And when she shrugged the linen shirt from her shoulders, his dream collided with reality.

"It had better be an ice cold bath," he choked out. "I don't think I can endure much more heat."

Feigning concern, Erica brushed the palm of her hand over his perspiring brow. "Have you taken ill, pirate captain? Perhaps you need a relaxing bath more than I." Delicate fingers freed the buttons of his shirt and then pushed it from his broad shoulders to silently admire the massive expanse of his chest. Then her hand wandered through the dark matting of hair that covered his ribs, tracing each one. "Shall I assist you? I have never played the handmaiden before. It might prove to be a fascinating duty."

His entire body roused to the feel of her wayward hand as it trailed over his hip and then slid over the waistband of his breeches to help him shed the last of his clothing. She was a seductress, so skillful and tempting that Dante was snagged in her enticing web. Her touch excited him, and he yearned for more of her familiar caresses. He groaned in torment as she moved closer, her satiny skin brushing lightly against his. Then his heart returned to its normal resting place, but Erica soon had it misbehaving again. He gasped for breath as the dusky pink peaks of her breasts skimmed his skin.

His eyes gazed into hers, and he glimpsed heaven in their blue horizon, a promise of relief from the maddening passion that churned through him. With a quiet smile, Erica steered him toward the tub and urged him to sink into the waiting bath. Dante swore steam rose around him as he settled into the tepid water.

Then Erica leaned across him to grasp her brother's forgotten razor, and she eased down beside Dante to shave his beard. She completed her ministrations with the greatest of care and then ran her knuckles over his jaw to inspect her work. "Now for your bath, sire," she murmured provocatively.

Dante was still suffering from a severe case of oxygen deprivation so he did not risk speaking. He merely responded. The light touch of her soapy hands was sweet torture as they glided over his shoulders and arms, stirring his passion. Then her fingertips delved lower, giving dedicated attention to every inch of his muscled flesh, and her hand gently folded around him, her bold caresses taking him to the brink of insanity and leaving him teetering dangerously on the edge.

His eyes fell to the ripe peaks of her breasts that glistened with water droplets. His hand touched what his hungry gaze beheld and then ascended to curl around her neck, pulling her closer. "Have you been practicing these same, devastating tactics on my crew?" he questioned, his voice ragged with desire.

Lips as red as cherry wine parted in a provocative smile. "I am considering opening a bathhouse when I return to New Orleans," she taunted as her hands continued to work their tantalizing magic. "It will serve weary male travelers, easing their tensions. Do you suppose men will take to the idea?"

Erica had not answered his question, but it didn't matter. Dante didn't remember asking it. Her exquisite massage dissolved all thought and he could barely recall *her* inquiry. "No doubt, it will become a booming business if you are the masseuse," he breathed hoarsely.

His compliment invited her to continue her pleasurable ministrations so Erica delighted in rediscovering his virile body by touch. Her hands scaled the taut muscles of his arms, investigated the corded tendons alóng his neck, and then leisurely slid down the sinewy slope of his shoulder. Again her exploring caresses tracked across the crisp matting of hair on his stomach, then it dropped to follow the hair-roughened planes of his legs. She was so engrossed in the feel of his masculine body that she was taken unaware when Dante hooked his arm about her, drawing her into the bath.

"Brazen wench," he growled playfully. "You know damned well what you are doing to me." His mouth slanted across hers before she could voice a retort, stripping the breath from her. "Bathhouse, indeed! I will have more than a bath before this night is out."

Erica had counted on that. She had spent too many painful nights strolling the deck with members of the crew, wishing Dante would venture from his room to voice his displeasure at seeing her in the company of those men. But he hadn't, and Erica had almost given up hope until he'd burst into her cabin with that dangerous look in his eyes, and on his face the wild, reckless expression that excited and aroused her.

Now she was in the magic circle of his arms, and she didn't care that streams of bath water were pouring over the edge of the tub onto the deck. She could do nothing but surrender to the tidal wave of emotion that flooded over her, leaving her hungry and impatient to satisfy a need that only Dante aroused.

It seemed he had suddenly sprouted an extra pair of hands. He was not missing an inch of her quivering flesh.

It did not occur to her that the water had grown cold since she was being so thoroughly heated. A wildfire raged through her veins, feeding on sensations that crackled like kindling.

"Lord, woman, what you do to me should be labeled a criminal offense," Dante muttered huskily, suddenly seized by a longing so fierce that he was almost mad with wanting of her. "And you will pay for arousing me . . . I assure you of that." His hand glided to her throat, tilting her head back so he could gaze into fathomless pools of sapphire and see her rippling desire match his own. "Did the others move you to passion?" His caress descended to enfold the full mound of her breast before his lips followed the searing path his hand branded on her quaking flesh. "Did you surrender to them without a fight? Did you lure all of them into your arms?"

Erica would have answered, but she was caught up in the sizzling emotions that shot through her like lightning, sending nerve-tingling sensations throughout her body. She couldn't breath, she couldn't think, she could only respond. She was hypnotized, bewitched, fully aroused by the feel of his male body straining toward hers.

"Answer me," Dante growled. "I must know if the others sampled your charms, if you responded to them."

Erica sputtered, attempting to inhale a breath as her fingers delved into the damp raven hair that framed his face. "Does it matter so much to you just now?" Her voice wavered with barely restrained desire. "Is the past more important than this moment, more important than what I feel for you when you hold me in your arms?"

Perhaps she is right, Dante mused. He no longer had a claim on Erica, and he had never interrogated another woman about her affairs with other men. Why should he make demands on Erica that he made on no one else? She had not asked for accounts of his previous encounters with women. But Erica is different from the rest, he reminded himself. It *does* matter. Pride would not allow him to become just another of her many lovers. He needed to be more to her. He needed to know that she felt something for him.

"I have to know where I stand with you," Dante rasped as he bent over her, sending water rushing over the edge of the tub. "It matters a great deal to me."

The smile that brimmed her lips melted his heart. It was mischievous and radiant, as were the sparkles in her eyes.

"You need not stand at all, my handsome pirate," she whispered as she curled her index finger beneath his clean-shaven chin, bringing his lips only a few breathless inches from hers. "I like you just where you are . . . and even closer would be better. . . ."

Her mouth feathered across his as her caressing hands roamed unhindered. Then her tongue traced his teeth before intruding to mate with his, even more subtly assuring Dante that, as intimately close as they were, it was not enough. As her body arched to fit itself to the hard contours of his, she breathed into him a fire that inflamed his soul. Emotions that had simmered for a tormenting week exploded within him and he was driven toward her by an instinctive need that blocked out all thought. He heard only the sound of her raspy voice, saw only her flawless face, smelled only the fresh clean scent of her.

Dante braced his arms on either side of Erica as his hips settled against hers. Then he became her possession for those moments that pursued and captured time. Their souls were forged as their bodies moved in rhythm to a melody that played only for them, and their hearts beat in harmony as they clung together in love's rapturous embrace. The fervent pitch of their passion rose toward the lofty pinnacle that, moments before, had seemed just beyond their reach, triggering ineffable sensations that spiraled higher and higher until the lovers were consumed by feelings that exceeded all other emotion, pleasures so satiating that they were held ecstatically suspended until their strength was drained. Then in timeless delight they soared beyond the horizon, reveling in rapture before drifting back to reality.

As passion ebbed, Erica felt herself descend gently into Dante's protective embrace. She grasped at the fragments of emotion that had burst and scattered about her, wishing those moments would never end. As she lay limp in Dante's arms, she became increasingly aware that they were bobbing in a bathtub built for one, and that it now held very little water.

The realization that they had made wild, sweet love in a wooden tub made her giggle. When Dante touched her she forgot where she was or what she had been doing. Her lashes swept up to see him crouched above her, his long legs entangled with hers.

"What do you find so amusing?" Dante cocked an eyebrow and then ran a tanned finger over her kiss-swollen lips. "Your moods baffle me, vixen. I am at a loss to understand you."

Erica squirmed about, seeking a more comfortable position, but there was none. "I think I shall invest in my bathhouse, but I will design a more functional tub. This one is a bit cramped to serve more than one use."

Dante laughed out loud when he spied the enchanting smile that curved the corners of her mouth upward, making her blue eyes dance mischievously. "Would you perchance need someone to assist you in testing its usefulness?"

Erica looped her arms over his shoulders and flashed him a provocative glance. "Are you acquainted with someone who might be interested in experimenting with such a new invention?"

His lips whispered over hers. "Mmmmm . . . a very close friend of mine would jump at the chance to become your subject, my lovely mermaid, so long as you don't employ several other men for experimental testing."

"He will need to supply a character reference," she murmured as she nibbled at his sensuous lips. "I am a mite particular, and I would never hire just *anyone* for the job since he and I would be working so closely together."

Laughter bubbled from his chest. "How much closer can two people get than this, *chérie?*"

Erica pressed wantonly against him, using all the techniques she had learned from her master instructor. "Shall I refresh your memory?" She purred the question.

Dante pried himself away, feigning indignation. "My memory serves me well. And do not think to take unfair advantage of me. I happen to have a ship to command, and I cannot tarry in this tub to curb your insatiable appetite. I am beginning to think no mortal man can, witch," he playfully flung at her.

"And I would not think to keep you from your appointed rounds, Captain." Her voice registered boredom, as though she could turn her emotion off as easily

355

as Dante.

Dante did a double take. He had expected her to beg him to stay. After being coaxed, he had intended to spend the night with her. Had she really tired of him that quickly? That was it? A splash in the tub and a hasty goodbye? This woman is incredibly fickle, he decided. She is more the rogue than I have ever been! Could any man tame this raven-haired tigress with laughing blue eyes and a smile that could charm a sea serpent?

Dante grabbed his breeches and pulled them on, wondering if he and Erica would be forever fighting over who was to wear them. That wouldn't surprise me, he thought sourly. "My original purpose in coming here was to inform you that we will dock in Pointe-à-Pitre, Guadeloupe in two days. I am counting upon you to stand in your brother's stead when it comes time to market the cotton and the other cargo we carry."

Erica beamed delightedly. At last she would be allowed to take part in the business dealings of the New Orleans Cotton Exchange. What her father had not permitted, Dante had. Obviously, he considered her capable of dealing with men. He *did* respect her intelligence. Erica loved him all the more for offering her a position of authority, and she would have bounded from the tub to embrace him if doing so would not have made her appear overanxious.

"I will hold out for the highest price the buyers are willing to pay," she assured him confidently.

A wry smile formed on his lips as his warm gaze wandered over her shapely contours. The buyers would say yes to any proposal this dark-haired beauty submitted, he predicted. Erica had an uncanny knack for making men forget business.

"I will count on that," he murmured as he pivoted toward the door.

"Dante?" Her soft voice halted him in his tracks, but when he glanced over his shoulder, half-hoping she would ask him to stay, Erica gestured toward the crumpled white shirt draped over the back of the chair. "You forgot something."

He snatched up the garment and then stalked out, muttering under his breath. Well, perhaps he did deserve this nonchalant treatment. He had shoved Erica from one man to another aboard the *Natchez Belle* and had then strutted about the decks with one attractive woman after another on his arm. Maybe this was Erica's way of repaying him for the way he had treated her, but dammit, he had been trying to prove a point to the willful chit. Unfortunately, she had failed to perceive it, and he was not about to spell it out for her. Erica had enough thinking to do since he had divulged her father's involvement with his mother. It was too soon to expect her to fully understand his motives, especially since he and Erica had gotten off to an awkward start.

He shook his head and then heaved a sigh as he climbed to the helm. Awkward start? The entire affair had been a tangled mess. He and Erica had come the full circle—in reverse. He had taken her to his bed, had tricked her into a marriage that had not lasted a month, and *now*, after all that had happened, he was attempting to court her. Would it have made any difference if their relationship had begun the other way around? Dante let his breath out in a rush as he lifted his face to the salty breeze and studied the stars that twinkled overhead. Somehow he doubted it. He was man enough to admit that he had met his match when Erica had stumbled into his life. But it

357

still stung his male pride to realize that Erica was as resourceful and capable as any man.

A thoughtful smile lingered on his lips, and the warm tingle Erica had hoped he would experience trickled down his spine. She had become the quiet smile when no one was around, the arousing sensation that could fire his blood on the coldest of nights. Dante would long remember barging into her cabin and discovering that bath tubs could serve dual purposes. A low rumble erupted from his chest as Erica rose before him, like a sea siren, capturing his attention and setting him adrift in a pleasurable fantasy. She had taught him things he had never known about love, things beyond his wildest imaginings. For a moment he tried to conjure up the face of a woman who could match Erica's lively spirit and entrancing beauty. But he couldn't. Erica filled his senses, and the sweet memory of the time they had spent together in a winged bathtub preyed heavily on his mind. She has really done it this time, Dante thought as he propped his arms on the railing and let his gaze drift over the silvery waves. Now he couldn't even enjoy a bath without thinking about her. Lord, the woman had touched every facet of his life, caressed every emotion. Indeed, the word "woman" evoked a vision of that feisty, sable-haired minx with eyes as blue as the sea and lips that melted like rose petals beneath his kiss.

Dante shook his head, trying to dismiss the lingering sensations and images that swarmed about him. But it was useless. Erica was holding his mind hostage, and it would take a battalion to march into her cabin and retrieve it!

Chapter 20

After checking her appearance for the third time, Erica inhaled a deep breath and then aimed herself toward the quarter-deck. All eyes were upon her as she emerged upon it, dressed in one of the stylish gowns she had brought along with her.

Reade nudged Dante, whose attention was also fixed on the goddess who gracefully floated across the deck. "She has bewitched the crew and its cap'n." He chuckled. "I used to think yore first love was the sea, but it seems this saucy wench has snared yore heart."

"And *you* are immune to the lady's charms?" Dante quipped sarcastically, dragging his eyes off Erica to focus them on his first mate. "I have seen you vying for her attention and for whatever affection she might offer. You have been her constant shadow since I carted her aboard. She has but to snap her fingers and you are at her heels, inquiring as to how high she would like to see you jump."

Reade shrugged off the jibe. "I won't deny it. I only find it amusin' that a mere wisp of a woman could have so much influence over men."

"Did it occur to you that the lady might have more intelligence than all of us put together?" Dante grumbled, his tone registering an undertone of bitterness. "She knows exactly how to handle this motley crew and how to keep them eating out of the palm of her hand."

As Reade himself eased back against the railing, his appreciative gaze took in Erica's physical attributes. And she has plenty of them, he thought to himself. "But that ain't what interests me most," he mused aloud. "Who can think about brains when yore distracted by such beauty?"

"I rest my case." Dante smirked. "While you are ogling Erica, lost to your lusty thoughts, she is busily devising ways to manipulate you. Have a care, Reade." He glanced meaningfully at his distracted first mate. "It would never do to lose your heart at your age."

"My age?" Reade crowed like an indignant rooster. "I ain't too old to fall in love."

"Obviously not." Dante chortled as he strolled away leaving Reade to contemplate his parting remark. "It seems to me, you just have. You have done nothing but shower Erica with compliments these past weeks."

Dante set aside banter and offered Erica his arm, his gaze focused on the two gentlemen who waited on the wharf of Pointe-à-Pitre, Guadeloupe. "I am counting on you, Erica," he murmured as he assisted her onto the gangplank.

Erica sorted through her repertoire of charming smiles and then displayed one of highest quality as she approached the two men awaiting them. A wry grin slid across Dante's lips as he watched her draw both men into her spell and then converse with them in fluent French.

On numerous occasions he had stood back to watch Erica weave her web around male companions, and on occasion he had been on the receiving end of it. Nonetheless, it still baffled him that he was stung by a twinge of jealousy when other men blatantly admired Erica.

When the two men started to lead her away, Dante frowned skeptically, but Erica quickly assured him that she was in capable hands. Actually, *that* was what worried him. The young Frenchman couldn't possibly have stood any closer to Erica. Charles Cadeau was suave and debonair, and Dante found himself mimicking the man's mannerisms as he watched the coach rumble along the wharf of Pointe-à-Pitre.

Heaving a disgusted sigh, he spun around to meet Reade's goading smile as he leaped onto the gangplank.

"What was it you said about a man losin' his heart at my age?" he mocked dryly. "Yore old enough to know better yoreself, Cap'n. My age compensates for my folly, but yores don't." Reade chuckled heartily when Dante's annoyed glare sliced him in two. "Yore in love with her just as sure as birds fly."

"I don't recall having said so," Dante grunted sourly.

"You didn't have to. I thought there was somethin' strange about yore behavior when I caught up with you on the steamboat." Reade frowned thoughtfully. "You've bin sayin' you want revenge on yore uncle, but I'm thinkin' that's just an excuse. I think it's the lady you've bin after all along."

Dante didn't respond. Instead, he wheeled around and stalked back to his cabin to await Erica's return, cursing himself for not insisting that he escort her. That confounded Frenchman seemed all too interested in Erica, and although he had placed the burden of marketing the cotton crop on Erica's shoulders, he did not expect her to make a personal sacrifice to obtain the top price.

Personal sacrifice? Dante grabbed the bottle of brandy and took a drink. Erica had done so much flirting and cavorting aboard the schooner she would probably welcome Cadeau's advances. Dante swallowed more brandy as the picture of Erica rose like a genie from the bottle. Yet if she had reappeared at that moment, he would cheerfully have choked her for what he imagined she was doing with Charles Cadeau!

"I don't like this one bit!" Dante scowled as he paced back and forth across Erica's cabin while she finished making her toilet. "I don't trust that French Don Juan."

A secretive smile pursed Erica's lips as she peered into the mirror, watching Dante prowl about her cabin. "Would you prefer to take your shipload of cotton and return to New Orleans?"

"No," Dante gritted out. "I would *prefer* that you conduct your meetings with that Frenchman and his father aboard this ship!"

Erica slowly turned to face him, arching a delicate eyebrow. "They invited me to dine with them and several of their friends this evening, and I can't very well refuse when your cargo is at stake, can I?"

Dante detested logic when he was in an emotional state. "I suppose not," he muttered acrimoniously. Then he surveyed the daring lavender gown Erica had selected for the evening. She reminded him of a dainty flower, ripe for the picking, and he was not about to turn Cadeau loose on her. "Don't set foot out of this room."

"But . . ." Erica could only get one word out before

362

the door slammed behind Dante. She threw up her hands in exasperation. "The man is mad," she spouted at the walls. "He doesn't love me, but he wants no other man near me. Why is he so possessive?" She looked at her mirror, wishing it would offer some words of advice, but none came and she was at a loss to understand why Dante had ordered her to remain where she was and then had stalked out of her cabin.

Within a few minutes, the door swept open and Dante stepped inside, dressed in a black silk waistcoat and tight black trousers. Erica's jaw dropped as her eyes took in the dashing gentleman who struck a pose and then bowed before her.

"Our carriage awaits, *chérie.*"

"Really, Dante, you are behaving like an overprotective father," she chided as she snatched up her shawl. "I am quite capable of handling Charles."

"Then I will merely sit back and watch," Dante assured her as he took her arm and steered her through the companionway.

As the handsome couple walked across the wharf, Charles's face fell like a rockslide. He had not anticipated competition for Erica's attention. Indeed, he had counted upon having her to himself after dinner. Forcing a smile, he nodded a greeting to Dante and then focused his undivided attention on Erica.

"*Sans aucun doute,* I am not the least bit disappointed that you came in Jamie's stead, *chère amie.* You look enchanting this evening. *Mon dieu,* you take my breath away," he murmured as he pressed a kiss to her wrist.

"Not completely," Dante grunted as he clutched Erica's hand, drawing it away from Charles's lips. "It seems that your French admirer is all too anxious to gobble you up," he said, his voice agitated, as he led her to the carriage.

"Mind your manners," Erica scolded as she wormed her hand from his viselike grasp. "Remember, your cargo is at stake. If you can't keep a civil tongue in your head, don't speak at all. You will accomplish nothing by needling Charles."

Clamping a tight rein on his temper, Dante parked himself across from Erica since Charles had scampered up behind them and had wedged himself next to Erica. His intentions were obvious, and it was all Dante could do to maintain his composure. Furthermore, it annoyed Dante that he could only decipher bits and pieces of Cadeau's conversation since the rogue continued to rattle on in French. Although Dante had only a meager command of the language, he was certain Charles was being too familiar with Erica. The man's a rake, Dante thought sourly. Obviously Charles didn't care that he had an audience while he whispered sweet nothings in Erica's ear. Dante was already tired of Monsieur Cadeau's company.

"C'est magnifique!" Erica declared as Charles escorted her up the marble steps of the sprawling Cadeau mansion. The surrounding gardens had received meticulous care, and the entryway was studded with ornate gold carvings. Never had Erica seen anything as extravagant as the Cadeau manor. She felt that she was walking into a palace.

"Naturally, this estate was your father's undertaking." Dante said spitefully; then he grunted when Erica gouged him in the ribs with her elbow for being rude and sarcastic.

Charles spared Dante an indulgent smile, one that

didn't reach his smoky gray eyes. *"Vous jouez de malheur. Au contraire, monsieur,* it was *I* who built this grand home and then sent for my father to occupy it with me," he explained, so arrogantly that Dante had to suppress an urge to plant his fist in Charles's smug face. "I do a thriving trade with Europe, and I was only too happy to share my abundant fortune with my father."

"Comme vous êtes bon," Erica interjected, favoring Charles with an admiring glance.

Just dandy, Dante thought disgustedly. Cadeau is a self-made man who can lay the world at Erica's feet, and judging by the way he is drooling over her, he would do just that, given half the chance. Confound it! Why couldn't she have been a plain-faced twit instead of a ravishing beauty? Dante asked himself resentfully. Didn't he have enough trouble without playing lackey to this distracting damsel and her overeager beau?

"Par ici, ma petite," Charles murmured softly as he slid an arm about Erica's waist.

While Dante was grappling with his disturbing thoughts, Charles ushered Erica toward the dining room, leaving him to follow them like a stray pup. After arranging the seating so that Dante would be at the opposite end of the table, Charles pulled out the chair beside his and gestured for Erica to take her place.

It was all Erica could do to keep from bursting into giggles as she watched Dante fiddle with the silverware. He was pouting like a small child who had not been allowed to have his way. She knew it went against Dante's grain to stand in the wings since he was such a forceful individual, but for the sake of his cargo, he had clamped a stranglehold on his tongue and had taken the seat Charles had offered him.

After they had dined sumptuously, Charles escorted Erica to the ballroom, took her in his arms, and attempted to sweep her off her feet while Dante propped himself against the wall and scowled. It was obvious that Charles Cadeau was accustomed to getting what he wanted, and it seemed to Dante that Erica was only too eager to let him have it. Damnation, this was no business conference; it was a whirlwind courtship. Dante was becoming tired of watching Charles charm Erica with his sugar-coated smiles. Finally, able to stand no more of it, he pushed away from the wall and weaved his way across the ballroom to reach Erica just as Charles was about to whisk her onto the terrace to tarry in the tropical moonlight with a devastatingly beautiful woman.

"S'il vous plaît, I should like at least one dance with *mademoiselle,"* Dante insisted as he cut Charles off at the door and maneuvered Erica toward the dance floor. "Surely you can tear yourself away from this bewitching young woman for a few minutes and allow the rest of us the pleasure of her company."

Dante's smile was so polite that Charles would appear the culprit if he protested. So he didn't. But he was silently smoldering as Dante drew Erica against him, holding her too tightly.

"Quand on parle du loup, on en voit la queue!" Erica muttered acrimoniously.

"Kindly speak to me in English," Dante demanded gruffly. "I am in no mood to attempt to translate. Save your softly spoken tongue for your French *roué.*"

"You are behaving like the very devil," Erica admonished as she pried herself away from Dante's suffocating embrace. "Are you trying to spoil everything? You are sorely testing Charles's temper."

"No more than he has tested mine," Dante countered,

a distinctly unpleasant edge to his voice. "What Cadeau wants from you has nothing to do with selling and buying cotton. If I were guessing, I would say he is more interested in having you inspect his bed linens."

Erica cast him a withering glance and then heaved an exasperated sigh. "You are meddling in my affairs and I—"

"Affairs?" Dante pounced on her choice of words, his mouth thinning into a tight smile that Erica expected to split his lips. "I believe that easily translates from French to English." His tone was riddled with contempt, and his flaming green eyes scorched her. "Had I known it had already come to that, I would not have allowed you to prance off with that foreign libertine in the first place!"

"His amorous advances and romantic tactics are no worse than yours." Erica was taunting him and loving every minute of it. "You have no right to condemn a man for attempting to take advantage of a woman when *you* are a master of the technique of seduction. I should know. You've practiced your skills on me from New Orleans to Natchez."

Dante bit back a sarcastic rejoinder, and he gracefully bowed out. *"C'est entendu, mademoiselle,* you have properly put me in my place, and it is certainly *not* at this tropical ball. I trust your admirer will see you back to the ship when the two of you have finished conducting your business . . . or whatever it is you intend to do. *Que dites-vous de cèdre? Adieu."*

Laughter bubbled from Erica's lips as Dante pivoted on his heel and stalked away. He certainly needs to polish up his French, she thought. He had just asked her opinion of cedar trees. With his weak command of the language, he had probably imagined that Charles had been making intimate remarks to her throughout the evening. Dante was living proof that a man with a little knowledge was a dangerous man. What he didn't comprehend, he presumed he understood. If Dante weren't such a rake himself, he would not be so suspicious of Charles, Erica reminded herself. What is good for the goose is good for the gander. Dante had courted his fair share of attractive women aboard the *Natchez Belle* while Erica had been stuck with groping scoundrels. Now she was being ushered about by one of Guadeloupe's most wealthy and handsome gentlemen.

"Il n'y a rien à craindre. I must admit I am relieved that you sent your guard dog on his way." Charles smiled as he strolled up behind Erica who was still watching Dante pick his way through the crowd.

"Pardonnez, mon ami, s'il vous plaît," Erica beseeched as she blessed Charles with a smile more radiant than the chandelier that hung above them. "He is really a very likable gentleman, but he imagines himself to be my guardian angel and he has a tendency to hover protectively about me when he feels my virtue is threatened."

Charles grinned like a hungry barracuda as he took Erica in his arms and waltzed across the floor, swaying in rhythm with the music, his male body aroused by the feel of Erica's shapely curves. His imagination was running away with itself, and Charles was prone to let it. The visions dancing in his head were getting the best of him. He wanted more than a business relationship with the enchanting Erica Bennet. She had a great deal to offer a man, and before they concluded their business transactions, Charles was determined to know how much.

* * *

"Good God, what happened to you?" Reade hooted as he watched Dante stagger across the deck, his silk waistcoat draped over his shoulder, his top hat set cock-eyed on his tousled black hair.

Dante attempted to focus his blurred gaze on his first mate; then he groaned as his stomach pitched and rolled like a ship floundering on a stormy sea. After bracing himself against the railing, Dante inhaled a breath of fresh air, then expelled it. "I have been doing some serious thinking," he mumbled, his words tripping off his thick tongue.

A wry smile tugged at one corner of Reade's mouth as he wrapped a supporting arm around the captain and steered him toward his cabin. Dante reeked of rum, tobacco, and cheap perfume. It wasn't difficult to recognize that thinking wasn't all Dante had been doing that night. A troubled frown etched Reade's brow when he remembered that Dante had escorted Erica off the schooner earlier that evening.

"Where's Erica? You didn't forget and leave her somewhere, did you?" he demanded.

"I would prefer to forget where I left her," Dante muttered, as he watched the towering masts of the schooner spin about him. Lord, he was drunk, but not nearly intoxicated enough to forget why he had stormed from the Cadeau mansion and had aimed himself for the nearest tavern. "That woman is a witch." His sluggish speech revealed his annoyance.

"Sure she is," Reade responded patronizingly as he herded Dante toward his cabin.

"I was a reasonably sane man until I had the misfortune to collide with that whirlwind of trouble," Dante muttered. Then he braced his hands against the

369

companionway before he fell on his face. "I'm swearing off women again." He drew himself up proudly and then grasped at the doorjamb to keep himself upright.

"A wise decision, Cap'n," Reade affirmed, biting back a chuckle. He hadn't seen Dante so inebriated in years, and never because of a woman. He's love smitten for sure, Reade concluded.

"Do you know where that minx is?" Dante growled as he collapsed on his cot. Then he answered his own question before Reade could reply. "She's dallying with that French Casanova at his grand, tropical mansion."

"Maybe she'll put ashore permanently. Then she won't cause you no more trouble." Reade smiled as he reached down to tug off Dante's boots. "That's what you want, ain't it, to wash yore hands of her for good?"

"You think I would leave her on the Leeward Islands and sail off after wading through hell to retrieve her from my uncle?" Dante snapped indignantly. He snorted derisively. "Hell no! I won't leave her sitting in the lap of luxury. She doesn't deserve that after the way she has behaved. I saved her from Sabin, but does she thank me? I rescued her on the eve of her wedding to that ruthless devil, but does she shower me with gratitude? No." Dante shook his head and then let it plop back onto the pillow. "She tempts me and taunts me and then strolls off with the next wealthy gentleman she meets."

"Maybe she's fickle," Reade suggested as he wrestled with Dante's other boot and then tossed it aside.

"Fickle?" Dante croaked. "That's putting it mildly. She toys with me and then casts me aside as if we were strangers. She was my wife. Does that mean nothing to her? What does she expect from me? I gave her my name, offered her protection, gave her expensive gowns.

Damnation! What is a man supposed to do for a woman that I haven't done?"

"Yore askin' me?" Reade chirped as he braced his hands on his hips and peered incredulously at Dante. "That question has baffled men for centuries. If you ever figure out the answer, let me know. I wouldn't mind some insight, even at my age."

When Reade had closed the door behind him, Dante stared up into the swirling darkness, cursing himself for allowing Erica to torment him. He had been so furious with her that he had gone in search of another woman, one who could ease his needs without entangling his emotions. But the moment he had taken the tavern wench in his arms, her flaming red hair had become a raven mane and her pale green eyes had turned to that mysterious shade of blue that could boggle a man's mind when he peered too long and hard into them. Dante had torn himself away from the maddening vision that materialized before him, thereby spoiling the pleasure he had hoped to find in another woman's arms. And the agonizing truth was that he hadn't wanted another woman. He had wanted Erica, and anyone else would have been a poor substitute for the spine-tingling sensations he experienced when he took her in his arms.

Erica . . . A vision of pure loveliness drifted above him. She was there, just beyond his grasp, her flawless complexion glowing in the lantern light, her mystical eyes compelling him to follow her, her sensuous lips parting in invitation. She was staring at him from the door of the brothel in New Orleans, that strange, haunting look on her face. She was storming across the deck, her eyes flashing with anger, her cheeks flushed. She was gliding across the stream, her curvaceous body bathed in moonlight. She was thundering across the meadow, her hair flying wildly behind her, her face beaming with the pleasure of racing against the wind. She was kneeling beside him, her silky caresses flowing over his eager body, smoothing away the tension, filling his veins with a passion that inflamed his very soul.

Dante was captivated by the many moods Erica had displayed. A mellow smile hovered on his lips as her image floated toward him, evoking a dream that carried him far from reality's shore and then set him adrift amid the fantasies and memories that warmed him, body and soul.

Part VII

Be still sad heart, and cease repining;
Behind the clouds is the sun still shining,
Thy fate is the common fate of all,
Into each life some rain must fall,
Some days must be dark and dreary.

—Longfellow

Chapter 21

A proud smile blossomed on Erica's lips as she lifted the front of her skirt and stepped upon the plank. Charles Cadeau had proved to be a shrewd business man. It had taken two full days to come to terms, but Erica had received a more than acceptable price for the cargo.

After informing Reade that Charles's crew would be arriving within the hour to unload it, she went in search of Dante. She found him stalking about his cabin, looking like a caged predator. His ferocity rivaled that of an injured panther as his frosty green eyes drilled into her.

"Where the hell have you been?" Dante growled, although he already knew the answer to his question.

"I have been trying to sell your stolen cargo, Pirate Fowler," she informed him, attempting to remain cheerful, even though Dante looked as if he would thoroughly enjoy strangling her.

"It does not take forty-eight hours to negotiate terms!" he thundered.

But Erica didn't cower. Holding true to form, she thrust out a defiant chin. "It does when one is dealing with Charles Cadeau," she insisted.

Dante's fuming gaze blazed over the fashionable satin gown that Erica had suddenly acquired. "It seems your French admirer has showered you with gifts. What services did you perform to obtain such an expensive garment, *mademoiselle*, or dare I ask?" His voice was cutting.

Outraged, Erica gasped and then slapped his cheek. Her face was as red as the crimson welt that appeared on Dante's cheek. It was insufferable of him to accuse her of bedding a man to secure better payment for their cargo! Erica hurled the money pouch at Dante's midsection and then stormed toward the door.

"You have your money, Dante. Do with it what you will, but don't expect my assistance ever again. I expected a simple thank you, not crude insults. You are most contemptible."

When Dante opened the pouch, his eyes widened. Erica had received a very high payment for the cotton, and he was now convinced that she'd offered Cadeau more than cargo to have gotten such an exorbitant price. Blind fury and jealous rage sizzled through him. For two days he had prowled about the ship, muttering epithets and fighting back the image of Erica in Charles's arms, but stubborn pride had kept him from going after her. Damn, she had turned him inside out. Clenching the purse in his fist, Dante would have sworn Charles Cadeau had paid generously in return for Erica's favors. He wrestled with his jealousy, but he couldn't control it. Damn Erica! he thought. How could she have slept with that honey-tongued *roué?*

"I may have stooped to stealing Sabin's schooner, but you obviously lowered yourself to Charles's bed," he declared harshly.

Erica was furious. She had gotten Dante what he wanted; how dare he imply that she had sold herself to Charles. It was such a ludicrous accusation that she refused to dignify his remark with a reply.

Dante took advantage of her silence and cocked a taunting eyebrow as he waved the money in her flushed face. "I can now afford the pleasure of having a hand-maiden bathe me. Shall I come to your cabin around eight o'clock this evening or have you decided to weigh anchor in Pointe-à-Pitre?"

Erica's blazing glare would have burned any other man, but Dante deflected her glower with his infuriating grin. "There is nothing I want in Guadeloupe, and if you want to soak, you can do it in the ocean, not in my cabin," she stated coldly. "I still reserve the right to refuse service to anyone, Dante Fowler. Take your money and go . . . straight to hell!" Her voice became higher and wilder until she was almost screaming; then she spun about and stormed away.

When the door slammed shut behind her, jarring the entire ship, Erica cursed Dante. She had tolerated Charles Cadeau's presence, strategically maneuvering around his amorous assaults, tactfully keeping him at arm's length without botching up their business dealings. Yet two frustrating days of playing cat and mouse with the amorous Frenchman had only provoked harsh ridicule from Dante. Erica was furious.

Nothing she did pleased Dante. Why had she bothered to try to get a better price for the cotton? She could have accepted Charles's original offer.

Erica threw up her hands in a gesture of futility. Loving Dante just isn't enough, she thought dismally. Maybe he and I are wrong for each other. We are both so strong willed and determined. After all, birds of a feather can peck each other to pieces.

She tossed the extravagant gifts Charles had bestowed on her on the cot and then tugged the pins from her hair, letting it tumble down. Sinking down on the edge of the bed, she carefully unwrapped the gift she had bought for Dante. As she gently lifted the carved replica of a schooner from its box, she was thankful that she had not broken the fragile model during her fit of temper. Should she give it to him after all the hateful things he had said to her? Perhaps he would presume that Charles had paid for it.

Well, let him think what he wishes, Erica thought stubbornly. She would sneak into Dante's cabin, leave the gift, and refuse to answer any questions about it. She was replacing the replica she had broken, as she had promised, and what he thought of her gesture was of little consequence.

She decided to cleanse her mind of that infuriating man, once and for all. She had fallen *in* love with Dante, and she would just have to fall *out* of love with him. It sounded perfectly logical. All she had to do was dwell on his numerous faults. Determined to do just that, Erica focused on the darkly handsome image that appeared before her. Dante was stubborn, wooden headed. He was arrogant, temperamental, insulting, domineering, deceitful . . . Erica breathed a perturbed sigh. It wasn't working. Each time she listed one of his annoying characteristics, one of his admirable qualities came to mind. He was a tender lover, a born leader of men, a conscientious business man, a humanitarian. . . .

Erica let her scarf flutter over the wooden model, and then she glanced through the window to see Dante assisting the crew with the cargo. She would take the gift to his quarters and then repossess her heart, by forgetting he existed. It might take time to recover from this one-sided love, but recover she *would*. And perhaps, one day, another man would come along to take Dante's place in her heart, and she would fall in love again. But the next time she would fall with her eyes wide open, then she would understand the sensations that gripped her and she wouldn't make the same foolish mistakes. No more tumbling pell-mell into love and then picking up the shattered pieces of her broken heart. She would be cautious and methodical, she assured herself. Love could be a reasonable and pleasant experience if she stumbled on the right man. Dante had taught her a valuable lesson and if she had any common sense at all she would profit from her stormy affair with the emerald-eyed rogue.

Clinging to that thought, Erica crept down the corridor, made her way to Dante's cabin to deliver the gift, and then returned to her own quarters, locking herself in.

She was determined never again to allow her heart to rule her head. She would have nothing more to do with Dante for the remainder of the voyage. Perhaps she shouldn't have been friendly with the crew in her attempt to make him jealous, but if he couldn't trust her when she insisted that she had slept with no other man, their relationship was worthless. Damn Dante! she thought. He couldn't see love when it was staring him in the face.

A troubled frown creased Dante's brow while he stood at the helm, squinting at the sun which was playing hide-and-seek with the dark clouds looming in the sky. The strange calm worried him. It invariably preceded a storm.

That is all I need, Dante thought disgustedly. He and Erica were practicing civilized warfare, sharing the same cramped space and pretending to be polite to each other. But the resultant strain was tearing Dante apart. He regretted having turned Erica loose in Guadeloupe, where she had been swept off her feet by Cadeau's foreign charm.

He and Erica were barely speaking, and Reade constantly taunted him because he'd insulted Erica after she'd turned a sizable profit on Sabin's cotton. Dante could repay Avery his share, hold out Sabin's as bait, and still make a profit for his troubles. Yet he had to resolve his differences with Erica. He simply could not forgive her for bending to Cadeau's will, and he was not about to thank her for replacing the broken replica because he suspected it had been purchased by Cadeau.

He felt he had made a mess of things. He had practically thrown her at Cadeau, yet he was furious with Erica for submitting to the man. What could he do now? Dante had spent ten days wrestling with that question, and still he had not come up with a workable answer. Several times he had attempted to go to Erica, but each time she had slammed the door in his face.

The rumble of distant thunder shook Dante from his silent contemplations, and he peered at the foreboding clouds that had swallowed the sun. A cold, brisk wind slapped him in the face, warning him of the furious gale to come. Then he glanced back to find Reade staring at the clouds, his expression grim.

"It don't look good, Cap'n," he muttered.

Dante did not appreciate hearing his fears voiced. "Did you order the crew to batten down the hatches and secure the ship for rough weather?" Dante's gaze drifted back to the angry sky.

"Aye, all we got left to do is haul in the sails when you give the word." Reade gestured toward the canvas billowing in the gusty breeze. "It don't look like we got a chance of outrunnin' this one."

Dante nodded his agreement. He had postponed tying up the sails, hoping the storm would veer northwest of them, but it had not. They would be forced to weather what had every indication of being a disastrous tropical storm. "Call out the crew. If we wait much longer the wind will send men flying from the masts. I should hate to lose a sailor in these shark-infested waters."

As Dante strolled over to relieve the helmsman and tie himself to the wheel, Reade blurted out a question. "Which one of us is goin' to keep an eye on Erica? She ain't got no idea how rough it can get."

"That will be up to you," Dante insisted as he reached for the rope and wrapped it around his waist. Tied to the wheel, he might be able to keep the ship on course. "I'm sure she would prefer it that way since she has had little use for me of late."

As Reade hurried down the ladder to summon the crew, he was unable to smother his anticipatory grin. He could picture Erica huddling in his arms during the blow. He had always been a man who seized opportunity, even in the face of disaster. If he drowned at sea, at least he would die with a smile on his face.

When he rapped on the door of her cabin, Erica was already pacing the floor. She had seen the crew scurrying about the ship and had viewed the dark clouds. She was disappointed to see the surly first mate staring at her. In this instance she would have preferred Dante's company, even if she had talked herself into detesting him. When she felt the inclination to huddle in a man's arms, she yearned to be enfolded in Dante's.

Although Reade had provided her with companionship during the voyage, Erica had never been quite certain she could trust him. Reade Asher was a crusty old sailor, and he was a bit unscrupulous at times so Erica had never completely let her guard down with him. Reade was a strange man. He could be considerate when doing so involved no personal sacrifice, but he was a mercenary at heart. He always looked out for himself first and others second. Still, he was a likable fellow, despite his flaws.

Erica indicated with a gesture that Reade should enter her cabin. "How long before the storm hits?" she asked point-blank.

Reade lumbered into the room and parked himself in a chair. "Not long. You ain't afraid, are you?"

"I would be a liar and a fool if I said I wasn't." Erica fiddled nervously with the belt on her breeches. "I've never experienced a storm at sea, but I'm sure they are far worse than the ones we've endured on land."

Erica jumped as if she had been stung when the wind suddenly howled, and as bolts of lightning sizzled through the sudden darkness, she shivered uncontrollably. When the schooner pitched and rolled, she braced herself against the wall, her eyes bulging, her heart catapulting into her throat. This is no time to fall apart at the seams, she told herself, attempting to bolster her courage.

Reade got to his feet and weaved across the room to the cot. "You better come sit with me before the furniture starts slidin' across the floor," he advised.

Erica complied, but not without reservation. She was

annoyed because Dante hadn't come to console her. He owed her that much, didn't he?

"I suppose the good captain has anchored himself down with a bottle of brandy," she grumbled, her tone laced with resentment.

"No, he relieved the helmsman and roped himself to the wheel," Reade informed her as he placed a protective arm around her.

"What? He's on deck in the middle of a storm?" Erica bolted to her feet. "You left him out there alone without trying to persuade him to remain below? What if he washes overboard?"

"What can I do to help him now?" Reade's tug on her arm pulled her onto the bed beside him. "I know better than to try to talk Dante out of a notion when he's made up his mind. Besides, you know I can't swim a lick. It's times like these when it's every man for himself, and I ain't about to start playin' the martyr."

Erica wormed free and dashed toward the door, visualizing Dante succumbing to a wall of water that surged toward the schooner.

"It's suicide to go out there now!" Reade screeched, but Erica paid him no heed. She was gone.

Reade grumbled under his breath and then braced his boot heel against the table that slid toward him. "Damned fool woman. If she had any sense she would be scared stiff."

But Erica was too overwhelmed with fear for Dante to consider her own safety. Perhaps Reade could stand by and watch Dante risk his life, but she couldn't. Being blown off course was a small price to pay for being alive, and Erica intended to tell Dante so. Her concerned gaze flew to the quarter-deck, where Dante was silhouetted against the turbulent sky. Panic gripped her as the raging wind threw her back against the wall, but she strangled her fear and edged toward the ladder. As the pounding rain pelleted her, Erica gritted her teeth and climbed upward, determined to reach Dante and urge him to seek shelter in his cabin.

Dante glanced over his shoulder to see a bedraggled Erica clutching the rail to keep from being blown overboard by the raging wind. Then his blood ran cold when she was thrown back against the mast as if she were no more than a feather in that gale.

"What the hell are you doing up here?" he roared to make himself heard. "Get below!"

Erica grabbed the rope to haul herself toward him. "Not without you," she yelled back at him.

Dante's head swiveled around as an avalanche of water surged toward them, and he snatched Erica to him just before the great wave crashed down upon them. "Hold on to me!" he ordered as he swung her over the ropes to position her between him and the wheel. "Little fool! Haven't I enough trouble without worrying about your washing overboard? Dammit, I already have my hands full."

Erica did not reply. She barely had time to throw her arms around Dante before the huge wave rolled down upon them, tilting the schooner dangerously. Erica held her breath for what seemed an eternity while the angry sea sought to plunge them into its depths. Although the driving force of the water threatened to rip her from Dante's arms and hurl her over the rail, Erica clung to him for dear life. Terror washed over her as her nails dug into the tense muscles of his back, and she was certain her lungs would burst before she could get a breath of air.

Relief flooded over her when the water ebbed, but it was short-lived. The schooner lurched and then dropped, and Erica felt as if she were dangling in midair. Then another wave slammed against the hull. For another long, frantic moment she could not breathe.

"Good God!" Dante gasped as he wiped the salt water from his eyes, only to see another monstrous wave rolling toward the starboard bow. He had weathered storms at sea before, but never had he faced anything like this. It would be a miracle if the oncoming wall of water didn't capsize the schooner. "Don't let go, Erica, no matter how strong the pull. Don't let go of me!" Dante ground out the words and then spun the wheel, turning the bow to meet the wave head-on. He couldn't risk being hit broadside by a wave as tall as the masts.

Erica squeezed her eyes shut, concentrating on his words rather than the fast-approaching water. She felt Dante's body tense as he whirled the wheel, fighting the current that sought to suck the ship into the cresting wave and then fling her downward. Erica's frightened scream was drowned by the roar of the raging sea, and she felt her grip weaken. As the ropes bit into her ribs, threatening to slash her in two, panic shot through her. Erica knew the end was near. Dante's handsome face rose above her, but she couldn't get to him. She was going to die, and Dante would never know how deeply she loved him. It was too late. She couldn't tell him because she was submerged in water. He would never know. . . . Darkness closed in on her as the supply of air in her lungs was used up. She was about to become one of the souls adrift in the sea. Her hands slid from Dante's waist . . .

*   *   *

Calling upon the last of his strength, Dante carried Erica's limp body across the wet deck. The air was oppressive in the wake of the storm, and Dante was still gasping after his near brush with death. A worried frown puckered his brow as he peered into Erica's ashen face. They had weathered the storm, but he had been unable to help her until he could free himself from the wheel. He prayed that she would survive.

After pushing open the door with his shoulder he laid Erica on her cot and then stripped off her drenched clothing. He noted that her skin was like ice and she was deathly quiet. He pushed away the morbid thoughts those observations evoked. Then he hurriedly retrieved quilts from the trunk. After peeling off his own clothes he lay down beside her, offering what warmth the covers and his body could provide. Silently he cursed Reade for not keeping Erica below. But then, what did he expect? he asked himself. Reade always allowed Erica to run wild. This time that could cost her her life.

The warmth from Dante's body roused Erica slightly and she inched toward the heat, but she could not control the chills that ricocheted up and down her spine. Her thoughts were dazed and distorted. Fragmented visions collided and then faded away. She drifted in and out of consciousness, often moaning softly when the pain in her ribs worsened.

Dante tenderly smoothed the renegade strands of hair away from her peaked face. Why had she come to the helm? She detested him. Dante shook his head and sighed wearily. He certainly didn't know why she had done it. He did not understand Erica.

The faintest hint of a smile raised the corners of his mouth as he bent his head to hers. "I have brought you nothing but trouble, haven't I? But then you have given me some in return." Dante kissed her gently, hoping for a response, but he received none. Her lips were cold and they did not warm to his touch. "We are an odd pair, you and I. We make each other miserable, yet I cannot imagine facing the sunrise without you. Don't give up, sweet nymph."

Cuddling her closer, Dante allowed his eyelids to flutter shut. As he gave way to exhaustion, he prayed that Erica would have the strength to survive. She must. The world would be bleak and dismal without this spirited beauty. Dante groaned as tormenting memories swirled about in his mind. Erica was being flung about like a rag doll while they were strapped to the wheel, and he feared he would wake to find that she had died. Yet he continued to hold her to him, denying the angel of death his prize.

Chapter 22

A groggy moan tumbled from Erica's lips as she propped herself upon one wobbly elbow. Then her clouded gaze focused on the man who sat across the room from her.

"I was beginnin' to wonder if you would ever come around," Reade declared to his dazed patient. "Are you feelin' better?"

"Compared to what?" Erica's attempt to tease him failed miserably because Reade had to strain his ears to catch her hoarse murmur.

"You still don't look too perky." A thoughtful frown creased his craggy features. "You had us worried the last few days, lass. And Dante raked me over the coals, but good, for lettin' you go on deck. Lord, he chewed off my ears and swore he'd cut me into bite-size pieces if you got the grippe after being exposed to the weather."

"I wouldn't have thought he'd care what happened to me," Erica mused aloud as she struggled to sit up. Goodness, she didn't seem to have an ounce of strength.

A wry smile tugged at Reade's lips. "He must. I never

saw him fuss over a woman the way he's doted over you these past two days. He was worse than a mother hen nestin' with her baby chick."

Erica was surprised. Surely she hadn't slept two days away. Reade must be exaggerating. After all, he was prone to spin wild yarns.

"He only feels responsible for me," Erica predicted. "I was a necessary inconvenience during this voyage."

Reade didn't contradict her since he had no inclination to play the matchmaker. His feelings for this blue-eyed nymph were too strong to permit him to hand her over to Dante. If Dante wanted Erica, he would have to win her heart.

"I was mighty worried about you," Reade insisted as he rose and crossed the cabin. Then he leaned over to run a callused hand over her cheek. He was relieved to note that some color had finally begun to creep into her ashen features. "I ain't a religious man, but I did some serious prayin' that first night when you was barely breathin'."

Such words from a man like Asher touched Erica and she smiled up at him. "Thank you for caring."

Reade tilted her face back. He was bewitched by her natural beauty, even when she was at her worst. "I've never had much use for women," he confessed. Then he grinned sheepishly. "Except when . . ." He paused to formulate his words, attempting to express his feelings in a manner that would not offend Erica. "What I mean is . . . well, being a man and all . . ."

Erica laughed huskily. "I understand what you are trying not to say, Reade. Believe me, I have learned how it is with men. I was married once, you know."

"No, I don't think you truly understand." Reade heaved a frustrated sigh and then began again. "I know

I'm not good for much, and I've done some things I'm not too proud of just to earn a little spendin' money, but I get this funny feelin' when I'm with you, even though I know I'm old enough to be yore father." He had never paid much attention to the English language, and the one time he would have liked to dazzle a woman with words, he found himself tongue-tied. "Confound it, Erica. I don't know how else to say this." Reade took a deep breath and then said quickly, "I think I've fallen in love with you."

Erica had not expected his profession of love, and it took a moment to regain her composure. "I'm flattered, Reade, but—"

"But you don't love me," he finished for her.

Her eyes met his. "As a friend," she said gently, determined not to leave him in limbo as she'd regretted doing with Elliot. That had been a mistake which Erica refused to repeat. "I am fond of you, and I do not want to hurt you." Her lashes fluttered down as she offered him a wan smile. "I hope we can remain friends, for I have enjoyed your companionship. You have been my companion many hours aboard this schooner."

Reade sighed as his hands dropped away from her satiny face. "It's prob'ly for the best anyhow. I ain't got much to offer you. I hope you will forgive an old man for makin' a fool of himself."

Erica watched him stroll toward the door. She said nothing; she was afraid to trust her clouded mind to produce an appropriate response. When the door closed behind Reade, Erica muffled a sniffle, but for the life of her, she didn't know why she felt like crying. She had never been prone to tears, but she felt as if pent-up emotions were about to burst free and she didn't have the strength to hold them back. A tear formed in the corner of her eye, then another. Finally, a steady stream of them trickled down her cheeks, and within moments, Erica was sobbing like an abandoned child.

At that moment Dante slipped into her room and immediately froze in his tracks. Erica crying? Her muffled sobs tore at his heart, and before he realized what he was doing, he was at her side, offering her a shoulder to cry on. But Erica pushed him away, preferring to bury her tears in the pillow. She was humiliated because Dante was watching her cry.

"Go away," she wailed. "Just go away and leave me alone!"

"Not until you tell me what has upset you." Dante pried her shoulder from the pillow and pushed her onto her back, forcing her to meet his concerned gaze.

"Nothing has upset me," she insisted through trembling lips.

Dante rolled his eyes heavenward. "Nothing?" he repeated skeptically. "You escaped molestation in New Orleans and then found yourself in a brothel with a man who refused to heed your plea for assistance, yet you didn't shed a tear over losing your innocence. You found yourself the stake in a gambling bet, but you didn't cry. I kidnapped you and brought you aboard this schooner without informing you of my plans until it was too late for you to return to shore, and even then you didn't succumb to tears." Dante eyed her speculatively. "Something drastic must have happened if you survived all that with dry eyes. Why are you crying?"

"I have heard it said that people stumble on mole hills, not mountains," she countered, muffling a sniffle. "This is but a mole hill."

Dante wasn't appeased. He was determined to have a direct answer. "If this were a mole hill you wouldn't have broken stride," he argued. "You don't crumble easily, Erica. Now, dammit, I want to know what is bothering you."

Erica was too upset to engage in a debate with Dante. She was exhausted and depressed; the struggles of the past two months had finally caught up with her. Why couldn't he let her wallow in self-pity for a while? She just felt like crying, and that was all there was to it. The stark realization that she and Dante had no more future than she and Reade had distressed her. She wanted to forget Dante, and to assure herself that her broken heart would mend, given the proper amount of time. She wanted to forget her struggles with Sabin and Charles Cadeau, and her terrifying experience during the storm.

"Just let me be, Dante," Erica ordered. Then she inhaled a shuddering breath and wiped her cheek, rerouting the stream of tears that flowed down. "You are the last person I want to see at the moment."

Dante was at the end of his rope. He had been through hell the past two days, wondering if Erica would survive. Watching her heart-wrenching sobs was simply too much for him, and he was annoyed that she refused to lean on the strong shoulder he offered.

Had Reade done something to upset her? Had he taken advantage of her in her weakened condition? The thought destroyed Dante's fragile control, and he grabbed Erica by the arms, shaking her until her head snapped backward, and her hair flew wildly about her.

"Dammit, I want to know what happened. What did he do to you?" Dante growled.

"Who?" Erica just stared at him when her head

stopped spinning. What the devil was he ranting about?

"Reade." Dante scowled as if the name left a bitter taste in his mouth. "Did he take advantage of you? I should have known better than to ask him to keep a watchful eye on you. The man lacks scruples. If I didn't need him to guide me to the treasure I would never have allowed him to tag along."

"Scruples," Erica scoffed. "How would you know about such things?" She flung his hands away and struggled to sit up on the cot. "You want to know why I'm crying? Very well, I'll tell you." She drew in a deep breath and then tilted her chin to stare down at him. "Because of *you*, not Reade. You are the most exasperating man I have ever met!"

"Me?" Dante hooted like a screech owl, then his eyes widened. "What the hell did I do besides save your life two days ago? Does that count for nothing?"

"You should have let me drown," Erica shouted as she pushed him away, sending him sprawling. "It would have been a fitting end." Then a confused frown settled on her brow as his earlier remark registered on her brain. "What treasure?"

"The one in Yucatán," Dante informed her as he gathered his feet beneath him.

Erica rolled her eyes in disbelief. Dante was willing to risk his life wading through savage-infested jungles on some wild-goose chase. "You are mad," she muttered.

"No, desperate," Dante declared, his voice rising testily. "If you weren't so busy sulking you might have considered *my* dire straits. *I* am the one who should be teary eyed, but you wallow in self-pity instead of offering me assistance. I must salvage my plantation, and repay my brother for his losses."

Erica was so infuriated by his harsh criticism that she was itching to slap his arrogant face. "And if *you* weren't so self-centered you wouldn't risk the crew's lives or mine to chase the pot of gold at the end of a rainbow." Erica gave Dante a scornful glance and then gestured toward the door. "Get out of my cabin. I have my heart set on crying myself to sleep, and you are interrupting what promises to be a perfectly miserable evening."

Dante growled under his breath as he pivoted toward the door. Arguing with Erica only made him all the more frustrated. "Fine. Have your cry, but I intend to do something about my predicament." Dante tapped himself on his swelling chest to emphasize his point. "At least *I* have not given up hope. Some of us are fighters; others are whimperers. I guess you know which category you fit."

"And some of us don't give others a fighting chance!" Erica hurled at him, flashing him an accusing glare.

Dante paused at the door, leaning heavily on the latch as his piercing green eyes surveyed her bedraggled appearance. At least he had put some color in her pale cheeks, if nothing else. Since he had already upset her, he decided to give her more food for thought.

"Come now, love, are you so naïve that you don't know that fighting chances are never *given*, only *taken*. Opportunity breezes by the man who sits and waits."

Erica was in no mood for a philosophical lecture, and she detested Dante's implication that she lacked courage. She was every bit as daring as he was, and she was not going to let Dante Fowler preach to her. He was not without faults. Erica had an urge to fling something at him, but she came to the conclusion that it would take a boulder to shatter his colossal arrogance.

Dante's dark eyebrow rose, mockingly. "No clever retort? I never thought I would see you speechless."

"I have finally realized that it is a waste of breath to argue with you. Debating a mulish man accomplishes nothing." Erica shot back at him. "Think what you wish about me. I couldn't care less."

Dante made an exaggerated bow. "Thank you for your permission, *chérie*."

After he exited, Erica sighed. Why were they constantly at each other's throats? Why had she ridiculed his fighting spirit? He was right, although it galled her to admit that. She must pull herself together and stand up for what she wanted. Dante was seeking treasure, she was seeking love. If she truly wanted Dante then she would have to ensure that he felt his life would be meaningless without her.

Erica drew herself upright and peered at her disheveled reflection in the mirror. First she would make herself presentable; then she would go to Dante, just as Reade had come to her. But she would use finesse. She would make Dante desire her, and then she would fight *with* him instead of against him. As he had said, one must never give up hope. Clinging to that encouraging thought, Erica set about dazzling him with her appearance, although she prayed he would look deeper and would find the love she was willing to offer. It lurked just beneath her defensive exterior, feeding on the dim hope that the time they had spent together meant more to him than a passing fancy.

"Cap'n! It's the headland of Yucatán," Reade yelled as he gestured to the southwest.

Dante turned his attention from Erica and focused it on the puffy white clouds that indicated land just beyond the horizon. If Reade's wild story of treasure was true, he could return to America with enough capital to replace the steamboat and keep the plantation on its feet. Although Dante had been tempted to take Sabin's share of the sale of the cargo, he couldn't. He wanted to regain his lost fortune by his own means, not by stooping to the same methods Sabin would have employed. Erica's father would be reimbursed immediately, but Sabin would have to bargain for his share of the profit; and Dante had already decided what his uncle would have to relinquish for the heaping sack of coins.

Lingering at the helm, Dante watched the land on the horizon grow larger, nurturing the hope that Reade hadn't dragged him on a futile search. But he was still plagued by the nagging thought that his luck had run amuck. If he sailed away empty-handed, Erica would consider him a fool. It is little wonder she has no use for me, he told himself. She managed better in Guadeloupe without me, and she might have fared well against Sabin if she had wed Elliot.

Although Dante kept searching for some glimmer of hope, everything looked bleak. He had attempted to light a fire under Erica, but now her depression seemed contagious. He had no chance of winning her respect after all he had put her through, and he had very little chance of finding the Mayan treasure that Reade had sworn was theirs for the taking. Perhaps I should have tossed myself overboard, he thought as he strolled across the deck, intending to sulk in his cabin. Erica would be far happier, and he would not have to tell Corbin the distressing news that their financial position was precarious because

Dante had bargained with the devil and lost to his deceit.

While Dante slumped in his chair drowning his troubles in a bottle of brandy, the door of his cabin creaked open and he jerked up his head to glare at the intruder. His breath caught when his eyes beheld the tantalizing vision gracefully poised before him. Erica's seductive figure was framed by golden lantern light. Her dark hair, a sparkling sea of ebony, rippled over her shoulders to curl temptingly over her full breasts, and her gossamer gown flowed loosely about her. Dante did not move a muscle for fear of breaking the spell and making Erica retreat into the shadows. He considered pinching himself to ensure that his drunken mind was not playing tricks on him. He didn't quite believe that Erica would come to him after he had insulted her.

Aware of his hesitation, Erica smiled gently and then eased the door shut behind her. "Am I intruding on your thoughts, Dante?"

Her silky voice drifted toward him like a stirring breath of wind, at the moment he became aware of the delicate scent of her perfume. Dante wilted back in his chair, his senses absorbing the sight and aroma that fogged his thoughts.

"No," he rasped, his voice ragged with desire.

A seductive smile traced her lips as she reached up to unclasp her Grecian-style gown. "I've been thinking about what you said this afternoon," she murmured.

As the wispy fabric slid lower, Dante sucked in his breath. The creamy flesh of her breasts rose and fell with each breath she took, and the gown threatened to tumble downward, exposing what his eyes hungrily devoured.

Had she come to torment him after he had ridiculed her? Was this to be the final retribution for his mistreatment? Did she intend to amuse herself by making him crumble and then walking away?

Erica silently approached him, her soft expression changing until her blue eyes danced with deviltry. Dante detected their lively glint and hurriedly backed away before she tempted him past resistance and then cut him to shreds for imposing himself on her. He could not stand close to her without yielding.

One of Erica's delicate eyebrows arched in amusement as Dante sought out the farthest corner of the cabin. My, but he was behaving strangely. He had come charging into her room, roaring like a lion, but now he was cowering like a lamb. Yet she had never known this powerful man to retreat. She recalled the night she had found herself in a New Orleans brothel, hiding behind furniture to protect herself from the handsome rake who prowled about her like a panther stalking his prey. But the tables had turned, and it was Dante who was searching for shelter.

"Are you afraid of me, pirate captain?" she taunted as she strategically positioned herself between him and the door.

"Certainly not!" Dante snapped defensively.

"Then why are you standing in the corner?" Erica stepped closer and flashed him a challenging smile. "I never thought I would see the courageous pirate captain cowering."

"I am not cowering. I am only suspicious of your reason for being here."

"Isn't it obvious?" Erica whispered as she allowed her eyes to boldly caress him.

She untied the belt at her waist, and her gown fluttered to the floor. When she stepped over it and walked toward him, wearing nothing but a mischievous smile, Dante squeezed his eyes shut, but the vision of her luscious body had already been branded on his mind. He fought his urge to clutch her to him, thinking that, no doubt, she was waiting for him to yield to the lusting beast within him so that she could fiercely protest his advances. Yet it was all he could do to stand his ground.

Her fingertips trailed over his rugged cheek, investigating the stubborn set of his features and then tracing the sensuous curve of his lips. Dante sucked in his breath as her teasing caress trickled along his neck to seek out the buttons of his shirt and push it away from his chest. He died a thousand deaths as the peaks of her breasts brushed over the dark matting of hair there, and when her body inched closer to his, he groaned. She was driving him mad with her taunting seduction, and Dante's resistance lowered when her moist lips trailed across the slope of his shoulder. To fan the flames of his desire her hands played over his chest and then the taut tendons of his back, stroking him and languidly caressing away his determined resistance. God, how was he to withstand the urges sizzling through him? But she is waiting for me to succumb, he told himself as sweet sensations surged through his body.

"Why are you doing this?" he choked out. "Why not shoot me and end this torment? There's a pistol in the desk. For God's sake, use it!"

Erica marveled at his perseverance. If he were caressing her, she would have surrendered long ago. But perhaps he wasn't as vulnerable to her as she was to him. That possibility in mind, she took his suggestion and retrieved the weapon. If she had to hold him at gunpoint, she would do so, but she wasn't leaving his cabin until she had what she wanted—Dante. She wanted uninterrupted hours of bliss to counteract the agony she had endured this past month. She scooped up his discarded shirt, shrugged it on, and then rummaged through the desk for the pistol.

Dante pried one eye open and then breathed a sigh of relief when she moved away from him, but he flinched when she turned about and rammed the gun in his abdomen.

"Since you are making this difficult, you leave me no choice. Now drop your breeches."

Dante gaped at her. Did she intend to strip him of his pride *and* his clothes before she blew him to smithereens?

Erica jabbed him again. "I do not have all night. Shed your pants or I will shoot them to pieces with you in them," she threatened, her blue eyes sparkling with amusement.

"You wouldn't," Dante challenged as his eyes involuntarily slid over the seductive enchantress who had already confiscated his shirt and who was now demanding his breeches. Surely Erica wasn't bloodthirsty. Bitter and angry, yes, but cold-blooded? Dante had pushed her so far that he was almost afraid to answer his own question. Although he was reasonably certain he could have snatched the weapon from her hand, he couldn't guarantee that it wouldn't explode during their struggle. And with Erica's aim, she could easily render him useless to any woman.

"Don't test me, Dante. I rarely back down from a dare," she assured him soberly, even though she was secretly amused by the wary expression on his face.

As Dante reached down to unfasten his breeches, the look in her eyes was more mischievous than vicious and the faintest hint of a smile lifted one corner of her mouth. That, and the fact that she hadn't blown him to bits, eased his tension. Perhaps she wants something other than revenge, he speculated. Besides, what do I have to lose? What sane man would deny a half-naked woman who aimed a pistol at him?

"Would it be too much to ask you to explain your motives, minx?" As his husky voice glided over her, Erica shivered at its seductive sound.

When he grinned, she had difficulty following through with her charade. As his features absorbed his disarming smile, it carved lines in his cheeks, and as his sensuous lips curved upward, Erica melted like snow tossed into a roaring fire.

"I want you to make love to me, and that will not be possible if you have your clothes on," Erica informed him.

"At gunpoint?" Dante croaked. "Really, love, that seems a bit unconventional, even for you. I will be happy to accommodate you . . . for a certain price."

"The same price I was paid in the brothel?" Erica's perfectly arched brow rose, and her smile was slightly taunting. "That price would be much too high in this instance. I lost more than my dignity that night. I am not taking *your* innocence," she reminded him flatly. "And I would hate to venture a guess as to how long ago you lost it."

The smile that played on his lips vanished as he stared into her eyes. "I cannot help what I am," he told her softly, "and I cannot change the past. But my price is that you and I make a new beginning, to forget the bitterness."

"You want a truce of sorts?" Erica studied him thoughtfully. "I suppose it couldn't hurt. Besides, if it doesn't work out, I can always resort to using your pistol on you."

"With just cause," Dante murmured as his outstretched hand folded over hers, then placed the pistol on the desk. "But first I should be allowed to plead my case, don't you agree?"

The warm glow of passion flickered in his eyes as his arm slid beneath the shirt to make bold contact with her smooth flesh, and Erica found it difficult to reply, his touch excited her so.

"Present your defense," she offered as her arms curled over his broad shoulders to toy with the shaggy hair that hugged the nape of his neck.

"With pleasure," he rasped seductively.

His lips hovered only inches from hers, stirring a need that had long gone unappeased, and then his mouth claimed hers, their breath intermingling. His probing tongue traced her upper lip and then glided into the hidden recesses of her mouth. As his kiss deepened his hard body pressed against hers, forging them together.

When his lips abandoned hers, Erica tried to cling to them, wanting the delicious kiss to last forever, but as his warm breath skipped across her cheek to seek out the sensitive point beneath her ear, he murmured, "That was but the first point in case." Then his fingers glided over the curves of her hips. "And here is but another reason I would prefer you didn't dispose of me just yet." His deliberate caresses trailed across her thighs and then ascended until his hands cupped her breasts while his kisses showered her shoulder with tantalizing sensations that quenched one need only to create another. "Because I *love* touching you like this. . . ." His voice revealed that his deliberate assault on her senses was having an equally devastating effect on him.

A tiny moan escaped her as Dante nuzzled his cheek in the valley between her breasts, suckling one pink peak and then the other. She cradled his raven head against her, overwhelmed by the musky scent that invaded her senses, the feel of his muscular body, and the explorations of his lips and hands.

"And because I *crave* to touch you like this. . . ." Dante's hand splayed over her abdomen to gently guide her thighs apart before it flowed upward like a rolling wave to curl around one rose-tipped crest and then the other. In the wake of his caress Erica sighed, and her lashes fluttered down to block out everything but the feel of his skillful hands sensitizing her entire body, inflaming her.

"You stir me like no other woman. Your very name evokes a longing that, once it is satisfied, leaves me with a deeper craving, continually fed, like an eternal spring." His voice was ragged, and his lips hovered over her flesh, weaving intricate patterns on her belly and then tracing her inner thighs. When his fingers delved into her womanly softness, a wave of pleasure washed through her. But his hand again scaled her abdomen before it ventured farther downward as his lips folded around a roseate bud and his other hand brushed over the other thrusting pink peak.

His hands and lips were everywhere, tasting her, caressing her, practicing exquisite torture. "I can't get enough of you," Dante murmured, his hands and lips investigating every inch of Erica's body as he rejoiced in the feel of her. "You're a fire in my blood."

Erica caught her breath as his kisses defined her waist while his knowing fingers probed deeper, leaving her burning with a hunger that originated in her very core. She was hot and cold, trembling. She wanted him so badly that her need drove out all thought. His caresses were sweetly tormenting; they spilled over her like molten lava.

Then he turned her to him, his manliness pressing intimately against her as his powerful arms slid over her hips to pull her closer. A groan of longing burst from him as he buried himself within her, his dark head nuzzling her shoulder, his lips lovingly nipping the trim column of her neck, his hot breath chilling her flesh.

"Erica, I need you. I want you as I have from the beginning . . ." he whispered raggedly.

As he moved gently within her, the flames of their passion burned hotter, firing them both with hungry impatience, and primal needs swept over them like a crowning fire. Their bodies blended, their hearts beating in frantic rhythm, he plunged deeply within her, seeking the ultimate depths of intimacy; and together they soared toward the far horizon, spiraling on pinioned wings through the rapturous expanse of the universe, touching blazing stars, and basking in the warmth of ecstasy, which had the heat of a thousand suns.

Erica clutched him closer as indescribable sensations shot through her, proclaiming the essence of her being. She was a living, breathing part of him and he was the warm flame within her, her reason for being, and a never-ending need that blossomed and unfurled like the velvet petals of a rose.

Then she hung suspended in a dark universe, living

and dying in the sweet splendor that consumed her, penetrating her every nerve and muscle. The enormity of her pleasure left her quaking and gasping for breath, as Dante again drove into her, clutching her to him as if he never meant to let her go, before a groan of utter fulfillment spilled from his lips to hers and his taut male body shuddered in rapturous release.

While the embers of their desire cooled, its warmth remained, assuring Erica that their passion, though temporarily appeased, could easily be rekindled into a raging blaze. She sighed contentedly as the haze of pleasure gradually dissipated; then her lashes fluttered up and she saw Dante's handsome face hovering above her.

As her gaze drifted about the cabin, an embarrassed gasp escaped her lips for their maddening craving for each other had been satisfied in the very corner in which Dante had backed himself. His sinewy arms were braced against the wall and hers were resting on his narrow hips. A becoming blush colored her cheeks as her eyes met rippling green pools surrounded by dark, thick lashes.

"It was my first time too," he said quickly as he interpreted the cause of her discomposure. "I suppose I became so involved in"—his raspy voice trailed off as he flashed her a roguish grin—"in pleading my case that I forgot where I was." His index finger traced her kiss-swollen lips; his eyes focused on their sensuous curve. "When I was a child and my mother ordered me to stand in a corner for misbehaving, never in my wildest dreams did I imagine it could also serve such an arousing purpose."

Erica laughed despite her momentary embarrassment. "No more than I imagined that a wardrobe closet could also serve as a cozy niche for kissing."

Dante's suggestive gaze shifted to the unoccupied bed, that place most often considered passion's nest, a place in which he and Erica had seldom satisfied their insatiable cravings for each other. The thought that they had done so on the grass, on a carriage seat, in bathtubs, and now in a corner amused him, and he chortled as he bent to kiss her velvety lips.

"Shall we try the bed, *chérie?* It seems we have made very little use of it."

Erica gave her head a negative shake as her hands glided over the broad expanse of his chest. "I still haven't decided if your case would *stand up* in a court of law," she teased, her sapphire eyes dancing with deviltry. "You have not allowed the prosecution its counterdefense."

Her wandering gaze flooded over his muscular physique, seductively measuring the width of his shoulders and the slimness of his tapered waist, then following the crisp dark hair that trickled down his belly. When her lips brushed over his male nipples and then trailed along the lean planes of his belly, Dante moaned. Her butterfly kisses and her taunting caresses, so light and exquisite, made him long to throw himself on the mercy of the court. If this was to be his punishment, Dante would not complain about making retribution for a lifetime. Lord, her sweet torture created one maddening craving after another. As her exploring caresses climbed his spine to investigate the hard muscles of his back, her lips returned to his for a fleeting moment. Then they fluttered over the line of his jaw to seek out the rapid pulsations in his neck before venturing to his chest to feel his runaway heart stampeding against his ribs. Her silent assault was so deliberate and thorough, so wildly disturbing, that it drove Dante to the brink of mad desire. She was savoring the feel of his male body with her fingertips and lips, creating a maelstrom of sensations that left him gasping to catch a breath. When her hand folded about him, boldly caressing him, he groaned with the want of her. His nerves spun into tangled twine, and as her lips stimulated his quaking flesh, he melted into liquid desire.

"I yield," Dante breathed raggedly.

It pleased Erica that she had such power over this magnificent man, and her hands continued to wander at will. "The defense rests?" she asked, a provocative smile pursing her lips.

"No contest," Dante affirmed as his hands moved up her arms to cup her face. "Do with me what you will. I am long past caring."

Then his mouth slanted across hers. Gone was his tender patience, lost in the swirling sea of sensations that engulfed him. His tongue eagerly sought to mate with hers as his fingertips delved into her raven hair, tilting her head back to grant him free access to the soft, moist lips that opened beneath his. Sinewy arms imprisoned her in a fierce embrace, and as he pressed her supple body to his, he forced her back to the wall, stealing her breath with his ravenous kiss, wedging his muscled leg between her thighs, and pressing flesh to flesh as the fervent heat of desire raced through him.

They became as one, touching, kissing, sharing the same erratic breath. Time stood still as they cascaded into the rapids of turbulent emotions which carried them into the whirlpool created by love's embrace. Then they were towed far beneath the currents of desire, and they were drowning in their ardent craving for each other.

Erica held her breath as tempestuous tides of passion pulled her along, pressing closer to Dante, arching to meet his hard thrusts, giving herself completely. When she cried out, Dante muffled the sound with his kiss as he drove into her, taking her with him into that dark, rapturous abyss where only their delicious pleasure existed.

When their bodies shuddered in sweet release, Dante collapsed against her and waited for his heart to slow. Making love with Erica was always so complete and so devastating that he had to regain his strength. She leaves no part of me untouched, he mused. Then, as he breathed against her swanlike neck, he realized that her pulse beat was gradually becoming normal.

Mustering the last of his energy, Dante scooped Erica into his arms and carried her to the bed, falling with her onto the sheets. If she had any intention of slipping back to her own cabin, Dante intended to let her know he did not want her to go. He had spent too many nights alone. Although they had resolved nothing, their need for each other had not ebbed, and he wanted to drift into sleep with Erica in his arms.

She voiced no complaint as Dante pressed one last kiss to her lips and then relaxed beside her. There was no place she would rather be than in the unending circle of his arms. Never again would she allow bitterness and pride to keep her from him. She loved him, so she would take each day and night as it came, enjoying the pleasures he offered. That will be enough; it has to be enough, she told herself as she snuggled against his shoulder and allowed her eyes to close. The love she felt for Dante could come only once in a lifetime, and when they went their separate ways, she would have to survive a broken heart, but she would cherish her memories of their spontaneous lovemaking. That decided, Erica followed Dante into deep sleep.

Chapter 23

A tender smile hovered on Dante's lips as the sun shone through the porthole, casting its dancing light on Erica's flawless features. The previous night had been beyond description, and even in the light of day his memory of the way she had made him burn with passion had not dimmed. His warm gaze claimed her creamy flesh, just as surely as his hands had possessed her shapely body the previous night. Tempted though he was to rekindle the flame that leaped through his veins, Dante carefully inched away to don the clothes he had shed at gunpoint when the bewitching minx had seduced him in her unique way.

Casting one last glance at the sleeping beauty in his bed, Dante quietly closed the door behind him and climbed the steps to the quarter-deck. His keen gaze swept the coastline, where dense forests cut a jagged line against the blue horizon. Before nightfall he would know if Reade's tales of fortune were true. God, how he hoped they were.

"We're 'bout ready, Cap'n," Reade informed Dante as

he ambled up beside him and then gestured toward the skiff he had lowered into the water.

As Dante prepared to take up the oars to row toward shore, a shadow fell over him and he glanced up to see Erica, garbed in breeches, shirt, and boots she had borrowed from a small lad on the crew, climbing down the rope ladder toward him.

"What the devil . . ." Reade's eyes bulged as Erica planted herself on the seat between him and Dante, her eyes fixed on the foreign shore. "She ain't goin' with us, is she, Cap'n?" he squeaked in disbelief.

"No." Dante's stern gaze focused on her determined face. "Get back on board the schooner," he ordered.

Erica paid him no heed. She had made up her mind that Dante was going nowhere without her. She intended to become his shadow, whether he liked it or not. Shoving the sack of equipment aside, Erica settled herself more comfortably on her perch.

"Erica, I said go back to the ship," Dante said more forcefully, but still she didn't budge.

"I have sailed the Caribbean and endured the worst of storms," she reminded him breezily. "Don't think for one minute that you can stash me in my cabin while you blaze your way through uncharted territory. Besides, last night you said—"

"I know what I said," Dante grumbled, flashing Erica a silencing frown. He had told her how she pleased him and how he longed to keep her by his side. But this wasn't the side-by-side companionship he'd had in mind, and she damned well knew it.

"Well, I don't know what you said," Reade snorted as he darted a glance at Erica and Dante, who were flashing silent messages with their eyes.

410

"It was a private conversation," Dante muttered sourly. Then he gave Erica the evil eye. "I want you back on the schooner where I know you will be safe."

Erica tilted a rebellious chin. "I am going with you."

Her words rang with determination, and Dante could tell by the expression on her face that it would take more than ropes and pulleys to pry her loose from her perch. When this stubborn chit made up her mind to something, a team of wild horses couldn't drag her from her obstinate stand.

"Very well then, I expect to hear no complaints," he declared in a patronizing tone. "This cannot be compared to a Sunday picnic in the park. It will be rough traveling, across rugged terrain, and once we go ashore, there will be no turning back."

"Yore lettin' her go?" Reade hooted incredulously. "Lordy, man, there's a jungle awaitin' us. I know. I've bin there before!"

Erica twisted in her seat to turn her pleading eyes on Reade and to bless him with a smile that would melt his resistance. "If I remain on board to sit and stew, it would cause me more distress than accompanying you to Yucatán." Her tangled lashes swept down to lightly touch her cheeks as a guilty expression settled on her exquisite features. "I fear my adventurous spirit has gotten the best of me, Reade. Please let me go with you. I promise not to cause trouble."

When her dainty hand folded over his, Reade's opposition dissolved. This feisty beauty was the only woman who had ever been able to sway him from his better judgment. Confound it, he was a silly old fool for allowing her to talk him into this, but he was powerless to resist her when she blinded him with that radiant smile. What

411

harm will it do? he asked himself. Erica seemed to be a delicate flower, but, in truth, she was made of sturdy stuff. She had proved it time and time again. She could endure the journey; she wasn't the squeamish type and she didn't cower when there was trouble.

"Oh, all right," Reade consented, breathing a defeated sigh. "The cap'n can't tell you no and neither can I."

Erica beamed delightedly, her gaze swinging to the canopy of trees and thick undergrowth that covered the headland of Yucatán. She was determined to remain by Dante's side, no matter how difficult the problems they faced, and she had never been one to turn her back on adventure. The mere thought of blazing a trail through uncivilized territory sent adrenaline spurting through her veins. She was most anxious to explore a land that she had only envisioned from descriptions in books.

As the rowboat cut through the water, Erica's anticipation mounted. Reade had assured her that the Mayas were a friendly but superstitious sort, not prone to cannibalistic tendencies so she did not fear that she would be served up for supper. However, he had purposely failed to mention the torture Mayas inflicted on unwanted visitors who seemed a threat to their existence.

When the skiff ran aground, Erica felt a knot of apprehension coil in her stomach. What if? . . . She stifled the thought before it grew into fear. Although the shoreline was abandoned, her active imagination pictured savages leaping from the underbrush to attack them. Keep a tight grip on yourself, Erica silently ordered as she stepped ashore to reevaluate the dense forest that surrounded them.

Reade gestured to the east and then grabbed a sack of equipment. "Yonder lies Chichén Itzá, the center of

Mayan civilization. They abandoned most of their other strongholds." His shoulders lifted in a shrug as he led the way through the sand. "I don't rightly know why. I never could figure why all them Indians congregated in one city. Epidemics maybe," he guessed. "Or maybe it had somethin' to do with their pagan gods. I s'pose makin' human sacrifices didn't please the great spirits like them Mayans thought it would."

"Human sacrifices?" The color drained from Erica's cheeks, and she broke stride. Lord, what had she gotten herself into this time?

"There!" Reade pointed to a cove lush with trees and greenery. "We can cut our way to the Well of Sacrifice. It's been abandoned for years. If a man didn't know it was there, he would never find it in all that vegetation."

Erica peered at Dante who hadn't shown any indication of fear. No doubt, he was envisioning the treasure Reade had promised was theirs for the taking. Dante was hoping that the fortune in the well would reimburse him for the losses Sabin's treachery had caused. He was determined to regain all that was rightfully his if it was the last thing he ever did. Erica swallowed hard as she surveyed the shoreline choked with dense growth; then she took a deep breath of the humid air. It was so heavy and sticky one could almost slice it with a knife. She prayed this wouldn't be the last thing she and Dante ever did. No treasure hunt was worth becoming a human sacrifice in the unclaimed territory of Chichén Itzá.

When they reached the cove, Dante swung his sack to the ground and fished through it to retrieve the machetes. He shoved one into Erica's hands, took one for himself, and handed another to Reade; then he directed her attention to the suffocating undergrowth that made Erica feel it would swallow them up when they set foot in it.

"We'll chop a path to the well . . . and cut down anything else that moves," he informed her, grinning wryly. "Are you certain you wouldn't have preferred to remain on the schooner?"

Erica clutched the heavy-bladed knife and set her chin determinedly as she marched toward the thick vines that reminded her of entwined snakes. "I am quite certain. I only hope Reade didn't dream all this up. I have imagined myself in many adverse situations, and some of them have even paralleled reality, but I never thought of myself as someone's midday meal."

"I told you they don't eat humans." Reade snickered as he wedged himself in front of Erica and swung his heavy sack over his shoulder. "But they do have other uses for women, if you want to hear 'bout them."

"No thank you," Erica chirped. She swallowed the lump that had suddenly risen in her throat and then followed in Reade's wake. She could well imagine what purpose she might serve, and she didn't want to think about it. We'll simply have to be careful, slip in and out of the forest without getting caught, she told herself, mustering her courage as insects swarmed about them, making their intolerable situation even more unbearable. But she did not voice a complaint about providing a meal for the mosquitoes even though they threatened to eat her alive.

After three hours of fighting the tangled brush, Reade pointed ahead of them. "There lies the well."

His voice was laced with excitement, but Erica and Dante could not share his enthusiasm. Before them, overgrown with vegetation were the remnants of a stone temple and a long, sacrificial platform that tilted precariously over a limestone sinkhole where the earth had collapsed into an underground river. The bottomless pit was almost two hundred feet in diameter, and its stone walls extended downward much farther than Erica cared to look. She became wide-eyed as Dante urged her closer and her gaze tumbled the full seventy feet to the fetid water below. God help her! This wasn't at all what she had imagined when Reade had raved about the Well of Sacrifice! She had pictured a small pit, not a monstrous hole in the ground!

Her knees went weak as she peered down into the gloomy murk, and she clutched Dante's arm for support when a helpless feeling made her heart pound and she felt that she was about to fall into the limestone sinkhole.

"I hope you have overcome your fear of heights." Dante chuckled as he shot a glance at Erica's white face. "Reade's supposed treasure lies buried in that muck."

Erica cringed at the thought of sliding down the limestone walls and ending up in that stagnant water. She was certain some dreadful creature was waiting to gobble her up. She braced herself for another glance over the edge as Reade and Dante rummaged through their packs to retrieve the ropes. When Dante hurled the lifeline over the platform and secured it to a gnarled tree, Erica's stomach turned inside out. God, why did she have to detest heights? Her one fear kept cropping up to torment her.

As Dante swung over the side and disappeared from sight, Erica held her breath and carefully inched closer, overwhelmed by the maddening feeling that she was about to leap to her death. When Reade tugged on her arm, Erica very nearly took the fall she so desperately feared, but she wheeled around and clutched at Reade, hanging on to him for dear life while he squawked in surprise. He hadn't expected to have the stuffing squeezed out of him.

"What's wrong with you? You know I wouldn't shove you in!" Reade complained as he pried her arms loose and then peered bewilderedly into her alarmed face.

Dante's laughter echoed up from the bottomless hole. "Oh Reade, I forgot to tell you . . . Erica is deathly afraid of heights."

Reade's mouth gaped open, and his eyes grew round as he surveyed the young woman who still clung to him like a choking vine. "You? I don't believe it. I didn't think you was afraid of nothin'."

His voice brought her to her senses, and Erica willed herself to release her stranglehold on him. "Only that," she rasped as she pointed a trembling finger toward the bottom of the pit. "I cannot seem to help it. When I stand too close to the edge, I have this overwhelming feeling that I am going to jump, even when I have no desire to do so. It is like a magnet pulls me on and I—"

Reade groaned and rolled his eyes. "Lordy, I can't swim and you can't look down without gettin' light-headed," he muttered in disgust. "We ain't gonna be no help to Dante at all."

His remark fired her determination. She decided that she would not succumb to her fear again, not in front of Dante and Reade, not when Dante needed a helping hand. Gritting her teeth, Erica grasped the rope and then knelt with her back to the cliff. She stretched out her legs to leave them hanging in the air as she inched over the edge, keeping her eyes focused on the ledge above her. She tried not to think of anything except moving downward until she could set her feet on something that didn't slope at a ninety-degree angle. And although her heart thundered and her breath came in short, ragged spurts, Erica slowly descended into the pit.

Relief washed over her when she felt Dante's steadying hands on her waist, guiding her to the boulder at the edge of the water. He brought her against his lean, muscled form and then turned her to face him. A frown furrowed her perspiring brow as she peered up to see a strange glow in his emerald eyes. Why was he looking at her like that?

Then his sensuous lips parted in a smile as his head came toward hers. Erica was pinned to the limestone wall as he pressed, full-length against her, and the kiss he planted on her mouth was heated enough to make the murky water steam. The weakness that had overwhelmed her as she'd walked down the wall couldn't hold a candle to the feelings that consumed her when Dante took her in his strong arms and kissed her senseless. If he had commanded her to walk across that monster-infested pool she would have done so, to please him. God, how she adored this green-eyed rogue who was the devil's own temptation. He filled her senses until they were attuned to the sight, feel, and manly fragrance that clung to him and then to her.

When Dante finally dragged his lips from hers, Erica blinked bewilderedly. "Why did you do that? And here of all places?" It wasn't that she didn't enjoy his flaming kiss—indeed, she would have requested a dozen more just like it—but they were up to their ankles in muck, standing in a foul-smelling pit seventy feet deep, and only God knew what detestable creatures were slithering about.

His shoulder lifted in a noncommittal shrug as he pushed away from the rock wall and pivoted on the partially submerged boulder to survey the muddy water. "Why did you come with me? Why did you scale that precarious wall when we both know your fear of heights?" He answered her question with questions of his own.

"Because I live for thrills," Erica responded, an undertone of sarcasm in her voice. "Now why did you kiss me like that in a place like this?"

Watching Erica descend the wall and seeing the sunlight catch her thin shirt to display her full breasts had, quite simply, sidetracked him. Erica had always been a distraction he couldn't resist, whether they were riding in a brougham in the rain or standing in a corner and fighting over who was to claim his breeches—or perched inside the bowels of the earth.

"I was pursuing a whim," was his belated reply. "And I thought you were sorely in need of kissing after your daredevil feat."

That matter settled, Dante turned his attention to the business at hand. He shed his shirt and boots and then slid into the murky water before flashing Erica one of the lopsided smiles that made her heart turn over.

"If I don't resurface in a few minutes, get the sweet loving hell out of here." His rippling green eyes appraised her shapely figure, not missing even the smallest detail. "I should hate to have such a lovely morsel gobbled up by whatever lies at the bottom of this well."

When Dante grabbed a clawlike tool to scrape up the

mud and then submerged himself in the dark depths, Erica turned quite pale. She held her breath and waited anxiously for him to reappear, to assure her that he had not provided a feast for the creatures that lived in the black abyss. Finally, after what seemed an eternity, his muddy head emerged and he wiped his face to flash her a wide, but grimy grin. He unfolded his outstretched hand and then rubbed his thumb over the solid gold ceremonial cup that he had confiscated from the silted pond.

Erica sank down beside him to take the relic, gazing at it in amazement. "Do you suppose Reade is correct? Could there be a fortune in the bottom of this well?"

"I think what waits in the mud can replace my losses," Dante assured her.

"Well, did you find anythin'?" Reade called as he leaned out over the sacrificial platform.

"Gold!" Dante's voice was vibrant with success, but he squawked in surprise when Erica jumped over him and disappeared into the murky depths.

"What the hell is she doin'?" Reade yelled as his alarmed gaze fell on Dante.

"Treasure hunting," Dante responded. "I do believe the lady has been caught up in the adventure."

"And no tellin' what else." Reade grunted as he squatted down to look farther over the ledge.

A secretive smile bordered Dante's lips as he laid the gold cup aside and followed Erica into the opaque pool. He was amazed by her courage. She was like the rare gem he sought. There seemed to be nothing she wouldn't try, except jumping off a window ledge into a tree. Any other woman would have drawn back from the rancid water, but Erica had jumped right in, ready to tackle whatever obstacles came her way. That wild vixen never ceased to surprise him, Dante mused as he groped in the mud, seeking the lost treasures of the well.

After two hours of digging in the silt, Dante and Erica had collected a sackful of jade and turquoise ornaments, alabaster vases, gold bells, pendants, silver and seashell bracelets, and several copper tools. One of their finds was a solid gold necklace, inlaid with huge precious stones that had made Erica catch her breath when she'd scraped the object clean. This item alone could cover Dante's losses, she thought delightedly.

Dante lifted the necklace from her hands and laid it around her neck. Then he sank back to view the bedraggled beauty whose captivating blue eyes sparkled brighter than the stunning jewelry that clung to her neck.

"Erica, there is something I—"

"Cap'n you better git up here!" Reade's apprehensive voice wafted way down to Dante, spurring him to action. "We got trouble!"

"You stay put," Dante threw over his shoulder as he scurried up the rope, bracing his feet against the limestone wall and pulling himself up hand over hand.

Erica tensed nervously as she watched Dante walk straight up the wall. She had certainly learned that when things went wrong they did so at the most inopportune moment. Had the Mayan Indians discovered them? Were they about to become sacrifices to the pagan gods who guarded the ancient ceremonial ground? Erica was imagining all sorts of horrible punishments: Dante being strung up by his heels, roasting over a blazing fire, even . . . Erica shuddered. She hated to think what else a tribe of angry savages might do to him.

Gritting her teeth, she grasped the rope and hauled herself upward, not daring to look down and apprehensive about what she would find when she reached the top.

Dante's mouth was set in a grim line as he and Reade squatted in the heavy brush beside the Temple of the Last Rites, watching a handful of Mayans step cautiously toward the platform that jutted out over the well. Fearing Erica would be spotted and seized by the Mayans, Dante gathered his feet beneath him and prepared to lunge from his hiding place to take on the entire search party. But Reade grabbed his arm and hauled him back into the brush.

"It's suicide to confront them now," he warned in a hushed voice. "They'll kill you before you could do anythin' to save her. Dammit, man, you just don't leap out of the underbrush when yore outnumbered ten to one."

"And if I don't try something, they might kill her," Dante muttered as he pried Reade's hand from his arm.

"And what good are you gonna be to her when they separate yore head from yore shoulders for scaring the wits out of them?" Reade shot back and then squinted through the brush. "Hell's bells!"

Dante followed Reade's gaze to see what had brought on his surprised squawk; then he groaned when Erica's muddy head slowly inched above the ledge. A murmur of shock rippled through the party of Indians. Dante could not tell for certain who was more surprised to see whom, but he was quick to detect the loss of color in Erica's smudged cheeks. Her alarmed shriek echoed around the limestone walls, adding several new cracks to those it had taken Mother Nature millions of years to create. Erica slid backward, and her flailing legs dangled in midair as she scratched and clawed for a grip on the lifeline. This is it, she thought as she gasped for breath, but she finally managed to pull herself up enough so she could swing one leg onto the platform. Her eyes immediately swept up to see the chieftain poised before her, his feet straddled, his dark eyes popping. The swarthy Mayan ruler wore a feathered, ceremonial headdress, and he reminded Erica of a plump ostrich. Circlets of gold and silver were clamped around his elbows and ankles, a white loin cloth barely concealed his hips, and a blood red cape cascaded from his shoulders. From the gold chain around his neck hung a pendant that closely resembled the one Dante had placed around Erica's throat.

Forcing what she hoped was a cordial smile, Erica drew her dangling leg onto the platform and then rose to her full height, determined to face disaster without displaying a trace of fear. She had no intention of meeting her maker with a look of horror on her face. Darting a quick glance around the area, Erica could only assume that Reade and Dante had been captured and whisked away. Soon I will be with Dante, she told herself, then she was stung by the dreadful thought that she might be tossed back into the well without ever laying eyes on Dante again.

The chief raised his ceremonial weapon, which was equipped with barbed tips, and for a moment Erica was certain he intended to hurl it at her. But when he spied the necklace she wore, his arm stopped in midair and he staggered backward as if Erica had suddenly knocked the wind out of him. His black eyes shot open wide in disbelief as his amazed gaze took in her mud-caked clothes. Then he directed an unintelligible remark to the other men who stood behind him, while Erica stood as still as a statue, wishing she understood what the chief was saying. The tension was so thick she could have sliced it with her machete, which she would have given anything to have had in her hands. She had the nervous feeling that she was going to need a weapon.

A quiet chuckle bubbled in Reade's chest, and Dante could have choked him for finding demented amusement in Erica's plight.

"The old chief says Erica must be the muse of the well since she wears the sacred jewels of his forefathers." Reade paused to listen as the Mayan ruler spoke to his men; then he translated for Dante who had half-collapsed in the brush. "The chief says the appearance of this goddess is a sign from the gods. No one has ever emerged from the bottomless well, and that's the proof that she's a spirit who has taken human form."

Dante smiled to himself. Surely fate had brought Erica along with them. She had gotten a high price for the cargo, and now she had kept the superstitious Mayans from disposing of them.

Although Reade and Dante knew that the Mayans posed no threat to her existence, Erica had no idea what was to become of her. Apprehension got the best of her, and the words gushed from her lips.

"What have you done with my friends? I wish to be taken to them." She gestured to the east, the direction in which Reade had said the heart of the Mayan civilization lay. "If you have killed them, then kill me as well." Tears welled up in her eyes as her control threatened to desert her. "God, Dante, where are you?" she wailed, her voice floating back to the well to come back at her from all directions.

The Indians retreated several more steps, and Reade shook his head in bewilderment. "Now the chief thinks the muse is orderin' him to leave the Sacrificial Well. Lordy," he chuckled. "Erica's screamin' out for help, and them Indians are backin' off as if she's spoutin' demands at them."

When the Mayans pivoted on their heels and scattered into the forest like a herd of stampeding horses, Erica's mouth dropped open and she stared incredulously after them. The rustling in the underbrush then drew her attention, and she jumped as if she had been snakebit. But an angry red stained her pale cheeks when Dante and Reade strutted out of the vegetation, grinning like two witless creatures. Her short-fused temper exploded like a keg of gunpowder. Damn them! They had cowered in the brush like frightened rabbits, leaving her to confront the savages. She would have expected as much from Reade, who always looked out for himself first, only considering his companions after he was assured that he had saved his own neck. But Dante? He had his faults, plenty of them, but he had never abandoned her when she'd sorely needed help. Obviously, however, now that he no longer had a use for her, he was content to sit back and let her fend for herself amidst the dark-skinned heathens who swarmed the forests of Yucatán.

Erica turned on him, her fury evident in the set of her jaw, her blue eyes blazing like torches. "You are despicable!" she hissed, venom dripping from her lips. "You left me out here all by myself while you slithered back under your rock. I was helping you dig up your treasure, and what thanks am I offered in return?" Erica's face bespoke her contempt. "*You* leave me to the savages!"

Dante could not suppress his wide grin. Erica was magnificent when she was breathing fire. No wonder the Mayans had turned tail and run. She could send birds to flight when she was enraged.

After bowing before her, Dante gestured to the necklace that encircled her throat. "Your ceremonial jewels saved us all, *chérie*. You were in no danger. The Mayans think you are a messenger from their god, an omen the high spirit has sent up from the bottomless pit to take on a human form."

His explanation took the wind out of her sails. "What?" Erica stared off in the direction in which the heathens had fled. "That is preposterous."

"Not to them," Reade interjected with a chuckle. "They got some funny notions about this well bein' filled with powerful spirits. No human who was ever tossed in it survived. When you crawled out of that pit wearin' that sacred necklace, them Mayans thought you was a spirit come to deliver a message to them."

Before Erica could decry such ridiculous logic, Dante grasped her arm and dragged her along beside him. "I think it's time we gathered our treasure. I don't relish the idea of confronting those Indians again. They may have considered you a goddess, but I doubt that Reade and I would fare as well." He directed Erica's attention to the sacrificial platform. "Guard the well, muse, whilst I descend into the jaws of hell to retrieve the gems."

Erica couldn't stay angry with him when he favored her with one of those disarming smiles that touched every craggy feature on his face. She adored Dante, and she had risked everything to be with him, even her own life, but when they had returned to New Orleans, he would sail back to Natchez. They had so little time. That thought sent her spirits plunging to the bottom of the well from which she had ascended.

"I can't wait to git my hands on them gems," Reade confessed, arousing Erica from her pensive contemplation. "Nobody would believe me when I said there was a fortune in Yucatán. Now they'll know I wasn't spinnin' wild yarns." When Dante scurried back up the rope, gathered his equipment, and aimed himself in the direction of their rowboat, Reade stared incredulously at him. "We ain't leavin' without searchin' the Temple of the Last Rites, are we? I'll bet my right arm them tombs are heapin' with treasure."

"I draw the line at diving into scummy wells. I have no intention of confiscating treasure from ancient tombs. We have enough wealth in these sacks to live out the rest of our lives in luxury." Dante's hard gaze fixed on Reade who was grumbling sourly at his decision. "Greed does strange things to men and I want no part of it."

Reade heaved a perturbed sigh and then fell into step behind Dante and Erica. "I don't see no harm in takin' advantage of the situation," he muttered. "We got Erica here to protect us from them Mayans. They won't question anythin' she does and we could—"

Dante wheeled to face Reade, holding him captive with his probing stare. "The answer is no. If you want to search the tombs, buy yourself a schooner and return for the treasure we left behind—it will be yours alone—but I have no desire to delay. I have business in New Orleans."

As Dante turned and walked away, Reade wryly smiled. Maybe Dante was right. Why share the fortune when he could have it all to himself? If he had further need of money he knew exactly where to find it. Content with that thought, he tossed his sack over his shoulder and quickened his step.

Erica followed Dante as they picked their way through the underbrush, loving him all the more because he had refused to disturb the ancient tombs. They had fished enough treasure from the well. Erica shivered repulsively at the thought of what they might find in the tombs. Thank goodness Dante had objected. Her near brush with death was still too recent to permit her to want to stare Mayan mummies in the face.

Chapter 24

A pleased smile lighted Dante's bronzed features as he eased back in his chair to survey the gold, silver, and priceless stones he and Erica had scrubbed until they sparkled. Now he could afford to pay for the loss of the *Natchez Belle* and the cotton crop. When he faced Sabin and Avery he would have the backing of his own wealth. He would not be at Sabin's mercy.

When Dante's pensive gaze drifted to Erica, he marveled at her flawless complexion and at the way the candlelight danced in her blue eyes, recalling each splendrous night he had spent in her arms. A faint smile brimmed his lips as his eyes traveled over her trim figure. She seemed so delicate, and yet she was such a free spirit, one so willful and determined that she refused to accept defeat. They had been to hell and back together, but she had survived it all. Could he set her ashore and let her walk away after he had settled his differences with Sabin? Could he bury the memories of these past few months, forget the pleasure and passion, the stormy arguments? Could he blot out all the emotions that coursed through him at the sight of her?

Erica's thick lashes swept up, and she smiled as she lifted a silver and turquoise pendant, offering it to him. "These precious jewels for your thoughts," she murmured. "I thought you would be sitting on top of the world after finding your treasure, but you are very quiet tonight."

Dante hesitated to speak his mind, for he was apprehensive about Erica's reaction. He never knew where he stood with this wild vixen. At times she was warm and responsive, but like the changing wind, her mood could alter and then her blue eyes would be snapping with fury. But after giving the matter a moment's consideration, Dante decided that confession might be good for the soul. He had attempted to walk an emotional tightrope where Erica was concerned, and doing so had brought him nothing but anguish. There came a time in the life of almost every man when he was forced to bare his heart, to bring his feelings out in the open and face them. Perhaps now was that time for him.

"You may not want to hear what I'm thinking, *chérie*," he rasped as he took the pendant and tossed it aside as if it were of little value. "But I think it is time that you and I came to an understanding. I have been evading the truth, and that is not fair to either of us."

Erica stilled the furious beat of her heart. Did he intend to inform her that she would have her freedom once they returned to New Orleans?

Dante looked her straight in the eye, took a deep breath, and then plowed on before he lost his nerve. "Erica, I want you to marry me again. I need you," he blurted out matter-of-factly.

Her face fell. What purpose was she to serve this time?

What scheme had he devised to avenge himself on his uncle? Enough is enough, Erica thought stubbornly. I will not become a party to another risky plot. The first one had almost proved disastrous, and she had no intention of finding herself the stakes in yet another mad challenge.

"No," she said flatly as she withdrew her hand from his. "Only a fool would make the same mistake twice. Wedding you once was quite enough."

Dante's pride collapsed. "Was it so bad sharing my name? I—"

Erica clipped off his sentence with a distasteful sniff. "It was not bearing your name I protested," she reminded him tersely. "It was the fact that you used me to challenge the devil himself. What purpose will our marriage serve this time, Dante? What game do you intend to play with Sabin?"

"Do you see me as such a cold, calculating man that I would need an ulterior motive for proposing?" Dante scoffed indignantly. "My lord, woman, you cut me to the quick." Vaulting to his feet, Dante paced the confines of the cabin and then wheeled to face Erica. "I have decided how and when I intend to have my revenge on Sabin. That has nothing to do with you, not this time. I very nearly lost you to him once." Dante threw up his hands in a gesture of futility; then he let them dangle loosely by his sides. "Have you no conception of the hell that has been my lot, of the jealousy that devoured me when you pranced off with that French Don Juan in Guadeloupe?" He bestowed a withering glance on Erica, who just sat there, staring at him as if he were the first man she had ever laid eyes on. "Don't you know why I threw you to every shark on the steamboat?"

"Well, I assumed—"

Dante cut her off after allowing her to squeeze in only a few words. "Because I wanted to make myself appear a saint in comparison to those scoundrels. I wanted you to accept me as your husband because I was man enough to please you, despite your reasons for wanting a hasty wedding. And do you have the foggiest notion why I used you for bait in my challenge with Sabin?"

Erica did know the answer to that one, and she hurriedly started to fling it at him, but he interrupted her again.

"To break my uncle's claim on you once and for all," Dante insisted. "I risked everything I held dear, just to have you. I broke my own vow never to wed a scheming woman. I had sworn never to wed unless the woman I loved returned my devotion. I was not about to suffer the heartache my father endured when my mother realized she had something more to offer a man than mere loyalty. Dammit, Erica, are you still so naïve that you cannot tell that I love you and have gone to considerable effort and expense to keep you with me? Why the hell do you think I've dragged you all over the Caribbean, if not for love? Now, you tell me, which of us is the bigger fool?"

Erica did not dare to trust her own ears. She stared at him in disbelief. Dante loved her? It was too incredible to conceive.

Dante scowled at her stunned expression. Then he grabbed a brandy bottle and poured himself a tall glass of courage. "I know it probably makes little difference to you that I fell in love with you on that first night you stumbled into my life in the most unlikely of places. But that is the irony of love." He chuckled bitterly, then tossed down his drink in his haste to pour another. "A man can search for love for most of his life, yet he finds it sneaking up on him from his blind side. I kept telling myself that my fascination for you would fade, that I could learn to fill the emptiness when we went our separate ways." Dante heaved a deep sigh as he eased his hip onto the edge of the desk and braved a glance at Erica. He smiled ruefully at the personification of his wildly wonderful dreams. "I tried to free myself of you with Elliot and then again when you met Charles Cadeau, but I don't think I can give you up, Erica." His voice was softer now, his gaze sketching her as if he were viewing a cherished portrait that had been stashed away for years. "I have seen you at your best, worst, and all angles in between. You have touched so many emotions that I can no longer imagine life without you. I died a thousand times during the storm. I knew fear the likes I'd never experienced—because I was afraid I would lose you."

Still, Erica could not speak, and Dante's frustration was mounting. He had spoken from his heart, yet she just sat there like a bump on a log, her mouth open, her blue eyes as wide as the ocean upon which they sailed. It was obvious to Dante that his confession hadn't fazed her. If it had, she would have responded.

"Well? Go ahead. Say it," he muttered resentfully. "Tell me I deserve to live with the misery of loving you while you can barely tolerate the sight of me. I know you think I've made a mess of your life, wedding you and then giving you up to my uncle, carting you off to Guadeloupe, forcing you to endure a tropical storm, causing you to risk your life in Chichén Itzá." He flung her an annoyed frown. "Throw something at me." Dante indicated the wooden replica she had replaced after demolishing the first one. "Launch the model schooner.

It means nothing to me if it was not given as a gift of love. Curse me; rant and rave at me," he urged. "But confound it, don't just sit there staring at me. I cannot stand another minute of this!"

Oh, how she loved this man. The very sight of him stirred her blood; his touch, his kiss, could melt her into liquid desire. Her heart swelled with so much happiness that she feared it would burst before she could murmur the words she had kept locked inside these past months. Tears of joy boiled down her cheeks and in a moment she was sobbing.

Dante slumped dejectedly. His confession hadn't pleased her. It had upset her. That was answer enough. He rose and strode toward the door.

Erica's broken voice crackled through the silence. "Dante, I—"

"You don't have to say anything," he insisted, forcing the semblance of a smile. "Your silence was answer enough. I will try to make the remainder of the journey as comfortable as possible for you, and I will see to it that you are free of your obligation to Sabin. It will be my way of repaying you for all the agony I have caused you."

He was leaving and she had not confessed her love. She couldn't let him walk away thinking that she despised him. Galvanized into action, Erica grabbed the machete and hurled it at the door, finding her mark, not six inches from Dante's shoulder. Dante flinched, settled wide, disbelieving eyes on the quivering blade, and then looked at Erica.

"Christ! When I invited you to throw something at me I didn't mean something as lethal as that!" His voice faltered.

"Blast it, Dante, why didn't you tell me how you felt in

the beginning?" she scolded. "Think of all the misery you could have spared us. There has never been another man who stirs me the way you do, not Elliot and certainly not Charles. I can barely remember when I *didn't* love you. It seems a lifetime ago."

It was Dante's turn to stare at her.

"Sweet merciful heavens. You accuse me of being naïve, but what about you? Don't you know when a woman loves you more than life? Would I have allowed you to use me in your challenge against Sabin if I hadn't cared about you? No," she answered for him. "I could have and would have found a way to leave you if I had wanted to. Yet I tolerated Charles Cadeau's suffocating nearness to ensure that you received a handsome price for the cargo. I followed you into the forests of the Yucatán and climbed down into the well when you know how I detest heights. If I did not love you I would long since have been gone, and you would not have been able to stop me."

Dante's face beamed like a beacon on a dark night. "You do love me, even when I have led you from one calamity to another?"

Erica rose from her chair and sauntered toward him to slide her arms over his broad shoulders. A provocative smile played on her lips as she tilted her head back, allowing raven curls to spill down her back; then she pressed close to his solid frame. The flame of love glistened in her eyes as she reached up to trail a dainty finger over the sensuous curve of his mouth.

"Shall I show you how much, Dante? I have tried to express my love for you on several occasions without voicing the words, but you seemed unable to decode body language." A hint of mischievousness flared up in her eyes. "Or perhaps I was not as thorough as I should have been."

"You have always been devastatingly thorough, but I was a bit of a cynic, afraid to trust my instincts, afraid to trust you with my heart."

Her sapphire eyes misty with emotion, she peered into his face, watching his chiseled features soften as he smiled tenderly at her. "Believe me, my handsome pirate. I had no conception of the meaning of love until I came to know you. And I will always love you, far more than you could ever love me."

"Not so!" Dante contradicted as his arms settled on the shapely curve of her hips. "A man has a greater capacity for love, and mine has been in storage much longer than yours."

Erica laughed aloud at his twisted logic. "Everyone knows a woman is more generous with her love than a man. She may be unable to match a man in strength, but she is more capable of love."

"Nonsense," Dante protested; then he proudly boasted. "My love for you is wider than the ocean upon which we sail."

"And mine is deeper than the seven seas," she assured him.

"Is it now?" One dark eyebrow rose suggestively as he clutched her closer, his lips parting as they closed the distance between them. "Why don't you show me your love and I'll demonstrate mine. Then perhaps we can decide who has won the battle."

"Battle?" Erica chortled softly at his choice of words. "Battling is *not* what I intend to do with you, not ever again." Her soft lips feathered across his, leaving him hungering for a score of kisses, just like the one she had offered him. "This contest may take some time."

"How much?" Dante inquired before lowering his lips to hers once again to sample a kiss more intoxicating than wine.

"The rest of our lives . . ." Her lips parted in invitation as his engaged her in something far more arousing than conversation. Yet just when Erica was prepared to surrender her last breath if he would have requested it, Dante dragged his lips from hers, his emerald eyes glistening with unmistakable love and desire.

"I won't be content to have you tonight or during this voyage, Erica. I want you forever. No matter what happens with my uncle, I mean to have you with me, and I don't care what I have to do to keep you. You are my world." His voice wavered with emotion as he pulled her against him, confirming his profession of love with a kiss so gentle that Erica half-collapsed in his arms.

His touch was like the warmth of sunshine as his hands glided over her ribs to fold around her breast, his fingertips teasing each pink bud to tautness before his moist lips whispered across her shoulder and then descended until his tongue flicked each ripe peak in turn. Streams of wild, sweet pleasure pulsated through, leaving no part of her untouched, and a coil of longing unfurled somewhere deep inside her as his relentless caresses and kisses skimmed her flesh, bringing her senses to life. She was achingly aware of the feel of the hard, masculine body pressed intimately against hers, the arousing scent of musk that clung to him and then hovered about her, the taste of his skin beneath her eager kisses.

Her fingertips explored his sinewy muscles, sliding down his powerful shoulders to spray over the broad expanse of his chest. Touching him excited her, so

Erica's adventurous hands blazed paths across his hair-roughened flesh, rediscovering every inch of his male body, knowing him by touch.

His lips trailed between the valley of her breasts, making fire dance on her skin, and she moved instinctively closer to the source of the flames. As his breath drifted from one thrusting crest to the other while his gentle hands traced intricate patterns on her abdomen, Erica moaned. The blaze was spreading like wildfire, making her burn with barely controlled desire.

"This is the beginning of forever," Dante rasped as his lips returned to hers in a ravishing kiss that stole the last of her breath from her lungs. "It will always be like this for us."

As he scooped her up in his arms to carry her to the bed, Erica tunneled her fingers through his thick raven hair, drawing his head back to hers. His words thrilled her, as did his touch, and another wave of rapture spilled over her as he nestled beside her. Again his skillful hands began to work hypnotic magic on her skin, gliding and curling over each curve and swell, sensitizing her entire body until she was drifting on a sea of bliss, far from reality's shore. She was where she belonged—in Dante's loving arms, exploring a universe where the rolling sea blended into the black velvet sky.

His knee nudged her thighs apart as his familiar caresses tracked across her hips in long, gentle strokes. And then his fingers delved into her feminine softness, sending her spiraling breathlessly onto yet another plateau. As his caresses wandered over her belly Erica sighed softly, then she caught her breath when his patient hands again tantalized her inner thighs. His intimate fondling was sweet agony, and Erica arched to meet his probing fingers, whispering for him to appease the maddening craving he had stirred within her. She could not be satisfied until he was a part of her, his hard, muscular body molded to hers; until they were moving as one, gliding in rhythm to the melody that played in her soul.

"Dante . . ." His name floated from her lips as her arms curled about his neck, drawing him closer, aching to possess and be possessed in the shared moments that pursued and captured time.

"I love you," he whispered back to her as his lithe body twisted to hover above hers, his eyes burning with a living flame. He held himself above her, the muscles of his arms bulging as he braced his hands on either side of her. "Send the world away. . . ."

As his hips settled between her thighs Erica groaned with pleasure, loving the feel of his body melting into hers. Sharing his embrace was paradise, as if she were basking in the warmth of the sun on a desert island. His kiss was like a gentle sea breeze drifting over her lips as he moved slowly within her, stirring sensations that defied description. His body roused to the feel of hers, his hard thrusts wafting them into the clouds. Then shimmering warmth channeled through them, bringing the sweet quintessence of passion's pleasure. Their love created unique feelings, fiery and ardent, yet achingly tender. They shuddered with delight. Then, when Erica was certain she could fly no higher, a wild, powerful sensation shot through her, and she could not contain the moan of ecstasy that broke from her lips to be captured by Dante's devouring kiss. Over and over again that sweet sensation came, ebbing and then cresting, draining her strength until she just drifted, living and dying in those rapturous moments.

Dante groaned with satiated pleasure as he clutched her even closer, holding her so tightly that she could barely draw a ragged breath. A warm, pulsating numbness surged through him as passion spilled from his soul, paralyzing him, and his heart thundered furiously against her naked breasts. He hadn't the strength or the will to move.

"I love you," Erica murmured as her lips lightly caressed his shoulder.

Slowly, Dante raised his head, a gentle smile brushing his mouth, curving the corners upward. "Keep telling me that for the next century. I will never tire of hearing it," he assured her, his voice husky from the aftereffects of passionate lovemaking.

Erica reached up to investigate the dimples in his cheeks, studying him thoughtfully. "I intend to, but I can't help but wonder if you will still love me when the new wears off and the challenge is gone."

A low chuckle erupted from his chest as he shifted to her side and propped his head on his hand. "I cannot imagine why I wouldn't. I loved you when you taunted and harassed me, drove me crazy with jealousy, and tormented me by refusing to allow me near you."

"But I will never give you cause to complain again," Erica promised as she snuggled closer, her wandering hand mapping the hard contours of his thigh and then sliding along the smooth muscles of his back. "Indeed, the only complaint you might voice is that you have fallen in love with a very demanding woman."

Dante choked when he glimpsed the suggestive gleam in her eyes. "My lord, woman, I give you my all, yet you ask for more," he taunted. "How will I chart our course home if I cannot set foot out of this cabin?"

A deliciously mischievous grin pursed her lips as her

hands swam over his muscular body, rekindling fires that lay dormant. "We can sail in circles for all I care. I have found my treasure. . . ."

And Dante had found his. Her caresses drove all thought from his mind. Suddenly he didn't care if he ever set foot on solid ground, not when he was cradled in the arms of the woman gentle enough to capture his heart and strong enough to keep it. Erica had become all things to him—the distant star just beyond his reach, the impossible dream that just eluded his grasp, the precious treasure at the end of the rainbow.

Her mouth opened on his, warm and insistent, persuasively gliding over the curve of his lips. His body came alive, fueled by the breath of love. As her hand flowed over the flat muscles of his stomach and then splayed over his thigh, Dante gasped; then her lips abandoned his to pursue the titillating course her hands had tracked across his hips. She inhaled the warm male scent of him, tasting him, savoring him as her wildly disturbing caresses aroused his desire, and Dante responded to this skillful seductress. Her light kisses fed the gnawing hunger of his passion and her gentle caresses created new cravings. A groan of sweet torment burst from his lips. He could stand no more of her teasing. He forged her flesh to his, and with masculine grace he rolled above her, intent on appeasing the maddening need that her kisses and caresses had evoked. He came to her with driving thrusts, as if he could not get close enough to the fire, as if he were flying into the sun, eager to be engulfed by its raging fires.

Dante knew how hot their flames could burn. Their fires leaped across his flesh and shot into his soul. His entire being was ablaze with white-hot sensations that engulfed him. And his love for Erica fed the fire, even when there was nothing left to burn. Intangible emotions crackled, like kindling, creating something from nothing, feeding the flames of desire.

And even in the aftermath of love, when the embers of passion smoldered, Dante knew that Erica's touch could reclaim the fire. His feeling for her transcended physical pleasure, yet the cravings of the flesh lay just beneath the surface eagerly waiting to be ignited.

A weary sigh escaped his lips as he pulled Erica back against him and laid his arm beneath her breasts. Within moments, he had yielded to her again, in his dreams.

Erica's lashes fluttered against her cheeks, but a strange sensation tapped at her drowsy mind and she tensed instinctively. A dark shadow hovered in the corners of her mind, and Erica instantly knew the source of her uneasiness. Their love for each other was strong. It could endure the test of time, but could it overcome the one evil that stood in the way of their happiness? Sabin . . . The mere thought of him sent a shudder through her. Erica cuddled closer to Dante's sleeping form, praying that their voyage to New Orleans was just the beginning of her new life with Dante. Now that she had earned Dante's love she couldn't bear to think of being without him. Yet Sabin would destroy what they had, if he could.

Blocking out that dreary thought Erica conjured up the sweet memories of their lovemaking. She would have to deal with Sabin eventually, but she was determined not to allow him to destroy the time she and Dante had before they docked in New Orleans.

Then she slept, recreating in her dreams the rapturous moments when she and Dante were one.

Part VIII

Treachery at first thought cautious, in the end betrays itself.

—*Livy*

Chapter 25

An apprehensive frown clouded Erica's flawless features when she gazed across the curling waves to survey the Mississippi delta. The days and nights she had spent with Dante had been a dream come true. But the sight of land on the horizon brought her back in touch with reality. Just beyond the gulf her father and Sabin Keary waited. She and Dante would be forced to deal with both of them. Although she would have preferred to travel upriver to Dante's plantation without notifying anyone of their return, she knew Dante would not avoid the trouble that awaited them. The thought of him tangling with his uncle dampened Erica's spirits, and it wasn't until Dante wrapped a possessive arm around her that she felt secure again.

"I wish we could—"

Dante pressed a tanned finger to her lips to silence her. "Sooner or later we have to face my uncle," he reminded her. He might well have peeked into her mind and plucked out the thought that lodged in it like a bothersome thorn. His hand curled beneath her chin, as he lifted her troubled gaze to his. "I have waited a long time to settle with Sabin, and you know as well as I do that our problems will never be resolved until he is out of our lives."

"But he is not to be trusted," Erica breathed in dismay. "Must I remind you how treacherous he can be? How will you? . . ."

Dante dropped a silencing kiss to her lips. "Let me fret over Sabin. When the time comes I will deal with him in my own way."

Erica chanced to lose everything she held dear, and to her it seemed more reasonable to let the sleeping dog lie. Although she was prone to argue about the coming confrontation with Sabin, she held her tongue, knowing she couldn't dissuade Dante once his mind was made up. Taking a deep breath, Erica hoped that whatever scheme Dante intended to employ on Sabin would meet with success.

After Dante had given the order to have the last sail tied to the mast, Erica, Reade, and Dante prepared to go ashore. Against her better judgment, Erica consented to confront her father first, though she was certain Sabin would get wind of their arrival and brew up trouble before Dante could confront his treacherous uncle.

When the carriage came to a halt in front of the Bennet mansion, Dante assisted Erica to alight and then turned back to Reade. "Take our luggage and book passage to Natchez. We will meet you at the dock."

As Dante and Erica ascended the marbled steps, Reade fished into Dante's luggage to extract the pouches of gems they had collected, stashing them in his pocket. A wry smile hovered on his lips as he ordered the driver to proceed to Sabin Keary's plantation.

*   *   *

"Erica . . ." Avery Bennet wilted back into his chair, the color gushing from his cheeks. "What are you doing here? You should never have returned to New Orleans after you escaped Sabin."

"We have unfinished business here, Avery," Dante declared. He retrieved the money they had received for the cargo of cotton and presented it to him. "Paid in full, a reasonable fee for the goods delivered in your son's stead."

Avery nodded mutely, but his eyes were still glued to his daughter. The look on her face assured him that she had been informed of the incident that had made him Sabin's slave.

"He told you, didn't he?" Avery blurted out. "You know what happened."

"Yes, I know," Erica affirmed. Then she moved slowly toward her father, a man who had been a stranger to her the past four years. "But I still do not understand why, Papa. Why did you allow Sabin to blackmail you? Surely you could have lived with the mistake and the rumors. That would have been no worse than allowing Sabin to manipulate you. Do I mean nothing to you? Is your pride more important than your own flesh and blood?"

Pain flickered in Avery's eyes as he glanced back and forth between the darkly handsome man who towered over him and his daughter who stared disappointedly at him. Could she ever understand the hell he had lived through? Could she possibly know why he had kept his secret at any cost?

Finally, Avery peered at the far wall, looking back through the window of time. The words rolled from the tip of his tongue, words that he had kept locked in his heart for four agonizing years.

"I was a lonely man, Erica. You had gone away to school and Jamie was a grown lad who no longer needed my attention. My life was empty, just as it had been since the day I lost your mother. When Sabin introduced me to Maggie Fowler, something in her stirred emotions that had laid dead and buried, feelings I had never expected to experience again." Avery unclenched his fist and let his hand drop limply in his lap as a rueful smile skimmed his lips. "Maggie was like a breath of springtime. Love that had withered long ago blossomed in me, and grew with each day I spent with her. I fell in love, even when I knew there could be no future with her. And she fell in love with me." He paused to dart Dante a meaningful glance. "We knew it couldn't last, that Maggie would return to your father. She never meant to hurt Dominique. She wasn't that kind of woman. Maggie was kind and caring, but neither of us could control what was happening between us."

Dante stood stock-still, listening to Avery's tale of a man and woman whose love for each other had destroyed many innocent lives. Could that happen to him? Could another man sweep Erica off her feet? The thought pierced Dante's soul. If he lost Erica, he would be crushed, just as Avery had been when he'd lost Maggie.

"But it wasn't enough that Maggie and I found something in each other that drew us together. Sabin was bent on spoiling the beauty of our ill-fated love. He sent a letter to Dominique, informing him that he had lost Maggie to another man and that she intended to divorce him. It was a lie," Avery swore, his aging face twisted with resentment. "Everything he told Dominique was a vicious, premeditated lie that only served to infuriate the man and cloud his logic."

Avery slumped back in his chair as if his confession had sapped his strength. Heaving a frustrated sigh, he continued. "Sabin had made Dominique blind with rage, but none of us realized his intention until they snowballed into disaster. Maggie tried desperately to assure Dominique that she had not been unfaithful to him and that she wanted to return to Natchez with him. Dominique believed her, but Sabin taunted him, laughing at him and insisting that Maggie had never loved him. Sabin's goading lured Dominique into a duel. He swore he would rid the world and himself of Sabin and his ruthless schemes." Avery squeezed his eyes shut as a haunted expression appeared on his face. "As long as I live I don't think I can ever forget that fateful day. Maggie was hysterical when Dominique rose to the taunt and consented to a duel. I tried to intervene, but Dominique was a stubborn man and his hatred for Sabin had festered for too many years." His tortured gaze lifted to meet Dante's condemning frown. "I assured your father that Maggie had done nothing to humiliate him, that Sabin was manipulating him, but the feud that he and Sabin had waged all those years drove him to that final clash from which only one of them would walk away alive. But know this Dante, and believe it"—his words were deliberate, his expression somber—"Although I deeply loved your mother, I never knew her as a man knows his wife. She was faithful to Dominique and he knew that. But it didn't matter. His bitterness ran deeper than Sabin's lies. Dominique wanted Sabin Keary dead."

Slowly, Avery rose to his feet and strode to the window. He peered across the grounds, lost to a world of forbidden memories, to a tragedy that had changed the course of his life. "None of us realized until it was too late that Sabin had meticulously plotted the duel. It began, shrouded in turmoil, and ended in catastrophe. It happened so quickly that we were stunned and dazed. When the pistols exploded and the smoke had cleared, Dominique was dead. While Maggie knelt over Dominique, Sabin retrieved both weapons and hurled them into the swamp, destroying the evidence that he had tampered with the pistols. Maggie was beside herself, wailing in torment, guilt-ridden. She blamed herself for Dominique's death, and before I could stop her she fled. I have not seen her since. And Sabin . . ." Avery breathed a ragged sigh, his voice quivering with pained emotion. "Sabin swore he would spread scandal from New Orleans to Natchez, that he would claim he stood in my stead because I was too much of a coward to face my lover's husband. He swore he would ruin the name of Fowler and Bennet, that he would make Maggie and me villains instead of the victims of his dastardly ploy."

"But *why* did you allow him to get away with that?" Erica demanded to know. It was still inconceivable to her that Avery hadn't forced Sabin's hand and denied the accusations.

Avery met her questioning gaze, his sad smile pathetic. "Do you know what it is like to love someone with every part of your being? Can you conceive of caring for someone more than life? I couldn't allow Sabin to tarnish those beautiful moments I had spent with Maggie. What we had shared was special. I wanted no man to destroy it." A tortured expression flashed through his eyes as he studied his lovely daughter, and Erica thought she saw tears misting his gaze before he regained control of his emotions. "I never dreamed Sabin would want you as his wife. At first I refused, but he vowed to spoil your repu-

450

tation as well as mine. He is a deceitful, vicious man. I had already witnessed one death due to his ruthless manipulations. Somehow it seemed easier for you never to know love, to live out your life in the lap of luxury, rather than find a man you loved and then watch him destroyed by Sabin's wrath. And when you returned from the East, so strong and independent, I feared another kind of trouble for you. I wanted you to remain submissive. It would have been easier for you to accept your lot in life. Sabin would have made you his queen, and if you never crossed him he would have placed you on a pedestal, treating you as if you were royalty. But things went from bad to worse, and because of my silence and my fears I have made a horrible mess of things."

Erica felt a lump rise in her throat. Avery's words pierced her. She understood the type of love her father had experienced, one so rare and beautiful that words could not do it justice. Now she feared that what her father had desperately tried to avoid would become reality. If Dante fell beneath that devil's sword, part of her would wither and die with him. She would not survive such anguish. No wonder her father had become a shell of a man, finding very little purpose in life except working and sheltering her in his home. He had feared that she would love a man, only to have him destroyed by Sabin. No wonder he'd complained about her willful nature, foreseeing difficulties that Erica had never imagined. Erica's heart went out to Avery, for she finally realized the mental torture he had endured. He had only attempted to protect her as best he knew how.

"Erica?" Avery's pale eyes clouded with tears as he clasped his daughter's hand, giving it a loving squeeze. "I have spoiled your life because of my foolish link with

Sabin. I was damned, no matter which course I chose. I could consent to your marriage to Sabin, or I could stand by and watch him destroy any chance you might have at happiness. I even prayed that you had fled from Natchez before we arrived, that Sabin would be unable to find you, though that meant I might never see you again." Avery tossed the money back to Dante, his gaze beseeching, his expression somber. "Take Erica far away from here, and don't ever return. I will bear my situation as I have these past years, but I don't want Erica near Sabin. She has twice stirred his wrath, and I can no longer trust him to control it. I fear his obsession with her beauty is a wicked one since he has been unable to tame her spirit. Please, Dante, at least grant me some peace of mind."

Determined green eyes locked with aging gray ones. "Only now have I come to fully understand your deep feeling for my mother," Dante informed him quietly. "I can forgive you because I have found the kind of love of which you speak." His warm, adoring gaze circled back to Erica, and he smiled softly as he smoothed a renegade strand of raven hair away from her face. "I married Erica because I loved her beyond all else. Because I wanted to sever all ties between her and Sabin forever, I risked everything in the challenge. But I failed to remember how ruthless Sabin could be." His attention focused on Avery, and his mouth became set in a grim line. "I cannot rest until I have found a way to beat him at his own game, to assure him that Erica is and always will be mine." Dante heaved a frustrated sigh. "No, Avery, I cannot, and will not, run from him. I won't spend my days in fear that Sabin will track us down and steal Erica away from me. Perhaps my father was a fool, but I, his son, know of no other way but to confront Sabin. I refuse to cower and run as if I have been beaten."

"If you love Erica as you say you do, you will consider *her* first and your stubborn pride second." Avery scowled. Damnation, Dante was bold as a lion, and this was one time it was wiser not to be. "Can't you leave well enough alone?" He had no trouble picturing his worst fears becoming a reality. Erica would suffer. Sabin's passion for Erica's beauty had been transformed into a need for revenge.

"Well enough?" Dante scoffed bitterly. "I can think of nothing worse than allowing Sabin to have the last laugh, to live with the fear that some day he will destroy my chance at happiness."

"Dante, please." Erica clutched at his hand. "You will be no less a man in my eyes if you turn your back on the past and begin a new life. I love you too much to lose you."

Dante gave his raven head a negative shake; then he let the money pouch clank on the desk. "I promised to meet Reade at the docks before we sail to Natchez. Are you coming with me or do I go alone?"

When he put the question to Erica, she stood frozen, indecision etching her brow. She was afraid to test Dante's love by staying behind and afraid to follow him for fear of watching him meet his death.

"I will send you away, Erica," Avery insisted. "Far away from Sabin. It is insanity to follow Dante, and I cannot bear to see history repeat itself. Don't fall into the same trap that snared me."

As Dante pivoted about and strode away, Erica found herself going to his side. She slid a hand in his, and her lashes swept up to let the expression in her eyes confirm her decision. She couldn't let him walk away; no matter what their future held, no matter what tragedy befell them.

Avery expelled his breath in a rush. Then he snatched up his hat, and stalked toward the hall, grumbling about his daughter's lack of intelligence. "Give me a moment to gather my belongings. I am coming with you. Youth." He grunted disgustedly, raking Erica and Dante with a sour frown. "Your fault lies in your age. You seem to think you can conquer the world. And if it should come to pass, I want to be a witness."

A pleased smile appeared on Dante's lips. "When we meet up with Sabin, I will be proud to count you among my friends, Avery. We will find a way to defeat him. *He* is his own worst enemy."

Although Erica wasn't certain what Dante meant, she didn't cross-examine him. They were due at the wharf, and she had to pack her belongings in record time. Once she and Dante were alone in their stateroom on the steamboat, she would question him about his plan, and she would inquire about the site he had selected for his confrontation with Sabin.

Reade ambled into the entryway of Sabin's sprawling mansion and then leisurely propped himself against the door casing. He grinned recklessly as his gaze swept the elaborate furnishings of Sabin's study and then anchored on the bony face and the hollowed eyes of the man who frowned sourly at him.

"Yore ship came in." Reade smirked and then reached into his pockets to dangle two leather purses of gems in front of Sabin. "And here is the treasure Dante retrieved from Central America—a fortune to cover his losses. Wouldn't it be a pity if it fell into the wrong hands and he received nothin' for his efforts?"

A wicked gleam glistened in Sabin's eyes as he pushed back his chair and then perused Dante's first mate. He knew the man to be a mercenary. He had dealt with Asher once before, and he was willing to do so again. They had met once in Natchez, and the outcome of their discussion had proved worthwhile.

"So my nephew found an innovational way to save himself from poverty, did he?" Sabin chuckled wickedly. "More's the pity that his state of well-being will be short-lived." He motioned for Reade to spread the treasure before him, but Reade tucked it behind his back and shot Sabin a cautious glance.

"These gems are yores *if* the price is right. I mean to have a fair amount of coin in exchange for the treasure, a fee to soothe my conscience for servin' Dante to you on a silver platter. If you ain't got the kind of money it takes to sell out an old friend I'll take my business elsewhere."

"Old friend?" Sabin eyed him skeptically. "If that is so, why are you so eager to betray him?"

Reade's shoulders lifted in a lackadaisical shrug. "For money," he answered matter-of-factly. "Why should I divide the fortune in half when I can have it all to myself? If a man don't look out for himself, nobody else will. It's a cutthroat world and I only seek to git by the best way I can. Dante's problems ain't mine and they never have been."

Sabin thoughtfully studied the bushy-haired sailor. Reade did seem determined to play both sides to his advantage. He would give him the price he asked. This temptation was too great to refuse.

"You have made yourself a bargain, Asher," he announced, and he rose from his chair to retrieve a heaping sack of gold coins, which he held up for Reade's inspection. "Spread your treasure before me and we will match its worth."

A grin as wide as the Mississippi stretched across Reade's weather-beaten features; then he strutted forward like a haughty peacock. "These ain't trinkets I have here. There's solid gold, silver, and precious gems worth a king's ransom."

Sabin's dark eyes grew round in amazement when he spied the treasures of the well. It would take almost all of his ready cash to afford the stones, but he was certain he could collect twice what he'd paid for them from a European buyer. Greed intermingled with deviltry in his smile as he clasped a ruby-studded pendant in his hand, picturing the look on Dante's face when he learned the jewels had been taken from him. Not only would he crush Dante, he would turn him against a man he had considered his friend. The realization that he had been betrayed and broken would send Dante into a rage; then Sabin would have his pesky nephew right where he wanted him.

After Reade had bargained for a generous price and had then sailed out the door with gold coins safely tucked in his pockets, Sabin sank into his chair to fondle the sparkling treasures spread before him. His wicked laughter rang through the halls of the mansion, like the pealing of a bell, a bell that tolled disaster for Dante Fowler.

"Again you will see that you are no match for me," Sabin jeered as he clutched a handful of jewels and shook his fist at the image that materialized above him. "I will destroy you just as I destroyed your worthless father."

His fiendish chuckle faded into silence as he scooped up the treasure and stuffed the pouches into his pockets. He would spring another devastating surprise on Dante.

When Erica, Dante, and Avery arrived at the wharf, Reade bit back a secretive grin and picked his way through the crowd to present Dante with tickets for their passage to Natchez. But a muddled frown replaced his delighted amusement when he found an extra passenger intended to travel with them.

"Reade, this is Erica's father, Avery Bennet. He intends to accompany us to Natchez." A sly smile pursed Dante's lips as he leaned close to Erica. "And the first order of business will be to make an honest woman of you."

When relief claimed Erica's flawless features, Dante dropped a feathery kiss on her lips. *Perhaps he does not intend to inform Sabin that he has returned to New Orleans,* she thought hopefully. Once they reached Natchez, she might be able to convince Dante to stay where he was, to forget his vendetta with Sabin. Sabin would never have to know that Erica had become his wife. Avery had guarded one secret for four years; surely he could contain another.

"I'll fetch another ticket," Reade called over his shoulder as he threaded his way back to the clerk.

Dante strode back to retrieve the armload of luggage they had collected at the Bennet mansion, but he jumped as if he had been stung when Sabin Keary stepped from behind the brougham, wearing a black cloak and a top hat. His smile would have made the devil himself cringe apprehensively.

Erica's blood ran cold when she saw the darkly clad figure loom beside the carriage. Quicker than a heartbeat she was at Dante's side, experiencing the same fierce hatred that coursed through Dante's veins. She itched to slap the hideous smile off Sabin's face. The mere sight of him made the hair on the back of her neck bristle.

"So we meet again." Sabin chuckled sardonically. Then he darted a glance at the shapely beauty who stood beside Dante. "We have a few matters to settle, nephew. I hope you did not intend to sneak aboard *The Lucky Lady* and steal off to Natchez without informing me of your arrival. It is time you paid the piper. I have grown bored with your games." With his cane, Sabin gestured toward Erica, his all-consuming gaze flooding over her and not missing one detail of her figure. "The lady is mine, as is the money you collected when you stole my schooner and sailed to the Leeward Islands."

A grim smile tightened Dante's lips, but it evaporated as he tossed the pouch of coins to Sabin. "Therein is the payment for your cotton, minus the expense for replacing the boat you sabotaged. I will not honor the bargain since you did not observe the terms." Dante looked his uncle straight in the eye and continued in a dangerously calm tone. "Erica is mine. By using deceit you forfeited any right you had to her."

Sabin was undaunted by Dante's decree. "And what will you offer a gently bred lady when you have nothing but a crippled plantation?" Sabin asked dryly. "Erica has no need of a pauper." He reached inside his cloak to extract the sacks of jewels he had bought from Reade Asher.

A gasp of disbelief burst from Erica's lips. So that is how Sabin knew where to find us, she thought bitterly.

Reade! He had turned on Dante like a vicious wolf. Her eyes circled the crowd, desperately searching for the first mate's face.

"The jewels are mine, Nephew." Sabin sneered, annoyed that Dante had not staggered as if he had suffered a low blow. "You have nothing left with which to fight me." A demented laugh bubbled from his lips. "You are too much like your father, a self-righteous fool." Still Dante made no move toward him, thereby thwarting Sabin's chances of cutting Dante down in self-defense. "Your mother tolerated Dominique, but I freed her from bondage. You accused me of putting her through hell, but if the truth be known, she is probably living out her life in seclusion, thankful that I saved her from that bastard our grandparents forced her to marry."

How Dante managed to stand Sabin's jeering insults without reacting was beyond Erica. She hungered to pounce on him, and she would have if Dante hadn't clutched her arm and drawn her to his side.

"Every mangy dog has his day," Dante snorted derisively. "Let this one rave, Erica. I'm curious to see if his bite is as bad as his bark."

"What will you do now, Nephew?" Sabin taunted. "Steal another ship and set off on another treasure hunt? How many times does it take a fool to realize he has been beaten? Your father was also a slow learner, but I cured him of that . . . eventually. You will fare no better than he did against me."

Erica was seething with rage, and she was about to hurl a barrage of hateful insults at Sabin when Dante spoke.

"Won't I?" Dante lifted one dark eyebrow. Then he glanced toward the front of the carriage. "Reade, step out here. It seems my uncle misunderstood your purpose in calling upon him."

A self-satisfied grin on his face, Reade swaggered around the side of the coach, and when he was in full view, he fished into his jacket to fetch the money pouch. "I followed yore instructions to the letter, Cap'n. Sabin took the bait just as you said he would." He gazed at Sabin, scornful mockery in his eyes. "Since you used me as a decoy when you kidnapped Erica, I was all too happy to return the favor, Keary. You deserved a taste of yore own medicine, and I was all too happy to serve you up a spoonful."

After Dante caught the sack Reade tossed to him he turned an infuriating smile on his stunned uncle. "One never knows whom one can trust, eh, Sabin?" Dante queried mockingly. Then he gestured toward the jewels Sabin clutched in his fist. "If I were you, I would be careful about selling those gems. Since they were taken from Yucatán, the Mexican government will be anxious to know what became of them. It would be wise to generously donate those relics to Mexico in a gesture of good will, unless you prefer to risk being fined for confiscating the treasures of an ancient civilization."

Rage sizzled through Sabin as he glared at the smug grin plastered on Dante's face, and on Reade's. It incensed him to be duped. The precious gems were worthless to him if he risked a fine for selling them. His mind raced, frantically attempting to devise a way to turn the situation to his advantage; then he used the only defense available to him.

"I will destroy your family's reputation," Sabin vowed vindictively as he glowered at Avery. "Your carefully guarded secret will be buzzing about New Orleans if you do not insist that Erica come with me. I will make you the laughingstock of the Mississippi delta. You will never be able to hold up your head when you walk through the streets."

Avery tilted a defiant chin. "No more, Sabin. Your threats are futile. Dante has taught me something about pride. Without it I was half a man, living beneath your tyranny. Spread your vicious lies; I don't give a damn. I know in my heart that I have done nothing shameful. It was you who murdered Dominique. And you paid Timothy Thorpe to sneak aboard the *Natchez Belle* and set it ablaze if it appeared that Dante might win the race." Avery was just gathering steam. He felt better than he had in years, venting the pent-up frustration he had harbored since Dominique's death. "Know this, you devious, black-hearted bastard. You will never sell another bale of cotton at the New Orleans Exchange. Take your business elsewhere. I would rather face bankruptcy than deal with the likes of you. You have poisoned everything you have touched, and my shame stems from allowing you to manipulate me."

Sabin's wild, furious gaze darted from one contemptuous face to the other. Rage boiled inside him, like lava about to erupt. He thirsted for revenge. He wanted to destroy these four who sought to ruin him and to bring down the vast empire he had constructed in the South. He had lost control of Avery, and Asher and Dante had tricked him into spending a fortune on jewels that could not be sold for profit.

"It seems *you* are the one in dire straits, Uncle," Dante flashed Sabin an intimidating smile that only served to stoke the fires of his temper. "Your word and your credit are no longer reputable. It seems you have gotten exactly what you deserve."

As Dante grasped Erica's arm to escort her to the steamboat, Sabin's eyes turned a fiery shade of black. He could not stand to be tricked after all the meticulous plotting he had done to gain control of Avery Bennet and to take his daughter as his bride. His temper snapped. Impulsively, he whipped his flintlock from his pocket and pointed it at his nephew's departing back.

"Dante!" he screeched maliciously. "Look at me. I want to see your face when I cut you down!"

Erica's heart stopped when she glanced over her shoulder and saw the bloodthirsty gleam in Sabin's eyes. "No!" she shouted, throwing herself in front of Dante.

Raising a courageous chin, Dante met Sabin's murderous glare as he maneuvered Erica safely behind him. "Do you intend to kill me with so many witnesses present, Uncle?" he questioned, his voice incredibly calm despite the weapon pointed at his chest. "Take a good look around you. There are two pistols aimed at your black heart." He gestured toward Avery and then Reade. "If I should die, they will ensure that I take you with me." A low chuckle erupted from his lips as his scornful gaze flickered over Sabin. "Think, man. Now that Maggie has disappeared, your fortune will become Corbin's and mine, should I survive and you perish." Dante paused, letting his words soak in. Then he plowed on. "Would it not be an ironic twist of fate if Dominique's sons inherited your wealth? It seems I will win, no matter what choice you make." A grim smile tightened his lips as he watched indecision settle on Sabin's wrinkled features. "Now you know the agony your victims endured when you snared them, Sabin." One dark eyebrow arched mockingly when Sabin did not cock the hammer of his flintlock. "Well, which is it, Uncle?

Who will control the Keary fortune?"

Scowling disgustedly, Sabin let his hand drop to his side. Then he wheeled about and clambered into his carriage. Erica breathed a deep sigh of relief as she watched his equipage career around the corner and disappear from sight. Dante had won this skirmish, but she had the uneasy feeling that the battle was far from over. She could not rest until she was certain that Sabin would never interfere in their lives.

"I think we should inform the authorities of Sabin's transgressions and have him arrested." Erica glanced at her father and then peered up at Dante, whose gaze was still fixed on a lingering image of his treacherous uncle. "Surely my father will testify that Sabin paid that roustabout to set fire to the *Natchez Belle,* and I will be all too happy to file charges against Sabin for abducting me from your plantation."

"I think Erica is right. Sabin deserves to be hauled to prison," Avery chimed in. "I don't trust the man. The sheriff can keep him and Timothy Thorpe in custody until you settle your business in Natchez. Then we can return to have them tried and sentenced for their crimes."

Dante stared thoughtfully at Avery; then he nodded agreeably. "A prolonged stay in a musty prison cell would do Sabin a world of good. All his plotting and scheming in solitary confinement will accomplish naught."

"I will remain behind to see to the matter, and then Jamie and I will catch the next steamship to Natchez." Avery's eyes glistened with amusement as he wagged a finger at Erica. "And do not think to wed this young man again until I can be there to give you away. I was deprived of that privilege the first time, you know. And I have no intention of allowing it to happen again."

"We promise not to repeat the vows until you arrive," Dante assured him as his arm glided about Erica's waist, hugging her tightly against him.

Avery looked Dante over, and then he nodded pensively. "I think this time my feisty daughter has met her match," he affirmed. "But, I must warn you, Dante, you will have your hands full."

Dante's loving gaze settled on Erica's exquisite face, and mesmerized by the way the sunlight sparkled in her eyes, he dropped a light kiss on her full pink lips before flashing Avery a careless grin. "Although I know full well you're right, I'm not complaining. I have already had a taste of life without her. I prefer to take my chances with this lively minx."

When Avery had bid them goodbye and had hurried on his way to order warrants for the arrest of Sabin and Timothy, Dante guided Erica along the dock to board *The Lucky Lady*. "I think your father and I have acquired a mutual admiration for each other. I can understand why my mother was so fond of him," Dante mused aloud. "I like the man . . . almost as much as I adore his daughter."

"You have restored his dignity; I can never repay you for that," Erica murmured, sentimental tears misting her eyes. "Thank you. I am in your debt."

"Ah, but you *can* repay me," Dante insisted, his emerald eyes dancing with deviltry. "And we will see to the matter when we are settled in our stateroom."

His suggestive gaze alerted Erica to the type of payment that Dante might find agreeable compensation and she tossed him a provocative smile. "Why wait until we are settled in? A debt made should be hastily repaid, don't you agree?"

A playful growl bubbled from his massive chest as he steered Erica along the main deck to the stairs that led to their cabin. "Brazen wench. The proper young ladies of New Orleans would be appalled to overhear you."

Erica lifted her shoulders in a reckless shrug as she grasped Dante's hand and led him up the remainder of the stairs. "Proper be damned. Besides, I have very little reason to pretend to be coy. You and I have been on familiar terms since the night we met."

Dante grinned with roguish anticipation as he followed Erica, his mind taking a lusty tack. "And what a night that was," he whispered seductively. "I should like to—"

"Cap'n, can I buy you and yore lady a drink to celebrate?" Reade interrupted as he lumbered along behind them.

"Later perhaps," Dante said absently, his eyes glued to the graceful sway of Erica's hips as she sauntered along ahead of him. "My lady and I have a few plans to make."

"Plans?" Reade snorted caustically. Just how blind did Dante think he was? "You got five days to make yore wedding arrangements. Surely you two lovebirds could—"

"No, we couldn't," Dante cut in as he opened the stateroom door. When he peered at the disgruntled frown stamped on Reade's face, he added, "We will join you for supper."

Reade grumbled as the door was slammed shut in his face. Dante is so head over heels in love with that raven-haired vixen he can think of little else except appeasing his needs, Reade mused as he aimed himself toward the saloon. He knew how Dante would be spending the majority of his time during the voyage, and it wouldn't be making plans or lollygagging around the deck and viewing the scenery. The only scenery that interested Dante was in his cabin. Reade was willing to bet his fortune that Dante would give Corbin full interest in another steamship so he could spend every available hour with Erica, not that he could blame him. But what the hell was he going to do with his idle time until they docked in Natchez? The answer to that question plagued Reade even more when he rapped on the stateroom door to inform Dante that supper was being served and he was met with a muffled, "Later, Reade."

Reade peered at the river, wondering how a man of Dante's powerful physique could survive on so little nourishment. Maybe there was a fallacy in the statement that man couldn't live on love alone.

Chapter 26

An excited smile enlivened Leona Fowler's lips as she peered out the window to see Dante's coach halt in front of her home. The past few days had been busy ones, but Leona had been delighted to assist Erica with the wedding arrangements. The place had been hopping: seamstresses altering dresses, Lilian offering suggestions, cooks preparing for the elaborate reception. Everyone was anticipating the marriage ceremony that was to be held the following afternoon. Except Elliot Lassiter, Leona reminded herself as she started toward the door. When Elliot had learned that Erica was back in Natchez and that she was to marry her first husband a second time he'd been beside himself. For the last few days, he had been in a drunken stupor, refusing guests, drinking all day, and waking to do the same.

Tossing that depressing thought aside, Leona reached for the doorknob. She had invited the wedding party to their plantation for supper, and she had finally convinced Corbin that the time had come for Dante to face the events of the past. Anticipation bubbled through her as Dante and Erica walked up the steps. They were a handsome couple. Leona could not think of a more perfectly matched pair, and she was elated that they seemed so fond of each other. Their love would be the key to understanding, something Dante had stubbornly avoided since that dreadful incident almost four years earlier.

"I suppose the two of you know Leona has been walking on air in anticipation of your upcoming wedding," Corbin chuckled as he placed his arm around his wife's shoulders.

Dante grinned down at his vibrant sister-in-law. "I knew you would want to witness the occasion. That is the only reason I decided to remarry Erica," he teased.

Leona chortled as she gave Erica a subtle wink. Nothing could be further from the truth, she mused as she watched Dante give Erica's hand a loving squeeze.

"Strange, he told *me* he was marrying me for my father's money," Erica taunted; then she wormed from Dante's grasp to seek out the woman she had come to know so well during the past few days.

"Where are your father and your brother?" Leona queried as she fell into step behind Erica. "I thought they were due to arrive this evening." It would spoil everything if the entire family was not present for this grand occasion.

"Lilian stayed behind to await their arrival." Dante answered for Erica, but he frowned when he detected the secretive smile hovering on Leona's lips.

Before he could interrogate his mysterious sister-in-law, however, Corbin grabbed his arm and propelled him toward the study. "I have been considering your offer," he remarked, thereby distracting Dante, who would have sworn Erica and Leona were up to something, judging by the way they scurried up the steps to avoid him. Corbin reached for the decanter of brandy. "Leona has convinced me to invest the money from the steamboat in the plantation. I have decided to settle down instead of navigating up and down the Mississippi."

Dante grinned mischievously as he stared at Corbin over the rim of his goblet. "A wise decision, big brother. You have left Leona to her own devices these past few years, and I agree that your purposes would best be served if you remained close to home. Indeed, Leona has been behaving very—"

"It *has* been like a second honeymoon." Corbin cut him off, certain Dante was about to give him the third degree about the way Leona had been smiling as if she were about to burst with a secret. "I never dreamed having our ship set ablaze could be a blessing in disguise."

Voices in the hall brought a quick end to their conversation, and Dante craned his neck to spy Avery and Jamie Bennet, Reade, and Lilian swarming into the entryway. He hastily set his drink aside and strode toward the door. "Excuse me, Corbin, I must make amends. My future brother-in-law and I are not on amiable terms. Since I had to threaten him the first and last time we met, I think it wise to assure Jamie that I am not roping Erica into an unwanted marriage."

Corbin frowned. He was itching to know why Dante and Jamie had gotten off on the wrong foot, so he followed in his brother's wake to meet their other guests.

Smiling cordially, Dante extended his hand to Jamie, who eyed him skeptically. "I want to apologize for my unethical tactics aboard the schooner," he blurted out before Jamie could open his mouth to utter a word. "I didn't think I had any choice but to take the ship by storm, and I wasn't sure you would approve of my intentions."

Jamie sketched the tall, darkly handsome gentleman who only vaguely resembled the swashbuckling pirate he'd had the misfortune to meet aboard the schooner. A wry smile twisted his lips as he clasped Dante's proffered hand. "Had I known of your plans, I would gladly have helped you," he declared. "Although I questioned your motives, I was silently applauding you for seizing Sabin's ship, especially when I learned who you were."

Relief washed over Dante's tanned features. "Had I known that you would have been with me instead of against me, I would have requested that you travel to the Leeward Islands with us. You could not have been as much trouble as your sister." Dante well remembered how furious he had been when Charles Cadeau had attempted to charm Erica out of her stockings. He would have preferred to spare himself the agony of his insane jealousy. "When she set off to do business with Monsieur Cadeau, I seriously wondered if I would ever see her again."

Jamie lifted an eyebrow and then chuckled at Dante's sour expression. "He is quite the ladies' man, isn't he? I have seen him wine, dine, and woo the most reluctant of women . . . and with considerable success." Jamie smiled rakishly. "And I shamefully admit I have employed his techniques once or twice myself. But Erica has dealt with his kind before. If I know my sister, she only considered him a challenge. Obviously, she was successful in her dealings with the man, or I would not be here to attend your upcoming wedding."

Dante flicked an imaginary piece of lint from his

470

jacket, then he struck a sophisticated pose. "I do believe I am the best man to control that unconventional sister of yours," he teasingly boasted.

Jamie's eyes sparkled with mirth, for he found Dante's playful raillery delightful. "I don't know how you managed to convince my father, but oddly enough, he made a similar remark this afternoon." And Jamie found himself in total agreement. There was something magnetic about Dante. His striking good looks, his forthright manner, his self-confidence, and his charismatic smile blinded others to whatever faults he might possess. "I only hope my father has alerted you to the fact that you will have no easy task controlling my sister for she has a fiery temper." He cast Dante a sly smile. "But then, if she *does* give you trouble, you can always threaten to feed her to the sharks once again."

Although Corbin and Avery were curious to know what Jamie had implied, a movement on the stairs caught their attention. Avery turned to greet whomever he was about to meet; then he sucked in his breath as the past flashed before him. The woman's smile recalled a forbidden dream. . . .

"Who is that?" Dante asked Corbin as he stared curiously at the shadowed figure of a plump, gray-haired woman who wore thick spectacles. A strange sensation flooded over Dante as his eyes strayed back to the foot of the stairs.

Corbin's grin stretched from ear to ear as he ushered his brother forward. "This is Madeline Perkins. She has kept a watchful eye on you these past few years, waiting for the right moment to make your acquaintance. I think perhaps now you can appreciate her . . . as you once did."

Dante froze in his tracks when Madeline removed the

thick spectacles and eyed him apprehensively. Reluctantly, she allowed Leona and Eric to guide her into the light that sprayed across the entryway. When she stood directly before Dante, she peeled off the gray wig and allowed the padded shawl to slide from her shoulders, thereby erasing a score of pounds from her trim figure.

"Hello, Dante. . . ." Her voice trembled as her moist lashes swept up to meet his disbelieving gaze.

"Mother . . ." Dante choked out the word, his eyes widening, his mind racing. He had often heard Corbin and Leona speak of Madeline, but until now he was unaware of the secret they had kept from him.

Maggie Fowler smiled as she watched confused reactions cross her son's face, and then she reached up to smooth away his troubled frown. "Corbin forgave me for what happened, but I was afraid you were far too bitter to accept me, to understand."

"But if you would have—" When Dante started to object, Maggie pressed a fingertip to his lips. She had rehearsed this speech a dozen times since Leona and Erica had convinced her to come out of hiding, and she knew she would never get through it if Dante interrupted her.

"When I ran away from Sabin's plantation that horrible day, I remained in seclusion for more than three months, allowing no one to know what had become of me. But I couldn't stay away from those I loved. I wanted to see my grandchildren grow, to know them and adore them. It was the only happiness I could have after what had happened. But Corbin told me it had been difficult for you to accept the tragedy, that you had become very cynical. I was afraid to face you again. I watched you come and go over the years, clinging to the shadows, sitting unnoticed when you ventured into Lilian's store. I hoped that one day you would meet a woman who could help you understand the feelings I experienced during my stay in New Orleans." Her teary-eyed gaze swung to Erica who also awaited Dante's reaction. "Erica has been a godsend. Without her and your strong love for her, I would never have dared to approach you." Maggie's lips quivered as she forced out the rest of the words. "Dante, can you find it in your heart to forgive me? I never meant to hurt your father. I had intended to return to him, to remain by his side, but Sabin—"

Dante scooped her up into his arms, crushing her against him. "It is you who must forgive me. I put you through as much hell as Sabin did. I'm sorry."

Erica muffled a sniffle as she watched Dante embrace his mother. For years Maggie had nestled in the corner of Lilian's mercantile, seeing her son come and go, studying him from a distance, learning about him from Corbin and Leona, praying that his bitterness would fade so she could come out of hiding and again take her place within the family she loved so dearly.

"Maggie?" Avery's voice was no more than a strained whisper as he walked toward the woman he had loved more than his pride; more than life itself.

Dante released his mother to Avery, watching as they clung together in silence.

"You can never know how often I have relived that day, wondering how I could have changed the tragic course of events," Avery murmured brokenly. "I've missed you so, Maggie."

Leona wiped the tears from her cheeks as she glanced back at Corbin who was still scrutinizing Dante's reaction. She noted that he was relieved to find pity in

Dante's eyes rather than bitterness. At last, Dante had come to understand the strong bond between Maggie and Avery. He now knew why both of them had so carefully guarded their forbidden love.

"Shall we adjourn to the dining room," Corbin suggested to the misty-eyed group. "We have further cause to celebrate tonight. I, for one, would like to feed my festive spirit."

As the guests surged toward the dining room, Dante grasped Erica's hand, detaining her and then enfolding her in his arms. "I owe all my happiness to you," he whispered affectionately. "Because of you, my eyes have been opened to the meaning of love."

His kiss was so gentle that Erica feared she would melt all over his emerald waistcoat. "I think we both learned a great deal about love from watching my father and your mother," she whispered when Dante finally dragged his lips away from hers. "They deserve to be happy after all the torment they have endured."

Dante nodded in agreement as his eyes settled on his ebony-haired enchantress, who was stunning in her gold satin gown. "They have my blessing." A wry smile pursed his lips as he watched Maggie and Avery. "Not that it matters," he chortled as he gestured toward the older couple who continued to hold hands beneath the table. "I don't think they know there is another soul in the world at the moment."

"Leona may be assisting with yet another wedding one day soon," Erica mused aloud as she ambled toward the table.

"By the look of things, I would say it cannot come quickly enough," Dante chuckled as he pulled out a chair for Erica and then seated himself beside her. "Perhaps we should suggest that they take the vows with us tomorrow."

Erica silently nodded her approval when she noticed the adoring look in her father's eyes. She had not seen him so content in years. The man simply could not stop smiling. It was a wonder that he didn't miss his mouth each time he raised his fork since his unblinking gaze was glued to Maggie. Erica seriously doubted that her father could taste his meal; his senses were too keenly occupied by the attractive brunette beside him.

Not until they had taken their meal and retired to the study, did Avery come to his senses. He drew Dante away from the conversation, into a quiet corner. A sheepish smile hovered on his lips as he peered at him and then stared at the far wall, as if something there had caught his attention.

"I have news from New Orleans, but I'm afraid I was so distracted by Maggie's appearance that it completely slipped my mind." His train of thought was sidetracked momentarily. "Speaking of Maggie, I wish to ask something of you."

Dante knew exactly what Avery intended to say before he said it. "Permission?" He flashed Avery a teasing grin.

Avery choked on his brandy. Had he been so obvious? Most likely, he thought to himself. He had been in a daze since the moment Maggie had shed her matronly disguise.

"Well . . . ah . . . yes . . . in a manner of speaking," Avery muttered after Dante had whacked him on the back to help him catch his breath. "Maggie and I would like to be married."

"I have no complaint about that," Dante assured him. "Why not say the vows with us? Erica and I would

475

be pleased."

Relief flooded over Avery's features. "I know it seems to you that I have behaved as less than a man these past few years, but it was because of Maggie that I did what I felt I had to do. I care deeply for your mother, and I will do all within my power to make her happy, to compensate for the years she suffered." He drew a quick breath and then declined Dante's offer. "I do not wish to give one bride away and take one for myself all in the same day. Maggie and I would like a small, quiet wedding with only our immediate family present."

"If that is your wish." Dante frowned curiously, letting the matter drop to pursue the comment Avery had made earlier. "What is the news from New Orleans? I suppose Sabin has hired a notable lawyer to defend him," he grunted acrimoniously.

"Timothy has been apprehended, but Sabin has not. He has never been in custody as we had hoped. I summoned the sheriff, but when we arrived at the Keary plantation, he was nowhere to be found. I'm afraid your uncle is still on the loose, even though we turned New Orleans upside down. When Jamie and I boarded the steamship, the sheriff still had not located him. I do not wish to spoil the festivities this evening, but I think it best that you are aware of the situation. Sabin can still cause trouble."

The news dampened Dante's cheerful mood. He had the uneasy feeling that Sabin planned to spoil their wedding. Dante had made a bitter enemy, and he knew Sabin would not rest until he'd exacted revenge. God, what was running through that devil's demented mind? Dante thought resentfully. He is probably lurking in the shadows, waiting for the opportune moment to strike.

The sound of a pistol shot made Dante wince as if he had been hit, and he glanced at Avery whose face immediately went white.

"Good God, is he making trouble already?" Avery's pained gaze flew to the door, and he prayed that Maggie and Erica were safe. Sabin meant to destroy his and Erica's chances for happiness. Avery could feel it in his bones.

"Dante Fowler! Get out here!" The booming voice came from the stoop.

Dante set his drink aside and hurriedly strode toward the door, bracing himself for the confrontation with his uncle. He pulled up short when he spied Elliot Lassiter standing at the bottom of the steps, his crumpled top hat askew, his blond hair disheveled. In each hand Elliot held a pistol. Having discharged one of them, he had reloaded it and had taken up another, intent on blowing Dante to smithereens if he refused to obey his demands.

"I have come to settle this matter on the eve of your wedding." Elliot squinted his glazed eyes, certain that Dante was moving to and fro. How could he take aim when his target was shifting before his eyes? "Dammit, stand still, Dante!"

Dante could not repress a grin. Elliot looked ridiculous. His clothes were rumpled, and his shirt was buttoned improperly. His shoulders slumped forward as if he would fall flat on his face at any second. "Your eyes are playing tricks on you, friend. I haven't moved a muscle. I think it's time we talked," Dante said calmly. "There are a few things you do not understand."

Elliot snorted. Then he attempted to draw himself erect in front of his rival, but the movement made him sway and it was a moment before he regained his balance.

"I didn't come to talk. I want you to relinquish your claim on Erica," he declared. Then he frowned when he saw Erica inch up beside his one-time friend. "Go back inside, woman. It would grieve me to wound you with a stray bullet."

Erica rolled her eyes when she heard Elliot's words trip over his thick tongue. He was so far into his cups that it was a wonder he hadn't drowned.

"Elliot, put down your pistols. You are too much the gentleman to threaten to shoot someone," she insisted as she marched down the steps, despite Dante's attempt to keep her by his side. "You are making a fool of yourself, and you will sorely regret this when you're sober."

"Dante is the one who made me look like an ass," Elliot protested. "You should be marrying me tomorrow, not him. And I have come to right that wrong."

"Erica, get out of the way!" Dante growled when she positioned herself directly between them. "Elliot doesn't know what he's doing. You could be hurt." When he stormed down the steps after her, Elliot moved to the right to give himself a perfect shot at Dante.

Erica laid her hand on Elliot's arm, demanding his attention. "You must listen to me, Elliot. I am marrying Dante because I want to, not because he forced me into it," she tried to explain.

"You are only saying that to prevent bloodshed," he muttered. "If Dante had been more of a gentleman and I less, *we* would be man and wife. He took unfair advantage of you, and I will not stand by and let that happen again!"

"Confound it, Elliot. I am in love with Dante," Erica shouted, hoping her words would reach his drunken mind. "That is the reason I married him the first time. I know I treated you unfairly, and I deeply regret it. I should have been honest with you at the beginning, but I was fond of you so I did not wish to hurt you. I was trying to use diplomacy with you, but—"

"He never gave me the chance to win your heart," Elliot grumbled bitterly. "Dante was too much of a coward to tell me of his intentions until it was too late for me to do anything." When Dante inched forward once again, Elliot became as alert as he could be, considering his drunken condition. "Hold your ground, Fowler. I am still contemplating your fate."

Dante halted in his tracks. Then he glanced over his shoulder, noticing the crowd that had gathered. Anxious faces were peering around the edge of the door, and the spectators were wondering if Dante would be buried before he could be married.

"Elliot, you must believe me," Erica pleaded. "If I had married you, I would have been living a lie. I could not have made you happy when I was in love with another man."

The truth stung Elliot's already injured pride. "I could have given you the world. One day you would have come to love me," he argued. "But he . . ." Elliot raised his pistol to gesture toward Dante.

"No!" Erica screeched. Certain Elliot meant to drop Dante in his tracks, she knocked the weapon aside, causing it to fire, the bullet shattering the glass in the parlor window.

Yelps of alarm echoed from the entryway as the guests poured out the front door. Dante lunged at his staggering friend who was as bewildered as everyone else when the pistol discharged. With a pained grunt Elliot landed flat on his back as Dante charged into him knocking Erica out of the way and sending her tumbling into the grass. The second pistol discharged into the air as Elliot and Dante wrestled. Although a crowd gathered about them as they sprawled in the flower bed, it was several minutes before Reade and Corbin could pry them apart.

"Dammit, you could have killed her!" Dante snapped at Elliot. Reade held him at bay, refusing to allow him to plant his fist in Elliot's grimy face for the fifth time.

"It wasn't Erica I had the inclination to shoot!" Elliot yelled back at him. However, the brawl had had a sobering effect on him, and his clouded thoughts were clear. "I trusted you like a brother and you betrayed me. How would you feel if your best friend stole the woman you loved right from under your nose, not once but twice?"

As Dante relaxed in Reade's bear hug, he heaved a sigh. "Just as you do, I suppose," he begrudgingly admitted. "Perhaps it seems that I deceived Erica and forced her to marry me, but I had my reasons and Erica fully understands them." He looked Elliot squarely in the eye. "It was never my intention to trifle with her. I love her as I have loved no other woman. Neither of us meant to hurt you, but our attraction was too strong. It began before you met her, and you refused to acknowledge our bond or to listen when Erica attempted to explain it. If you love her as you say you do, you will allow *her* to choose between us. We will leave this decision to Erica, and when she takes a husband the loser will gracefully bow out and will cause no more trouble."

"I will agree to that if you make no attempt to lure her to your side," Elliot stipulated. "You must allow her the freedom of choice without influencing her."

"I am agreeable to those terms," Dante affirmed, and then he glanced at those surrounding them. "Erica?" A puzzled frown furrowed his brow as he waited for her to wedge her way through the guests. But she didn't come. Was she lying unconscious in the grass, trampled by the

480

bystanders who had gathered to watch their fisticuffs? "Erica?"

Silence fell like a cloud of doom as Dante searched the shadows to find that Erica had vanished into thin air. A feeling of dread overcame him as he stalked around the corner of the mansion and spotted a handerchief lying in the grass. Then a growl of pure rage erupted from his lips. He crushed the monogrammed handkerchief in his fist, catching the pungent odor of the chloroform that had been used to render Erica senseless. Sabin Keary had crept from the shadows to steal Erica away. Like a creature of night, he had pounced on his prey and had dragged her off to his lair.

Dante wheeled around to meet the shocked faces that peered back at him; then he held up the handkerchief. "Sabin has come for Erica. If he harms her, I swear I'll kill the miserable bastard." His hard gaze narrowed on Maggie who dropped her head, refusing to meet her son's furious glare.

"I once defended my brother, but I will no longer. He has destroyed too many lives; it is time for him to pay." Maggie raised tear-rimmed eyes to Dante. "You must find Erica and ensure her safety. I do not expect you to consider my brother after what he has done."

Dante dashed toward the stables with Reade, Corbin, and Elliot in fast pursuit, none of them certain of where to begin their frantic search. Although Dante was trying desperately to outguess his uncle, he was so blinded by rage that the task seemed impossible. In the back of his mind, he knew Sabin had counted on that. Dante cursed that heartless devil as he thundered down the path toward Natchez, wondering if he was traveling in the opposite direction from Sabin, fighting back a haunting vision of the man abusing Erica.

Chapter 27

"Faster!" Sabin bellowed at the driver of the carriage as he watched Erica rouse from her drug-induced sleep.

His plan to abduct her had worked splendidly, thanks to the brawl that had kept the Fowlers and their guests preoccupied. Sabin would have staged such a fight himself had he considered how effective a tactic it would be. Now he had what he wanted—Erica—as bait. He would hold her hostage, demanding that Dante return the money he had paid for the Central American treasure and that he would drop all charges against him. Once Dante had met his terms, Sabin would take his captive and flee West to build a new empire. But at the moment he must concentrate on more immediate plans, Sabin reminded himself as he watched Erica's head roll from side to side as she moaned groggily.

Once they reached the steamship and embarked, Dante could not catch up with them. As soon as Erica was stashed away for safekeeping, Sabin would send the ransom note to her bereaved fiancé. The fool! Sabin chuckled to himself. Dante had thought he'd had the last laugh on Sabin Keary, but he would soon realize that was not the case. Dante would have nothing when Sabin finished with him.

As Erica's mind cleared, she blinked and then winced when she found Sabin sitting across from her. It only took a moment to recall what had happened. A bony hand had clamped over her mouth, and her senses had been assaulted by a handkerchief doused in chloroform. Erica reacted instinctively, lunging at Sabin, itching to get a stranglehold on his skinny throat. He squawked as a roused tigress scratched at his face as if she meant to tear it to bloody shreds.

"You little bitch!" he screeched as he shoved her away, sending her sprawling on the floorboard.

Then Erica's breath caught in her throat as she stared death in the face. Sabin's eyes were spitting black fire as he whipped up his cane, pressing his thumb against the ivory handle. Erica gasped when with a quiet click, a razor-sharp knife was projected from the bottom end of the walking stick.

"Would you like to have your lovely face marred beyond recognition?" Sabin sneered as he jabbed at Erica.

As the carriage careened around a corner, knocking Sabin off balance, Erica scrambled onto the seat. She shrieked as Sabin recovered enough to slash the hem of her gown with his makeshift sword. When he retracted the blade and came at her again, Erica sucked in her breath. The sharp knife sliced across her arm, but her pain became a throbbing numbness as she grasped the cane, deflecting yet another deadly attack.

Erica screamed bloody murder as Sabin leaped at her, his dark eyes demented. As the point of his knife stabbed into the seat, barely missing her left shoulder, Erica threw herself toward the opposite side of the carriage. Shrieking, Sabin grabbed at her clothes in an attempt to drag her to him, but she scrambled onto the seat, intent on jumping from the racing carriage before Sabin cut her to pieces.

"Come back here!" Sabin snarled. He clutched the end of the cane, and using the handle as a hook, he hauled Erica back the split second before she leaped. "Dante will have no way of knowing whether you are dead or alive when I demand my ransom. If you tempt me I will dispose of you."

A tiny moan of pain bubbled from her lips as Sabin yanked her back against his chest and clamped his fingers around her throat. Then her eyes widened in alarm as he twirled the cane to lay the blade against her neck.

"Dante will hunt you down and kill you like the vile vermin you are," she hissed venomously as she strained against him, only to feel the point of the knife gouging her skin.

She was trapped! She could not move without risking being sliced to shreds. Each time the carriage was jostled by the rough road, Erica felt the sharp blade press deeper into her throat, and she cursed herself for being unable to elude him before he'd chained her to him. Now, at any moment, she might have her head separated from her shoulders, and she had the dreadful feeling that Sabin would delight in doing just that.

Sabin's wicked laughter chimed in the wind as they rumbled toward the docks of Natchez. "At last you realize you cannot defeat me," he jeered as he eased himself back onto the seat, holding Erica so tightly against him that she couldn't draw a breath without almost choking on it.

When the coach came to a halt, he herded Erica along the wharf, his left arm hooked beneath her breasts, his right hand securely clamped on the cane to keep the blade against her neck.

"If you make the slightest sound it will be your last," Sabin declared threateningly as he aimed her toward the waiting steamship.

Erica glanced about her, frantically searching for a means of escape. But despair overwhelmed her when she found herself hustled across the gangplank and onto the main deck of a steamboat. Dammit, where was Dante? Did he know what had become of her? Would he ever catch up to her when he had no idea which direction they had taken?

An evil chuckle erupted from Sabin's chest as he shuffled Erica up the steps. "Don't bother searching the shadows for your lover," he jeered. "He will not come to save you. He has lost you forever."

Erica opened her mouth to respond, but Sabin's gnarled fingers dug deeper into her throat, strangling her biting remark. Lord, how she hated this demon. His mind was poisoned, and evil spurted through his veins. Somehow she would find a way to rid herself of him, she vowed as Sabin roughly dragged her up the steps toward his cabin on the boiler deck. Yet, she had the apprehensive feeling that she had seen her last sunset. If she lived through this nightmare she would be surprised. Only a miracle can save me, she thought disheartenedly as Sabin weaved his way around the deck chairs and then paused in front of his stateroom to retrieve the key from his vest pocket.

The sound of Erica's frightened scream reached

Dante's ears and he wheeled his horse around, his alert eyes scanning the darkness, his ears pricked to perceive the source of the shrill voice that wafted its way toward him. Dante's heart hammered furiously against his chest as he gouged his mount in the flanks, aiming him toward the distant sounds. He prayed that he would reach Sabin before he'd brutally disposed of Erica. When Dante saw the glowing lights of the wharf ahead of him he urged his steed to its swiftest pace, leaving the other three men in a cloud of dust in his haste to reach Erica. He was driven by fear and fury, emotions that were tearing him to pieces, bit by excruciating bit. Erica's haunted face kept materializing from the shadows, and her raspy voice was calling to him from afar. But he couldn't travel fast enough, and she'd been snatched away from him by such an evil force that Dante wondered if he would ever see Erica alive.

When he arrived at the dock, he pulled his laboring steed to a halt and vaulted down, watching in dismay as thrashing paddlewheels propelled the steamboat upriver. His tortured gaze swung from the boat to the abandoned landing, in the hope that Sabin had been too late to get aboard. But when his eyes returned to the riverboat, despair closed in on him for he saw two shadowy figures scurrying along the upper deck.

"Erica!" Dante's voice boomed out like thunder, shattering the silence of the night.

It startled Sabin, and he eased his grip on Erica in order to crane his neck to watch the four men congregated on the wharf. She immediately took advantage of Sabin's preoccupation. Flinging herself away from her captor before he could slash her with his knife, she ran for her life, her heart pounding against her chest. She screamed Dante's name, over and over again as she dodged through the maze of deck chairs, snatching up the front of her skirt to keep from becoming entangled in them. As Erica dashed toward the stern of the ship, her wild blue eyes locked with Dante's across the narrow distance that separated them. They were so close, but an ocean might have stood between them. A sense of hopelessness overcame her as the steamship cut through the water on its way to St. Louis.

"Damn you!" Sabin scowled as he hurried after Erica.

Dante's overworked heart slammed against his ribs as he watched Sabin whip a pistol from his pocket and aim it at Erica's fleeing back. God, he meant to kill her!

Reade gasped in horror as the light from the deck brought Sabin's darkly clad figure into view, glimmering on the barrel of the pistol clamped in his hand. He pulled his own weapon from his coat and tossed it to Dante who was frantically glancing about him, berating himself for not taking the time to arm himself before he'd thundered off after his ruthless uncle.

"Yore a better marksman than I am," Reade choked out. Then his eyes flew back to the steamship and he held his breath, praying like he'd never prayed before.

At that moment Erica pulled up short, uncertain of which way to turn to avoid being recaptured by the demon racing after her.

"Jump, dammit!" Dante shouted at her.

Jump? Erica had not even considered that means of escape. She braved a glance over her shoulder to see Sabin steady himself before he fired at his target. A lump of fear lodged in her throat, but Erica peered over the lattice railing at the muddy Mississippi churning below her. There are times when it is best *not* to look before one leaps, she thought. Jump? The very thought left her dizzy and light-headed. Her eyes dived back to the murky depths, she wondered if it always had to come to this? She was forever finding herself with no escape except taking a plunge. God, why was she plagued by this unreasonable fear of heights? No doubt, in hell she would have to inch along narrow ledges that towered high in the air.

"Erica!" Dante's bellowing voice roused her from her troubled contemplations, and she fastened her gaze on him instead of on the swirling water below her.

"If you try to jump I'll kill you." Sabin cocked the hammer of his pistol. "I swear I will. If I can't have you no man will."

The deadly ring in his voice made an eerie sensation dart up and down Erica's spine. She clamped her hands on the railing and swung one leg over the side. What do I have to lose? she asked herself. If diving off the steamboat doesn't kill me, Sabin's bullet surely will.

"For God's sake, jump!" Dante yelled at her as he took careful aim at Sabin.

Erica's blood-curdling scream pierced the air the moment both pistols exploded. It didn't matter that Dante's aim was accurate or that Sabin clutched his chest as he toppled over the railing to disappear into the dark depths, taking the treasure with him and returning it to the mud and silt from which it had come. It didn't matter that Sabin would no longer threaten Erica because she was mesmerized by the invisible force that pulled on her, compelling her to give way to the impulse that had always tormented her. She was falling, arcing through the air like a shooting star—dazed, helpless, oblivious to all except an overwhelming fear that she was plunging to her death. Hopelessness flooded over her as the water hit her with a hard slap, and she thrashed wildly about, desperate to reach the surface, fighting to keep her lungs from bursting. She gasped for breath, but none came. Her heart had catapulted into her throat, strangling her. Then she was towed into the river's current to follow Sabin to his death.

"Dante . . ." Her voice was no more than a strained whisper when she fought her way to the surface a second time.

As the force of the current curled about her, taking her under again, Erica surrendered to the swirling darkness and her eyes fluttered shut. She was drifting on a tranquil sea, rolling with the waves that lured her farther from shore . . .

Dante's arm encircled Erica's waist, drawing her limp body against his, and then he swam toward the wharf with Erica in tow. Panic gripped him as her head rolled lifelessly against his shoulder. Had Sabin's bullet found its mark? It seemed an eternity before Dante reached the shore.

After Reade squatted down to lift Erica from his arms, Dante dragged himself onto the pier. A concerned frown furrowed his brow as he peered at the bedraggled beauty. Carefully, he eased her face down so he could inspect her back. He was certain he would find a fatal wound. Relief washed over him when he found no trace of a bullet wound, and when Erica stirred slightly, he sank onto the wooden planks, clutching her in his arms, soothing her as he would a frightened child.

"Erica, can you hear me?" Dante murmured as he rained kisses on her ashen cheeks.

She groaned and moved toward the warmth of his body. She was so terribly cold, so weak. She drew in a ragged breath, then opened her eyes to see Dante's face hovering above her. The faintest hint of a smile brushed her pale lips as she reached up to smooth the raven hair across his forehead.

"I love you," she whispered softly; then she nestled in his protective embrace.

Elliot heaved a defeated sigh as he watched Dante and Erica cling to each other. It is true, he mused. Erica *does* love Dante. She had called his name when she was running from death, and when she had plunged into the river. He had made a fool of himself. Erica had tried to tell him that Dante held the key to her heart. If he hadn't been so blinded by love, so determined to win her affection, he would have seen that Erica was drawn to Dante, even in the beginning.

"And I love you," Dante murmured back to her. "I was so afraid you wouldn't jump, not even when your life depended on it." A proud smile pursed his lips as he ran his fingers through renegade strands of hair, smoothing it away from her exquisite face. "But I think you have overcome your fear of falling."

Erica nodded wearily. Then she placed her arms around Dante's neck as he scooped her up to set her on his horse. "I have taken more falls these past four months than I have endured in a lifetime." A provocative smile caught the corners of her mouth, curving them upward. "But none of them were as easy as falling in love with you."

Dante felt the heat of her body as he swung into the saddle behind her. His moist lips traced a warm path along the swanlike column of her throat. "I only hope it will be difficult for you to fall *out* of love with me. I don't think I could endure that, not after what I've been through to have you with me."

Erica chortled softly as she cuddled against the broad expanse of his chest. "Put your fears to rest, love. That will never happen," she assured him.

"I would see some proof of that statement," Dante growled seductively as his free hand caressed her breasts. "Just as soon as I get you home."

"How fast can this nag run?" Erica inquired, grinning mischievously as she glanced back at the raven-haired rogue whose mere touch could make her burn with desire.

As Dante and Erica thundered off into the night, Reade shook his head in wonder. Then he glanced at Corbin and at Elliot. "A man in passion rides a mad horse." He snickered. "And Dante has been sufferin' from that malady since that wild witch was spirited into his life."

Corbin's eyes swung to Elliot who had not uttered a word since Erica had professed her love for Dante. "I believe it was meant to be," he said pointedly. "No woman has ever affected Dante the way Erica does. I cannot blame you for being bitter, Elliot, but you saw with your own eyes the way it is between them."

Heaving a sigh, Elliot nodded slightly. Then he fixed his gaze on the silhouettes disappearing in the distance. "I envy him," he confessed. "But I no longer hold a grudge. Erica was right. She would not have been happy if she had married me, and I could not have forced her to live a lie. Erica has too much zest for life. I would have detested myself if I were the cause of her misery."

"You are a good man, Elliot." Corbin smiled sympathetically.

Elliot snorted and then settled himself more comfortably in the saddle. "Not good enough for that lovely hoyden," he grumbled. "As much as I dislike admitting it, Dante is the better man."

"Don't be too hard on yoreself," Reade chided. "I even fancied myself in love with that lively chit and I was old enough to know better. But it's plain that those two have eyes only for each other, though they gave each other fits before they finally admitted they was in love. Gittin' Dante to say the words was worse then pullin' teeth. I oughta know. I tried like the devil to git Dante to admit it 'cause he stalked around the schooner like a wounded lion until he told Erica what was in his heart."

"Well, at least they finally came to terms," Corbin said quietly as he caught the faint sound of horse hooves in the distance. "And perhaps our lives can return to normal. Between the two of them, they have kept us all in chaos."

Reade chuckled at Corbin. "If you think life will be quiet with Erica around, yore sorely mistaken, my friend. That woman don't have a docile bone in her body. Why, she even insisted on accompanyin' me and Dante into the forests of Yucatán, and she helped Dante dive for the treasure. Erica ain't one to sit back and let adventure pass her by. She—"

"She traveled with you on your expedition to Central America?" Elliot's eyes were wide with disbelief. Perhaps he didn't know Erica as well as he thought he did. The sedate life of a banker's wife would never appeal to a woman who would cut her way through an insect-infested jungle to retrieve a buried treasure.

Reade was quick to note that he had a captive audience so he promptly began to describe the high-points of his adventures on the headlands of Yucatán. "You shoulda seen her," he said. "Me and Dante was hidin' in the vegetation, tryin' to figure out what to do

492

when them Mayans came swarmin' out of the forest with their weapons. Erica rose up out of that ancient Sacrificial Well like a muse and them Indians . . ."

By the time the threesome reached the plantation, Corbin and Elliot were shaking their heads in disbelief. Reade had painted a vivid picture of the trials Dante and Erica had endured, and he had described adventures beyond their wildest imaginings. Corbin was silently wondering if Dante and Erica would be satisfied to manage a plantation after living life at such a frenzied pace these past few months. How could a man tame a wild-hearted woman like Erica and keep her content? he asked himself. Then he smiled when he heard the soft whinny of the steed tethered by the stream that meandered through the pasture of Dante's plantation. All Dante has to do is love her, he thought, as he heard soft laughter in the brush. The lusty rogue hadn't even had the patience to ride the extra mile to a soft feather bed, Corbin thought to himself. No doubt, Dante and Erica were frolicking in the stream. A secretive smile bordered Corbin's lips as he swung from the saddle and ambled up the steps to his manor. Perhaps he and Leona should practice some of his brother's unconventional techniques. The idea had some appeal, and Corbin fully intended to lure Leona into the darkness. Just as soon as he'd explained what had happened so that Maggie and Avery knew Erica was safe, he would send his guests on their way.

An apprehensive frown distorted Maggie's features as Corbin approached her. She nervously clutched Avery's hand, preparing herself for the worst, for she was certain she had lost a son and Avery had lost his only daughter.

"Are they—" Maggie began.

"Erica and Dante are safe," Corbin informed them. Then he watched Maggie and Avery cling to each other in relief.

"Thank God," Avery choked out, relaxing for the first time since he'd learned Sabin had abducted his daughter. He eyed Corbin's grim expression anxiously. "And Sabin?"

"Dante was forced to kill him when he tried to shoot Erica in the back," he explained, carefully surveying his mother's reaction.

Maggie nodded mutely, blinking back the tears that threatened to cloud her eyes. Throughout the years she had tried to find some small amount of good in her older brother, but Sabin had always been a lonely, bitter man. After he had killed Dominique, Maggie had given up on him, certain that wickedness poisoned him. It tore at her heart to think Sabin had caused so much misery by manipulating so many lives.

"It seems only fitting that the empire Sabin built by evil means should again become a home filled with love," Corbin mused aloud. Then he offered Maggie a faint smile. "Sabin's inheritance and properties are now yours, Mother. I pray that you will restore to the Keary plantation its former honorable reputation."

Maggie glanced hopefully at Avery. "Would you object to beginning our new life on my grandparents' homestead? If you would prefer—"

"As Corbin said, it seems fitting that we transform into good something that has long been shrouded in evil," Avery murmured, his heart in his eyes as he peered at Maggie. "I intend to spend less time at the New Orleans

Cotton Exchange, and I would be delighted to assist you in making the necessary changes in our new home."

"Father, the hour is late," Jamie interjected when silence fell upon the room. "I think perhaps we should travel to Dante's plantation. After all, tomorrow will be a very busy day."

Avery was not anxious to relinquish his grasp on Maggie. It had been almost four years since they had been together and they had plans to make.

Noting Avery's hesitation, Corbin steered Jamie toward the study. "I doubt that you need to rush off just yet." He chuckled. "I don't think your host and hostess will be on hand to greet you."

A worried frown settled on Jamie's brow. "Is there something you are keeping from Maggie and my father? Was Erica injured during her encounter with Sabin?"

A wry smile skipped across Corbin's lips as he thrust a drink in young Bennet's hand. "She suffered only a few minor bruises and some cuts," he assured Jamie, muffling a chuckle when the young man frowned again. "It is just that I saw your sister and my brother veering off toward the creek . . . to do whatever lovers do on the eve of their second marriage."

The twilight of understanding dawned in Jamie's eyes as he studied Corbin's outrageous grin. He downed his drink and then shoved the empty glass into Corbin's hand. "In that case, I should like another nightcap. I would hate to embarrass my future brother-in-law by appearing on his doorstep long before he is prepared to accept guests."

Corbin snickered as he handed Jamie the entire bottle of brandy. "By the time you polish off this, I should think Dante will have had ample time to finish whatever

495

it is he is doing in the moonlight."

Jamie eyed the tall bottle speculatively. "By the time I consume this much brandy, I seriously doubt that I will care whether or not Dante and Erica are there to greet me."

While Jamie plopped down on a chair to celebrate his sister's upcoming wedding, Corbin checked his watch, calculating that it would be well past midnight before he and Leona could be alone together. When Leona wandered by the study door to bless him with a smile, Corbin settled back in his chair, assured that the time he and his wife spent together would be well worth the wait.

Part IX

All thoughts, all passions, all delights,
Whatever stirs this mortal frame,
All are but ministers of Love,
And feed his sacred flame.

—Coleridge

Chapter 28

A puzzled frown knitted Erica's brow when Dante reined their mount to a halt long before they reached the mansion. She twisted around in the saddle to see him grinning in roguish anticipation, and she cast him a provocative smile.

"What is on your mind, sir?" she purred, as one delicate finger traced the sensuous curve of his lips.

"I happened by this stream one night to find a bewitching nymph swimming in the moonlight. I thought perchance I might see her again since the moon is full." His full lips whispered over hers, and his questing hand glided along her thigh, sliding the damp fabric of her gown upward to reveal a long, shapely leg. "I hope that sweet nymph hasn't gone into hiding. She is what dreams are made of, and I yearn to share one with her." His voice was ragged with desire.

"She is somewhere hereabout," Erica assured him as she undid the buttons of Dante's shirt so she could run her hands over the crisp matting of hair on his chest and feel his heart beat faster when she caressed him.

Dante groaned softly as her hands dropped to trace the lean contours of his belly, then traveled upward to explore the slope of his shoulders. "Fetch her for me and quickly," he requested as Erica's taunting lips played across his collarbone, then ventured along the column of his neck. "I have been too long without her."

Erica laid her head against his arm as she peered up into Dante's shadowed face, watching his emerald eyes burn with that living fire that enthralled her. "Twenty-four hours?" she mocked lightly. "Sir, you must have the lusty appetite of a dragon."

Dante's playful laughter drifted through the overhanging limbs of the trees to be carried off by the wind. "I never can control the beast in me when I am near you, nymph."

Erica slid to the ground and strolled along the bank of the stream, leaving a trail of garments behind her. "Then I shall see if I can locate this mystical siren you seek."

Dante could not remember dismounting, but he was following a trail of strewn clothing through the underbrush. He gasped in awe when he glanced up to see Erica standing by the edge of the rivulet, her alabaster skin glowing in the moonlight, a beckoning smile hovering on her lips. As his eyes fell to the rosy tips of her breasts and then feasted on the graceful sway of her hips as she walked into the water, his blood pressure soared. Ripples sparkled like tiny diamonds in Erica's wake as she stretched out to glide across the rivulet, and Dante hurriedly peeled off his shirt and tossed it aside, his hungry gaze fixed on the enchanting sylph who cut through the water in front of him. His black boots landed on the grass atop his shirt.

Amusement bubbled from Erica's lips as she watched

Dante wrestle with his trousers, but her laughter died when he walked toward her. His lean, powerful body had the grace of a panther, and his muscles flexed as he closed the distance between them. The moonlight enhanced the massive wall of his chest, and as Erica's eyes dropped to his narrow hips, she felt herself dissolving in the water. Dante was magnificent. He was her knight, the essence of virility, a dark-maned lion of a man who had often saved her from disaster. How she loved him! A wild, exhilarating sensation sent her spirits soaring as he swam toward her to enfold her in his strong arms. The fresh manly scent of him invaded her senses, and Erica moaned in exquisite pleasure as he pressed her to him.

"Mmmmm . . . I'm addicted to the taste of you," Dante whispered hoarsely as he nibbled at the corner of her mouth. "Your lips are like fine wine, and I long to drink my fill." His mouth rolled over hers, searching its hidden recesses, while his wayward hands glided over the alluring curve of her hips. "The aroma of springtime clings to you." He inhaled her womanly scent and drew a shuddering breath as his lips traced a flaming path along her neck.

Erica surrendered to the tantalizing sensations that washed over her as Dante lifted her until she was floating on the water's surface. His skillful kisses feathered over the tips of her breasts, his tongue flicking each taut bud, while his free hand journeyed along her shoulder and then followed the trim curve of her waist. Then his loving caress ascended to encircle her dusky peaks before it trailed lower to investigate the trembling flesh of her thighs. Erica groaned in pure pleasure as Dante's hands and lips rediscovered each sensitive point on her body, bringing her senses to life. His intimate caresses triggered

501

each and every nerve ending until she cried out with the want of him. But still he continued to arouse her, driving her to the brink of insanity.

"Will you tire of me when my hair turns gray and a younger man with a striking physique catches your eye?" Dante asked as his lips brushed over her satiny skin. "Will you still profess to love me when these eyes no longer claim the keenness of youth and my stature is stooped by the weight of the years?"

How can he question my fidelity? Erica said to herself. She could not imagine *not* loving Dante, could not remember when she didn't love him. "Do you perceive my love as a shallow emotion, a fascination that will wither with time?" she whispered as she cupped his head in her hands and stared deeply into bottomless pools of emerald flame.

A rueful smile pursed his lips as he peered into her flawless features. "You have a passion for living, Erica. How can I know that when Father Time has slowed my pace you will not become bored with me? What assurance do I have that you will remain loyal, that someone will not come along to make you regret you are tied to an older man? Although I cannot blame my mother for her fascination with your father, I cannot help but think his appeal was far greater since my father had passed his prime." Dante's arms encircled Erica, hugging her to him as if he feared to release her. "You have become a living, breathing part of me, Erica. What frightens *you* torments *me*. That which gives *you* pleasure delights *me*. I could not bear to let you go, yet I could not bear to subject you to unhappiness." He tilted her head back, sending a waterfall of ebony hair over his shoulder as he stared deeply into captivating eyes of liquid sapphire. "I want

502

you to be very sure before you speak the wedding vows tomorrow. I want you to be certain that what you *say* you feel for me is a love that can stand the test of time, an emotion so strong and unbending that you are willing to spend the rest of your life with me, even when I am old, gray, and hard of hearing."

Erica could not foresee the future, but she was not a fool. She knew in her heart that a love as all-encompassing as theirs would come along only once in a lifetime. She knew what she wanted in a man, and Dante had far exceeded her expectations. Erica would have erased every skeptical thought from his mind if it were possible to do so. Didn't he know that he was the only man on the face of the Earth who could truly make her happy? Would she have stood by his side while they waded through hell if he didn't possess her heart and soul?

Her eyes expressed the overwhelming love she felt for him as she met his probing gaze. "You cannot compare us to Maggie and Dominique. Theirs was a marriage of convenience, a contract for the benefit of both families. You and I have vowed to remain faithful to each other because of the love that binds us together, not because of mutual financial benefits." Erica sighed tremulously and then blessed him with an adoring smile. "Dante, I have given you no cause to doubt my devotion. There has been no other man in my life because I have wanted no other man. My love for you has no beginning and no end. You have become my world, my reason for being. I have already followed you to the edge of civilization and back again. What more must I do to prove that I love you beyond all others, that you are more dear to me than life?"

Her expression was so sincere, her voice so soft and

raspy, that Dante would not doubt her profession. The emotions swimming in those fathomless pools of blue were proof enough. "I have never been a man who could be satisfied with doing anything halfway. It has always been all or nothing for me. Can you possibly imagine how very much I love you?" he murmured as he gathered her in his arms and carried her toward the shore.

Erica laid her head against his sturdy shoulder and then flashed him a smile that would brighten the darkest of nights. "Enough to whisper those very words when *I* am wrinkled and gray?" she challenged. "Will your eyes stray when I am round with child?"

Dante's eyes danced with deviltry as he set her to her feet and ran his hands over her curvaceous body. "I shall delight in studying the many facets of Erica Fowler," he assured her. "And I anticipate that it will be a very exhausting study," he growled seductively. "One it will take years to complete." The rakish smile evaporated as he drew her down onto the lush grass that formed a soft carpet beneath them. Then Dante propped himself up on one elbow, and he bent over her, his lips only a few breathless inches from hers. "Feed this eternal fire that burns within me, my lovely nymph, lest I be forced to take to the stream to cool the lusty flames that are devouring me."

"I have never denied you," Erica whispered, her voice quivering with barely contained emotion. "Nor do I ever intend to. I love you, Dante, now and forever. . . ."

When she set her hands upon him, Dante closed his eyes and mind to everything but her languid caresses. Her soft lips fluttered over his skin, fanning the flames of passion until he burned, inside and out. Each touch, each kiss, said I love you. She knew how to please him and please him she did, as her lovemaking aroused every nerve and muscle in his body. Her feminine scent invaded his senses, and his heart thundered in response to her intimate touch. Then he groaned with the pleasurable torment of wanting her, totally, completely.

Erica lifted her face to his, her full lips parting invitingly as his mouth slanted across hers and his arms glided around her hips, molding her to the male hardness of him. Erica surrendered in wild abandon to the overpowering strength that pressed intimately against her, returning his devouring kisses, savoring the feel of his skillful hands, and reveling in the splendor of a boundless love. Their bodies melded, and their passions raged, consuming them in a blaze so intense it must run its fiery course. Endearing words spilled from their lips while they made wild, sweet love beneath a blanket of twinkling stars. They spiraled and glided in a secluded Eden, giving, taking, sharing a love that would last an eternity, creating a dream within the realm of reality, one that would endure a lifetime.

Erica belonged to Dante, and he belonged to her. One was incomplete without the other. They had endured the worst of times; they had a right to happiness. Erica was content to remain forever in his arms, staring into flames of emerald green that warmed her soul and set her heart ablaze.

In the aftermath of love, Dante pulled her onto his chest, chuckling softly at her ebony hair hovered about them like a silky canopy, shutting out the rest of the world and leaving him content to remain beneath its fragrant shelter.

"Your father and brother will think me an inconsiderate host," he whispered hoarsely, his voice heavily drugged with the aftereffects of passion. "It is their first visit to my plantation, and I am not there to receive them."

Erica dropped a feathery kiss on his sensuous lips before she traced the rugged lines of his face, memorizing each handsome feature. "A gentleman would never shirk his responsibilities to his guests," she agreed as her absent caresses wandered across his hair-roughened chest. And then she graced him with a disarming and very seductive smile. "But then, I would never think to label you a gentleman. You, Dante, are very much the rogue. My father and brother can fend for themselves a few more minutes. . . ."

"Give me one good reason why I should delay returning home," Dante requested. "I may not be the perfect gentleman, but I do have a few shreds of decency!" His voice registered mild offense.

Her lips fluttered over the tendons of his neck to investigate his muscular shoulders, and her breasts pressed wantonly against his naked chest as her wandering hand explored the hard contours of his belly and then ventured over his thigh. "Is this reason enough to postpone our ride to the plantation?" she breathed against his skin.

Dante's throaty chuckle drifted across the rippling creek. "That is reason enough," he assured her as he pressed her to her back and then grinned down into her bewitching face. "Take me back to paradise, *chérie.* The servants can tend to my guests."

As her lips melted against his, Dante yielded to the rapturous emotions that stirred his soul. He had sailed the seven seas in search of a woman who could match his passions and satisfy his craving for adventure. Now, he

506

no longer yearned to set sail across the wide oceans, not when this raven-haired siren was nestled in his arms. Love claimed his heart, and he had discovered a world of indescribable pleasure when he'd found this spirited beauty. Taming Erica had been an adventure in itself, yet no treasure could compare to the love that glistened in those mystical pools of sapphire. No voyage could offer the thrill of feeling her velvety flesh molded to his.

And as their souls touched and intertwined, Dante was engulfed by a fire that blazed hotter with each ardent kiss and caress. They were a flame in the wind, living fire fed by fervent passion; and nothing could deplete the eternal source from which their fierce love sprung. Erica had presented him with every conceivable reason why he should not leave her, and as Dante had received them, one by one, the lovers had skyrocketed to a paradise beyond the distant stars.

"I will always love you," Erica declared as they shared passion's sweet release.

A satisfied smile hovered on Dante's lips until she kissed it away. He believed in Erica because he had come to believe in love. For Dante, they were one and the same. . . .

Each month you'll receive 4 brand new Zebra Historical Romance novels as soon as they are published. Look them over *Free* for 10 days. If you're not delighted simply return them and owe nothing. But if you enjoy them as much as we think you will, you'll pay *only* $3.50 each and save 45¢ over the cover price. (You save a total of $1.80 each month.) *There is no shipping and handling charge or other hidden charges.*

—————— *Fill Out the Coupon*——————

Start your subscription now and start saving. Fill out the coupon and mail it *today*. You'll get your FREE book along with your first month's books to preview.